THE KINDNESS CURSE
Magic to Spare, Book 1

Michelle L. Levigne

Ye Olde Dragon Books
P.O. Box 30802
Middleburg Hts., OH 44130

www.YeOldeDragonBooks.com

2OldeDragons@gmail.com

Copyright © 2021 by Michelle L. Levigne
ISBN 13: 978-1-952345-35-7

Published in the United States of America
Publication Date: June 1, 2021

Cover Art Copyright by Ye Olde Dragon Books 2021

Chapter One

"I hate magic. I hate majjians," Merrigan said for what felt like the thousandth time since the seer, Clara, had turned her world upside down.

She tripped over another branch across her path through this unending, dark, tangled forest. Six hours ago, she had been riding in her carriage, following a tidy plan to save her kingdom. All she needed was a little cooperation from a seer who owed the late king of Carlion some loyalty. Her caves were in his kingdom, after all.

Merrigan stopped short, stunned to see sunlight and a road a few steps away. It wasn't much of a road, packed dirt full of ruts, and a ditch between her and it.

Five hours ago, her carriage stopped in front of the series of caves where Clara consulted pools of vision.

More than four hours now, Merrigan had stumbled through a tangled, shadowy forest, with birds shrieking overhead and squirrels and other creatures running through the branches. She was positive the roots reached out on purpose, to trip her.

Clara had done this to her. Threw her out into the forest, so far she couldn't find her way back to her carriage. Put her in these rusty black, dowdy clothes. Granted, she was a widow, but she was the *queen*. She had a right, a *duty*, to dress stylishly. At least Clara had changed her light slippers to heavy black boots. Sometimes, unfortunately, common sense and comfort did trump style.

Her legs ached and her joints creaked and her arms felt too thin. Even her hair felt wrong. She couldn't adjust the thick, canvas strap slung across her chest, and the heavy carpetbag bumped her hip with every step. Her arms simply wouldn't cooperate. She felt hollow, drained. What had Clara done to her? And why?

Everything blurred from the point the woman stepped from the shadows and looked at Merrigan with those depthless, pale eyes. Still, the implication was painfully clear.

"I'm cursed," Merrigan whispered. Getting across the dratted ditch in front of her was far more important than remembering what that arrogant majjian had said to her, just before rainbow streaks of magic twisted around her. A thousand thorns shredded her clothes and skin, then dropped her in a muddy patch of open ground in the center of the forest.

The sunshine slanted down at an early afternoon angle on the rough road. More like an overgrown path. Perhaps this was a lane to the main highway. She cringed at the mental image of someone from the court in Carlion seeing her here.

What was that creaking noise, rattling and dragging, coming toward her? Merrigan looked over her shoulder, anticipating some horrific monster made of bits and pieces, animated just long enough to torment her. Yet nothing moved in the shadows. The sound didn't come from the forest. Was it too quiet?

All except for the sounds of frogs.

Merrigan shuddered and focused on the road so she wouldn't hear if those frogs dared to speak to her. She had ordered all the frogs in Carlion turned into frog legs for breakfast, to silence them. She had grown sick of frog legs long before the kingdom ran out of frogs. Yet she still sometimes heard frogs creak-croaking her name, in the stillness between waking and sleeping.

"No, no, no," she whispered, and turned to face forward. She refused to look down into the ditch, if any frogs hid there.

Movement to her right wrung a tiny shriek from her. Was that a wagon? Yes, it was, and the source of the sound. Not a monster.

She had been an overly imaginative fool. Leffisand would laugh, if he could see her now. Of course, if her late husband could see her now, she wouldn't be out here in the forest, would she? She wouldn't need to consult a seer to fix the problem of having no heir.

Fury helped Merrigan take that leap to cross the ditch.

Her legs betrayed her, just like everything else today. She hit her knees on the edge. An unqueenly shriek escaped her. She dug her fingers into the dirt and debris and stopped her slide backwards. Thuds and voices cut through the panicked heartbeat in her ears. Big, strong hands caught hold of her arms with bruising force and lifted her up with astonishing ease.

What had happened to her, that she was so thin and frail?

"Here, now, Granny, be careful." The man smelled of metal and salt and the stables. He chuckled as he slung her half across his shoulders and strode down the road a few steps. She landed with a thud and a squeak on the back end of the wagon. "What are you doing way out here by yourself?"

"Here?" She looked down the road ahead of her. "Where am I?"

"You're on the main trade road between Schoebern and Wyndalbern."

"Where?" She shook her head when the big man frowned at her like she was an idiot. "What kingdom is this?"

"Bern-Lyceum."

"That's -- that's on the other side of the world!"

"What do you mean, *other* side?"

"Bern-Lyceum is on the western continent. Armorica is the center of the world."

"If you say so." He spat, barely turning his head. Laughter bubbled up behind her, and she turned enough to see four rough, bearded male faces, all of them tanned and dirty, with dirty hair and sloppy caps. Peasants, of the lowest sort.

"I know so."

"Yeah, and if you're so smart, why didn't you know what road you almost fell off of into the ditch?"

"I need to get to the nearest port. Dratted majjians! How dare they interfere? How dare they send me flying across the world? The inconvenience. The lack of respect!" Merrigan muffled an unqueenly shriek. She wished he stood closer to her, despite the peasant aroma. She wanted to kick this sneering, filthy man. All the trees she had struggled past. Especially Clara.

She would like to kick Leffisand, for going to war with a magic apple tree and getting himself killed, so she had to deal with all these inconveniences and indignities.

"The nearest port, eh? That's a long walk, Granny. Heading in the wrong direction, too."

"Oh, what do you know?"

"More than you." He grinned, revealing several dark teeth.

"You will take me to the port."

"I will, eh? And why should I?"

"Because I am the queen of Carlion, and I must return to my kingdom immediately."

"Should take you to a healer. Addlepated crone."

"I am not talking nonsense." She pulled herself upright and gave him her most queenly glare of disapproval. "You will take me to the nearest port. Immediately."

The idiot laughed, bending down with the effort, and putting his face in her reach. She slapped him. His laughter stopped short and he rubbed his cheek, visually measuring her head to foot.

"Should slap some sense into you, but one as ancient as you would probably break in half, turn to dust." He took another step back. "Probably some faerie trick. Push us hard until we do something rude, then slap a curse on me and mine." He turned, glaring at the entire forest. "Won't fall for it, that I won't! The word's getting around. You faerie folk are too big for your britches. Day's coming, you get judged like you been judging all of us."

Merrigan shivered, remembering angry old women, shouting at her mother on the steps of the palace of Avylyn. She remembered the things Nanny Tulip had said in the quiet of dusk, and the things she learned from the dark, old books her nanny put under her pillow, to fill her dreams and teach her while she slept. She agreed entirely. The faerie folk and other magical-gifted folk -- the majjians -- were unforgivably cruel, judgmental, and arrogant.

The man caught Merrigan around her waist and set her back down on the rough road with a thump. "I won't be falling for no tricks and judgment from faerie folk. Ain't going to give you the last of my food and water, and ain't going to curse you, even if you do sound half-mad. Just going to leave you where I found you."

"But I am the queen of Carlion. I order you to help me!"

"Keep telling that tale." He stomped to the front of his wagon. "You'll get a ride to the madhouse." He climbed up onto the driver's bench and clucked to his massive, muddy horses.

The old man with him stood up enough for Merrigan to see his hunched back and bald head. He muttered something, and the young men with him guffawed.

"Great-grand says you aren't even pretty enough for him!" one of them called, as the wagon started forward.

"How dare you!" Merrigan ran after the wagon a dozen steps, though she wasn't quite sure what she wanted to do.

"Just a wrinkled old crone. Not enough of you for tinder," he called. More guffaws rang out, bouncing off the trees and mud.

Merrigan stopped, her knees threatening to fold. She trembled so, she feared if she sat down she would never get up again.

"I'm not," she whispered, as the wagon bumped down the road

and faded into the distance. "I'm tall and raven-haired, with gray eyes and roses in my cheeks and I can dance all night and all day until the musicians beg for mercy." She shuddered, fearing those brute peasants had been speaking the truth. The clothes she wore were certainly fit for a crone.

After thinking until her head hurt, Merrigan turned and made her way up the road in the opposite direction. She certainly didn't need to meet those brutes in the next town and have them laughing at her and pointing fingers. Half an hour later, a family of farmers in a much cleaner wagon, pulled by two smaller horses with flowers woven into their manes, approached from behind her. A man with a cheerful voice called out greeting to her and offered her a ride before she could even think to ask. The farmer and his sturdy wife and three daughters, all of them browned by the sun and almost unbearably cheerful, addressed her as Granny, with some respect. That confirmed, but in a nicer way, what the brutes had said. The girls adjusted the sacks of cotton and fleece filling the wagon, which they were taking to town to sell, to make a soft seat for her. They offered her a cool drink of water from a clay jug and included her in their unbearably cheerful chatter about all the things they wanted to do when they were in town.

Merrigan was still smarting badly from the mockery of the brutes in the first wagon, so she kept her silence and let them believe she was tired. Their consideration for her comfort was most gratifying. Yet these people were strangers, not her servants. What was wrong with them, to be so kind to a total stranger?

When they reached the town, the smallness of it stunned her. The way the girls had talked, she expected a major city, with an enormous merchant district. This place boasted only four streets of merchant and artisan shops. She counted only four inns, a barracks and a courthouse. Merrigan didn't doubt the circuit judge only rode out here once every four moons. There was a town square, with a well, a dancing floor, and a dais for musicians. How could the girls have been so pink-cheeked with excitement over ... this?

She forgot her disdain for this disappointment that called itself a town when she stepped down from the wagon. She looked down into a watering trough between her and the steps up to the raised walkway around the town square. Merrigan stared, horrified, at the sagging jowls and pale skin, the red-rimmed eyes that looked like ashes rather than the dusky crystals praised by simpering courtiers. Leffisand had always teased that he preferred her eyes filled with sparks, ready to flame with righteous indignation. Her eyebrows and eyelashes were nearly nonexistent, her nose was twice as long and had a definite downward hook. She saw a protruding mole on her chin, another on her cheekbone and a third between her eyebrows. Her hair had once been so lustrous thick and dark that court poets described it as midnight velvet stolen from the skies. Now it was thin to the point she feared she had bald spots, and that peculiar shade of white that was no color at all.

Clara had indeed cursed her. Who would ever believe her when she said she was the queen of Carlion?

Yet that filthy brute who accused her of working with faeries had given her an idea. People still expected to be rewarded by majjians if they did outstanding things or ridiculously simple kindnesses. Didn't they? If the folks hereabouts thought faeries were interfering, then she could convince the fools that helping her would earn them a reward from the fairies. Or hedge witches. Or minor enchanters. Or faerie godmothers.

If all else failed, she could follow the stories of magic at work until she found the nearest majjian and request help. As long as that person hadn't heard what Clara of the Pools had done to her. There had to be some rivalry among majjians. If she was lucky, she would find someone with a grudge against Clara, and convince them to help her to spite the seer.

"Are you all right, Granny?" the farmer's wife asked, gripping Merrigan's elbow as if she thought she was about to fall over.

"Perfectly fine. Just thinking deep thoughts."

"Where do you plan to go from here?"

"I would like to see the world. Now that my husband is gone, and his property has gone to his kinfolk." She caught her breath, knowing that was happening in Carlion right that moment.

She had never met any of Leffisand's relatives, other than his wretched healer cousin, Rafal, until the funeral. The greedy graspers insisted Leffisand was an evil, scheming brute who had exiled them. They were likely stripping the palace of its riches. That horrid Rafal had likely proclaimed himself king. Did anyone pity her, as the childless widow? No. She had no claim to the throne because she hadn't given Leffisand a child. So she had gone to Clara for help. Why did the woman take offense that she had lied about being pregnant, so she could stay queen? How hard would it have been to give Merrigan a child conceived through magic? Why was it so horrid a thing?

What right did Clara have to call her selfish and cruel and arrogant, and condemn her to wander the world until she learned kindness? A queen who was kind and generous was weak, simply asking people to trample over her. Kindness would make her a target for the cruel and arrogant and selfish.

Just like her mother, Queen Daylily. Hadn't being kind ultimately killed her mother?

"Yes," she said, catching her breath, fighting not to shudder with her fury over the injustices that had hit her, one after another, until a lesser woman would have crumpled. "I want to see the world. I want to find magic and wonder and see incredible things."

"Well, you are equipped for travel. Do you have a cloak for when it rains?" The farmer's wife gestured at the heavy bag that had been hanging at Merrigan's hip this entire time.

Of course, she hadn't looked into it. Who had time, when they were struggling to escape a barbaric forest and find civilization? Merrigan let the farmwife check her possessions, to see if she was supplied. She had a shawl, extra stockings, extra underclothes, a spare shirtwaist and skirt, an eating knife, and a few slim bound volumes. Merrigan couldn't believe Clara could be so kind, and knew her love of books. A moment later, she knew she had been right. The first book was a collection of homilies on thinking virtuous thoughts and acting with generosity and honor.

The other two volumes were poetry, and tales of the actions of majjian folk. Merrigan wondered if the book had been there before or after she resolved to find someone with magic to pity her and help her. Was Clara taunting her, helping her, or warning her?

The farm family insisted she should share their dinner at the finest inn in town. Then they asked a merchant friend to help her on her journey, by letting her ride in his wagon to the next town on his route. Merrigan thought that was highly generous of them, and quite unexpected. She was just stunned enough to listen to the prompting from her childhood memories. Her first nanny, Starling, had gently scolded her to always say her thanks. No matter who had been kind to her. No matter how grand or small the gift. She thanked her benefactors with graciousness far above their station, climbed into the back of the merchant's wagon, and fell asleep.

Oddly, she dreamed about the farmer family on their journey home in the moonlight. *A star fell from the sky. The girls cried out with childish pleasure and made wishes for each other's happiness. They drove up the lane to their farm and found their dogs digging in the garden, just uncovering a small wooden chest. When the farmer pulled it out of the ground, he found it full of coins as silver as the light trailing after the star.*

Merrigan woke feeling quite discontent. Perhaps it was just a dream, but she almost wished she had accepted the offer to go home with them. Were they so foolish they would have shared the treasure with her? With just a handful of those silver coins, she could have hired a carriage to take her to the nearest port and booked passage to Armorica on a fine ship.

Yet what good would it do her to return to Carlion, when it was no longer her home?

Perhaps she should go home to Avylyn?

"Oh, yes, return in this wretched state, to live in hiding and shame until Father persuades some majjian to restore my proper face and form?" She snorted in a most unqueenly manner.

"Awake back there?" the merchant called from the front of the long, enclosed wagon. He sounded far too jolly for so late at night.

In point of fact, when she climbed out from the interior of the wagon, Merrigan found she had slept the night through and it was early morning, that sparkling time when dew covered everything. She settled on the long driver's bench and allowed the merchant to offer her some breakfast: weak, sweet wine, an apple, and a hunk of bread spread with sweet, soft cheese. His assistants, who had slept on the flat top of the wagon, called down good morning to her and chattered nonstop about the town up ahead of them. It was much larger than the one she had left behind. They were sorry to tell her she was still several days of travel away from the nearest port. One said he admired her for following her dream to see the world, and he wished her strong legs and the endurance to see everything her heart desired. Merrigan thanked him regally, taking the blessing at face value, no matter how crudely stated. Perhaps when she had regained her place -- and her face -- she might send back to this crude little country and reward him. She would astonish them all with the realization they had had a queen among them, and didn't know how to treat her properly.

His talk of following her dream reminded her of her dream of the farm family. She asked the merchant about his friends, what sort of people they were. His words dismayed her.

"Aye, they're the most generous folk, and it seems like whatever they give away, they get it back double. Nicest folks you ever want to meet. You'd think there are majjians watching over them. They do something nice and helpful, beyond what an ordinary man would expect, then something good falls on them. When bad things happen, they take it in stride, and whatever they lost is paid back double. Like they're being rewarded for suffering." He nodded for punctuation. "That kind of thing happens to old Tom, regular as rain falling from the sky."

Merrigan made polite noises, and demurred when the merchant offered to tell her stories about Farmer Tom and his family. She had made a terrible mistake. She should have accepted their rough hospitality and gone home with them. They were such generous and goodhearted simpletons, she could have told them her entire sad story, and they would have helped her. They might have even pleaded her case with whatever majjian had taken the family under his protection, and mended her life for her.

That settled it. She had to go back. She asked the merchant to turn around and take her back, she had changed her mind and wanted to accept the family's invitation. He laughed for a moment. Why did people think it was all right to laugh at her?

"I'll be glad to help you, Granny, but I have my route to keep. People are expecting me to deliver what they ordered. You can ride with us, but it'll be more than two moons before we get back to Tom's place. Is that all right with you?"

What could she say? Of course it wasn't all right, but telling them that wouldn't do her any good. She didn't look like a queen, so who would tremble in fear of disappointing her? She thanked him and agreed.

At the next town, the merchant's big sons helped her down from the wagon and treated her to a fresh meat pie from their favorite vendor. Then she walked away without a word of goodbye. Perhaps she should have said thanks, but she feared they would try to stop her. Perhaps say she was crazy, like those brutes the day before. Merrigan set off for the far side of the merchants' square, where dozens of wagons were unloading, and pointed herself at a wagon that seemed aimed back the way she had come.

The world spun around her, the lights flickered and the ground slid from under her feet. Merrigan let out a most unqueenly shout.

Until you turn, you are forbidden to return, while ungrateful thoughts linger in your mind and pride in your heart, Clara whispered in her memory.

Merrigan landed on her knees in a patch of violets along the side of a tree-lined road. She heard nothing but the whisper of the wind through the leaves, and far off, the songs of sleepy birds. She turned around and settled on her bottom, drew her knees up to her chest, hid her face in her knees, and waited for the tears to come.

None came. Apparently, she was too wrinkled and dry and shriveled up to even cry in frustration.

So she wasn't allowed to go back, once she had turned her back on rustic hospitality and generosity? What common sense was there in that? Where was the justice in the world?

"Fine, then. Have it your way. I'll find someone to take pity on me and help me, no matter how much you interfere," she whispered.

Such words would have had greater effect if she had leaped to her feet and stomped out of the violets and headed down the road. Merrigan was too tired, and somewhat achy from her landing, so she made herself comfortable and sat and thought for a time. When no wagons came down the road after nearly two hours, she got to her feet and resumed walking.

By nightfall, she found her way to a village small enough that people noticed the elderly stranger among them. They offered her shelter in the little building that served as a general meeting hall and chapel. The bread and butter, mug of milk and bowl of porridge provided weren't up to her standards, but she said nothing. Demanding better because she was a queen would earn her mockery. She curled up on the bench cushion the circuit judges used, wrapped herself in the blankets several people offered for the night, and told herself she was quite comfortable. She was, compared to how she could have spent the night.

She finally fell asleep, trying to persuade herself that she liked the silence and solitude. The porridge reminded her of her nursery days, before Nanny Starling fell from grace and Nanny Tulip took over. Her dreams were full of her long, secret, magical correspondence with Leffisand, and all the advice he had given her, helping her to grow wise and insightful, to become a queen worthy of him. He had taught her the truth behind all the tales of faeries and godmothers and other majjian folk. He claimed they were lies, sweetened to trick people into trusting magically gifted folk. The witless, ignorant and undeserving always expected to be helped, rather than picking themselves up by their own bootstraps and fighting for what they wanted.

As the days and moons passed while she journeyed, Merrigan thought long and hard about the things Leffisand and Nanny Tulip had taught her. The truth behind the tales of majjian folk. While she trudged from village to town, she had many chances to see majjian injustice at work. It galled her to realize some of the too-sweet-for-their-own good twits who helped her with a loaf of bread, a coin, a ride down the road, were often rewarded soon afterward.

If faeries were waiting around every corner to reward every village idiot and simpering twit for performing charity, why did none of them show up just ten minutes earlier and help *her*? She was Queen Merrigan of Carlion, daughter of King Urson and Queen Daylily of Avylyn. Surely she deserved their help.

By the third moon of her unfair exile on the other side of the world, Merrigan decided the imbeciles and goody-two-shoes of the world had an unfair advantage over the clever girls and boys who wouldn't stand for any nonsense. Granted, the sweet girls and boys were the ones who actually noticed the shriveled old woman in need of food or a place to spend the night. Several times she considered going back to tell them she was a queen under a terrible curse, and ask if they would put in a good word with the faerie or pixie or minor wizard who had just rewarded them.

Each time, she mentally slapped herself. *Asking* for the help that should have been hers by right galled her.

She chewed so long on the injustice that had been meted out to her, she got past the sharpness of the ache. She learned to examine the whole situation with less emotion, and tried to determine where the mistakes had occurred. Possibly, she had done something wrong. Of course, not anything bad enough to warrant what she now suffered. Perhaps she was being punished for something Leffisand did? Was being stupid a crime? Or perhaps her husband had been a little too clever, a little too lucky? Could he have brought his ignominious demise on himself because he had broken several rules of magic? She had been deprived of her throne, her home, her beauty, because of something *he* did?

She would be safely at home in Carlion if she had produced the heir to the throne. Could it be the fault hadn't been with her at all? Perhaps Leffisand was denied an heir because of underhanded things he had done? Things she knew nothing about? After all, she had heard the rumors. There was the whole magical apple tree debacle, and the accusations that Leffisand had been involved in the death of his first wife, Fialla. Merrigan didn't believe any of it, otherwise she never would have married him, but … what if?

If that were the answer, it simply made her whole situation more unbearable. She suffered for the crimes of others. She had been robbed, cheated, when she was innocent of wrongdoing.

In the very next village, she looked at the villagers with new eyes, and watched their interactions, seeking the innocent and cheated among them. Surely there would be a kindred soul here? There had to be, since injustice filled the world.

She decided the blacksmith was dangerous. He had a thin smirk on his thick face, when he settled at the village well and watched the young people dancing that night. He had a way of looking at people that made her skin crawl. Merrigan asked the baker's daughter about the blacksmith the next morning, when the girl gave her fresh bread dripping with butter and honey. The girl looked in all directions before leaning closer to whisper that the blacksmith was new to their village. He had arrived last fall, claiming he was the long-lost younger brother of their smith, who had just died. No one could dispute him, because the brother had indeed been gone for nearly twenty years and no one could remember if he looked like his older brother or not.

They accepted him and let him take over the smithy. The four orphaned sons of the smith were only half-trained. They needed a teacher. The village needed a blacksmith. Nobody could fault the man, but nobody was entirely happy with him, either.

Merrigan did not believe in coincidences. Chances were the new smith had arranged for the death of the old one and came in to take his place. Probably by magic. That was just the way the world worked, according to Leffisand and Nanny Tulip.

The elderly, she had discovered by this time, were easily ignored. Merrigan settled under an apple tree where she could see and hear the activity at the smithy. Before the morning was half-gone, she was enraged at how the man ordered the four boys around, as if they were slaves. If she was right, he was a fraud, stealing their inheritance. Just like her kingdom had been stolen from her. She had to bite her tongue not to shout a command to stop, whenever he slapped the boys with the heavy leather gloves used for handling the hammer and tongs. Or when he swung a bar of red-hot iron perilously close to one boy who didn't respond fast enough to suit him.

"Hello, Merrigan."

She stiffened at the sound of that damp, warty-sounding voice. It couldn't possibly be -- could it? She looked down, bracing herself, and nearly didn't see the tiny, brownish frog sitting on a pillow of moss only a few steps away from her. Thank goodness, it wasn't Veridian, prince of frogs.

"What do you want?" She started to slide away, then stopped herself. She refused to admit that the sight of a frog, especially a talking frog, made her distinctly uncomfortable.

"Why are you scowling at those poor boys? Are they too noisy for you? Too dirty? Too ragged?"

"Not them." She could have bitten her tongue, to be caught conversing with a frog. What had conversing with Veridian in her mother's secret garden ever done for her? "Their uncle. I'm sure he's stolen the smithy and their inheritance. There's just something about him I don't like."

"Well, there's some hope for you yet." The frog let out a croaky chuckle. "You're right, he did steal it. He's selling the boys as slaves, at the fair in Blintytown tomorrow. I heard him promising them to a one-eyed man who stopped here three days ago."

"You have to do something. That's unfair. This is their home, not his."

"What can I do? Besides, you're the only person here who can hear me."

"What can I do?" she echoed, only half-heartedly mocking him. "I'm a stranger. People may be kind to the elderly and frail, but they don't listen to them. Especially not strangers. I'm quite tired of being laughed at and called mad."

"Forewarned is forearmed." He hopped away while Merrigan tried to decide if she should kick him, or even risk warts by picking him up and flinging him away.

She fumed, chewing on his words, until the blacksmith walked away at noontime to get his meal. The boys were left to tend the forge, and he left nothing for them to eat. That just added fuel to the fire inside her. Ordinarily, Merrigan believed in letting peasants cheat and trick and steal from each other and reduce their numbers so their betters didn't have to look after them. However, those boys looked so helpless, and so young, and there was just something appealing about them, under their dirt and bruises. Forewarned? Would it be enough to warn them?

The baker's girl came around the smithy from the back way, with a basket covered in cheesecloth. Her furtive look gave Merrigan a good hint of what she was doing. She wasn't surprised at all when the girl whistled softly and stayed in the shadows of the trees, close to where Merrigan sat. The boys came running and she quickly handed them bread with thick slabs of cheese, and an apple each. They thanked her with much nicer manners than Merrigan would have credited them, and she blushed prettily and turned to leave. Then she saw Merrigan sitting only a dozen or so steps away.

"Oh, Granny, I'm sorry. If I had known ..." She looked back over her shoulder at the boys, who had emptied her basket.

The youngest looked up and his gaze met Merrigan's. She shivered and lost her breath for a moment. Was that tingle in her fingertips a sign of some majjian nearby, watching? Of course, it would be the youngest who looked at her, looked at the remaining bread and cheese and the apple in his hand, and moved away from his brothers. Why was it always the youngest chosen for magical tasks and help? More important, why wasn't she granted such protection and help, since she was the youngest daughter of the King of Avylyn?

Chapter Two

Merrigan was hungry enough, she wanted to take all the bread and cheese and apple he offered her, but what if there was some majjian watching? She wanted to gain a few sympathy points. She refused the apple, telling him a growing boy needed something in his belly. What he had offered her was more than enough. Even though it wasn't. Then she told him what the frog had told her.

"Oh, I believe it." The baker's daughter looked in all directions, as if she feared the false blacksmith would come upon them at any moment. "No one likes him. The entire village knows how he treats you and your brothers, but what can they do? If he's your uncle, he has authority over you and the forge."

"We can tell the magistrate and the judge and the king's soldiers, when we go to the fair," the boy said. His brave little smile made Merrigan's heart ache, just for a moment.

Why was it always the brave and honorable and hopeful who got hurt the worst in this world?

The girl promised she would tell her father, and he would warn other leading men in the village, and they would do something. The one-eyed man would not claim his new slaves. She hugged Merrigan and hurried away. The youngest boy thanked her again, quite gravely, and insisted she take his apple before he ran off to tell his brothers.

Merrigan decided now might be a wise time to get up and leave. No matter how careful the good boys and girls were, they always told the wrong person what they knew, and who had been helping them. Something about that man made Merrigan quite sure he would hurt her if he knew what she had done. That really wasn't fair, she silently complained, as she hurried down the road. After all, she had only passed on what the frog said.

How desperately she wanted to stay around and watch the feathers fly. Just imagining the ruckus that would soon enfold the village occupied Merrigan's thoughts for at least an hour. She chuckled and hurried along the road, grateful that all the walking she had to do had restored her youthful vigor and endurance. Not that she thought she would need to dance until dawn any time soon. She considered lingering in the general area to find out what happened to the blacksmith. As a child, she had found it entertaining to eavesdrop on the nobles of her father's court, or ambassadors, or ministers in the council, and then stir up trouble by leaving notes, revealing what everyone's rivals or enemies had said or planned.

"Why not?" she muttered, after glancing over her shoulder for at least the twentieth time since hurrying away from the village.

Merrigan stopped and looked back the way she had come. Did she really want to go back? One village looked pretty much like another, which was depressing enough in itself. She needed to move on from small villages and towns and find decent-sized cities. Some place large and sophisticated enough that when she mentioned Avylyn and Carlion, people actually knew what she was talking about. She needed to find an ambassador or diplomat with the intelligence to believe her, and help her get home. Once she returned to Avylyn, surely her father could find someone with enough magic to break Clara's curse. What use was it being the most powerful king in Armorica if he couldn't get a curse lifted?

Still, wouldn't the leading men of this village feel some obligation of honor and arrange to get her to the nearest city? She had helped defenseless boys escape slavery, hadn't she?

"They owe me. Four brothers with hammers against one nasty, loud-mouthed uncle who might not even be their uncle? They should have stood up for themselves long ago. Their father died under mysterious circumstances. Shouldn't someone have been suspicious about the convenient timing? Idiots like that don't deserve any help. Especially from someone like me, who certainly needs far more help." With a snort and a sharp nod for punctuation, Merrigan set off down the road, back the way she came.

Dizziness washed over her. For several unpleasant moments, she felt as if she had been turned toes-over-nose. The sunlit road around her vanished in a haze of gray, with silvery sparkles at the edges. The bread and cheese she had eaten turned into hard lumps that bounced around in her stomach.

Drat and double drat!

Too late, Merrigan remembered Clara's confounding and

contradictory words.

She went to her knees in the grassy verge along the side of the road. Merrigan knelt there, gasping, until the ground steadied underneath her. When she raised her head, the oaks that had lined the road had changed to pines. The sunshine of early afternoon had faded to evening, with low-slanting rays and that bluish tint in the air that always promised a refreshing chill. Or at least, a refreshing chill when there was a palace to retreat to, and servants who brought warm shawls without being told.

Merrigan struggled to her feet and took several steps up the road. A much nicer road than the one she had been on two minutes ago. No deep ruts from wagons traveling in rainy weather, churning up mud. This road had large quantities of gravel ground into it, creating a sturdy surface. Amazing how much she had learned about road construction just from trudging down one road or cow path or trail or mislabeled king's highway after another.

It just isn't fair!

The momentary urge to weep made Merrigan realize how thirsty she was. She fumbled in the bag that bobbed and bumped against her bony hip with every step and pulled out the apple the boy had given her. The sweet-tart juice filled her mouth and she paused, stunned to discover she had a full set of teeth. All the gaps and loose teeth that threatened to snap if she bit into anything harder than week-old bread -- fixed. For all she knew, Merrigan had her own good, firm, white teeth back.

"Well, what do I make of this?" she murmured, after chewing the mouthful of apple and thoroughly enjoying it. In fact, she hadn't enjoyed a fresh, firm, juicy apple in far longer than she could remember. The problem with Leffisand's rebellious magical apple tree had quite put her off apples. What had she been missing? "Is this a reward, or just another nasty trick?"

Merrigan gnawed on the puzzle of what had happened, why, and the implications for her as she trudged down the road. After all, evening was coming and she had no intention of spending the night in this unknown forest with nothing but the remains of this apple, the extra clothes in her bag, and her walking stick. She had to find a town. Surely this visibly better road meant a good-size town of some wealth or standing had to be nearby.

This had better not be just another aspect of her totally

undeserved punishment. Did Clara honestly think she, Merrigan, Queen of Carlion, would be grateful to have her own teeth back? Or consider being able to eat an apple a reward? Who would be so foolish and gullible to think that dropping her on an unknown road was helping her? Perhaps some foolishly honorable kingdom-less prince would consider the change an improvement, but not Merrigan, Queen of Carlion. Reward? Hah!

She fumed over the unfairness of her situation as she moved from one town to another in the days that followed, always trying to find one larger and more aware of the kingdoms of the world. Why did she have to depend on the kindness of the little people for food, for a bed by the fire on rainy nights, for a ride in their cart? She was a queen -- surely justice decreed that wealthy merchants and town officials should be sent to help her along the way. Didn't the leaders of the community deserve a chance to be rewarded for helping her? Why didn't majjian folk hereabouts give them a chance to better themselves by helping Queen Merrigan?

No, it was entirely unfair that enchantresses and faeries always sided with the undeserving. The too-sweet-for-her-own-good twit who couldn't recognize that people were trying to steal the magic key left to her by her dying mother. Or in the case of an impoverished-but-noble young man, the map to a hidden kingdom where a princess lived under an enchantment, just waiting for a good-but-simple youth to break the spell.

How, with all the odds stacked against them, could any of those sugar-coated, cockeyed optimists continue to help old ladies and drowning puppies and enchanters in disguise who needed a pure soul to fetch some magical item? Merrigan just didn't understand. To make matters worse, several times she turned away with a loaf of fresh bread or climbed down out of a farm wagon and saw some majjian swooping down to reward whoever had just helped her. It wasn't fair. Couldn't they see her, standing there bold as life, desperately in need of help?

Finally, she had to have an answer. Certainly four moons of living under Clara's entirely unfair curse had earned her a few answers? Especially with winter approaching. Her chance came when a boy gave her a ride on a decrepit old donkey and helped her down at the intersection of five roads. The nearest town was called Smilpotz. He apologized profusely and explained that the man who had taken the mill that belonged to his family for ten generations had convinced the local judge to forbid him to come any closer to town than the crossroads.

The boy gave Merrigan a loaf of bread, three copper coins, and the names of several people in town who would help her for his sake. He wished her well. She thanked him -- it was only polite, after all -- and headed down the gravel-packed road wide enough for three carts. At the point where it turned to enter the trees, she glanced back, and saw him heading back the way he had come.

She wondered why, despite her habit of trying not to think about anyone she had left behind. Most especially not someone who had all the earmarks of downtrodden-and-deserving like this boy, on the brink of manhood.

Merrigan's next step faltered. She understood. He had retraced his steps for the last two miles to give her a ride to Smilpotz. His decrepit little donkey certainly hadn't needed her negligible weight on its back. From the deflated condition of his food sack and the lack of jingle when he gave her the coins, the boy certainly hadn't been able to spare either food or money, yet he had given them to her. What was wrong with him?

She froze as a faerie appeared, not thirty steps away. At least, she assumed the coldly handsome man with a face carved from black diamonds, with sapphires for eyes and silver for hair, was one of the Fae. He watched the young former-miller take the time to check his donkey, adjusting the few sacks tied to its back. The boy pulled out a bowl and spilled water from a water skin into the bowl, then held it for the decrepit creature to drink.

"He could have offered me some of that water," Merrigan muttered.

The Fae turned and stared at her, freezing her with the blue fire in his eyes. She shivered, feeling as if her crone disguise had been stripped away. He could see her, Merrigan of Avylyn. Even more chilling, she had the distinct impression he didn't like what he saw.

Then the Fae smiled, bright and glacial-cold. Merrigan cried out. She *tried* to, but the sound caught in her throat. He turned into *her*. The crone she was now. He called out with a creaky, frail voice, and hobbled down the road after the boy. Her voice didn't sound that bad, did it? Oh, the injustice!

The imposter commended the boy for being willing to help

people, even though the mill that had belonged to his family for so long had been stolen by a cheat with false documents and a lying judge in his back pocket. The imposter then consoled him for endangering the health of his donkey, who was lame in one leg and shouldn't have taken even the weight of a shriveled old woman.

"I could have told you one leg was off, just from the bumpy ride," Merrigan muttered. Stunned that she could speak now, she tried to move. No luck. All she could do was watch and listen. She was probably invisible, too.

Oddly, she felt a tiny flicker of some discomfort that wasn't related to the ache in her bottom from sitting on the bony spine.

Still, I could have walked this far on my own. It's not like I couldn't make it. Who did he think he was, making an old woman ride that awful, knobby old thing? Maybe trying to win a reward?

As much as she tried to make herself believe that, Merrigan couldn't. The young man had been entirely too kind, too considerate of her, to be faking it. She knew from long experience how to tell the difference between true gentility and false manners. The ones who stooped down to help a threadbare old woman, with expansive gestures and loud voices, only did so when they had an audience. The food they gave her, even if it was higher quality, didn't taste nearly as good as the simple fare shared by someone who couldn't afford to share.

Strange. Why hadn't she noticed that before? Maybe she was losing her mind, under the weight of this dratted curse.

Merrigan's grumbles halted when the look-alike resumed his otherworldly, cold good looks. His chuckle was entirely too warm and pleasant to be real, when the miller's son dropped to his knees, stunned with wonder. At least the boy had the sense to be frightened. He might not be quite as much an imbecile as others who didn't deserve magical help. However, when the boy stood up, wearing fine clothes, and climbed onto the donkey that had been turned into a massive white stallion, that was the last straw.

"Excuse me?" Freed from magic once the boy rode away, Merrigan stumbled forward, through a berry bush. "What about helping someone who really needs it? Or do you have some awful grudge against old women?" She stomped down the road toward the Fae, who simply stood there, hands clasped behind his back, getting a little taller with every step she took. By the time she reached him, his head was even with the treetops. "Maybe our time has passed, and we don't have a right to help? Don't trust to appearances -- isn't that something you're always--"

"I know exactly who you are, Merrigan of Avylyn," the Fae said, his voice deep enough to shake the ground.

"Don't I need help too?"

"You need even more help than that good-hearted young lad, but there's the pump principle involved here." His smile was a glacial smirk. "You probably don't know what a pump is, do you?"

"Of course I know," she snapped. "I've had to pump my own water when I'm thirsty. The rudeness of some people, filling troughs and buckets for themselves, but when I step up and need some water, suddenly I'm invisible."

"No, you're just as visible as all your servants ever were. Your fellow travelers are in a hurry, and since they're used to having to fend for themselves, they think everyone else can do the same. Have you ever heard of asking -- not ordering, but *asking*?"

Merrigan knew better than to snarl that she was a queen, she shouldn't have to *ask*, she shouldn't even have to order. People should just be on the alert, watching for her slightest need. She didn't look like a queen, after all. She didn't sound like a queen.

"I ask plenty of times." Her hands shook just at the memory. The memories of the times she had to lower herself to beg for a piece of bread, for some cheese, scalded her soul.

"At least now you know you have a soul," the Fae man said.

She trembled. The cold running through her had nothing to do with her usual fury when some majjian saw into her thoughts.

"Back to what I was saying." He chuckled and bent down so his eyes were even with hers. They burned bright. "The pump principle. It's called priming the pump. When a pump has sat idle for some time, you must put water in before you can get water out. All your life, you've been taking from the pump. You're as dry as some pumps that haven't given water in years." He stood up, his smile even colder. "You're a smart girl, Merrigan. So smart, you've been very stupid. Think about it. What would Nanny Starling say about the predicament you've gotten yourself into?"

"Nanny -- How dare you!" She shuddered hard enough she nearly went to her knees.

"Think about what you just heard." He gestured down the road to the spot where he had rewarded the miller's son.

Then he vanished in a haze like hoarfrost that fell down on the road and dusted Merrigan's black dress with white. She shivered. Any other time, she might have welcomed the chill. Black clothes were hot, and it was an unusually warm, pleasant fall day.

"Pumps," she muttered. For a moment, she wished the boy had offered her a ride on his big, strong horse, but she had too much sense to take a chance on a beast that had been magically transformed. "Just where am I supposed to find a pump? And where am I to find water to prime the pump if the pump is dry?"

She shuddered and looked down the direction the miller's son had gone, then slowly turned to look at the intersection of five roads where she stood. The stone pillars standing between the roads indicated the towns each road led to, and how far away they were. The boy had to leave the closest town, Smilpotz. If he had told her his name, she couldn't remember. Smilpotz was just beyond the woods, according to the markers chiseled into the stone pillar. The town where his ancestors had run the mill that now belonged to a cheater with a dishonest judge in his back pocket.

"I know what it's like to be cheated out of what belongs to me," Merrigan muttered. "Will it make you happy if I do something about it?" she said, just a little louder, to the now-vanished Fae. That didn't mean he was gone. Someone who meddled in the lives of others likely remained nearby to see what she did with his unwanted advice.

If she had learned anything from Leffisand's mistakes, it was that majjian folk had to be treated with far more respect than her peers. Much as she admired Leffisand and understood why he took such pains to protect the treasures of Carlion, she had to admit that her late husband had made rather large blunders. For instance, the Gifting of his great-uncle. He should have ingratiated himself with the old healer, and played on their family connection. The doddering, idealistic fool should never have Gifted his healing magic to that milk-and-water, goody-goody farmer princess.

"Enough." Merrigan shook herself for good measure. Wasting time nattering over things she couldn't change and people she couldn't bring to justice only drained her.

Very well, she would go to the town that had cheated the miller's son and set the balances right. Maybe that would please the

Fae and earn some help in the future. Maybe all she had to do was help someone, to earn a champion who would perform some magical quest to rescue her. She tried to ignore that totally unreasonable sense of guilt at not knowing the miller lad's name.

Merrigan straightened her shoulders as much as she could and set off down the road to Smilpotz. At least there was enough gravel packed into the road that the mud wasn't too awful, and she had shoes she didn't mind getting muddy. Not like they were satin slippers, or her favorite dancing shoes with the blue crystals. Leffisand had said it was like she danced on water when the light glistened on them. He would be horrified to see her walk through the mud in those particular slippers.

Then again, if he were here, she wouldn't be in this mess.

"Leffisand," she said with a sigh, as she trudged down the road. "For such a clever man, you were rather an idiot, weren't you?"

An odd twinge threatened a headache. Honesty compelled her to admit the true idiot ... was her. If she had just held her ground and not depended on so many panicky lies, she wouldn't have had to run to Clara for help. What fools ever got the idea that a woman who stared into pools of water could give them useful advice?

"You made this mess, Merrigan," she said as she reached the crest of the small hill and could see down the slope to the decent-sized town of Smilpotz. "Now it's up to you to fix it."

~~~~~

Judge Brimble's large, recent inheritance was the talk of Smilpotz. Merrigan sat on the steps of the bakery, enjoying a freshly baked roll and a lovely, cold cup of milk, and listened to the gossips who had gathered on the steps of the apothecary next door. The people discussing the same subject on the steps of the millinery across the street were even louder. Being turned into an old woman had taught her the joys of being nearly invisible, and the wealth of information that came from listening to people who talked far too freely for their own good. Merrigan had observed that some people proved the reliability of their information or opinions by raising their volume. She wasn't sure if she should be comforted or worried that it was the same among peasants as it was among courtiers.

The louder voices across the street informed her that Judge Brimble wasn't happy with the tailor who ran the best of the two fabric shops in town. His apprentice had gone home to tend to his
~~~~~

dying father, so it was just the tailor, his wife and daughter to handle all the orders. The mayor's daughter was getting married in a fortnight, and the tailor was halfway through a large order of clothes for the bride, and for the wedding party. No matter how much the judge offered to pay him, he couldn't put aside the order because then he wouldn't finish on time.

The gossipy old women on the steps of the apothecary changed their chatter, in competition with the millinery gossips. The judge was far too talented at making people miserable if he didn't get what he wanted. He had already hinted the tailor's young daughter was just the sort of confection he liked. After money, fine clothes, and food, of course. Brimble would find some way to threaten the tailor's family until they either turned over their daughter to placate his injured pride or abandoned the wedding clothes.

"Poor child," one silver-haired, hawk-nosed old gossip said with a sigh. "Someone should do something. Judge Brimble is getting too big for his britches. In more than one sense!"

That set off a chorus of giggles among them.

Merrigan gritted her teeth. When she was younger, she had lost several serving maids to the predations of nasty old courtiers who insisted on having sweet young serving maids for their wives. Even worse, her father never believed her when she insisted the girls were going into dangerous situations. He always accused her of being selfish, and five serving maids just to attend to her needs were far too many.

The foul-tempered wives with delusions of grandeur always seemed to drive the serving girls away in no time at all. Then to make matters worse, they generated false stories that the girls had fallen in love and left to get married and settle down in the country. When Merrigan tried to find the girls, certain they needed rescuing, those vicious old nobles started rumors that the girls had actually gone into their employ to escape serving *her*.

Well, here was one serving girl Merrigan could rescue. Technically, the tailor's daughter wasn't a serving girl, and hadn't fallen into danger yet. It was just a matter of time. Merrigan wondered if she could remember that spell Nanny Tulip had taught her, for enchanting collars so they choked their wearers at the appropriate time. She had learned that spell after her mother died and after Nanny Starling fled in disgrace, and her own sisters and brothers grew critical and ignored her. Nanny Tulip had taught her about minor magics and how a princess deserved to be treated. She helped her wreak small bits of revenge on anyone who slighted her or treated her as if she didn't have a brain in her head.

Unfortunately, Merrigan hadn't used the spell in years. She hadn't needed to, after she married Leffisand, because his courtiers knew how to give her proper respect.

In that moment, the whisper of a plan seeded itself in her mind. She chuckled, positive it would be deliciously clever and properly nasty, as the old lecher deserved. He had to be the judge who had helped cheat the miller's son.

"Are you finished, Granny?" The baker's assistant bent down to Merrigan where she sat on the steps. "Would you like more?"

"No, thank you. It was lovely." Merrigan didn't mind giving a compliment to the rosy-cheeked boy. She had seen him take the bun from the long tray fresh from the oven, when his master told him to help her as she walked into the bakery. Such kindness touched her heart. Maybe when she got her looks and her kingdom back, she would send someone with a gold coin to reward them.

That would certainly make liars of the people who called her an ungrateful brat.

She got up off the steps and made her way to the tailor's little house at the far end of the main street of Smilpotz. Her steps were slow, in contrast with her racing thoughts.

Her mother had taught her to sew, as an entirely proper occupation for a princess. She enjoyed sewing. As a child, Merrigan had loved taking scraps of cloth and bits of braid and beads, and turning them into gowns for her dolls. She had also enjoyed the admiration and envy of the other girls her age among the nobility in the court of Avylyn. Sewing in her mother's garden had been among the happiest parts of her childhood. She hadn't been that happy in many years.

Merrigan stopped in the middle of the street, startled by the single tear that trickled hot down her cheek. She blotted it with the back of her fingerless black glove and muffled a sigh.

Nanny Tulip, however, believed sewing wasn't a proper occupation for a princess. Except when used in magical pursuits, such as the choking collar. Merrigan could never reconcile the conflict between her mother's teaching and her beloved nanny's.

Well, Nanny Tulip would certainly approve of the plan that slowly clarified in her mind. She had been a stickler for propriety. Judge Brimble was abusing his power. A mayor and a wedding certainly trumped a fat old lecher's desire for a new wardrobe.

"Can I help you, Mistress?" Master Twilby, the tailor, rose from his chair behind the long worktable in the front room of the house and shop as she stepped up to the open door.

"Would you have some work for these old fingers?" Merrigan held out her spindly hand, proud that it didn't shake. "I don't need much, just a blanket, some bread, and a roof over my head."

"Sorry, but even though we could use some help, it wouldn't be for long. The boy who works for me is due back in ten days."

"Oh, that would suit me perfectly. I just need a place to rest my feet, catch my breath, so to say."

"Can you sew seams?"

Merrigan most definitely did not want to sew boring seams. What she wanted was the fancy work, the ruffles and embroidery and stiff collars -- especially the collars. However, she needed to get her foot in the door. Then Master Twilby would see the common sense of handing over the fancy work to her, and leave the drudgery to his daughter and apprentice. It would be easy. Peasants were so simple-minded and so easily led.

"Faster than the dawn, and straight and tight. So tight it'd take you a fortnight to rip one out," she added, tipping her head at that slight angle guaranteed to convince him she was adorable, if not slightly daft.

For some reason, everyone assumed the slightly not-right-in-the-head were trustworthy and good-hearted. Merrigan couldn't see it herself. She was positive most people only pretended to be daft to avoid doing an honest day's work, or to perform some deception. As she did now.

Master Twilby would thank her someday, when he learned the truth.

She imagined him kneeling before her, shaking in terror when he realized he had hired Queen Merrigan of Carlion to sew seams. He would profess undying gratitude for her help in protecting his daughter from that lecherous Judge Brimble. It made such a pleasant mental picture, Merrigan almost missed the quick, low discussion between Master and Mistress Twilby when the lady of the house came in from the kitchen. She had the impression the wife was far more willing to hire the old woman. Perhaps just because she was an old woman who needed work.

Just for that, Merrigan took extra pains with the test job they gave her. Let them doubt her ability to do anything she set her mind to. Master Twilby's smile and slow nod of approval, as he inspected the vest she had put together in good order, generated a warmth in Merrigan's chest she hadn't felt in a long time. Actually, she couldn't really remember the last time she had felt it.

By dinnertime, she and Mistress Twilby had done the main seams on the matching vests for the mayor and his two sons and future son-in-law. He was a minor nobleman in Carnpotz, a major city twice the size of Smilpotz. Merrigan thought the brocade for the vests entirely suitable for a wedding. The mayor's daughter had good taste. Merrigan was grateful for the subdued color scheme. After all, she didn't want to suffer eye strain the entire time she labored in the tailor shop. She intended to be given Judge Brimble's wardrobe order, as soon as Master Twilby realized he could now handle both jobs.

Mistress Twilby became almost chatty, as they put away the vests to make dinner. Merrigan faced a moment of dread. She wouldn't have to cook, would she? She had never learned, and had no interest in learning. It seemed so utterly messy, and rather alchemical. Cooking made her think of enchanters working in dark, damp dungeons, throwing together potions. Spells were fine, but potions and all the cutting and mixing and the smells and vapors made her uneasy. She would prefer to avoid magic of any kind for the rest of her life, thank you very much. After this curse on her was broken, of course.

To her relief, Mistress Twilby asked her to set the table while she and Fern, her daughter, took care of the final preparations. Merrigan learned that Mistress Twilby had assembled their dinner that morning, putting everything into an enormous cast iron pot and then sliding it into the oven to cook all day. It was a simple matter of pouring mugs of cider for everyone, cutting bread, and dishing up an amazingly delicious, hearty stew.

Perhaps there were some benefits to taking gainful employment. Hot food and sitting with the family. Welcomed by them. Included in their chatter, even if it was of plebian things like the town gossip and sewing the mayor's daughter's wardrobe. All of it was rather ... surprisingly ... pleasant.

After dinner, the sewing continued. She didn't really mind. The kitchen was warm and well-lit and Mistress Twilby provided hot tea with plenty of honey. Master Twilby praised the straightness and tightness of her seams, and asked if she would be so kind as to teach Fern the trick of it, now that the girl was old enough to move on from piecing and pinning. Merrigan didn't mind teaching her at all. In fact, it was quite easy to be gracious.

The odd, tight feeling in her chest did give Merrigan pause. She couldn't quite understand the wet warmth in her eyes, either.

"I hope you don't mind, Mistress Mara," Master Twilby said, as he came back into the kitchen with a thick, ragged-edged book, the cover so worn she couldn't read the title. "We do enjoy some reading in the evening, especially after a good day's work and getting back onto schedule, thanks to your opportune arrival."

"Of course not. I assume this is some volume of edifying homilies?" Merrigan frowned when a giggle escaped Fern. What had she missed? The snotty little thing wasn't mocking her, was she? Such a deceptive child. Just a moment ago, Merrigan had been sure she was the sweetest, most attentive child she had ever met.

"Fern," Mistress Twilby scolded softly. To Merrigan's amazement and slight irritation, she chuckled, then reached over to pat her arm. "In some sense the stories my husband reads could be considered educational. There's always a chance of running into someone with magic, or who has been enchanted. Though the chances aren't as strong as they were in my grandfather's day. But yes, the tales could be considered educational."

"I don't care if they're educational," Fern announced with a sharp nod of her head. Then she astonished Merrigan by snuggling up against her on the long, padded bench by the stove where the three women sat. "They're fun. You like stories about magic spells and heroes and maidens trapped in durance vile? Don't you?"

"I -- I --" Merrigan swallowed hard, confused by that odd, twisting, warm sensation in her chest. "I adore such stories, actually."

Granted, she had adored them more when Nanny Tulip and Leffisand hadn't been teaching her the truth behind the mask of glamour in tales of majjian folk.

To her delight, the first story Master Twilby read was one she hadn't heard before. Honestly, the lack of common sense of some Fae -- blessing the goody-goody sister so every time she spoke, flowers and jewels fell from her lips? That was a blessing? And for what -- for being polite and giving an old woman a drink of water? Didn't the silly child owe such kind actions to the elderly as a matter of course? Then, the stupidity of the mother, to send her more ambitious child to the well, with orders to be nice to the next old lady. So what happened when the Fae returned, this time dressed as a queen? The girl was put out because she wasn't the old lady who would bless her with an utterly inconvenient and messy gift.

Who in their right mind would consider that a gift? The girl would have to spend the rest of her life with a trough or a feedbag affixed under her mouth, to catch whatever fell out. Graces help her if she were a chatterbox! Imagine the mess during polite dinner conversation, and then the hazards to people around her on the street or during social events. Pity the people who stepped on the jewels she didn't catch. Then of course, the Fae didn't recognize that the other daughter was confused because the encounter didn't go as expected. She wasn't ready to face nobility, which Merrigan imagined could be a most unbalancing experience. The Fae proved just how temperamental her kind were, when she cursed the second girl to drop toads from her lips whenever she spoke.

Education, indeed! Merrigan wondered if such tales were more for the education of the parents than the children. If they could warn their daughters and sons to act with more common sense when they went into the woods, or stay out of the woods altogether, the world would be a calmer, more sensible place. When she was queen again, she would see if something could be done about that. If magic and majjians couldn't be controlled, perhaps all magic should simply be eradicated.

That thought gave her an odd shiver. It felt close to something she had overheard in an argument, long ago. Some insistence that magic was being wasted, and people shouldn't be allowed to fling it about as they wished. Magic needed regulation, or it would entirely run out. Had Nanny Tulip said something similar?

A distant rapping on the front door startled Master Twilby, two minutes into the second story. He stood, nearly dropping the book. Mistress Twilby went entirely still, except for her fingers, which curled and crushed the vest she had been hemming. Master Twilby hurried out of the kitchen. Only Fern seemed unconcerned.

"Who would come at this time of night?" She hopped off the padded bench and stepped over to the stove where the pot of tea kept warm. "Would you like more tea, Mistress Mara?"

"Thank you, child, that would be lovely." Merrigan reflected that it was easy to be gracious to a sweet girl with lovely manners. With the proper clothes, her hair in a more becoming fashion, she would make an enchanting little handmaiden. Merrigan sighed as she held out the large earthenware cup to be filled. By the time she regained her kingdom, Fern might be married, with children, and no longer a delightful, pretty little creature.

Fern paused in putting the teapot back on the stove. She frowned, glancing toward the door into the tailor shop at the front of the house. "Who is Father talking to?"

"Little pitchers have big ears," Mistress Twilby murmured, her hands shaking. She never looked up from her sewing, as if suddenly her life depended on finishing the hem.

Chapter Three

Merrigan focused on listening. The other man's voice was deep and too hearty. He sounded like several members of her father's court who were entirely too certain of their value in the world, their power and influence, and their right to stomp on anyone who didn't give them their way. Such people had thought they could stomp on her, when she was a child. Merrigan had taught them a thing or two and enjoyed it.

"If there is any justice in this wretched, magic-sickened world," she whispered.

"Is something wrong, Mistress Mara?" Fern asked, coming back to the bench.

"Not if I can help it." Merrigan smiled, though the effort hurt her face. How she loathed having to hide her feelings, when there was no one to tremble in the face of her anger. She put down her sewing and got up to find Master Twilby.

A man stood on one side of the long sewing table, hands braced on it, leaning over the table and making Master Twilby cower back a step. He was exactly like those odious courtiers Merrigan remembered. Big -- big shoulders, big hat, big voice, big nose, big triple chin, big belly. The tone of his clothes was big as well, the colors just a shade too bright, and too many colors together, for Merrigan's taste. His tall walking stick was ebony, with an ivory handle in the shape of a lion's head. Too ostentatious for this size of town. It lay on the table in front of his braced hands, like a dividing line between him and Master Twilby.

"I don't understand why you are so unreasonable. It's a perfectly sensible solution," the man said, his jolly smile entirely too big. How could anyone talk and smile at the same time? Maybe that was what made his voice so big?

"What you are asking, Judge --"

"Ah, so this is Judge Brimble?" Merrigan swept into the room as she used to sweep into one of Leffisand's meetings with the council of lords. He had always found great amusement in her ability to interrupt the meeting at the most crucial time, intimidating the nobles dimwitted enough to resist his plans for the country. She just wished she had her full skirts and long train. The simple black dress and widow's cap utterly ruined the effect.

Still, from the widening of the judge's eyes, the straightening of his shoulders, she hadn't quite lost her touch. Maybe he had no idea why, but he felt intimidated.

This will be fun.

"Master Twilby, have you told him our plan yet?" Merrigan held out her hand to the judge as she once used to do with ambassadors and visiting princes.

Judge Brimble was just provincial enough to frown at her hand for a moment before reluctantly, with the grip of a limp fish, bowing over it. She supposed she should be grateful he didn't kiss it. No one liked being kissed by a limp fish.

"What plan is that?" Brimble said, his voice only at half the previous volume.

"I assume you have come here to ask once again about Master Twilby fitting in your entirely necessary order for clothes to befit your station, despite the previous and honor-bound commitment to take care of the mayor's daughter's wedding clothes."

"Err ... yes, exactly." His piggy eyes -- the only things about him that weren't big – narrowed, and he looked her over as he released her hand. "And you are?"

"Mistress Mara, formerly of the courts of Avylyn and Carlion. I sewed for the royal family in Avylyn and came to Carlion when Princess Merrigan married King Leffisand. With all the upheaval after the death of King Leffisand, well ... the wise flee before they can be caught up in turmoil they had no part in causing." She nodded her head once, in what she thought a sage manner.

"Sewed? For royalty?" Judge Brimble turned to Master Twilby. "And when were you going to tell me such a talented woman worked for you?"

"Did you give him time?" Merrigan asked, as Master Twilby's mouth flapped several times and no words came out. "I only arrived today. Such a pity you weren't informed. So depressing, the lack of the niceties in these provincial backwaters. But you, sir, I hear you aim for bigger and better things. Your wardrobe must reflect your potential. Master Twilby and I have been working out a plan for me to design your new wardrobe. All done as discretely as possible, so as not to incur the wrath of the mayor. Master Twilby didn't want to make promises to you, raise your hopes, before he had anything solid to offer. A man of your stature, after all, shouldn't be disappointed. Master Twilby had considered putting me in charge of the wedding clothes, but then he decided your new wardrobe had higher priority."

"Yes ... yes, of course." Judge Brimble's face brightened and he let out a satisfied chuckle that shook his massive girth. "Clever, Twilby. I appreciate you putting my feelings ahead of your profit. Shows you have more common sense than most people in this benighted town. No wonder you hesitated over my suggestion."

"What suggestion was that?" She fluttered her eyelashes at him and took a step closer, as if inviting him into her confidence.

"He wanted me to send Fern to live at his house and tend to the sewing. He thought it would give us more room to work, and save time, running back and forth." Master Twilby gave Merrigan several sidelong glances. Almost as if he feared her.

"Splendid idea," she said, and fought hard not to burst out laughing. She hoped her face wasn't bright red from her repressed mirth. So unbecoming.

"It is?" The poor tailor's voice cracked, and he went whiter than his starching powder.

"That will support our decision to be discrete. If I live in Judge Brimble's household, no one needs to know that I am actually in your employ. Everyone will believe that I have been hired by the judge. He can let my credentials be known -- entirely by accident, of course, because a man of his stature has no need to brag about the talents of those in his employ. No one will know that you put the judge ahead of the mayor, or that the judge is paying you for my services. In fact, providing for my room and meals will cut down on the higher fees I usually charge for my services."

She fought more laughter when Judge Brimble's mouth and eyes twitched at mention of "higher fees." She had pegged the man accurately. A miser about paying decent wages, but lavish with his own comforts. If he thought he was saving money by having her under his roof, that was his error, and made willingly.

"I'll leave the two of you to work out the final arrangements. Dealing with money is so tedious," she said, dropping a curtsey to them both. Merrigan was certain both men held their breaths as she swept out of the room.

Mistress Twilby burst into tears and flung her arms around Merrigan, after she told her what had happened. She found it rather irritating and slightly discomfiting when the woman insisted that she must have been "sent." Stuff and nonsense -- she had made the choice. No one had made her come to this town. She was inflicting a little justice on Judge Brimble for her own satisfaction, and for the sake of the miller's son -- she still couldn't remember his name. Merrigan still needed to find the man who had stolen the mill from him. He had done it with the help of the judge, so she was one step closer to her goal.

While it was lovely to have the gratitude of the Twilby family, being in the judge's household would make it easier to find the man who had taken the mill. When she had dealt with that cheat, then she could leave Smilpotz. Perhaps when she got out onto the main road, that alarmingly handsome Fae would be waiting for her, ready to grant her some much-needed and highly deserved help.

Everything was working out perfectly.

~~~~~

Judge Brimble's servants were suitably cowed, for the most part, from the moment Merrigan walked through the door, early the next morning. She arrived before there was enough traffic on the streets of Smilpotz for anyone to see her leave the tailor shop and walk to the judge's house. The household staff consisted of two overweight, pock-marked serving girls who seemed to find the floor fascinating; a bald, swarthy-skinned cook with a peg leg and eyepatch, who had the audacity to wink at her; an elderly, stiff-backed seneschal who looked down his nose at Merrigan; a pasty-faced clerk who looked like he should still be in school and not studying for the law under the auspices of Brimble; and two boys who saw to the stables and drove the judge's carriage. The house sat on the far edge of town and was large enough to impress Merrigan. Four stories tall, built of stone, the narrow window slits gave the impression the manor house had originally been a fortress.

She decided the judge was indeed too big for his britches as soon as the seneschal took her on a tour of the premises to find the perfect room to set up her workshop. He had entirely too many rooms for a man who had yet to find a wife and, according to town
~~~~~

gossip, preferred to entertain in the largest tavern in town, instead of his own home. Half the bedrooms didn't have any furniture. The windows were shuttered and then sealed with waxed sheets of linen. They all smelled musty. The servants lived in the back of the house on the second floor, with plenty of room between them and the judge's living area. He occupied the front of the house on the first two floors, occupying a massive bedroom, another room twice as large for his wardrobe, a sitting room, an office, and a dusty dining room. One other room was of note, but as Merrigan learned quickly, he never really used it. The library sat on the second floor, spanning the office and the dining room below it.

Merrigan lost her breath at the sight of the library. Between the floor-to-ceiling shelves jammed with books, the thick curdles of dust over everything, and the knowledge of just what a perfect location that was to listen in on everything transpiring in the office, she wasn't sure which detail impressed her most. Or maybe it was the delight of seeing the seneschal go white when she declared she would use the library for sewing, and he had to have it thoroughly cleaned. Immediately. After all, when she had chosen all the fine cloth for the judge's new clothes, the material had to be handled in spotlessly clean surroundings.

The seneschal couldn't argue with her, because it only made sense to use the library. No one else was using it, as attested to by the curdles of dust that turned all the thick leather book spines the same drab shade of gray. The windows between the bookshelves provided light from the south and east. The three long study tables in the middle of the room could be pushed together to form one long worktable to handle several pieces of clothing in various stages of assembly. The thick-cushioned chairs were a bonus. It was as if the library was made to order.

She decided to move into the library, once she saw the parsimonious bedroom allotted to her. The cushion on the deep window seat would make a much more comfortable bed than the thin pallet on a narrow frame waiting for her.

It wasn't as if the judge would be inconvenienced. From the thickness of the dust, he hadn't consulted his library in years. To carry out his duties properly, he would need to continually consult the volumes of law. Yet he obviously didn't. Her father prized men who kept learning, who weren't ashamed to admit they didn't know something, then sought to learn twice as much as they needed to carry out their duties. Despite his softer qualities, her father was a wise man and a good ruler, and Merrigan trusted most of his assessments of people's worth. The King of Avylyn would loathe Judge Brimble just as much as she did. Yes, such a dunderhead deserved the punishment she would levy on him and his co-conspirator.

The two stable boys came to fetch her shortly after the cleaning effort started. Merrigan left the two serving girls battling the thick layers of dust with damp rags. She followed the boys outside, to the back courtyard, where the judge's coach waited. He was pacing in front of its door, eyes bright and step amazingly light for such a big man. When he saw her, his arms spread wide and Merrigan cringed at the horrified thought that he might try to embrace her.

Of course, he didn't know a beautiful young queen hid behind the decrepit husk of Clara's curse. His emotions ruled him, not lust.

"Mistress Mara." He bowed to her, and straightening, pulled a leather pouch from his pocket. "I entrust you to obtain everything necessary for creating my new wardrobe. The lads have been instructed to take you as far as Carnpotz, if need be. Here is my letter of introduction with my seal, so no one will dare say no to you. In fact, dear lady ..." His eager-little-boy expression dimmed as he looked her over. He sighed. "I think perhaps your first stop should be to procure better clothing for yourself. It is a tragedy that the failings of others put you in such dire circumstances. How shall I put this delicately for a lady of your great talent?"

"I do not look the part. Some people might think I lied about having handled Queen Merrigan's clothes personally?" She kept her voice dry and light. She had found that softening her tone effectively made people with booming voices stop booming.

"Indeed. You do understand."

Merrigan understood very clearly that if the judge weren't in such a dreadful hurry to have his new clothes, he might have showed some common sense and investigated whether an old, white-haired woman named Mara had indeed been a seamstress for the courts of Avylyn and Carlion. That kind of investigation could take moons, and require crossing the ocean. She had been counting on the judge's impatience and vanity to keep him from investigating. Only a fool took a total stranger's word as fact. This was another proof of her theory: people assumed the elderly, frail, daft, and very young were trustworthy and truthful.

"I do understand, Your Honor." She took the pouch of coins. It was satisfyingly heavy and didn't jangle as she slipped it into the bag still slung across her chest. "I do thank you for trying to be delicate about a woman's vanity." She fluttered her eyelashes for good effect, and nearly burst out laughing when the judge shifted backward half a step.

Did the self-obsessed fool think she flirted with him?

"I shall repair my outward appearance so that I will not embarrass you, if anyone should remember who bought the material for your splendid new wardrobe. I shall make sure every penny is devoted to my task. The outcome shall be most satisfactory for all involved."

There -- let anyone take apart her words and prove she promised to spend all the money on him, rather than putting as much as she could into her own pocket. This further ensured that he paid for his part in cheating a decent-if-gullible young man out of his inheritance. That would satisfy the Fae who had presumed to lecture her. Just because he had magic in his blood, that didn't give him the right to criticize. If Merrigan hadn't learned the painful lesson of dealing very carefully with majjian folk, she might have told him a thing or two about the twisted, unreasonable expectations of the magical races in general.

Merrigan's estimation of the judge's foolishness increased when she found a basket packed with food for the journey, tucked into the carriage. The man was falling over himself to please her, without any proof of her skill.

She had plenty of time on the carriage ride to plan her actions for the next few days. Servants knew everything within a household. They became invisible to their employers and they saw and heard things that many people kept hidden from their own spouses and children. Their invisible, all-seeing position made servants rather valuable -- once trained properly.

As the first step in gaining the confidence of the entire household, Merrigan rapped on the roof of the carriage, asking the boys driving it to stop. Much as she would have preferred to keep the provisions to herself, she shared the meat rolls, honey cakes, and the thick stone bottle of cold milk with the boys. It was amusing to see how their eyes lit up, and to observe the visible shift in their attitudes toward her. Such simple, malleable people, these peasants. She had to assume the judge was so cavalier about the treatment of his servants, any kindness earned their admiration. If she could simply remember to continue such treatment with the entire household staff, she would have them eating out of her hands. A somewhat disgusting thought, if taken literally. In short order, she would have their confidence and they would help her in taking down the judge. Destroy sweet young girls like Fern Twilby, or cheat the miller's son of his inheritance? Not while an intelligent, determined woman was anywhere in the neighborhood.

The first shop she visited was to provide herself with better clothes than the rusty black widow's weeds. While Merrigan would have loved to indulge in the deep jewel tones she saw on one rack of bolts of cloth, the material was too expensive and fragile. She had learned the value of having sturdy clothes while living on the road. Besides, the rich burgundy or the deep emerald green, while perfect for her coloring when she wore her own face, would look utterly ridiculous with her pale, sagging skin and white hair and washed-out eyes. Much as it galled her, Merrigan chose from the clothes the shopkeeper offered. She assumed the unfashionable clothes were discards from people who no longer wanted or needed them. Along with fresh new underpinnings and much better shoes, she chose two complete outfits in dark blue and a rich gray with hints of purple. Both were too large for her, but the shopkeeper gave her a box of pins for free. She used them to adjust the blue dress so she could wear it out of the shop and present a much better image to the other merchants she would have to deal with today. Once she altered her new clothes, she would be quite well-dressed, even if on plain and simple lines. She would prove her talent, even before the judge walked about in his new clothes.

Now, if only she could remember that spell Nanny Tulip had taught her, for making collars that choked their wearers days and moons after she had made them.

~~~~~

The library was so utterly transformed when Merrigan returned to Judge Brimble's house that evening, it astonished her into a good mood. She did love the smell of fresh lemon wax and floor polish and the aroma of cleaned leather. The bindings of all
~~~~~

those lovely books shone with quiet splendor as she walked around the library, inspecting the cleaning job the two serving girls had done. The library in her father's palace had been her favorite place, her retreat from an unkind, critical world, and her heart had ached a little when she saw the neglect inflicted on this place. The stable boys moved the tables into position in the center of the room, under the massive oil lamp chandelier, under her direction. Then they brought in the packages from four different shops, full of all the supplies Merrigan needed for her tailoring work.

The fresh, hot meal the girls hurried to bring her, before she could even ask, raised her spirits even more. Merrigan thanked them and, according to her long-term strategy, asked if they wanted to see all the lovely fabrics and thread and buttons and trimmings she had bought. When she offered to teach them fine sewing, to better their stations, the girls clasped hands and muffled little squeals of delight. Merrigan knew she had them in the palm of her hand. With some surprise, she decided they were actually pretty, under their dull clothes and an extra stone or two of weight.

Judge Brimble was entirely too jovially pleased with the choices in cloth and colors and patterns, when he came to inspect her purchases the next morning. Merrigan feared he might embrace her this time. Fortunately, she was already hard at work, using the sharp new scissors bought with his money. He never asked her how much everything cost, though he did care which merchants she patronized and who might have seen her in his carriage. He also complimented her on the improved image she presented in her new clothes. Merrigan almost felt a flicker of sympathy for him, when she thought of the tidy stack of silver coins tucked away at the bottom of her bag of buttons and trimmings. Between a mixture of respect for and fear of Judge Brimble and casually mentioning that she had been a seamstress to royalty, many shopkeepers and merchants offered Merrigan lower prices on her purchases. She knew they depended on her to come back, and likely planned on improving their reputations by boasting that they had sold to her. Whenever Judge Brimble came into Carnpotz, they could point to his clothes and say that the material came from their shops.

Master Twilby expressed his gratitude for Merrigan's intervention with a basket of fruity pastries, fresh from Fern's clever little hands, when he sent over Judge Brimble's measurements. That saved her the somewhat distasteful task of having to get close to the man and touch him. Now all she had to do was make patterns to suit the current fashions.

Judge Brimble was in such a jolly mood that his voice boomed through the house all morning. Merrigan sat in her library, measuring, marking, cutting, smiling, and listening. The pipe for the heating stove in Judge Brimble's office connected with the pipe for the library stove. It perfectly funneled sound up to Merrigan for her to hear every conversation he had there. She had plenty of paper and ink and ten fine quill pens that the serving girls had procured for her. Flora and Fauna. She made sure to remember their names, since it was important to her plan. Whenever something interesting came up in the judge's meetings, Merrigan made notes. She didn't learn any plots that first day, or even hints of plots to cheat other people, but she did learn quite a bit about the town of Smilpotz. The judge considered himself not only admired, but well-liked. He treated all his visitors with a jolliness that had Merrigan gritting her teeth several times. Even with a floor between her and them, the tones of the many voices, the hesitations, the broken sentences taught her the people coming before Brimble might respect him, but from fear and desperation, not admiration. Her father, by contrast, had ruled Avylyn with justice and honor, and the people had been intensely loyal by choice, not through intimidation. Bribes and threats didn't work well on people who were loyal to an admirable man.

What Merrigan heard solidified her resolve to have Brimble taken down a few notches, his benefactor mask torn away. He simply was not admirable. Not like her father. And not just because she owed the miller's son a good turn.

"Why can't I remember his name?" she muttered, nearly skewering her finger with the needle she had been trying to thread. "Oh, bother ..." She sighed, put down the needle and thread, and rubbed at her temples.

She had been sitting too long. After what felt like years of walking from village to town, she wasn't used to sitting for more than half an hour at a time. She felt restless. Oddly, she thought she might miss, just a tiny bit, being outdoors and on the move.

"That can be fixed easily enough," she muttered, looking around the massive library. Two or three circuits of the room, and then she could concentrate on the judge's conversation with the baker, who was upset over someone spreading false tales about finding ashes in his bread. Merrigan knew those were lies, because she had thoroughly enjoyed the light, tasty bread the baker had given her for free. A man who adulterated his flour and lowered the quality of his goods wouldn't give away free bread. Cheats didn't have that generosity of spirit. Anyone with a bit of common sense could figure that out in two seconds.

She circled the room twice, making a game of walking as silently and lightly as thistledown. The baker had been disturbed by the rumors enough to confront the people spreading them, to demand proof that the bread they had eaten was bad. Merrigan snorted at hearing that. If the bread was bad, they should have returned it and demanded their money back, instead of just complaining. Any fool knew that. Talk was no good without proof.

"Told you so," she muttered, when Judge Brimble echoed her thoughts, but in more formal, legal language. Then the baker said the people he confronted had only repeated what others said.

Her attention caught on something on the far side of the library. A stray beam of sunlight had moved across the wall as the afternoon aged, and landed on a jumble of old papers tucked into a corner bookshelf. She found that odd, because Flora and Fauna had done a splendid job of cleaning. Even odder, while the papers seemed jumbled and discolored and dusty, there was a sparkle in that dustiness. Still listening to the now-boring conversation in the room below her, she crossed to that odd bookshelf. Why hadn't the girls straightened out those papers while cleaning? Why did the papers sparkle?

She shuddered at the idea that bit of glitter in the air might be magic. Merrigan shook her head. While there was plenty of magic in the world today, much of it was in the hands of solitary enchanters who preferred to be left alone, or in the hands of interfering, judgmental busybodies. Or people like Clara, who never took into account the dreadful circumstances that forced people to lie to defend their rights. Nanny Tulip had told her stories about the wars between great and powerful majjians who tried to impose standards on all others who worked magic around the world. Many had vanished, either drained by their battles or simply because they no longer cared. According to Nanny Tulip, the dreadful results of their battles remained in the world, and the non-majjian suffered for it. The chances of encountering some magic in Judge Brimble's too big, too ostentatious house were very small.

"I should have guessed," she said on a sigh, when she reached the corner bookshelf and discovered a sheet of wavy, green-tinted glass across the nook in the shelves. Corner bookshelves were useless for storing books, because most of the books were tucked out of sight. They were most often used for hiding things, or getting useless things out of the way.

Merrigan lightly ran her fingertips along the frame holding the glass in place, seeking the latch. Someone at some time had decided that jumble of papers was worth putting away behind the glass. She suspected Brimble might not have entered the library since he inherited it, and didn't know this corner and those papers existed.

"I do wish I could find a latch of some kind," she muttered, and stepped back to let the fading light stream past her. It sparkled on the glass and the papers behind it, and Merrigan let out a sigh of exasperation. There, where her fingers had pressed not two seconds ago, was a hinge. She looked on the opposite side of the frame. There was an indentation, allowing her to slide three fingers in between the frame and the bookcase and tug the glass door out. Now why hadn't she seen that before?

She opened it slowly, anticipating a swirl of dust from the movement of air. A loud creak. She jumped and froze. No, the creak came from the judge's office. She smiled at her jumpiness. Who would walk into the library without knocking first? Wasn't the library her domain now? Besides, she doubted anyone in this household cared about books.

Merrigan, however, loved books, all the treasures of knowledge and secrets and useful information hidden inside them. A soft moan of dismay escaped her -- that wasn't a jumble of papers sitting on two shelves, covered in dust that had filtered in behind the glass panes.

That was a *book*, cruelly ripped from the binding, the pages tossed into uneven piles. She held her breath as she brought the piles out and put them on the table under the light from the chandelier. This was an old book, hand-written. Such odd, old-fashioned, looping handwriting. The yellowed vellum pages were stained by water and what might just be mud. The ink had run in some places -- the words still legible, though -- and in others were dimpled from water. She found the broken binding and empty wooden cover panels and torn pieces of the leather cover buried among the pages. Merrigan's hands shook from anger as she lifted a few pages to examine. Why would someone so utterly destroy a book, and yet save the pieces?

"I suppose some idiot destroyed it in a fit of rage, and someone else salvaged it, intending to fix it." She lifted a few more pages, squinting at the loopy handwriting and old-fashioned spelling. The pages had headings, so she sorted through the first twenty or so pages and put them into groupings by the headings. That would certainly help in re-assembling the book.

Merrigan stopped short at that thought. Why would she even want to assemble the old book?

After a few moments of internal debate over the waste of time versus doing something she would enjoy, which Judge Brimble hadn't paid her to do, she put the papers down and dug out the broken cover. Merrigan move slowly, delicately. Not because she expected the book to be valuable, but just because it was a book.

She saw writing on the spine. Tiny and faded, but retaining enough golden sparkles to make the letters legible. The fact someone had written with gold ink had to mean it was valuable.

"Of the great secrets of this land," she read aloud, slowly piecing together the words. "I do like secrets." She put the cover down slowly, carefully, spreading it out flat so the inside surface faced upwards.

The book waited for its torn pages to be put back into place. Like a hand waiting to be filled.

She shuddered from some feeling she couldn't understand, and shut the glass panel with a careless, soft thud. Merrigan fought the urge to stick her tongue out at the piles of pages, and walked back around the table to resume her sewing. She had work to do, a little bit of justified punishment to levy.

Oddly, when Fauna brought her supper tray, the girl didn't notice the broken book lying at the far end of the long worktable. Even more odd, Merrigan kept looking at those papers all through her evening of sewing. She imagined sewing the pages back into the binding with the same ease as she sewed the first seams of the snowy linen shirt. She couldn't push aside the thought of reweaving the book together, even when she was tired enough to lower the chandelier on its long chain to blow out the oil lamps. She left just one lamp to light her way to bed in the thick chair cushions piled in the big, deep window seat. Sighing with satisfaction, she adjusted the clean blankets that smelled of lavender, and closed her eyes, falling swiftly into sleep.

Merrigan heard a voice through her dreams, whispering, pleading with her to fix the book, and promising her rewards beyond her wildest imagination.

She didn't believe in wild imagination. She believed in common sense and having a careful plan and making calculations and carrying through. And not trusting in anyone but herself for success, as she had learned through bitter experience.

Still, would it be so bad, hedging her bets?

When she woke the next morning, she dismissed the night's dreaming and pleading and considerations as just that -- dreaming. Yet the idea of putting the book back together lingered at the back of her mind while she cut out the material for a second shirt and basted the pieces together. During her noon meal, she overheard the judge laughing with someone about the baker's frustrations with all the lies being told about his wares.

That decided her.

The book had to be valuable, to someone. She would repair it and take it with her when she left, and serve Judge Brimble right if it turned out to be a treasure he had overlooked. The man was odious, and his cruel treatment of a book just proved it.

She had to do something to punish the egotistical bag of hot air, since she still couldn't remember Nanny Tulip's handy little spell for choking collars. After a full day of listening to that man talk, the false joviality in his voice, comforting and advising one man over problems that provided amusement to someone else two hours later, Merrigan wanted to do more than frighten him. That was all the collar would do -- choke him a few times, frighten him, turn his face red and cut off his voice at inopportune moments. Eventually the spell would wear off, or he would throw the collar away. She couldn't do anything permanent. She had never been able to do anything permanent.

"That's the problem, isn't it?" she muttered as she put aside the tray with her half-eaten meal and picked up the pieces of the first vest. "Only simpletons get permanent. Granted, if they have the wisdom to protect it. Most of them do learn to be a little more alert. Why can't I get permanent? My problem is that I get soft and rely on other people. I never should have trusted Leffisand to hold onto the kingdom. Or his own life, for that matter. Oh, Leffisand, why did you have to be so stubborn? Would it have been so bad to let that noble idiot cousin of yours heal you?"

Merrigan stopped, the words catching in her throat, at the sight of three, now four, now five, drops of water on her sewing. She wasn't crying, was she? She hadn't let herself cry in years. It was such a waste of time and energy. Someone always came in and caught her crying, and that was simply embarrassing.

Sniffing and then swallowing hard, to ensure a sob didn't escape her, she got up from the table, walked around it three times to steady herself, and blotted at her eyes. Rubbing only added to the redness from tears, and that simply wouldn't do. Whatever was wrong with her, to get so weak and weepy?

Before she quite knew it, she had a bundle of pages cradled in one arm and had sorted several dozen according to the headings of the pages. Oddly, she found the motions somewhat soothing. She glanced at the headings and sorted and her mind drifted. At least she wasn't dithering over Leffisand and his foolish --

"Scorch it," she muttered, and nearly threw the papers down. "Just when I was starting to feel better. I wish I could -- no, I don't really want to forget about Leffisand entirely. Those few years we had together were rather enjoyable. I liked life in Carlion much more than I did back home." A sigh escaped her. "I don't want to forget Leffisand. After all, what use would it be trying to get my kingdom back if I couldn't remember why I was Queen of Carlion? No, I just wish it would stop hurting so much."

She paused in reaching for another stack of pages to sort. Odd, how this work was going much quicker than she had anticipated. Merrigan could have sworn someone called her name. Her real name. She was going by the name Mara. False names were much better for protecting her dignity. It wouldn't do for someone she had met along her exile travels to show up in Carlion, expecting payment for the piddling little good deeds they had done for her.

Merrigan paused, half the pages sorted, caught between the urge to fling them across the room and to sort faster. What was wrong with her? It was like there was an argument in her head, correcting her every time she spoke her thoughts aloud.

"Granted, Leffisand employed far too many lies and nasty tricks, but wasn't he justified in punishing people who got in his way? He was the king. He had to protect his throne, his kingdom, his people … his lies." Merrigan looked at her empty hands and the sorted piles of pages. Somehow, she had gotten through the first stack of ripped-out pages and had ten piles of pages now. She rubbed at her temples. She actually felt a little better, as if she were accomplishing something important.

"Poor Fialla. She simply wasn't the right wife for Leffisand. Much too sweet and good-hearted and weak. King Conrad would have been a much better choice for her." Another snicker escaped her. "Thank goodness he ran away in horror when someone proposed he ask for me. The only one who really wanted me was Bryan, and he …"

Merrigan closed her eyes to wish away the image of a long-forgotten, handsome, young face. She hadn't thought of Prince Bryan of Sylvanglade in years. Had it been ten, or more than that? At least he had never formally proposed marriage. The youngest son of a large royal family in a small kingdom, he had no chance. Even before she learned to always consider power and never accept anything less than an heir, she had known better than to encourage Bryan.

It just showed how low she had fallen in the world, to think of him now. Better to concentrate on other things. Such as all the handsome crown princes who had looked at her and either shuddered in fear or stomped away in disgust and wounded pride when she refused them. Conrad of Jardien had been one of the former.

Chapter Four

Merrigan sat in front of the piles of pages, rested her head in her hands, and let out a few odd, teary chuckles. It was the dust from the pages that got on her hands. The paper dust got in her eyes. That was where the tears came from.

Someone whispered behind her, "If that's what you want to believe, go ahead. It'll just make everything take a little longer."

"Who asked you?" she snapped, and looked around, making her neck ache a little from the sharp, quick movements.

She was losing her mind. There was no one else in the room. While it was all well and good, and rather relaxing to be shut up in a library all day, she might just need someone to talk to. Or at least to hear some voices other than Judge Brimble pontificating and lying and mocking, his voice coming in hollow tones from the room below her. She had thought the plan was brilliant at the time she came up with it, but Merrigan saw flaws in it now. Sitting still all day, sewing in solitude, with servants to bring her tea and check if there was enough oil in the lamps, had seemed a wonderful, intelligent plan at the beginning. Now, though ... she might just be losing her mind, if she was hearing voices in her head. And worse yet, voices arguing with her, correcting her. No one had dared correct her since her mother died and she lost Nanny Tulip.

"Oh." Flora peeked around the door, instead of coming in to pick up the tray with her empty dishes. "Didn't you like the stew? Or the apple dumpling?"

"Hmm?" Merrigan rubbed at her face and got up. Yes, she simply needed to get up and walk and get her blood flowing a little faster. "Oh, yes, they were delicious. I'm simply not used to eating so much at a sitting, and so regularly."

"Are you all right, Mistress Mara?" The dumpy serving girl peered up at her, wrinkles of concern around her eyes and mouth.

"It's rather quiet in here. When I was -- when I had a home," she corrected quickly. If she said, "when I was queen," she would find herself locked up in the local madhouse, with others whose minds had been broken by too much magical interference. "My husband used to play his fiddle in the evenings when I did my sewing. Or he would tell me stories." She certainly couldn't admit she had a music ensemble to play soothing music, and someone else to read stories to her, when she had a headache or couldn't sleep.

For the first time, Merrigan wondered what those servants did when she didn't need them for days at a time. She rubbed harder at her temples. Such thoughts were just more proof she was slowly losing her mind. Was that part of Clara's curse? Drive her insane, so she spent the remainder of her days huddled in a dark corner somewhere, whimpering and talking to herself?

"I don't suppose there are any books of fables or humorous journals in here?" She gestured at the shelves of books. Judging by the bindings, the dyes in the leather still fairly strong, they had seen little sunlight or use since they had been bought and shelved.

"There might be," Flora said with a little shrug and a glance around the room. Her eyes widened a little. "It must be lovely to be able to read anything you want."

Most likely, Judge Brimble never gave his servants permission to read during their off time. Another reason to dislike him. The King of Avylyn wanted all his people able to read, and Merrigan had admired her father so much for that. He had established libraries in every major town throughout his kingdom. The surest way to protect the people from the lies of seditionists or infiltrators from enemy kingdoms was to enable them to read the laws and proclamations sent throughout the kingdom. Libraries and programs to teach children how to read engendered a sense that their king valued them. Merrigan disagreed with how much her father valued the peasants, but she understood the strategy.

She loved to read. She loved the freedom and the protection that reading offered her. This was just another item on the list of things she disliked about Brimble. Deny his servants the simple joys of reading?

"Are you all right?" Flora asked again, putting the tray down and stepping over to pat Merrigan's arm. "Should I ask Cook for a headache powder for you?"

"No, I'm quite all right. I just have so many thoughts going through my head ..." Merrigan glanced down at the tray. She hadn't realized until now that she hadn't finished her meal. That was foolish. The stew and the apple dumpling were both delicious, and she did adore apple dumplings -- despite the whole debacle with the magic apple tree. "Perhaps I should try to eat a little more."

"I could ask Cook to warm it for you, and give you more cream to pour on it," Flora offered, picking up the tray again. She chuckled. "He'd do anything for you, I'd wager."

"Excuse me?"

"Oh, it's not that obvious, but Fauna and I both think he's gone sweet on you, just in two days. We heard him talking to the big iron cauldron he uses for heating wash water, asking himself what Mistress Mara would like best to eat. He's never done that before."

"Talked to the cauldron?"

"Oh, he talks to it all the time. Some people think he used to be an enchanter, back about a hundred years ago. There's talk about enchanters that used to live in these parts, but there was a huge war. The losers were swatted like a bunch of snotty little boys, and had their magic taken away." Flora leaned closer, her voice dropping to a whisper. "There's even talk that this used to be the castle of one of them, or at least what's left." She giggled. "No, I meant Cook never cared about what any of us would like to eat. We all like him, never fear, and he's rare fun in the evenings when the judge is out. Seneschal is grandfather to Rosco and Oscar, and the three of them play fiddle and pipes and drum, so we have dancing. You'll join us next time we have the house to ourselves, won't you?"

"I'd ... I think I'd like that," Merrigan admitted. How odd, that her heart would race for a few beats, then slow, race, then slow, all during the girl's spurt of babbling. Did it really disturb her -- or worse, flatter her -- that the one-eyed cook seemed sweet on her? She should be offended. After all, she was Queen of Carlion.

Cook didn't know that, did he? All he saw was the thin, somewhat ragged old woman.

"Would you do me a favor?" she asked, as Flora headed for the door with her meal tray.

"I'll heat up the apple dumpling and bring it right back, don't you worry."

"Besides that. Could you just mention, in Cook's hearing, that I'm a recent widow and still grieving my dear husband? I wouldn't want to insult Cook, you know. Just discourage him, a little. My husband ... well, my world was utterly destroyed when he died."

That much was the absolute truth, and it felt oddly good to say it to someone besides herself. Merrigan found her headache had completely gone as she sat down to resume her work. Perhaps it was the fresh air, since Flora left the door halfway open, or perhaps having an actual conversation with someone. Or perhaps it was the sympathy in the girl's round, pale face.

Sympathy from a serving girl? Welcoming that sympathy? How Merrigan had fallen from her glory days.

She sighed and glanced at the pages in their semi-neat piles at the other end of the long table. "You keep quiet -- I'm not complaining, and I'm even a little bit ... well, grateful is too strong a word, but it is nice having someone feeling sorry for me. I'm just stating the facts of the situation, that's all."

Her work went quickly, despite an odd need to look up and make sure the pages were still there in their piles, every dozen stitches or so. Merrigan had half the seams basted together by the time Flora returned with a fresh apple dumpling, a saucer of thickened, sweetened cream to spoon over it, and a little pot of steaming fresh cinnamon tea to go with it. The girl winked at Merrigan as she put the tray down on a little side table she pulled up next to her chair.

"Flora, do you know how to read?" She put her sewing down in her lap. If that chat earlier had done her good, she would have regular chats with the serving girls whenever she could.

"Enough to read the road markers walking to Potzwheel, or Grimblpotz, and get the right papers from the judge's desk when he's already out in his carriage and needs something." She rolled her eyes, with a smile. Merrigan guessed the judge was rather disorganized and sent his servants back multiple times for things he had forgotten -- and too lazy to get out and fetch them himself.

"Would you like me to help you read better?"

Flora's eyes got big and sudden tears made them glisten. "Oh, Mistress Mara, that would be so wonderful. But how would you have the time?" She gestured at the bolts of cloth and spools of thread and all the other supplies for the judge's new wardrobe.

"In the evening, after your chores are done, you can come in here and read to me, and when you come to words you don't understand, we'll figure them out together."

Merrigan didn't quite understand the warmth in her chest

when the girl accepted with delight and then scurried out to tend to her duties. She rather liked the sensation. While of course her first motive had been to have some company, she found she didn't mind the thought of helping the girl improve herself. After all, once she could read, maybe she could find some place better to work. Wouldn't that serve Judge Brimble a bit more justice, losing another handy, downtrodden servant?

On second thought, maybe she should offer to teach Fauna and the stable boys -- Rosco and Oscar, yes, she could remember their names too. If Judge Brimble was helping to cheat other people besides the baker, he deserved to lose more servants. Merrigan rather hoped the next people he hired were servants he deserved.

That evening, the seneschal brought her supper tray and a curious contraption of iron rods, a framework that stood over a fat candle with four wicks. He nodded to her and put the framework and candle down at the far end of the table, next to the piles of papers. He returned perhaps ten minutes later with a small pitcher, a covered pot, and a handful of narrow brushes, which he also put down by the frame and candle and left again, all without speaking to her. Merrigan didn't know if she should consider that odd or not. While the seneschal had been polite to her, the extent of their conversations thus far had been to make sure she had everything she needed, nothing more.

When she finished her dinner, she got up and went to investigate the materials. The pitcher held water, and the covered pot fit perfectly into the frame sitting over the candle. Merrigan lifted the covering, which was a bit of hide held in place with some cord wrapped around the lip of the pot. The smell of the yellowy-brown substance in the pot was vaguely familiar. Merrigan touched it with the tip of her finger. It felt somewhat sticky, but a dry sticky that didn't come off on her finger. She put the pot over the flames of the candle. Common sense said the water was to go in the pot, perhaps when the flame had heated the contents enough to melt?

"Dunderhead," she muttered, smiling, as the pieces came together.

The pot held glue, with brushes to spread it on the binding of the book, to hold the pages in place. She hadn't gotten that far in deciding what to do after sewing the separate piles into bundles, and then somehow affix everything back into the binding. The excited little thrumming in her chest spread to put a smile on her face she could actually feel. She sat down to arrange the first pile of sorted pages into some kind of order. If only whoever wrote this book had taken the time to number the pages, that would have made the task so much easier. Of course, Merrigan admitted, the writer had never anticipated someone would come along and desecrate the book by tearing out all the pages, soaking it in water, and treading on it. Still, the job wouldn't be that bad, since she did have clues, starting with the headings on the pages. The headings were all at the outer edges, on the right edge on one side of the page and the left edge on the other side. It was the only way she could tell which side was the right facing page or the left. Unlike newer bound books, the outer edges were as uneven as the inner edges where they had been torn out of the book.

Now came the tedious part. Reading the last full sentence on the bottom of the left facing page to try to match it with the first sentence at the top of the right facing page. In several places she was lucky, because whoever wrote the book, or perhaps more accurately, the journal, ran out of room at the bottom of the page and split the word, to continue on the next page. Merrigan tried not to pay attention to what the sentences were actually saying, because she didn't want to ruin the fun of reading the book when it was finally assembled. She couldn't stand people who would flip through books, reading a paragraph here, a paragraph there, the start of a chapter and the end of the chapter, and then read the entire last chapter before they started reading from the beginning. What fun was that?

When Flora came to retrieve the dishes, Merrigan asked her if Fauna would care to practice her reading as well. That earned her another wide-eyed gasp of gratitude. Honestly, the girl was pretty, with that flush in her cheeks and her eyes sparkling. She took the tray away and promised they would both be back in twenty minutes, thirty at the most. That bought Merrigan more time to sort through this first pile of papers. She had purposely chosen the thinnest pile. It seemed to narrate an encounter between a rather accident-prone young man and a foul-tempered herbalist with dreams of being a powerful wizard. That was far more of the story than Merrigan wanted to know. She was pleased there were only twenty sheets of paper in the pile. The first page of the bundle and the last were easy enough to identify, because the right facing side began halfway down the first page, and the left facing side of the last page only had five lines on it. That left her eighteen sheets to arrange. She had everything in order before the girls came back to the library for the night's reading.

"I am not taking the chance of having to do you all over again," Merrigan muttered, looking down at the neat bundle sitting on the table before her. Thirty piles, some of them twice as thick as the pile she had sorted. She hadn't thought it would be such a large book, judging by the binding.

She decided to use one of the longer pins to hold the papers together. Though she hated to poke holes in the pages, there was no remedy for it. Besides, she would have to poke numerous holes when she sewed them together before gluing them. Something made her hold her breath and brace -- for what, she wasn't sure -- when she inserted the pin through the sheets.

A sensation riffled through the room, not quite a sigh, but definitely the impression that someone let out a breath he had been holding, when she bent the bundle of papers and inserted the pin again, neatly fastening them together. Merrigan dropped the papers on the table and stepped back, rubbing her fingertips on both hands together.

For a moment there, she could have sworn she felt warmth flash through the dusty old yellowed papers, there and gone again.

"Too long alone," she scolded herself. "Or maybe the fumes from the glue are too strong." She sighed and bent to blow the flames out on the candle. What had she been thinking, letting the glue warm and melt when she wouldn't be ready for days to do the gluing?

Ten minutes later, as she followed the girls down the bookshelves, looking for a book simple enough for them to practice their reading, Merrigan looked over and saw the flames under the glue pot were still lit. She scolded herself for carelessness and walked over to blow them out again. This time, she put the warm pot of glue down on the table, to make sure she blew directly on the flames. Then Merrigan walked back over to help Flora and Fauna pick out a book.

All in all, she was pleased with the evening. She finished putting together the second shirt and cut out a vest. The girls helped each other figure out words so she didn't have to stop to help them often enough that it grew annoying. They read to her from a clever book about the antics of silly, harmless talking animals trying to set up a kingdom so they could be "just like people." Merrigan remembered that book from her childhood and enjoyed hearing it again. Her sojourn here might turn out more pleasant than she had anticipated. If only she could remember that choking collar spell.

~~~~~

The next four bundles of papers Merrigan put together, working her way up from the smallest, all seemed to have the same type of story, just from the little bit she read to match the pages together. Each dealt with a traveler of some kind, whether an adventurer or someone who had lost his or her home through foolishness or a cruel trick. That young man or woman then encountered someone of varying magical strength. There was an accident or argument, or the majjian tricked the traveler into helping him or her find or retrieve something. That was always far more detail than Merrigan wanted to learn. She didn't want the story to be spoiled when she could finally sit down and read through the book. Preferably in a pleasant, clean, comfortable inn, where she could indulge in a few days of reading luxury.

By the third bundle of pages, she no longer had the sensation of someone in the room holding his breath, waiting for something to happen when she fastened the sorted papers together. As she arranged the fourth bundle, Merrigan made a disheartening discovery.

While it was easy enough separating the different sections of the book by the headings on the top of the pages, and then putting the pages into order, Merrigan had no clue yet to the order of the sections, to assemble the whole book. What came first? It would be highly irritating and inconvenient if she read one section and then read another, and realized the second should have come before the first. Books had to make sense. If they weren't a collection of individual, unrelated stories, then the sections or chapters had to lead one into another. What was learned in one chapter had its roots in the previous chapter. The journey had to go somewhere, and it had to make sense.

"Bother," she muttered, as she finished pinning the fifth bundle
~~~~~

together and looked at the next pile to be arranged. "I don't suppose there is an index anywhere among any of you?"

She wasn't about to give up on the task now, a quarter of the way through. Less than a quarter, really, since the gluing and stitching would likely take as long as the sorting itself had taken. Still, knowing she couldn't confidently glue the sections into place rather took away the growing sense of accomplishment, the visible progress that mitigated the tedium. How could she consider the task accomplished if she might have to rip the bundles out of the binding and rearrange everything again?

"I suppose I could just put the pieces in and find some ribbons or even sew a case to hold everything together, and not glue it until I was sure ..."

That solution didn't feel right, either.

"Bother," she snarled, and put the pile of papers down and stomped over to the other end of the table, where she found relief in cutting out the pieces for three pairs of trousers. There was something highly satisfying, almost soothing, in the crunch of the scissors going through the thick cloth, of cutting apart the long, dignified, richly dyed material.

The problem of the order of the book sections gnawed at her all through the basting process and dinner, and made her somewhat short-tempered with Flora and Fauna during that evening's reading. The girls didn't seem to notice she sighed each time they asked her to help them figure out a word. That irritated her, too.

When the silence grew too long, she looked up to see the girls stood at the other end of the table, examining the papers. A shriek of warning caught in her throat as Flora gently flipped open a bundle of leather and wood, the battered cover and binding.

"Mistress Mara, what's all this writing in here? It looks like words, but I don't know any of them," the girl said.

Merrigan's hands trembled as she put down the trousers. Her knees wobbled as she walked down to the far end of the table. The scolding rising up hot in her throat cooled and died away when she saw neither girl had done anything more to the torn binding and covers, hanging together by a few thin, worn pieces of leather and many torn threads. With delicate motions, she tugged the leather of the front cover into place on the inside, left face. Odd. She could have sworn there was very little of the leather left when she first found the mangled book. It looked almost whole now, if faded and stained and threatening to wear through in a few spots.

Flora was right. There was writing on the leather. Not just writing, but a list. The first few words on each line were the titles of the bundles she had sorted. Merrigan's mouth relaxed into a smile. Her pleasure died as she deciphered the next few words on each line. Someone, in a different hand, had made notes to rearrange the list, so that the first item on the list wasn't the first section of the book. In fact, it had been designated the third, then changed to the twelfth, then the eighth. The same had been done to the other sections, their positions changed and changed again.

"Someone was very disorganized and very messy," she finally said to the girls. Merrigan could smile at them, though, because hadn't her discouraging problem been solved?

She should have looked at the cover, instead of nattering herself into a headache.

The odd thing was, she could have sworn she *had* looked at the pieces of the cover. Not only hadn't there been a list the first time, but far less leather existed in the cover. Was something wrong with her eyes?

~~~~~

The list danced through her dreams. When she woke up long before dawn, Merrigan had a plan firmly in mind. She could almost laugh at herself, how she obsessed over fixing a book that was little more than a collection of tales of idiots who ran into majjians and fell into rewards they didn't deserve. Still, she had a gurgling in her throat that threatened to turn into humming, as she put the glue pot back on the candle to warm and melt, then hurried to wash with the water left in her basin, neatened her hair, dressed, and settled down to work on the book before her breakfast arrived. Between the sunrise creeping through the windows and the oil lanterns in the chandelier, there was more than enough light.

She felt positively buoyant this morning. By rights the prospect of another day putting together grand new clothes Judge Brimble most certainly did not deserve should have made her feel much abused. Repairing the binding and cover of the book felt like enormous progress.

The glue had softened enough that it was easy to stir it around
~~~~~

with a little water and the stick end of a brush. Merrigan's hands stayed steady and her touch was delicate and sure, as if she had done this sort of thing a thousand times, as she spread glue on the wooden boards of the cover, stretched the leather into place and pressed it down with a firm but gentle touch. She had thick books ready to put on the mended cover boards to hold the leather in place while the glue dried. Odd. She couldn't remember taking them off the shelves. A chuckle escaped her.

"Mindless obsession. How Leffisand would laugh if he saw me now." She sighed, realizing she didn't feel the usual resentment that came with thinking of him.

There was innate satisfaction in repairing something that had been so tragically damaged. While the cover dried, held in place, she searched through her supplies for the thickest, strongest thread and the sturdiest needles, and prepared them, then set them aside. She knew exactly how to repair the binding to make it ready to take the bundles of pages. Before the seneschal brought her breakfast tray and the two fresh pitchers of water, one hot and one cold, she had two more piles of pages sorted into order. The sorting seemed to go more quickly with each pile, as if the pages were arranging themselves.

The morning sewing flew by. Merrigan caught herself a dozen times with a childhood song bubbling in her throat as she stitched and pinned and turned seams and thought ahead to what piece of the judge's wardrobe she would work on next. Working on the book had become a reward for completing tasks, rather than escape from the drudgery of sewing.

When she took a break midway through the morning, she sorted another pile of pages with ease, hardly paying attention to them as she listened to the judge speaking with a new visitor. Merrigan nearly dropped the bundle in the process of pinning them together when she heard the word "mill." What she had overheard before suddenly made sense. Right below her feet was the man who had cheated the miller's son.

For another half hour she stood right there, where the voices came up strongest through the floor and flue pipe. She sorted another pile of pages and listened. The oily glee of the man made her want to stomp downstairs and shout for the captain of the guard to come drag him away and throw him in prison for a year or two. What right did he have to take that mill? It belonged to the miller's son, just like the throne of Carlion belonged to her -- she was the queen, wasn't she? So what if she hadn't given Leffisand an heir? She had earned it. Just consider all the frustrations she had endured, the whispering, the mockery from her siblings, the marriage proposals from second and third and fourth-born princes who might have been handsome and talented and brave and nice, but they weren't going to be kings.

Just like Bryan.

Merrigan sank down into the nearest chair, her heart thumping at an odd rhythm. She hadn't thought of Prince Bryan in years, and now twice in less than a week. She had been six when they first met, when he came to Avylyn with his father's delegation for the conference of allied kingdoms. He hadn't been old enough to go to the welcoming ball that first night any more than she had. Just like her, he had snuck out of bed and found a dark spot in the highest balcony looking down on the Great Hall to watch the festivities. They had spotted each other and crept through the darkness to meet halfway and sit. They had spent much of his visit exploring the palace, finding hiding places to listen to the conference, and exploring the countryside around Avylyn. She looked forward to him coming back with the delegation from Sylvanglade every year for the conference.

For a few years all had been fine between them, despite her mother dying and Nanny Starling being forced to leave. Nanny Tulip had been tactful, but she had made it clear that Prince Bryan was unacceptable as a future suitor, therefore he was not acceptable as a playmate. Despite her vow to never betray their friendship, Merrigan's attitude toward Bryan changed. She wasn't sure when it happened. Nanny Tulip was right, of course. Merrigan learned that Bryan's oldest brother had made an unwise marriage alliance. His promised bride was under a curse, made dangerous when her father tried to find a way to break it without following the proper order of things. Nanny Tulip was adamant that curses could not be rewritten or sidestepped. Those who tried to bend the rules or ignore them usually ended up even worse off than if the curse had been fulfilled. The bride's curse could damage Sylvanglade and extend to the royal family, and to the kingdoms of the brides of the royal brothers.

When Bryan stopped coming to Avylyn, Merrigan couldn't remember. That was all for the better, she supposed. As Leffisand told her, royalty did not have the luxury of marrying to suit themselves. They had kingdom concerns to answer to. Merrigan could not settle for anything less than a king, or a crown prince. Bryan, being the fifth-born son, simply didn't make the cut.

"Bryan," Merrigan whispered.

What was wrong with her? Why did she let thoughts of Bryan, no matter how much fun he had been, distract her from her entire purpose for being in this house?

"Bother," she said, a little louder, and went down on one knee to help her focus and listen to the voices below her feet.

The two conspirators talked about having dinner that evening. Then she heard the scraping of chair legs on the floor of the office. The dratted man was leaving.

"No more woolgathering," she scolded herself, and turned to stomp back to her chair to resume sewing.

Something caught her attention, from the corner of her eye. Merrigan looked and pressed her hand against her chest. Her heart thudded so fast and hard her breastbone felt bruised.

Every pile of torn pages had been neatly arranged and pinned. When and how had that happened? She was sure she was only halfway through the chore.

"Just proof that this peasant atmosphere is stultifying to my mind," she declared, keeping her voice low. "Spells of unconsciousness ... while continuing the work." A shudder worked through her. "Spells, indeed..."

How could she have been so oblivious?

"I won't be manipulated," she declared, bending down so her nose almost touched the closest pile of pinned pages. "I am here for a purpose, and you will not distract me. And you most certainly will not force me to spend any more time in this wretched, middle-class house than I absolutely have to."

She turned, stomped down the length of the table to her chair, and picked up the half-finished pair of trousers.

Wait. Hadn't she just cut out the pieces of the trousers this morning, right after breakfast? How could they be ready for the hems and reinforcing work? Merrigan shuddered as she looked down the length of the table and saw all ten shirts and five vests and three more pairs of trousers, all assembled and waiting to be fitted to Judge Brimble to make the necessary tucks and darts and hems. When had that happened?

"If there are any sprites or brownies hiding hereabouts," she said, pitching her voice to carry, yet stay soft enough that someone standing out in the hallway, on the other side of that closed door wouldn't hear her. "I think you should reveal yourselves now. It's very impolite. I am a queen, after all. Even if I don't look like it. You owe me the courtesy of introducing yourselves before you interfere with ..." She glanced at the clothes lying on the table and easily calculated all the hours of work that should still have been lying ahead of her. "Before you help me and save me a great deal of time and effort. It's disconcerting to have things changed and manipulated, that's all I'm saying." The pressure in her throat was almost frightening. Something wanted to force words out, and something else wanted to keep them back. "I do thank you," she said at last, her vocal cords feeling rather strained.

No, I thank you, a soft, somewhat buzzing voice said at the back of her mind. *Fair's fair, don't you think? You're helping me, so it's only right that I help you.*

"Who are you -- where are you?" Her gaze went to the bundles of pages. Merrigan half-expected them to leap up into the air and assemble themselves into the book in another moment, with a gaudy display of magical sparkles and shimmers, for good measure.

That's right, Mi'Lady. I'm the book.

"Why haven't you spoken to me before this?"

Because you didn't give me permission. Or rather, you weren't ready to listen. Oh, and because I wasn't assembled enough to do more than listen. Quite frankly, until you took me out of that wretched enspelled cupboard and started sorting my pieces, I wasn't even able to listen.

"Enspelled?" Somehow, that was much easier to think about than the other implications swirling through her head. Merrigan wondered if she had read too many tales of magic as a child. Or maybe not enough. What, exactly, was she supposed to do?

A magic book.

She was talking to a magic book.

Something magical ... was *helping* her, even if it was with something so small and mundane as sewing.

The book had just acknowledged she had helped it. Did that mean it owed her something?

Enspelled, as in the glass kept almost everyone from seeing me there, and ensured that what little magic I had left in my binding couldn't reach out and catch anyone's attention. It was destiny, Mi'Lady. Maybe the many layers of spells wrapped around you guided you to find me. Is it impertinent of me to say how delighted I am to have someone as clever and determined and pretty as you rescuing me?

"I am most certainly not pretty. Just goes to show how all that ripping and water damage and mud staining your pages interferes with ..." She sighed. What was she doing, talking to a book? How could a book, even a magical book, see her? It didn't have eyes!

Of course you're pretty. You only have the illusion of old age and bad hair and a stooped back wrapped around you. The spells only change people's perceptions of you, and how you interact with the solid, real world. There's a very strong anti-looping spell on you, and a one-way spell, and an aversion spell, so people sort of bounce off you, until some serious changes occur in ... well, we'll deal with that later. Since I am magic, and under a few curses myself, I can see through all the shrouding and shielding and don't-notice-me spells disguising you. You're rather pretty. Or you could be. You need some work.

That assessment didn't bother Merrigan as much as it should have. Maybe because she felt so breathless at the news. She wasn't truly old, wrinkled, pale, stooped, thin, and shaky -- she only *seemed* that way. Underneath everything, she was still herself.

"All right," she said, taking a few deep breaths that didn't dispel that knocked-breathless feeling. "So now you can talk to me. Now what do we do? What do I need to do so you can help me break all these spells you see on me?"

Sorry, Mi'Lady, that's the problem. I can't. No one can. You have to break them by abiding by the conditions woven into the spell. Someone very strong, very wise and experienced, wove that spell. I can't even unravel the one that ensures no one but you can ever see the conditions written into the spell that dictate how it can be broken.

"Then what good are you?"

Silence.

Merrigan put down the trousers and waited, dread slowly growing on her. She hadn't just destroyed her first chance at fixing this utterly unfair, unjust, undeserved mess, had she?

"I'm -- please see this through my -- you've rather -- this is all a shock. If I insulted you, I'm ... I'm sorry."

A rap on the door startled her so she leaped to her feet, dropping the trousers. Merrigan bent to retrieve them and jumped again when the door creaked open. She felt nearly sick with the fear that someone had been standing outside in the hallway all this time, listening.

Perhaps someone with a talent for throwing his voice, as the puppeteers had done during festivals and galas when she was a child? Pretending to be the book, talking to her. She had utterly made a fool out of herself just now, hadn't she?

Oh, please, book, please, be real!

"Luncheon, Mistress Mara," the seneschal said. His droopy, wrinkled, yet comfortingly dignified expression never wavered as he brought the tray to her end of the table and put it on the little side table. He didn't look at her as if he feared she was losing her mind, or worse, he didn't look nastily jubilant over the trick played on her.

"Thank you. It smells delicious. Please pass my compliments to Cook," she murmured.

The seneschal jerked, just slightly. His eyes widened, just as slightly. Then one corner of his mouth quirked up in what had to be an enormous smile for him, and he nodded to her.

Now see, that's growth. That's change. That just created the teeniest, tiniest crack in one part of one layer of the spell on you, the voice commented, as the library door thudded closed.

Chapter Five

"What was?" Merrigan reached for the teapot. She hoped it had been allowed to steep nice and long, because she needed something strong and bracing.

Thanking him, thanking the people who did something nice for you.

"That was just being polite," she muttered, and inhaled with delight as she smelled rich spices in the steam rising from the cup. How could Cook know she favored that particular blend of spices and black tea, with hints of jasmine?

Merrigan stopped with the cup nearly to her lips. How had he found the tea? It came from some far southern kingdom on this continent, ringed by high, snow-filled mountains. The short season when merchants could reach it made any exports highly prized within the continent, much less to Armorica. She only knew that because her father had had to sit her down and give her a lecture with a map of the world, to explain to her why her favorite tea was only available half the year. No matter how she scolded and stomped her feet, they couldn't get her any more if there wasn't any to be bought.

How often have you been polite lately, Mi'Lady?

She wrinkled up her nose at the pieces of the book, then took a long, slow, leisurely sip of the tea. A whimper of delight -- and yes, gratitude -- escaped her.

"This has been a most surprising and stressful and yet ... gratifying day," she murmured.

We're just getting started, Mi'Lady. Now, the sooner we get me thoroughly assembled, and you finish making those clothes and complete your quest, the sooner we can head out onto the road and find your cure.

"You will help me?" Merrigan moved to the book's end of the table, so she could speak softly. It wouldn't do to be caught talking to the book and end up in a healer's house for the gently insane. Not when hope had finally been awarded her. "Wait -- what quest?"

You did a good thing, choosing to find some justice for the miller's son. His name is Corby, by the way.

"Not for him, exactly." She put down the cup, hating the momentary trembling in her hands. Merrigan bent down, resting her elbows on the table to get close to the piles of pages. "I know what it's like to be cheated, and that Fae was so judgmental." She sighed. "I knew I had to do something. It all just made me so angry. But how did you know?"

For someone as thickly woven with spells and orders and conditions, every choice you make, every reaction to directions or help offered, it's written into the spell. As easy to read as -- the voice snorted -- as a book. Now, what have you done toward helping Corby?

Merrigan told him, her hands automatically getting to work on the book again. He sighed with relief as she took the cover and spine out from the books holding them flat. Under his directions and with the help of magic she felt humming through the papers, she sewed the pages into packets and slipped them into their proper order and place in the binding, gluing everything together with an ease that was very clearly magical.

"Why couldn't you have fixed yourself before this?" she asked, more curious than grudging, as she rubbed her fingers together to peel off the glue sticking to them.

"Too wounded to have much magic left. The enspelled glass of the cupboard blocked me, and the glue pot was too far away." The book sighed, then a chuckle escaped it. "I'm audible again! Oh, what glory."

"I still can't tell -- are you a boy or a girl?"

"Yes."

Merrigan opened her mouth to retort that it hadn't answered, then the humor struck her and she chuckled.

"The truth is, Mi'Lady, even being a magical book, I am limited. I need hands to carry me, and tell me about things beyond my ... well, as you remarked earlier, I don't have eyes or ears, but I am able to see and hear and smell for a limited distance. Sometimes it's better not to know all the fine details of the magic involved. As for being a boy or girl ... well, my previous master called me Bib. That sounds more like a boy's name than a girl's, if you feel more comfortable assigning one or the other to me."

"I'd much rather think of you as a 'he' than an 'it,' if that makes any sense," she admitted.

"And there's another fine crack in the spell. You're making

incredible progress in creating your own freedom, Mi'Lady."

"When you said previous master ..." She hesitated to voice the nebulous idea churning up through her middle.

"You are the master of the book, now, after saving me from dreamless waiting, with just enough awareness that I could have screamed if I had the energy." Bib's voice thickened, so Merrigan had a good idea of just what he had suffered.

"How long were you ...?" She gestured at the corner shelves where his ravaged pieces had been tossed.

"No idea. I think I don't want to know, either. What are people saying about this place? As far as I can tell, only a small part of my old master's castle remains. Quite a few of the books who were my old friends are gone. The ones that have replaced them." He made a rude snorting noise that earned a grin from her. "Didactic, pedantic, self-righteous, and quite a few contradicting each other. The problem with books of the law is that if they aren't given regular fresh air and sunlight, they get ingrown, with an inflated sense of their importance. Especially when they're still clean and glossy years after being printed. The law was made to be a servant, not a ruler. Kings need to learn that lesson as well."

"You mean to tell me, all these books in here are somehow aware, even if they're not magic?" She tipped her head back and slowly turned, surveying the shelves reaching up to the ceiling, all filled with thick, unused books.

"All books have the *potential* for magic. It depends on how they're used, and the spirit of the people using them." Bib sighed. "Listen to me, nattering on and on. Priorities, Mi'Lady. First, we solve the problem of the people who cheated young Corby -- and yes, the man downstairs a short time ago is the ringleader. Master Swickle. Judge Brimble is just a vainglorious and willing dupe in the plot. From what I overheard, they're now turning their sights on the baker, to take over his shop. Swickle's cousin wants to be a baker, but doesn't want to invest any money or even the time to learn how to bake. They've been working to undermine the baker's reputation. The cousin has a dozen relatives who will claim to be sick from eating the baker's bread. They'll even claim one of them died, poisoned. The baker will have to turn over his bakery to them to keep from going to prison. They won't strike until they figure out how to force the baker and his family to stay on and work for them."

"That's insidious!" Merrigan trembled, thinking of the delicious bread the baker had offered her, for free, when she stepped into his shop. He had given her fresh, not leftovers, as she knew most businesses did when it came to poor, penniless travelers looking for charity.

She thought of the rosy-cheeked baker's assistant, who had offered her cold milk without being asked or ordered. She thought of that sweet young boy working for a man who would lie and cheat to steal someone's livelihood. Such an idea made her furious.

"What should we do?"

"I'm still regaining my strength. While the glue is still wet, I don't dare try anything strenuous. Let me think on it." Bib's pages ruffled slightly, startling her. "Ah, that feels good. I haven't been able to stretch my limbs, so to speak, in a dragon's age. And dragons aren't all unfriendly, I might add. Quite a few can be very stout, loyal friends, with a wonderful wit. If we could befriend a dragon, Mi'Lady, I'm sure he or she could shred the spells binding you and set you free in no time."

"One thing at a time, Master Bib." Merrigan picked up her cup and walked back down to the sewing end of the table. Finishing this sewing job was necessary before she could leave this house and find someone such as a dragon to help her.

The trousers were finished and lying on the table next to the other pieces of clothing. The everyday clothes were finished and ready for fitting. Now she had to work on the fine new robes for Judge Brimble to wear to court -- two robes for everyday wear, when he sat on the bench in Smilpotz, then a grander robe with thin silver braid on the sleeves and collar, for when he was called to special cases requiring a panel of judges in Carnpotz. These three robes would be in staid black. A fourth set of robes would be in deep, dark crimson, with black slashes on the sleeves and bracketing the collar, trimmed in crimson and gold braid, for the few times when Judge Brimble would attend the High Court.

"Thank you," she said, giving Bib a chipper curtsey as she reached for the stack of thick black cloth sitting on one of the smaller study tables, now pushed up against the bookshelves.

"We're partners, Mi'Lady. As soon as you started to help me, that gave me the energy and magic to help you, which gave you more power to help me, and in turn gave me more magic to help you. Enchanters have searched for centuries for a self-sustaining source of magic power. Simple people without any magic at all have possessed that secret for just as long."

"Are you part philosophy book?" She spread the cloth out with a smile. Merrigan hoped he wouldn't give her miniature lectures like that all the time -- and tried not to think it too loudly. It wouldn't do to insult and irritate the first real friend she had found.

~~~~~

When Flora and Fauna came to the library that evening, Bib took over helping them with their reading. Merrigan continued with her sewing while the girls read to her, this time from a book of fables about magical events in the country itself. The first time Fauna had difficulty with a word, Merrigan nearly dropped the robe she was hemming when her own voice asked Fauna what letters were in the word. She certainly hadn't spoken. Slowly, she glanced up to see if the girls were looking at her. They weren't. They sat in one of the massive cushioned chairs big enough for them both to share, with the book open between them, bent over the page. She thought it rather endearing how Flora ran her finger across the bottom of the line and mouthed the letters with Fauna as she recited them to Bib. He was a very good mimic, apparently.

Neither girl ever looked up, and Merrigan felt some gratitude that he had taken over. Not that she would have minded getting up and stepping over to the chair to lean over the girls and look at the word. A chance to stretch her legs would be welcome. Still, it was pleasant to have someone read to her, to let her mind wander a little, and have someone else tend to the teaching. She was more than willing to admit she wasn't the most skilled in teaching. Then again, why should she need the talent at all? She was a queen -- other people were responsible for teaching underlings how to do their jobs. The day she had to teach a servant how to serve her, she would seriously fear for the state of the kingdom that would put her in such a position. Something was wrong.

Well, of course something is wrong, she scolded herself. *Look where I am. Oh, Leffisand, why did you have to be such a fool? You had to go haring off and make even bigger mistakes, take bigger risks to cover them. Why couldn't you have thought of me first, for a change? Sometimes a king's life is more important than his reputation or his kingdom.*

Now who's turning philosophical? Bib said, directly into her
~~~~~

mind, even as his impersonation of her coached Fauna into pronouncing "vainglorious."

It's not philosophical, it's common sense. Why couldn't Leffisand have included me in the plot so much sooner? She sniffed and glanced up at the book that sat innocuously on the corner of the table next to her, half-covered with the skirts of the robe. *Eavesdropping is rude.*

You think so loudly, Mi'Lady. Bib chuckled, the cover of the book lifting a little to allow the pages to riffle in a whispering sort of sound.

Merrigan preferred carrying on a conversation with Bib outside of her head. Besides his tendency to eavesdrop, it disturbed her to do so much thinking. So when Flora and Fauna finished their reading lesson for the night, she was relieved. She bade them goodnight, remembered to thank them for the hot water they brought up to the library for her to wash with -- odd, to consider hot water a luxury -- and closed the door firmly to ensure no one would overhear her. Then with one shielded lamp sitting on the table, she curled up in the window seat bed, with Bib perched on a pillow on a chair nearby, and settled in to talk.

She asked how he had come to be torn apart.

"It's an odd tale, Mi'Lady. To begin: Under ordinary circumstances, the magic that infiltrates my pages requires that I only answer the questions asked of me."

"Despite all the tales in all those books," she gestured to one bookcase that contained nothing but tales of magic, the breaking of curses and the foibles of enchanters, "I find nothing ordinary about magic of any kind. You are most certainly magical. And rather extraordinary in your own right," she added with a smile.

"A lovely compliment, Mi'Lady. I thank you." Bib riffled his pages in a buzzy sort of laughter. "Yes, under ordinary circumstances, I am limited in my powers of speech. I only speak when spoken to, and only answer the questions asked me. It takes the presence of a majjian somewhat stronger than a hedge witch to break the geas and allow me to have intelligent conversations." He sighed melodramatically.

Merrigan chuckled. She liked the warm feeling from sharing genuine laughter with someone, not staged, public-face laughter.

"I assure you, Bib, I have no magical powers to speak of."

"No, Mi'Lady, but you are *permeated* with magic. It radiates from your flesh and bones. Now that's a consideration I hadn't taken into account until now."

"What?" She sat up, just when she was starting to feel deliciously drowsy. "You have an idea how to break my curse?"

"No, Mi'Lady. It just occurred to me that once we break the curse, there won't be any magic enfolding you, and we might not be able to talk, really talk, anymore."

"Oh." She lay down again and tugged the blankets up to her chin. "That's ... that's rather sad. We've only known each other a day, but I suppose when you've been sorting through someone's innards like I have with your pages, that produces a kind of ... intimacy." She echoed his last sigh. "I truly think I will miss you when that happens, Bib."

"Thank you, Mi'Lady. On the bright side, the curse may be on you long enough, magic soaking into you, when it's broken, enough magic will remain to allow me to speak freely."

"I Imm ... yes." Merrigan would much prefer to break the curse before any more magic soaked into her. The mental image was of swamp ooze clinging to her skin. "So, I assume the inability to do more than respond to questions led to you being destroyed?"

"The previous owner of this house, Judge Brimble's uncle, discovered my ability to speak. A curious, sad family history. The uncle's father cheated his brother, Judge Brimble's grandfather, out of his inheritance as the oldest son. As I recall, there were several brothers in between the heir and the cheat. His trickery earned him a curse. Odd, if you think about it. Usually the youngest sons are the good ones, the heroes and recipients of majjian help."

Merrigan reflected that she was the youngest, and the various local magical folk never went out of their way to help her. Maybe that was the problem? People had scolded her for her attitude and her siblings referred to her as "the brat." She sensed she had been cheated of her magical birthright as the youngest, the favored one. Wasn't that enough to sour anyone?

"The curse kept the previous two owners of this house from enjoying any success in the family way. The great-uncle found eight wealthy maidens to agree to marry him. Each one vanished, either carried off by a black knight or running off on a quest of her own before the wedding could take place. His son was adopted, though they always denied it. He went to a foreign country for a year, then returned with a tale of marrying an enchanted princess. Supposedly the day their son was born, she vanished, turned into a black swan. People stopped believing him when no black swans ever came to visit the baby. There are rules to magic and curses, and usually a loophole that leads to breaking them."

"I wonder how long it will take to find the loophole to break mine," Merrigan murmured into her pillow.

"Be that as it may," Bib continued, "the curse kept the adopted son from finding any joy in wife and children. He ended up adopting his orphaned cousin or nephew or whatever Judge Brimble was to him. The house and all the books, mostly law books by this time, came back into the possession of the proper bloodline."

"That doesn't explain how you were torn up and looked like you had been dropped into several mud puddles."

"Painfully accurate guess, Mi'Lady." He sighed, the pages riffling louder, so Merrigan felt a slight breeze. "Brimble's uncle didn't ask the right questions, so I couldn't give him the answers he wanted. He became so frustrated with me, he tore a few pages out of me at a time, to loosen my tongue. His own words. The fool. When it was just a few pages at a time, I had the strength to repair myself. He tried to burn some of my pages, but I killed the flames. Eventually, he got so infuriated that he took me outside and ripped pages out by the handfuls and threw me into the hog pen."

"How awful! I'm so sorry. You must have suffered terribly." In her travels, she had encountered far more hog pens and the attendant stench than she cared to remember.

"While I have the power of speech, Mi'Lady, fortunately I lack a sense of taste or smell unless I can borrow the senses of the people I serve, if they so permit by an act of will."

"I will keep that in mind." Such an ability might come in handy.

"A protective spell brought me back to the library while I repaired myself. By this time, most of the family fortune had vanished, and the uncle only came into the library when he needed another rare book to sell. He was nearly apoplectic when he saw me sitting on the reading stand where I belonged. Much bedraggled and worse for wear, but in one piece again."

"Oh, dear," Merrigan murmured, envisioning what likely came next. Mostly because, she was oddly ashamed to admit, she would have done the exact same thing. She had never ripped apart books, but she recalled destroying other things that had failed her. "He tried again, didn't he?"

"Five times. Until he learned he had to rip all the pages out of me so I couldn't repair myself. Each time, he rode farther away, trying to defeat the magic that brought me home."

To her surprise, Bib chuckled. More accurately, he snickered.

"What's so amusing? I can't imagine any of those experiences were pleasant for you at all. You didn't actually feel yourself being torn apart, did you?"

"Yes, and no. It wasn't how I imagine you would feel if say, someone peeled off your skin and then pulled off your arms and legs, but yes, it's a disquieting sensation to feel yourself going to pieces. Accompanied by maniacal laughter. My only consolation was that each time that wretched man saw me again, he had an apoplectic fit. The fourth time, he was confined to his bed for two moons. Most of that time, he was unable to speak. Quite fitting punishment, if you ask me."

"Indeed." She reached out and stroked the cover. "Am I imagining things, or is it the candlelight, or is your cover ... thicker? The colors darker?"

"My repairs are still progressing, Mi'Lady. Your sympathy, your discomfort on my behalf, comfort and strengthen me. Hastening the healing."

"Oh ... well ... I'm glad I could be of help." She wriggled a little, feeling somewhat squirmy inside. Being helpful to someone was a good thing, wasn't it? It wasn't like she was breaking any sort of rule for being a queen. Was it?

Merrigan scrambled for something else to focus on, to get her mind off the odd thoughts that seemed to focus beams of uncomfortably warm light back on herself.

"The glass -- in the corner case -- it had a spell on it?"

"Oh, yes, indeed. That was part of the curse put on me by the enchanter who -- no, let me back up in the story. When that despicable, temperamental old man --"

"Why don't you ever say his name? You always refer to him as the uncle, but never his name. Don't you remember?" She found it amusing, despite her own inability to remember people's names.

"I don't want to speak it. I loathe him. Even more than I loathe the enchanter who put me behind that enspelled glass. Now, as I was saying ..." Bib paused, and Merrigan wondered if he expected her to interrupt again. "When that fiend recovered from his last fit, he promised all the magical books remaining in this library to an enchanter who could deal with me. He offered me in the bargain, but the man didn't want me." He snickered. "He had once fought with the enchanter who made me. He refused to even touch me, and declared the world was safer if I remained within the confines of the ruins of my master's castle."

"So the stories are true?" Merrigan sat up again and looked around the shadowy library. She thought about the rows upon rows upon shelves upon stacks of books in this library. What were the chances that a book of magic could be found in here that would break Clara's curse? Then she sighed and curled up again. "The enchanter took all the books, didn't he?"

"Oh, no indeed. There are a great many books of magic still here. He couldn't remove them any more than he could remove me. Despite the punishment cast on the warring enchanters, binding their magic until they could act with proper civility and concern for and duty to others, some magic remained in effect. My previous owner put a spell on all his magic books so no one could take them from his castle without his permission. Even if he died."

"Oh. Then ... When we take care of the judge and the miller, I won't be able to take you with me, will I?"

Odd, how disappointing that was. Merrigan admitted she had grown quite fond of Bib in such a short time. He was amusing and clever and kind, and he flattered her without making her feel he was maneuvering for something to benefit him rather than her.

Bib chuckled, several ripples of his pages, before saying, "Oh, you must take me with you, Mi'Lady. I think it was ordained. But let me finish my story. The enemy enchanter created the glass to seal the corner cabinet that held my pieces. Only someone with magic, from outside the household, outside the town of Smilpotz even, could find me. Ask anyone in the household. They'll tell you that corner is solid wood, not glass. The uncle was mightily relieved when he came in here to remove some ancestral silver plate and couldn't see me. He searched all over the library, and kept walking right past me. I think there was a don't-notice-me spell in force. The spell was intended to keep my first master from finding me, if he ever regained his magic. A codicil in the spell says my rightful owner cannot take me up again until other hands, disinterested hands, someone with justice on their minds, repaired me. Then I could leave the ruins of this castle, either with the one who saved me or with my original owner."

"How long have you sat there, waiting? Judge Brimble is ... well, he's so huge, it's hard to tell his age, and I'm very sure he dyes his hair and paints his face."

"Well, perhaps two centuries since my master was defeated and exiled, and maybe thirty years or so since my pages were entirely ripped from my spine."

Merrigan winced at the imagery. "And no one has seen you, even come near you?"

"Well ... I have my suspicions. Several people with magic have visited this house. I'm very sure Cook has inherent magic, but chooses not to use it. Although, some would say that cooking is a kind of magic all its own."

"Certainly far more useful than most magic," Merrigan retorted. That earned another rippling chuckle from him. "How do you know Cook has magic?"

"He used to come up here. Streamers of magic would follow him around, soaking into the books that were sleeping -- that's what magic books do when no one has used them in decades. They sleep. Cook has enough magic to leave a trail, and it ... I don't know, it soothed the other books. Made it easier for them to sleep. You don't want a magic book to wake up from a bad dream or simply wake up cranky or furious at being ignored. No, indeed, Mi'Lady. A few times, he stopped and put a hand on the glass, and he looked right at me. He never said anything, but there was such sorrow flowing off him, through the wards of my prison."

"Bib ... what if Cook is your original owner, but he couldn't get through the glass to take you out and repair you?"

The silence from the book lasted so long, Merrigan feared she had said something to offend him. Or worse, hurt his feelings.

That just showed how low she had fallen, to be concerned about the feelings of a book.

"I think ..." he said slowly, when he finally did speak, "I think, Mi'Lady, I should like to get out and see the world, when the time comes for you to leave."

"We still don't have a plan yet to punish the judge and

Swickle." Merrigan lay down again and snuggled up under her blankets. There was that warm spot again, pure pleasure that Bib wanted to go with her.

Perhaps it was pitiful, to be happy a book wanted to be with her. Then again, she had always preferred books over people when she was a child.

"We can't leave until we do something about them," she continued, as a yawn thickened her voice. "And time is running out, if you consider how quickly the sewing is coming along. That was you again, helping me, wasn't it?"

"Always delighted to oblige, Mi'Lady."

"I think you just enjoy showing off."

"What I enjoy is being able to do things, move things, help people, after sitting idle for so long. There's nothing more dreadful, more depressing and destructive to the soul, than being unable to help others, unable to fulfill my purpose in life."

Merrigan swallowed hard, to keep down the urge to ask what exactly her purpose was. Had she ever had a purpose, other than to be a queen, standing beside a powerful king? Now it seemed … well, not useless and empty, but limited. Lonely. Truth be told, there was something cozy about being here in this library, her world made so very small, surrounded by her handiwork.

I'm sleepy and worn out from a long day of work, that's all. Merrigan turned her mind toward the challenge of finding proof to use against Judge Brimble and Swickle.

"We need an excuse to get into his office and look through the papers," she murmured, after a long, comfortable, deep silence had fallen on the library. One nice thing about Bib was that he didn't feel the need to keep talking when there was nothing to say.

"You get me into the office, Mi'Lady, and I will take care of searching all the papers right under the big buffoon's nose. He'll never notice. My master once remarked that ordinary, un-magical people have a remarkable talent for blinding themselves to magical, un-ordinary things around them, so they don't have to admit that magic is everywhere. Some people are happier believing magic always happens to other people, in other kingdoms."

"Bib, you're brilliant." Merrigan smiled at the sleepy, muffled tone of her voice.

"Thank you, Mi'Lady. In what way, exactly?"

"I'll take you with me to the office and insist the judge has to be fitted for his new clothes there, instead of his bedroom." A shudder worked a chill through her comfortable, sleepy warmth. "I certainly wouldn't want to go into his bedroom, even looking as I do now."

"Don't be too certain about that. Your hair seems more gray than white now. But yes, Mi'Lady. Brilliant idea."

Merrigan couldn't get her eyes open, couldn't seem to drag herself awake enough to think about what he said. Something about her hair? Then a moment later, she forgot what it was as sleep claimed her in a long, luxurious, comfortable slide down into dreams.

~~~~~

Judge Brimble was delighted, effusively so, when Merrigan knocked on his office door midway between breakfast and luncheon, and announced she was ready for the first fitting. Bib suggested she not only ask the seneschal to help her bring the clothes to the judge's office, but be present during the fitting. The seneschal didn't just act as the head of the household, directing the servants and paying bills. He also served as the judge's body servant, attending to his clothes, bringing him wash water, shaving him, and other assorted tasks that two or three other servants would normally have attended to. The judge was not as wealthy as he appeared to be. Or perhaps it was simply difficult to get enough servants willing to work for him.

Merrigan delegated the seneschal the task of helping the judge in and out of his nearly finished clothes, behind an enormous modesty screen. She was so grateful for that screen, she didn't wonder about the incongruity of it being in his office until after she went back upstairs.

The freedom to stick Judge Brimble with pins at regular intervals during the fitting helped her find some enjoyment in the otherwise humiliating exercise.

"Well?" she muttered, as she carried Bib back upstairs more than three hours later, sandwiched between the trousers and the shirts, while the seneschal carried the robes and vests.

Oh, Mi'Lady, in the parlance of the street thugs -- who, I might add, come here regularly to take odd jobs for the judge -- he will never know what hit him. Bib rustled his pages, and the soft, dusty laughter
~~~~~

sounded thicker and somewhat congested. Merrigan hoped that was a sign of just how many pieces of paper with necessary proof he had managed to confiscate while she was busy pinning and adjusting and stabbing Judge Brimble.

"It might just be fun seeing his schemes fall apart and all his cheating come back around to choke him," she said with a sigh, once the library door was closed behind her and she was alone with Bib again. "Still, I doubt it would be very safe to remain once the feathers start to fly. What other magical powers do you possess, besides the ability to rifle through someone's desk drawers and ledger books and remove papers without anyone seeing?"

She chuckled and sat in her sewing chair, and lightly stroked his cover. If she wasn't mistaken, the leather seemed several years newer than it had been last night. It was now a lovely shade of blue with streaks of green, like a semi-precious stone.

"Books contain unlimited wisdom," he said, "for those who know how to use it properly, and who are willing to take the time to study and learn."

"And ask the right questions? Bib, if I ask you here and now to point out to me anything I need to know but don't think to ask, will that cover any lapses?"

"If only the judge's greedy bully of an uncle had thought of that." He chuckled hard enough to flip himself open. A dozen sheets of paper in cramped handwriting slid out onto the table. "Mi'Lady, you and I have passed to a much higher level of friendship and partnership. I shall always try to offer information that hadn't occurred to you, and point out areas where you might be blind or mistaken."

"Good. I must admit, when I was a child, I had a rather nasty temper. I wouldn't like to be so provoked that I threw you off a bridge or tried to rip out your pages in a thoughtless moment." She patted the open page. "That's not a threat. Please don't take that as a threat."

"None taken, Mi'Lady." His pages rippled, and more papers slid out on either side of where he lay open.

Soon a sizable stack had piled up to the right and left of Bib. Merrigan could only shake her head. The papers piled up higher than his usual thickness, and yet he hadn't looked any larger or felt any heavier when she carried him back to the library.

"That's useful magic." She chuckled. "I don't suppose you were used by a pickpocket at any time in your past?"

That earned laughter from Bib, and he regaled her with some silly stories of his first master. In their early days together, they had traveled the world, and the adventurous young man had secreted items within his pages. Some were done to inflict justice on people who cheated others, such as Swickle. Others were somewhat selfish, such as stealing a meat pie or a piece of bread or cheese from a shopkeeper who looked at the young man's travel-worn clothes, assumed he was a beggar, and refused to let him enter the shop to buy.

He finished two stories before Flora came up with the tray of Merrigan's noon meal. Merrigan bit her tongue against complaining that it was an hour late. She knew she had made the judge late for his meal, and as this was his household, he had to be served first. He probably demanded twice as much to eat, since he had had to wait. She was further silenced by the realization that admitting her fault didn't sting quite as much as the last time. She didn't feel the need to complain that if people knew who she really was, they would treat her better.

How odd.

"Well, now we have the evidence. What do we do with it?" she mused, after demolishing her meal. Cook's fare was always delicious, but today he had outdone himself. "There is no higher authority in Smilpotz than the judge, and we certainly can't present the evidence to him."

"We go to the next highest authority, the Overseer of Judges, in Carnpotz."

"And just how do we convince him of the truth of our story?" She nudged the dirty dishes out of her way so she could slouch properly, elbow on the table, chin on her fists.

"Well … I suppose we can …" Bib sighed. "I must confess, I've been so enthralled with the idea of getting out of here and seeing the world with you, I quite didn't think that far down the road. So to speak."

"I don't suppose you know the kind of man the Overseer of Judges is," she mused aloud. "Is he the kind to be astonished or afraid or even think he's losing his mind if some magic happens right in his lap, instead of in the next town or country?"

"What are you thinking, Mi'Lady?"

"Who would argue with a magic book?"

"Only fools, Mi'Lady."

"Bib." She smiled and sat back. "Playing obsequious does not suit you."

"Yes, Mi'Lady." He chuckled, his pages rippling hard enough to flip himself closed again. "I see where you are going with this. If we walk into the Overseer's office and I disgorge all the papers in front of him, he can't very well argue against the evidence that I am magic. That ought to convince him of the truth of our story."

"If only we could find the miller's -- Corby." She nodded, pleased that she had remembered his name. "If only we could find Corby and have him back up our story."

"We could take the baker with us, as he seems the next target of the nefarious schemes."

"No, we won't take him -- we'll ask to ride with him." She glanced down the length of the table. On one side were all the papers, all the signed documents, the town records that Brimble and Swickle had rewritten, alongside the originals. On the other side of the table were the clothes that needed to be finished before she could leave the judge's household. "We have one more day to make our plans."

Chapter Six

That evening, Merrigan looked up at the sound of the library door creaking open to see Cook with her supper tray, instead of Flora or Fauna. He paused in the open doorway and looked around the room. For just a flicker of time, he wasn't the iron-gray, stooped man with the weathered face and a stained leather eye patch. He was taller, younger, straighter, with two eyes that shone like emeralds, and flickers of purple magic spun around his outstretched hands, cradling a bowl full of rose-colored smoke. Then he was simply Cook again. He limped a little as he walked down the length of the table. His gaze raked over the books on their shelves with regret, rather than the awe Flora and Fauna displayed when they looked at them.

"You'll need this," he muttered, his tone soft and earthy, almost gritty, as if it came from deep underground. He put down the tray and shrugged one shoulder, letting a thick strap slide down, attached to a sturdy, thick shoulder bag, such as foot travelers or apprentices used to carry their masters' equipment.

His hand brushed over Bib as he set the bag down next to him, and Merrigan shuddered, fully expecting him to snatch up the book and walk out.

"Thank you," she said, her voice softer and weaker than she liked.

"I'm not him." Cook winked at her, which was odd, since she had always thought it difficult to wink with only one eye.

"Not who?"

He gestured around the library, then spread both arms, taking in the household. She understood. He meant the enchanter who resided here when this had been a castle.

"What happened?" She reached as if to catch hold of his sleeve, then thought better of it. "Who are you, if you aren't him? You know about ..." She rested her fingertips on the edge of Bib's cover.

Cook smiled, and again she had a glimpse of the young man he had been, strong and ruggedly handsome and full of power.

"I am usually blocked from coming in here, until I have learned my lesson thoroughly and permanently."

"Usually?" she prompted.

"Some of us take longer to learn our lessons than others. I suppose the higher the heights of the fall, the longer the climb upwards again. The wise learn from the mistakes and foolishness of others, Highness."

She shuddered. Hearing this man acknowledge her rank, her position, was entirely different from hearing Bib say it. Merrigan wondered why it frightened her.

"Learning is more than gathering facts and knowledge. Learning leads to wisdom, but we stopped at knowledge, like a dragon hoarding gold and jewels, only to sleep on them."

"Where is ..." She gestured as he had done, indicating the former castle.

"It doesn't matter, except that we each must learn a bitter lesson. I am pleased to note that I have ... paid, learned enough, to see a little of the spells swaddling you like a baby. Yes, that is an apt metaphor. You must be reborn, remade."

"How long have you been suffering?" she whispered.

"I don't really know. Time passes strangely, for those under enchantment."

"That is so unfair."

"There is no law that says magic that teaches a necessary lesson must be fair. At least," he added with a smirk that made his remaining eye brilliant green for a few seconds, "not fair while the spell is in force. When the change is complete, well ... let the enspelled judge."

"I don't want --" She squeaked as he pressed a gnarled, calloused finger against her lips, silencing her.

"It is useless to complain, and no one to appeal to for a change in judgment. I had to wait more than a century before I learned that. Learn from me, Highness. Don't waste your energy complaining or fighting. Focus on learning and becoming better than you were."

"Why are you telling me this?" Merrigan muffled the urge to shriek in a most un-royal manner.

"Learning requires passing on knowledge, especially lessons learned through pain. I would not wish my lessons on anyone. Not even the enchanters who were once my enemies." He executed a graceful bow, so utterly incongruous with his crooked form. He turned and went to the door. "I daresay we shall not see each other before you leave, which I recommend you do quickly. Your hair is darkening. Leave before someone notices the change and suspects you of magical doings. It could be uncomfortable."

Then he stepped through the door and out of sight. Merrigan couldn't even hear his footsteps moving down the hall. Then again, she hadn't heard him approaching the library.

"Well," she said, letting out a deep breath she hadn't realized she had been holding.

"Indeed," Bib said.

~~~~~

Rosco showed up to take away the dinner tray and announced that he had been told to take a message for her to the baker. Before she could ask, "What message?" Bib's pages riffled and a piece of paper slid across the table toward her. She gave Rosco the note and thanked him.

"So, be prepared to flee for our lives tomorrow?" she said, when the door had closed again.

"Once we give the documents to the Overseer, we don't dare come back."

~~~~~

Merrigan reflected there were some benefits in having very little to call her own. She could leave the house with her two bags hidden under her cloak, and no one to suspect she had no plans to return. She put the finished clothes on the table, neatly folded, ready for pressing, and wished for a moment that she had left some undone details on each piece. She never had remembered the spell for the collars, but yes, this judgment falling on the judge was far better than choking him for moons to come.

"I don't suppose you can arrange for the seams to start unraveling once we're far away and safe?" she murmured as she looked around the library one last time. Bib just riffled his quiet, papery laughter.

In the kitchen, she asked Flora and Fauna to take care of pressing the clothes, then announced she was going to do some shopping in town before she returned to finish the last bit of hemming work. Cook nodded to her, but didn't turn away from the soup he was stirring. When she climbed into the wagon with Rosco and Oscar, she had to fight not to take one final look and wave a cheerful goodbye to this rather sad, if grand household.

The baker looked thinner, when Merrigan walked into his shop. He finished sliding a tray of buns into the tall rack standing next to the counter, and his welcoming smile struck her as somewhat pitiful. She remembered overhearing him talking to Judge Brimble about his bakery suffering because of the nasty rumors. And then how the judge and Swickle laughed together over those same rumors and the baker's reaction.

This man had been kind to her, without knowing she was a queen. Didn't that deserve some reward?

"Why did you want to ride with me to Carnpotz?" the baker asked as he led her to the small, rather flour-dusty wagon behind the bakery. "How did you know I was going today?"

"I overheard you telling Judge Brimble. I was working in the room over his office."

"Ah." He offered her his hand to help her climb up, and tugged a pad over onto the seat before she sat down.

"I want you to know," she said, once they had put two streets between them and the bakery, "I think all those lies people are telling about your shop are awful. Your bread is the most delicious I have ever eaten."

"Thank you." He patted her hand. "You didn't say why you need to go to Carnpotz."

"Actually, I'm fleeing the judge. The things I overheard discussed in his office make me fearful for my life."

"What sort of things?" He frowned, but Merrigan suspected he wasn't quite as surprised as he should have been.

"He helped Swickle cheat that good boy, Corby, out of his inheritance, for one thing."

"Hmm, I don't find that hard to believe at all. Why would that frighten you?"

"I'm an old woman alone, a stranger in these parts. We all know from the fables that cheating and lying and injustice eventually ..." She sighed. "They gain enough weight that eventually some magic intervenes. I don't want to be blamed when that justice strikes. Judge Brimble is not so foolish it wouldn't eventually occur to him that someone sitting above his office could hear all his schemes."

"Hmm. Wise."

They rode in silence for another hour, until she saw the sign indicating Carnpotz was over the next hill.

"You should know," she said, touching his arm, "that I overheard Swickle and the judge plotting to take over your bakery. They're the ones spreading the nasty stories about your bread."

"I am not surprised," the baker murmured. He pressed his hand over hers on his arm. "Yesterday, he claimed he wanted to become partners, that he would provide the flour and ensure the quality was of the best. He offered me a contract to sign, and then was most upset when he learned I could read."

"He was counting on your not knowing what was in the contract," she guessed.

"Took it away before I could read anything, and said he would bring it back for me to sign in a few days, after I had time to think about his generous offer." He nodded twice. "I guess I'd be signing away my livelihood. Thank you for warning me."

"Would you do something for me?" she said, after the wagon had climbed to the top of the hill and the much larger town of Carnpotz spread out before them.

"Gladly."

"I have been helping the serving girls, Flora and Fauna, practice their reading. If the Overseer believes me and acts against the judge, will you make sure they find good positions elsewhere, and continue their studies?"

"Again." He patted her hand. "Gladly."

Merrigan couldn't understand why she felt like crying. At the same time, a curiously light sensation settled in her chest. What was wrong with her?

She was out of that gloomy, stifling household, back out in fresh air and sunshine. She had a friend to advise her and help her, someone who understood her. Why shouldn't she be in a better mood than she had been since long before Leffisand died and she lost her throne?

~~~~~

"It's the curse," Bib whispered, once he and Merrigan were alone in the room where the Overseer's secretary had led them.

"What do you mean?" She nearly leaped up from the wooden bench with the dark blue cushion that was very welcome after the long, bumpy ride into Carnpotz. "Are we going to be imprisoned?
~~~~~

They can't force you to disgorge the papers, can they?"

"Oh, forgive me, Mi'Lady. Not that kind of -- well, let me start over. I didn't mean to frighten you. Didn't it seem a little too easy to gain an audience with the Overseer? You're not even a resident of this kingdom. Anyone can tell that by your accent. So why should a penniless, frail widow be allowed to see the Overseer, who is obviously very busy?"

"They decided anyone who came with a complaint against Judge Brimble, especially a foreigner, has to be lying and needs to be punished right away. Oh, what was I thinking, to try to make anything right? That Fae who advised me to do something, to pay back the help I received, he's in on it with Clara, isn't he? He deliberately set me on the wrong path."

"Mi'Lady, no, no."

Bib's words didn't penetrate her heart-thudding moment of panic, but the suspicious hint of laughter in his voice did. Merrigan nearly burst into tears right then and there. Bib wasn't part of the plot to destroy her, was he? Why had she been such a fool to believe he was her friend?

"No, Mi'Lady, the curse isn't to hurt you and keep punishing you, but to guide you in, as you said, making things right. The curse isn't really a curse, if you think about it long enough. Clara did it to help you."

"Hmph. Clara's kind of help, I can do without, thank you very much." Still, now that she sat and thought about it a moment, Bib might be right. "So we gained our audience without any waiting or trouble because the curse is fiddling circumstances in our favor?"

"Let's call it a spell, Mi'Lady. Much easier on the ears. And quite frankly, if the wrong people hear you say you're cursed, they'll never give you a chance. Imagine all the princesses who never would have been kissed to awaken from an enchanted sleep if everyone considered them cursed, rather than enspelled. Princes and knights on quests must be triply cautious. I could turn your hair white again with tales of otherwise intelligent, talented, brave young men who thought they were lifting a spell and got themselves tangled in a curse that refused to be broken. *Enspelled*, not cursed."

"Semantics." Merrigan snorted, then managed a somewhat unsteady smile. "Thank you, Bib. It's so good to have a friend with some common sense."

"Delighted to be with you, Mi'Lady."

Despite Bib's reassurances, Merrigan tensed the first time a door opened and another servant came in. This one was a woman in a simple, dark green dress, white cap and white apron. She inquired if Merrigan was hungry or thirsty, and when she said she was, brought her a large wooden mug of cider and a napkin with three warm, honey-glazed pastries. Now Merrigan could believe magic worked on her behalf. Certainly, if she was about to be accused of some crime, she wouldn't have been treated like a guest.

Another servant, this time a balding man with an enormous moustache that gleamed with wax, led Merrigan out of the reception room. He took her down the hall to a double set of doors. They swung open as the man approached. Merrigan saw a man and woman, just a little older than Master and Mistress Twilby. They stood in front of a tall man wearing somber black robes and an old-fashioned short, white-powdered wig. That had to be the Overseer. The man shook the Overseer's hand, and the woman curtsied. They glanced once at Merrigan as she followed the servant into the room, then they turned and left by a door on the opposite side of the room.

"Well, so you are Mistress Mara," the Overseer said, after he had gestured for her to take one of the seats facing him. "I was wondering when I would see you here."

"Excuse me? You -- you have?" Merrigan clutched the shoulder bag holding Bib, pressing him against her side. Maybe he had been wrong after all? Had someone lodged a complaint against her? "You know me?"

"Oh, indeed. Judge Brimble made sure everyone knew he had a foreign royal seamstress making his clothes." The Overseer's voice was deep, with a rumble that hinted at both contained amusement and anger. Merrigan found that highly confusing. "You can understand why a stranger who goes to work in the home of a high official would be investigated."

"And what did you find out about me, Your Honor?"

"I employ a very clever young woman to flitter from town to town and gather up the images of people I want investigated. She uses magic to peer into the hearts and the dreams of such people. She had to resort to simple pen and ink to capture your image because you are so thickly shielded with magic, her own magic refused to work."

"Please, Your Honor, I'm not a spy."

"And yet you come to me straight from Judge Brimble's household, naming yourself a plaintiff."

"I didn't intend ..." Merrigan took a deep breath to steady herself and gain a few more seconds to think. If she was utterly honest, she had indeed gone into the judge's household to spy on him -- just not for a foreign country.

"Mi'Lady?" Bib riffled his pages, nudging her arm where it lay across him, in the bag on her lap. "Shall I speak for us both?"

"Yes, Bib. Please do." She reached into the bag and put him on the massive desk between her and the Overseer. The man tipped his head to one side and didn't appear at all startled to see the book, or what happened next. All he did was listen, his face entirely unreadable.

Bib flipped open and proceeded to empty himself of all the documents. He explained what they were, and why he and Merrigan had taken them. She thought he spoke rather like a minister in a king's council, with a compelling combination of brevity and elegance. He then backed up and narrated how Merrigan arrived in Smilpotz, challenged by a Fae to find some justice for young Corby. Then he explained how she had overheard first the baker's complaints and pleas for help from Judge Brimble, then later heard the judge and Swickle laughing about the baker's plight and making plans to worsen the situation. He finished by repeating what the baker had told Merrigan on the ride to Carnpotz that morning.

The Overseer studied her in silence, over the tips of his steepled fingers, so long that Merrigan was ready to slap him, just to get him to blink. "You have been given a quest by someone magical, I presume? Other than the Fae who gifted the lad, Corby."

"Yes, I suppose you could call it that," she said.

"My assistant said she couldn't decipher all the layers, but it was applied with uncommon wisdom and purity of heart."

Merrigan swallowed hard, rather than release a thoroughly unladylike snort. She had enormous doubts about the "purity" of Clara's heart -- or whether she had a heart at all.

"She believes much of the spell muffling you is to protect you. I agree."

"That's ... comforting."

For some reason, the Overseer found that amusing. He spent the next hour asking questions to bring out more details of the official complaint against Brimble and Swickle. He admitted that complaints had been registered against Swickle over several years, but no one had been able to bring him evidence. The knowledge that Brimble participated in the schemes explained the difficulty in finding any justice.

"A bitter truth that the whole countryside must learn," the Overseer said, as he stood and crossed the room to pick up a small copper bell, "is that the longer justice is delayed and lies replace truth, the heavier justice will strike when it finally does so." He rang the bell and returned to the desk, to offer his hand to help Merrigan rise. "I must presume you do not wish to return to Smilpotz."

"No, and there's no need. I finished my work and I have all I own in the world right here." She bent and picked up the bag with her few possessions, her new clothes, and the empty bag for carrying Bib.

"Forgive me, Mistress Mara, but I will need you to return, for the investigation. You will, of course, be housed at the expense of the tribunal, and a servant will guard you at all times, so there is nothing to fear. But I do need you to go back there."

"I understand."

Merrigan hoped the Overseer would understand when the spell of no return wouldn't let her retrace her steps to Smilpotz.

~~~~~

Four days later, after being housed in a nice, sedate inn, Merrigan climbed into a very large coach with the Overseer, four secretaries, six officers of the court, and massive boxes of documents and inkwells and ledgers. They were escorted by other court officials in open and closed carriages, and three dozen mounted soldiers. A good twenty people had been found to testify how they had been cheated out of gardens, horses, shops, or homes, and couldn't prove it wasn't entirely legal.

The coach rolled heavily and smoothly and slowly away from the Overseer's massive house, through the central square of Carnpotz, and toward the main road that cut the kingdom in half going north and south. Merrigan tucked herself as far into the corner as she could go without sliding between the cushions, and
~~~~~

trembled in anticipation of what would happen next.

"Mistress Mara?" The Overseer looked up from the massive journal spread open on his lap, took the spectacles off his long nose, and frowned at her. "Are you feeling well?"

"Very well, sir. Why?"

"You look ..." His frown deepened. "You look rather ... transparent around the edges."

"It's started," Bib announced.

Most of the other people in the coach flinched at the voice coming from the bag sitting on Merrigan's lap. The Overseer had specifically requested she tell no one about Bib.

"What has started?" the Overseer asked.

"More dratted magic. I was hoping for a reprieve, for a worthy cause, but ..." Merrigan spread her hands in helplessness, and saw they were indeed turning transparent. She clutched the bag holding Bib with one hand and the nice, new, larger bag for her possessions, supplied by the Overseer. "It seems I'm not allowed to retrace my steps. Please be kind to Flora and Fauna and Cook and --"

The carriage turned upside down around her. A moment later Merrigan decided she had turned upside down, instead. She tumbled around for a few breaths, then landed in a loud rustling and an explosion of spicy green scent. When the world stopped tumbling, she opened her eyes, checked that both her bags were there, felt for her cap and her shoes, and looked around.

She sat in the middle of a candlespice bush, the feathery fronds dropping spicy-sweet powder all over her. More black powder rained around her, tossed upward by her landing.

"Mi'Lady? Are you all right?" Bib asked.

"That depends on your definition of 'all right.'" Merrigan turned carefully to get onto her knees, and from there to her feet.

She still felt somewhat wobbly and faintly dizzy, so she moved with caution and took deep breaths, fighting the hints of impending nausea. Then there were the tickly, feathery, long fronds of the candlespice bush that clung to her, tangling her legs, shifting when she took steps, so she couldn't be sure she could stay upright.

At last, she stumbled her way free of the bush, which had to be at least fifteen feet wide and high -- on the small side, for a candlespice, actually. Merrigan's heart caught in her throat as she recognized the classic markings of a crossroads. From the broken bricks tossed into the ditches bracketing both roads, and the visible signs of patching with new bricks, she guessed this had to be a major roadway. What kingdom had she landed in?

"Bother," she muttered.

"What's wrong, Mi'Lady? Where are we?"

"You tell me." She dug Bib out of the bag and let both bags drop as she clasped the magic book in both hands and held him up, facing the tall stone pillar with mile markings and arrows pointing in all four directions, accompanied by city names. "I have no idea where these cities even belong."

"Hmm ..."

She did not like the sound of that.

"Have we found another limit to your magic, Bib?"

Merrigan stopped short, startled by the snap and sharp edges to her voice. What was more disquieting? The familiarity of it, like stepping into a favorite old ball gown from two years ago, full of comforting, delightful memories -- or the realization that she didn't really like it? In essence, the ball gown smelled like someone had loaned it to a number of people who chose perfume over soap.

"Focus," she muttered, and held Bib up a little higher, closer to the signpost.

"I'm trying, Mi'Lady. Forgive me, but I think there have been some changes in boundaries and kingdoms and the names of towns and roads since I was essentially put into storage. My original master would update me regularly, feed me maps and reports on the political doings and wars in other kingdoms, so I knew who was who and what was where and ..." He sighed. For a few terrifying seconds, his cover turned spotty with wear. "I am sadly out of date. I must syphon information from other books or documents to catch up. I fear I am not much good as an advisor if my information is behind the times."

"It's not your fault," she said, hating the tight cords underneath her voice, and the effort it took to comfort him.

After all, who was the queen and who was the servant bound in the book, here? He was supposed to be looking out for her, not the other way around. By rights, she should have at least one servant just to carry Bib, so she didn't have to endure the weight of him, riding in that bag that bounced on her hip with every step she took.

But that was the problem with all this -- nothing was right.

They stood there long enough that her arms got tired and she cradled the book against her chest.

"There's nothing to do but pick a direction, a destination, and start walking. After the good deeds we did, certainly we've earned some help from someone magical, don't you think?" he offered.

"Hmm, I suppose so." Merrigan sighed, slightly nauseous from the surge of anger that curdled through her belly.

What kind of fool had she been, to feel so utterly disappointed at this turn of events? She was under a curse, no matter what game of semantics Bib tried to play. Curses never let up so easily. What made her think that getting involved in the petty crimes and political games and lies of a minor town in a minor country would earn her a reprieve? Landing in a candlespice bush certainly proved there was no mercy extended in her direction.

With a decisive nod, she tucked Bib back into his bag, adjusted the straps of her two bags, and stepped up to the crossroads post, to study the names of the cities. Wardenkraft sounded pleasant, even friendly. Then again, maybe it was because the marker said Wardenkraft was only two miles away, while the other towns were eight, six, and twelve miles away, depending on the direction she walked. She had to be a pragmatist, after all.

Perhaps those trees looming closer to the road, maybe half a mile away, harbored someone magical. Even if it was just a handful of pixies, or a brownie. Brownies always wanted to be helpful, didn't they? Merrigan considered limping, to gain some sympathy from anyone watching. While that might work with simpletons, like farmers and goose girls, that wouldn't work with magical creatures. They would see the spells woven around her, get suspicious and wonder why she was shrouded in magic. Merrigan dearly hoped curiosity would get her some sympathy, if not bring someone close enough to investigate.

"Bother," she muttered, when she walked far enough for the woods to close in on both sides of the road, and the paving was replaced by pebbles and dirt, then plain dirt. Merrigan found the lack of wheel ruts highly discouraging. "Bib, should I turn around?"

"It might be wise, Mi'Lady. You are vulnerable to any highwaymen or common thieves lurking in the shadows hereabouts. Even as poor and feeble as you appear to be, you do have two bags under your cloak. Someone might be desperate enough that whatever they take from you will make them richer."

"I do wish you would stop with the philosophy." Merrigan stopped and looked over her shoulder.

She glimpsed some sort of structure among the shadows. As she took a few steps closer, an errant gust of wind moved branches overhead, letting a beam of light reveal a simple slanted roof over a well, with several buckets hanging from the support posts, and two cranks to raise and lower the buckets on ropes.

"I don't suppose the water is enchanted, and if I drink some, it will break the spell?"

"We need to expand your education, Mi'Lady," Bib said as she followed the little beaten dirt path from the roadside to the well. "More often, an enchanted well will only make your situation worse, unless you drink from a special cup, or you have a magic coin to appease the guardian of the well, or you know the right words to say to convince the water to help you. You're better off if it's just plain water."

"I'm thirsty enough to appreciate plain water." She stepped up onto the platform of boards surrounding the round wall around the mouth of the well. "How do you propose to expand my education?"

"I could tell you stories as we walk along. It will certainly pass the time. Oh, and maybe if we're in a safe town, where some greedy magistrate or mayor or merchant doesn't try to take me from you, I could earn you food and shelter by telling stories. I'm sure even the simplest villagers would pay to hear a magic book talk to them."

"Bib, you are brilliant." Merrigan swayed for a moment at the thought of staying in a decent inn, and people waiting on her.

She looked down into the dark depths of the well. The water was far enough down, lost in shadows, she couldn't catch the slightest glimmer of the surface. She reached for the handle to lower the bucket.

"What do you think you're doing?" a young girl called. "You're supposed to wait for me to help you."

Merrigan looked around and located another path coming toward the well from the opposite direction of the road. A girl, maybe fourteen years old, dressed in bright clothes, probably her festival outfit, trudged down the path, lugging a silver pitcher.

"Oh, dear," she muttered, sensing she had stepped into a fable, but not quite sure which one and where she had entered. "Are you supposed to help me? Dear?" she added. After all, she looked like an old, skinny, helpless widow. Might as well play the part.

Did she have a part to play in this particular story? Merrigan hoped not. She was a queen, which meant she was the one who did the manipulating of others. No one manipulated Merrigan of Avylyn and Carlion.

"That's what Mother told me to do. I'm supposed to come to this old well that nobody goes to anymore, unless you're in trouble, and be polite and sugary like Drusilla and draw water for a ragged old granny, and she'll reward me. Then maybe we'll have enough money she can leave Drusilla's lazy old father and we can go somewhere far away and be better off." The girl plunked the silver pitcher down on the stone lip of the well. The pitcher rang slightly off-key, indicating the silver wasn't pure. Definitely a lower-class family. "You're not ragged, and your hair isn't that disgusting shade of white that really isn't white, so maybe you aren't a granny?"

"Oh, not yet. What's your name?" She settled on the edge of the well, careful to sit forward so she wouldn't topple in. If this was indeed an enchanted well, whoever lived in it would not be happy at having an uninvited visitor.

"Pearl."

"Well, Pearl, let me guess. Drusilla got sent to this well for a punishment, am I right?"

"Every time her nasty old father gets Mother angry, she makes Drusilla do twice as many chores as me -- and he doesn't even notice! Who needs a lazy old useless father like that?"

"You are so right, dear. Let me guess. When Drusilla came here, an old lady was waiting and she asked for a drink of water, and Drusilla was, as you put it, sugary and gave the woman water, and the woman turned into a Fae and rewarded her?"

"Every time she talks, three copper pennies come out."

Cheapskate Fae.

Bib chuckled, his voice muffled by the bag and her cloak.

"Mother hopes since Drusilla used the old copper pitcher and she got copper coins, if I used the silver pitcher, I'd get silver coins."

"I'm sorry, dear, but that is not how all the stories go. You're lucky you ran into me, an ordinary old woman ..." She slid off the lip of the well and gestured for Pearl to follow her. "With a magic book," she announced, pulling Bib out of the bag, and putting him down on the bag on the edge of the platform. "Bib, my dear friend, please tell this poor deceived child what always happens to the well-dressed stepsister who gets sent to the well after her idiot stepsister gets all the good rewards."

Pearl jumped back a step when Bib flipped himself open. Her eyes widened with wonder as the words on the pages swirled around and resolved into line drawings to illustrate his stories.

I didn't know you could do that, she thought to him.

Not to be cheeky, Mi'Lady, but you didn't ask.

Merrigan managed a smile. She wasn't ready to laugh just yet.

Bib went through three variations on the same theme -- the stepsister with the father was downtrodden and abused by the stepmother, the father paid no attention, and the daughter of the stepmother followed the instructions to the letter, prepared to be polite and sweet to an old lady. But of course, the Fae changed the rules halfway through. When the Fae woman showed up dressed like a queen, the poor stepsister, confused by the change and positive that she had lost her opportunity, was in a bad mood when she offered water to the royal lady. This always resulted in something nasty happening to her, in direct contrast to what her stepsister received -- snakes or toads falling from her lips, instead of the jewels and flowers her stepsister received.

"That's not fair," Pearl murmured, when Bib finished his story and flipped closed again. "Drusilla isn't that bad. I mean, yes, she can be stupid sometimes, but look at her father. I'm sure Mother would take her with us when we escape, if she didn't think the law would accuse her of kidnapping." Turning, she sat on the edge of the well platform.

"What am I going to do? Mother is packing, ready to flee on the next coach to the capitol. We shouldn't even have to leave. It's our house, but that stupid old man wasted all the money my father left us and then he sold Mother's jewels and ..." She sniffled. "And for some reason, everyone in town thinks Mother is evil and we abuse Drusilla horribly. The fact is, nothing would get done if Mother wasn't constantly reminding him and arguing down our bills with the merchants. Drusilla is just too stupid to be mean-hearted and I don't mean to be angry with her all the time, because I did like her at the beginning, but she tries my patience so!"

Merrigan was quite impressed by the girl's self-control that she didn't burst into ugly, sloppy sobs that would turn her into a red-eyed, snotty mess in minutes. Still, she knew how much comforting a fourteen-year-old needed. Especially one so level-headed and yes, generous, because she seemed to like her idiot stepsister despite her flaws. She patted Pearl on the back and put her arms around the girl and let her cry against her bosom. Just until the tears started to soak through the front of her dress.

"Is there anything valuable left in the house that you can sell quickly? Starting with that pitcher?"

"A few things. So much disappeared, so fast, but one day I caught Mother putting a few things into hiding so ..." Pearl nodded. "Yes, I think so."

"The most important thing is to leave. Get as far away from here, away from people who know you, as you possibly can. If your stepfather doesn't know about the copper pennies, then take Drusilla with you. She might as well pay her way."

"Leave a note for your stepfather," Bib said.

"Why?" Merrigan nearly shrieked. "So he can follow them?"

The important thing was to get the women away from that horrid, selfish, lazy man. The sooner Pearl and her mother got away from him, the better. It was too bad they had to take Drusilla, but if they left her behind, her father would marry a truly wicked stepmother with three ugly, cruel daughters. That was how the fables worked. They would make the poor girl talk nonstop until they were rich.

"Tell him Drusilla met a prince on the way back from the well. Make sure it's a prince from a kingdom at least a moon's travel away. Tell him Drusilla eloped, and you and your mother have gone to find a wicked enchanter to reverse the spell of the copper coins. No one will expect the three of you to be together."

"I suppose that makes sense." Pearl rubbed at her eyes. "But what if he decides to go look for Drusilla and live off her and her prince?"

Chapter Seven

"Do you think any prince will suffer a madman showing up on his doorstep, calling himself his father-in-law, and demanding to be taken care of in a style he doesn't deserve?" Merrigan said. "If he stays in the house and dies of his own laziness or goes looking for Drusilla and the prince, either way, you're free of him. All that matters is getting away. Remember the stories Bib told you, so you avoid more traps. Be kind to Drusilla, keep her out of trouble, and make her keep her mouth shut when strangers are around. You don't want anyone knowing the source of your income, do you?"

"No." The girl wiped her face on her apron, sniffed a few more times, then startled Merrigan by flinging her arms around her for a short, hard hug. "Oh, you are better than a faerie godmother! How can I ever thank you?"

"Just be happy -- and move quickly." Merrigan tried not to shudder as she carefully freed herself from the girl's hug. Part of her liked it, and part of her was repulsed, and another part of her was trying to whisper that she was a fraud. Merrigan couldn't understand why she should think such a thing. Maybe the strain of the day was crumbling the edges of her mind?

Pearl thanked them again, bowing several times, and almost forgot to snatch up her silver pitcher as she hurried to leave. Merrigan stayed where the girl left her, watching and waving, urging her to move faster, until Pearl vanished into the shadows of the forest.

"Do you think she'll be all right?" She gathered up Bib and slid him back into his bag. "It's so unfair, how the clever girls, especially the daughters of stepmothers, are always accused of being nasty. Why are stepmothers always evil? Why don't we hear any stories about evil stepfathers? Doesn't anyone realize the good-hearted dunderheads who get all the magical help are also stepsisters?"

Merrigan slid the strap of Bib's bag over her head and settled it against her hip. Then she turned to walk away from the well.

And ran right into a Fae.

A woman, with jewel-toned, sculptured beauty. She was all in blues and greens, including her skin and hair, and stood at least fifteen feet tall. Her arms were crossed over her chest and she scowled down at Merrigan. One foot tapped against the pebbles of the path the same way busybody old harridans in her father's court used to when they thought they could stand in judgment on her.

"Just what did you think you were doing? Who gave you the right to interfere with Fae justice?" the woman said. Her voice rang like wind chimes made of jewels.

"Justice?" Merrigan squeaked, wobbling between infuriated and terrified.

"That young snot needed to learn a good lesson. Along with her mother."

"What lesson?" Bib called, so loud the book vibrated against Merrigan's hip.

The Fae woman scowled deeper, then snapped her fingers. Merrigan let out a shriek as the strap lifted off her shoulder and the bag flew up in the air. Bib bounced out of it and opened, landing in the woman's outstretched hand.

"If you would so kindly oblige, Lady," Bib said. "See what I learned from the girl."

His pages turned as if blown by a high wind. Whatever he showed the Fae woman, her scowl faded, then her lips pursed and she slowly shook her head.

"I thought something was off. The girl looked well-fed and her clothes were clean and decent and she didn't look at all afraid. She did say she was sent to the well as a punishment, though."

"It seems the people hereabouts think there's something odd about the well," Merrigan offered. The Fae woman seemed more approachable. As her scowl faded, she shrank, so now she only stood ten feet tall.

"It's been nearly thirty years since anyone has come to it. There's no chance to catch up on gossip and really know what's going on ..." She sighed and tossed Bib up in the air. He slid back into his bag, which settled gently around Merrigan's shoulders. "Still, it isn't your place to interfere. There's a balance to things. When you place a blessing, someone else gets a curse."

"So it doesn't matter that someone who doesn't deserve a curse gets one anyway? What happens to the girls who get pushed into a place where a curse lands on them, and they didn't do anything wrong? Her mother is more at fault, for marrying a worthless man with a dunderhead for a daughter. Is that fair to Pearl? Is it fair that the children of people who get cursed end up inheriting that curse? Is it fair when a king makes idiotic choices and gets himself killed and his queen can't hold onto the kingdom? Is that fair?"

"I know who you are, Princess Merrigan. Your story is written in the magic tangling you."

"Tangled is a very good word! And I'm Queen Merrigan."

"Another holds the throne, and you never produced the heir to the throne, so you are not queen mother. You are once again Princess Merrigan of Avylyn."

"That's not quite fair."

"Fair?" The Fae woman shook her head, and for a moment it looked like she might laugh. "You need to grow more before anyone can have a discussion about what 'fair' means. That's not why I'm here. The debt you need to pay is a large one. If you keep interfering in the spells and reformation of others --"

"Interfering for the sake of justice! Would it have hurt you to go look at the girls' family before you started flinging blessings and curses around? Did you hear what she said, about her stepsister and her mother? She actually likes the little idiot. Since when does that happen?"

Merrigan shrank back as the Fae woman grew taller again, doubling her original size before suddenly turning transparent and fading into the breeze. She waited a minute or two, then cautiously reached out and snatched up her cloak, to wrap it around herself.

"Bib, do you think it's safe --"

"To flee? I think it might be wise to try. Whether you'll be allowed to ... who knows?"

Merrigan deliberately retraced her steps, hoping the spell against returning would activate and yank her somewhere far away, out of the reaches of the Fae woman.

She walked down to the main road, turned right, and set her feet toward the town farthest away, according to the mile marker. If someone were fleeing from her and needed a place to hide, she would expect them to go to the nearest town.

The magic codicil against returning never took effect.

When the Fae woman appeared in the road ten steps in front

of her, Merrigan suspected she was the reason why the spell didn't yank her away.

"Just because you were right this time -- this time -- doesn't give you the right to interfere in a process established by tradition," the Fae woman began.

"Wouldn't it use up less magic if you straightened people out while they're still children?" Bib offered. "Convince them it's better to be friends with their stepbrothers and stepsisters, that there's more profit in working with the good boys and girls."

"Hmm, that … does sound sensible." A weary smile softened the Fae woman's face. "You're right, book. Intervening sooner in the process would certainly use less magic."

"How many downtrodden girls and boys cheated of their inheritance can you marry off to kings and princesses? There's a limit. Eventually, you'll have to kill off someone's husband or wife, or convince the royalty to have dozens of sons and daughters to marry all the good boys and girls you help, and even then there's a limit to the number of kingdoms you can parcel out."

The Fae smiled, and that smile sent shivers through Merrigan deep enough to freeze her marrow. She nodded and grew taller, until her head stretched above the treetops.

"You are a very wise book. Whatever you do, Princess Merrigan, I would advise you to hold onto that book, no matter what it costs you. Listen to him and learn from his wisdom, and … well, there's a very slim chance, a complicated chance, that you can break free of the spell before your required hundred years end."

"A hundred years?" Merrigan yelped. "Why a hundred years?"

"It's written into the spell. As I said, there's a chance. A very slim, complicated chance. You'll have to work very hard. Hold onto the book and learn wisdom." Then the Fae woman faded into the green shadows and silence of the road.

"A hundred years?" She wobbled and thought for a moment her knees would fold and deposit her right there in the middle of the road. "Bib, why a hundred years?"

"Unfortunately … well, it seems to be a traditional number."

"We'll see about that." Merrigan took a couple deep breaths, straightened her shoulders, stiffened her knees, and took another step down the road. "If there's a chance, no matter how slim, then I'll find it. I will not -- I cannot --" Her voice cracked. "I will not spend the next hundred years looking like this!"

~~~~~

Bib advised her to travel in her black widow's weeds and to save her nicer clothes for when she reached a decent-sized town. If she wanted to be taken seriously and have people treat her as more than a beggar, then she needed to present herself as a seamstress looking for employment. The best advertisement was to look not only neat and respectable, but to have a sense of fashion despite her circumstances. When Merrigan stopped to rest on the unpleasantly long walk to the town of Wylder-by-the-Sea, she used the sewing supplies she had made sure to take with her, to adjust her secondhand clothes to advertise her sewing skills.

That gurgling little croon of happiness came back into her throat as she sat in the sunshine and snipped and stitched and used trimmings she had bought for Judge Brimble's clothes but never used. She was quite pleased with her new look, especially when Bib helped with his limited magic, making the adjustments go so much faster. Anything related to his physical state, he could manipulate. Since she had used glue and thread and needles and cloth and pins to fix him, he could "adjust" other such materials, just like he adjusted paper and ink. The closer they got to Wylder-by-the-Sea, a decent-sized port, the more newspapers and other printed materials he could view, long-distance. That included colored prints of the latest fashions from other kingdoms, which the local tailors and seamstresses posted in the windows of their shops to lure in customers. Merrigan adopted what appealed to her from those images Bib displayed in his open pages.

"You, Mi'Lady, look like a respectable, clever woman who is still able to hold her head up high, despite how badly life and luck have treated you," Bib assured her, as they reached the outskirts of Wylder-by-the-Sea.

The five-day journey by foot had taken only a day-and-a-half because several farmers and merchants had stopped to offer her a ride until the next crossroads. There was something to be said for looking like a respectable person down on her luck, rather than a beggar, Merrigan realized. People were more willing to help those who hadn't been down very long. She didn't think that was quite fair. Didn't the people who were worse off need the help more?

"I hope you're right. No more sleeping under the stars for me,
~~~~~

thank you very much," she said, lowering her tone as a coach with its windows open passed her. The young lady who leaned out the window of the coach got a scolding from an older-sounding woman, and withdrew into the shadows, but not before smiling and waving at Merrigan. Such a nice, polite girl.

"You are fashionable and well-dressed, and anyone who refuses to hire you as a seamstress is a fool," Bib responded, once they were semi-alone again.

They weren't alone enough for extended conversations for quite some time after that. There were always people around them. Bib resorted to talking into her thoughts. Merrigan could respond in her thoughts, but the effort gave her a headache, which made her cranky, which didn't bode well for convincing someone to give her a job and a place to sleep.

Once they entered Wylder-by-the-Sea, she had far more success finding a room in a boarding house -- run by a cheerful, painfully neat old woman and her hulking, mentally weak son -- than she did finding employment. Merrigan knew better than to admit she had enough coins to support herself in decent but frugal comfort for several moons. She paid by the week, and begged her kindly landlady for advice on finding a shop that would hire her and be patient when the rain made her fingers ache.

That's laying it on a little too thick, Bib had scolded her, laughing softly, as Merrigan set off to visit the first of six tailor shops Mistress Coppersmythe recommended.

Not thick enough, Merrigan retorted four hours later, when she had visited each shop and couldn't get anyone to hire her. From some of the glances the tailors or seamstresses gave her clothes, she suspected they were jealous. She was visibly more fashionable, even in her sedate colors and secondhand clothes.

Too thick, Bib insisted. *We're heading into cold weather, and winter is always worse on the coast, with all the damp in the air. They don't want to take you on and then have to coddle you when your fingers stiffen up, and pay you a day's wages for half a day's work.*

"What am I to do?" she said aloud. "Someone in this town has to hire me. I refuse to be a beggar," she added, stamping her foot.

"Good for you, Granny." A massive, black-bearded man hobbled up to her. An elaborately carved peg replaced one leg from the knee down. "What sort of work do you want?"

"I'm a seamstress."

"Don't suppose you know the proper seams for fixing sails or how to reweave nets, do you?" He grinned wide enough for her to see three gold teeth among the black forest of his beard. "Now, no need to look so stunned. I was just joking with you. Might be able to find you some honest work at that, if you don't mind sailors."

"I don't know. I've never really met any."

To her astonishment, he bowed -- a little jerky and rough, but it was an actual bow -- and then offered his bent elbow like any courtier. Granted, most courtiers she knew were only half this man's girth and only two-thirds his height, and only one-tenth as hairy. Bemused, Merrigan tucked her hand into his elbow and then they were off. For a man with a peg leg, he trotted along through the crowded streets of Wylder-by-the-Sea at a decent pace. She was somewhat breathless when they rounded a corner and came within sight of the sea, far at the end of a long row of docks bracketed by ships at anchor. To her right was a sprawling inn that looked like it had been added onto at least four different times through the decades, judging by the visibly different styles of construction and colors of paint. It sported a wide sign that arched over the double doors, proclaiming it the Bookish Mermaid.

Those who couldn't read could still identify the inn by the enormous carving of a mermaid on the roof of the entryway, surrounded by stacks of books, spectacles on the end of her nose, and holding an equally enormous book, open, strategically placed across her bosom.

"Gorgeous sight, ain't she?" the man said, as he guided Merrigan to the tall steps leading up to the door.

She had noticed that as they got closer to the water's edge, the buildings stood higher above the street and the stairs grew taller. Merrigan wondered if, at the water's edge, the stairs would rival the grand staircase in her father's palace.

"Astonishing," she said, tipping her head back to study the mermaid before they passed under the roof line.

"My great-granny posed as the model. My great-great-granddaddy made my great-granddaddy marry her about three days into the carving," he added with a wink. His chuckle shook Merrigan just enough she clutched at his arm to keep from falling off her feet. "People still talk about the ruckus that followed, when he found out it was a trick so he *would* force them to get married. My great-great-granddaddy had a good sense of humor, though. People say he was still laughing about the trick on his deathbed."

"Everyone loves a happy ending." Merrigan was somewhat relieved when they stepped through the double doors of the Bookish Mermaid and the man released her. Was everything about this place going to be massive?

"Tiny! Just what do you think you're doing?" a black-haired woman shouted from the far end of the long room.

Yes, Merrigan decided. Everything about the Bookish Mermaid was massive. Long tables set with heavy crockery. Four fireplaces big enough to roast an ox, down the two long sides of the room. Wide bookshelves jammed with books and scrolls and piles of newspapers everywhere. The woman standing in the doorway with an equally massive, blazing white apron covering her clothes, could only be called small when compared to the man. Everywhere else, she would be called statuesque.

"I found you a lady to help with the sewing, Ma." The man snatched his sailor's stocking cap off his head, jammed it into his coat pocket, and wrapped an arm around Merrigan's back to hurry her down the aisle between the long rows of tables.

"Goodness, you didn't kidnap her, did you?" The woman gestured for them to come through the door into the room beyond. Later, she told Merrigan everyone called her Ma, so she might as well also.

The dining room was only about half-full, and most of the people ignored them, either concentrating on their meals, which smelled incredibly delicious, or reading. Merrigan had never been in such a quiet dining room. She remembered too many tantrums when she had brought a new book to a meal, and her father or some high-ranking servant had insisted she engage in conversation with her brothers and sisters. Here, reading while eating was not only permitted, but appeared to be encouraged.

We have to stay here, she thought to Bib. *No matter what it takes.*

Oh, definitely, Mi'Lady. He sounded somewhat distracted. She wondered if he was already harvesting information from all the books and newspapers surrounding them.

Once in the other room with Ma and Tiny, Merrigan entered the heart of the Bookish Mermaid. One side of the room was a living area, with more bookshelves and long couches full of pillows and quilts for cozy reading, while the other side, taking up three-quarters of the room, was the kitchen. Four stoves, two roasting fireplaces, and two baking ovens. Eight people of varying ages hurried about among long worktables, working on various pots and bowls and platters. Two boys stood on stools in front of a massive sink long enough to bathe a horse, washing a pile of dishes taller than them.

"Are you sure you're all right?" Ma asked, as she guided Merrigan to sit in one of the thickly cushioned reading chairs. "My boy has a good heart, but he doesn't always think, or explain. I can see from your clothes, you're a lady, and you're used to fine sewing. We do need a seamstress, but most of your work would be mending. We don't have much call for new clothes or even for making over old into new and stylish."

"You and your son and your kitchen crew?" Merrigan asked.

"And the girls and boys who clean the rooms and do the laundry. And my man and older boys and girls, when they're in port. We'd keep you busy, but we'd pay you well. Room and board included."

"It sounds like you're offering me the position without knowing anything about me."

"My Tiny may be the runt of the litter," Ma said, reaching up to pat her son on his massive arm, "but the faeries kissed him in his cradle. He's a good judge of character."

"Runt?" Merrigan fought not to choke.

"Just a joke with my Ma," Tiny said, his face going red. "Beauregard is the runt. That's why he gets to be the cook on Pa's main ship -- 'cause he fits through the doorway of the galley when nobody else does."

"Now, now, lad, enough about us. The lady here is right, we know nothing about her and we're overwhelming her talking about us." Ma sat back more comfortably in the chair facing Merrigan's. "Where be you from? What sort of sewing have you done?"

"I sewed for Princess Merrigan of Avylyn, and then I sewed in the court of Carlion, when she married King Leffisand." Merrigan shivered when Ma just frowned at her words.

Just her bad luck -- she had come into one of the countries that considered Avylyn an enemy nation. Come to think of it, she still hadn't found out the name of this country where she had landed.

Bib? Where are we?

I'm sorry, Mi'Lady, I was having so much fun talking with the other books -- the country is called Swyfflbyrne and so far it looks like no one here -- at least, none of the books I've looked into -- knows anything about Avylyn or Carlion. You're very far from home.

Indeed. Merrigan took a deep breath and clasped her hands tight enough to threaten the seams of her black lace fingerless gloves. "I realize those names mean nothing to you. Perhaps someone from one of those ships out in the harbor, coming from over the sea, can verify that Avylyn and Carlion do exist. The truth of the matter is, when the king died and the queen ... well, the queen fell into a great deal of trouble. It seems some inimical magic caught me up and threw me around, and ... I'm really not sure how I ended up in Swyfflbyrne. You probably think I'm a madwoman, but I have no idea how to prove to you I'm not lying."

"You could show me to them, Mi'Lady," Bib said aloud.

"Who's that?" Tiny said, turning around so fast he wobbled on his peg leg.

"My ... my only real friend in the entire world." Merrigan tugged the bag up onto her lap and pulled Bib out, to sit on top of the bag. "He's a magic book."

"Ah, now we love books here." Ma chuckled. "As if you hadn't noticed already."

"Yes, I did, and that's why I would dearly love to be able to stay here." Merrigan didn't mind that for some odd reason, her eyes felt very wet. If tears convinced these people to give her a job and a place to stay, she didn't mind displaying such weakness.

"I assure you, Mi'Lady is a good seamstress, and she has indeed been in the royal palaces of Carlion and Avylyn," Bib said. For emphasis, he flipped open to blank pages and wrote the same words he spoke. "Since you love books so much, may I assume this is a reputable, well-mannered establishment, where Mi'Lady will be safe?"

"Just see what happens when people don't behave themselves," Ma said with a chuckle. "We're an oddity, since we don't allow heavy drinking or cussing or spitting or wenching. You'd be surprised how many folks appreciate having a quiet, clean place waiting for them when they step onto dry land. Well, I may be considered a fool for taking the word of a book, but only a fool ignores magic when it sits in front of him. Have you had your nooning yet, Mistress --" She frowned, but it was a bemused frown. "Now don't that beat all? I never did get your name."

"Mara," Merrigan said. Since she was likely very far away from Smilpotz and Carnpotz and Judge Brimble, she doubted tales of what she had done to contribute to his downfall would ever reach this place. It would be wise to stick with a name she was used to using already.

"Welcome to the Bookish Mermaid, Mistress Mara. Have you had your nooning yet?"

"No. I've been rather busy looking for employment."

"Well, no one goes hungry if they work for the Mermaid. You stay right here and we'll share our first meal together, and then we'll get you settled. Have you anything to your name besides the book -- and does he have a name?"

"Bib," he responded.

"Biblio," Tiny said with a chuckle. "It means book!"

An hour later, Merrigan had eaten the first bowl of fish stew that she actually enjoyed, and moved into a comfortable, clean room on the fourth floor of the Bookish Mermaid. Ma explained that while it was a chore to climb all those stairs, she put the staff on the fourth floor so they could be as far from the noise of guests as possible. The heat from the stoves and fireplaces in the winter made the rooms cozy, and they were high enough to catch all the good, cooling winds off the sea in the summer. Tiny ran to Mistress Coppersmythe's boarding house while Merrigan and Ma ate and discussed her duties and pay, and came back with Merrigan's bag of clothes and sewing supplies, as well as Mistress Coppersmythe's feebleminded son, who worked evenings in the Mermaid's stables.

That odd, warm, full and yet feathery light feeling settled into Merrigan's chest as she unpacked her few possessions in her tiny, cozy room. She would spend her days in the main room off the kitchen, mending clothes of guests and workers and family, and if she cared to take on any sewing of new clothes for guests, she was free to do so and make her own arrangements for payments. Ma insisted that everyone who worked for her learned to read, so there was always someone practicing their lessons in between chores, reading aloud in the main room. Sometimes newspapers, sometimes history books, and sometimes books of fables and adventures. Ma admitted with a blush and a twinkle in her eyes that her entire family preferred the fables and adventures.

Yes, Merrigan thought, she would be not just comfortable here, but she could be happy. At least, as happy as a queen who had lost her throne and her husband and her beauty could possibly be.

~~~~~

The winter passed in warmth and comfort, and though Merrigan preferred to stay on the sidelines, Ma's loud, happy, busy household and enormous family wouldn't allow it. They drew her in and made her one of them, and didn't push when she declined to talk about herself. She loved to read, so that made her one of them. She was happy, except for the times that she remembered who she used to be and what awaited her. While she enjoyed life at the Bookish Mermaid, the thought of still being here after one hundred years was enough to make her take to her bed and snarl at people. Only once did her foul spirits get bad enough that Bib had to scold her. The shock of it seemed to snap something back into place inside her head and heart. The odd thing was that apologizing to everyone for her bad mood and sharp tongue seemed to do her even more good.

Tiny and Ma and the rest of their vast family laughed it off and blamed the winter weather and being housebound with the stormy sea crashing within earshot of the inn. Their understanding and easy forgiveness brought her close to tears as well. Merrigan hoped they were right, and it was only the weather.

They were proved right when the days lengthened and warmed and her temper stayed even. Dreams of the past didn't plague her and she could hold off the memories during the daylight. Spring in a seaport was a busy, invigorating time of the year. Merrigan thought about spending the next ten, twenty years here. Maybe it wouldn't be so bad.

"If you can arrange to sleep through the winter," Bib teased her, when she finally mentioned the idea to him.

Merrigan managed to laugh, despite a twisting in her belly. He was right, of course. Bib was always right. Would she have to leave this comfortable place that valued her, just to stay sane?

Before she could work herself up to seriously contemplate booking passage on a ship to Armorica, Merrigan ran into a real
~~~~~

mermaid on the steps of the Bookish Mermaid.

Elli, as Ma's family came to call her, simply because they couldn't pronounce her real name, didn't have a tail and she wasn't wet. However, the signs were unmistakable. Her silver-and-gold hair, cropped short in frizzy curls, had a greenish tint, her eyes were enormous, and anyone who watched her blink saw she had two sets of eyelids. Most telling, she had several long, thin gill lines down both sides of her neck. She stood in the street in front of the steps of the Bookish Mermaid, in clothes two sizes too large. She swayed in time with the lapping of the waves against the pier, staring at the wooden mermaid, and weeping green-tinted tears.

Besides, if she hadn't been able to guess from all those clues, Bib told Merrigan the odd-looking girl was a mermaid.

"How did she get up there?" the girl asked, when Merrigan stopped to get a closer look, since she had always wanted to see a real mermaid. Her voice had a creaky-squeaky quality to it, but made bearable because she spoke in near-whispers.

"Well, when Great-granddaddy Pug finished sculpting her, I imagine it took a team of men with pulleys."

"Sculpting?" She blinked several times, looking between Merrigan and the wooden mermaid. "What kind of magic is that?"

"She thinks the emblem of the inn is a real mermaid, enchanted and imprisoned," Bib explained.

"Oh, hello, book," the girl said, addressing the bag that always hung at Merrigan's hip.

While she trusted everyone who worked at the Bookish Mermaid, Merrigan had an innate distrust for anyone who loved books as much as she did -- because if she would steal a magical book, wouldn't everyone else? She trusted Ma and Tiny to know that Bib was a magic book, but they agreed with her that no one else should know. This mermaid-on-dry-land had some magic of her own if she knew the voice that came from inside the leather bag was a magical book. Then again, how smart could this girl be, if she couldn't tell the difference between a relatively decent wooden sculpture and an enchanted maiden?

"I'm sorry I didn't sense you there," she continued. "I'm afraid my magic is very slow in regenerating. Just about as slow as the growth of my hair." She sighed, and several more green-tinted tears trickled down her cheek.

Merrigan glanced around, wondering why no one noticed. Several regular customers of the Mermaid strode past her, heading up the stairs for an early lunch. They tipped their hats to her or greeted her by name, and barely gave the mermaid a second glance. Or maybe, she should wonder why she *did* notice.

"It's because you're in close contact with me, and a little of my magic is rubbing off on you," Bib explained, as soon as the thought solidified in her head. "And no, it would take more than your dreaded hundred years before enough magic rubbed off to break the curse -- err -- spell."

Merrigan could almost have laughed at how Bib slipped up. He insisted they call Clara's curse a spell or enchantment.

"The you-don't-really-see-me spell is the first thing that grew back. Why did you cut your hair?" he added. "I'm sorry, we haven't been properly introduced. The enchanted lady who has agreed to take me as her traveling companion is Princess Merrigan of Avylyn, and I am Bib. What is your name and why are you on dry land with short hair?"

Later, Merrigan decided the most unsettling part of the entire encounter was that she didn't have a screaming fit when Bib called her a princess rather than a queen. Maybe she had finally grown used to the ugly truth.

"I am --" The girl let out a series of squeaks and clicks, with a few Human vowels and consonants thrown in, which was where Ma grabbed onto the name "Elli," a short time later. "I am from the Great Ocean, so far removed from this port that I can barely smell the water of my home." She gestured out at the high tide water, the stone breakwalls that protected the harbor, and the ocean beyond.

"Mi'Lady," Bib said. "Perhaps we should take this conversation indoors? Eventually, people will wonder why you are standing here, since they know you. Once they concentrate hard enough, ask enough questions, eventually the spell protecting our new friend will wear thin. We don't want to have a crowd of sailors overwhelming us. They go slightly crazy when there's a chance of a real mermaid within their grasp."

"Why?"

"Even poor relations such as I am can dive deep enough to retrieve sunken treasure," the girl said, a short time later, as they settled into the living area. The clatter from lunch reaching full speed was enough to make their conversation relatively private. "All they have to do is cut off a strand of my hair as long as their arm and hold onto it to make me obey their will."

"That's horrendous!" Merrigan cried. She clapped her hand over her mouth and glanced over her shoulder. None of the many workers on the kitchen side of the room even glanced up. "Is there no way to set you free? Is that how you lost all your hair? How quickly does your hair grow back?"

To be perfectly honest, right after the revulsion that shot through her at the thought of filthy, salty, tar-smeared sailors cutting off a woman's hair to control her, a flash of excitement pushed it away. All those riches lying on the bottom of the ocean, just waiting to be brought up to the surface -- why couldn't or shouldn't she have some of that? She imagined gathering enough gold to travel the world and pay the strongest enchanter she could find to break Clara's curse. The problem was that the mermaid sitting in front of her didn't have hair as long as Merrigan's fingers, let alone her arm.

Then another thought struck her.

"Poor relation? You aren't a princess? I thought all mermaids who came up to the surface were daughters of the Sea King."

"Ah, so that's what you are," Ma said, gliding in to join them. "I suspected, but my eyes aren't as good as they used to be, and this old charm has had a lot of use over the years." She rubbed the necklace of sea glass that circled her ample neck three times. "Here you go, dearie. This might help," she added, as she handed the girl a steaming cup that smelled like salt and seaweed and a very old crab.

She settled down with them. Merrigan paused to fight down the flash of irritation, because wasn't this *her* mermaid, her discovery? What right did Ma have, sticking her nose into what was turning out to be an interesting story? Then as Merrigan listened to Bib filling Ma in on what they had seen and learned so far, and the struggle to figure out how to pronounce the girl's name, she reasoned that of course, Ma had every right. She was the queen of the Bookish Mermaid, just as much as Merrigan had been queen of Carlion. How would Merrigan feel if someone brought a stranger into her palace and tried to keep information from her? After that, she could smile with the others as they decided that Elli was the easiest name to use for the girl. By this time, Elli had drunk half of the brew Ma had thrown together for her, and Merrigan could have sworn that most of the dry, frizzy look to her hair had smoothed out. Unfortunately, no instant hair growth. Her skin took on a faintly silvery cast, almost a glow, and she looked ... well, "damper" would be the best word Merrigan could come up with.

"Every Sea King has a dozen daughters, at least, for every son they produce," Elli said, when they returned to the explanation of how she had come to be so far from her home territory under the waves. "Despite the losses we incur every generation, from foolish maidens who go up to the surface and fall in love with some handsome land-walker who pretends to be a prince, there are at least nine or ten daughters who take a mate and produce another daughter or two or three. My great-great-great-great-grandmother was a daughter of the Sea King." She sighed and her tears had an even stronger green tint as they plopped down into the last mouthful of the brew in her cup. "You'd think with all the land-walker blood in me, between her and my mother, I would have had the sense to stay away from the surface."

"Excuse me -- land-walker?" Merrigan interrupted.

"With all those women in the water, it's not that easy finding a merman willing to settle down and take responsibility for his mate's mother and sisters and nieces, besides all the daughters they're likely to produce," Bib said. "The usual tactic is for a mermaid to come up on dry land for fifteen, twenty years, pretend to be a Human woman, take a husband -- generally an old, retired sailor -- and have several children. When he dies of happy old age, she takes her children and returns to the sea. The really lucky ones have a son or two with their Human husbands, which gains them quite a lot of prestige under the waves."

Chapter Eight

"That sounds ... well, that sounds rather sensible." Merrigan wondered if that was where she had made her mistake. There had been a few older kings looking for second wives who had been interested in her. The dangers of becoming a stepmother and automatically being blamed for anything that went wrong in the lives of her stepchildren had been the main reason for refusing to let the emissaries present their courting gifts.

"Not sensible enough. Not where I was concerned," Elli said. "My bad luck was to run into a real prince. I should have taken that old sailor with a fleet of small boats, who took rich people out on overnight trips up and down the coast. He didn't care about treasure, and I did like the paintings he made."

"Since when is it bad luck to marry a real prince?" Merrigan said with a chuckle.

"*Run* into a prince," Ma corrected her gently. "That's the problem, isn't it? He cut off your hair with a magic knife, to ensure you couldn't regain your tail and swim away from him."

"Ughsalla the Sea Witch gave it to him. She's had a grudge against my family line since my great-great-great-grandmother went to another sea witch to trade her singing voice to win a prince and live happily ever after. Ughsalla has always wanted to be in the Storm Surge Chorus, but her voice is only suited to creating typhoons." A few more green teardrops slid down Elli's cheeks and plopped into her cup.

"We need to get that knife back," Ma said. "Can you think of any other way to make her hair grow back and regain her tail, Bib?"

"No, I'm sorry." Bib riffled his pages, flipping up and then down again in a shrug. "I've been ransacking all the books I have ever visited that even mention mermaids. They disagree on so many details, some so ludicrous I could laugh until my pages tear out. However, they do agree that any change made to a mermaid through magic must be repaired by that same magic. Especially a magical tool."

"How do we get that knife?" Merrigan said. "What kingdom is that wretched prince from?"

The prince, it turned out, was now the king of Quibblshtahn, a small kingdom north of Swyfflbyrne. When Elli ran away from him, he didn't suffer a broken heart, but proved he was a vindictive, spoiled brat. In his search for a royal bride, he crossed the Great Ocean to Armorica. He left the magic knife, encrusted with jewels, with his bride's father in the tiny kingdom of Seafoam. Since Elli couldn't swim or buy passage on a ship to take her there, she couldn't retrieve the knife.

Merrigan could barely hold back a squeak of delight at that bit of news. She actually knew where Seafoam was in Armorica.

"You know the king of Seafoam, don't you?" Bib said, during a lull in the conversation when Ma got up to fix another cup of restorative tonic for Elli.

"I know *of* him," Merrigan said.

She trembled a little when Ma stopped, two steps away from her chair, and fixed her with that look she knew all too well from her nursery days. The look her own mother and Nanny Starling both gave her when she had secrets and they were on the verge of finding out. She had learned early that a wise child told those secrets, because no matter how naughty she might have been, the longer she took confessing, the worse her punishment.

"I never met the previous king," she hurried to add, feeling as if the words were being squeezed out of her. "I did see his silly daughters when they came to court. None of them were good-hearted enough to make their silliness bearable." At least, that was Merrigan's impression of the princesses of Seafoam on their one visit. She had been perhaps five years old at the time. They had been ridiculously obvious in their attempts to make one of her older brothers fall in love with them.

"You met princesses." Ma sat down, not quite frowning, but concentrating on Merrigan so her gaze had weight.

"I told you, I sewed in royal courts." She trembled, unwilling to admit to Ma, especially, that she was under a curse. Somehow, she didn't want Ma to get the wrong impression of her.

"That's the answer," the woman said after several more moments. She smiled, nodded twice, and picked up the cup to go get Elli's tonic.

"Answer?" Elli watched Ma cross to the kitchen side of the long room, then turned back to Merrigan.

Before she rejoined them, Ma sent one of the dishwashing crew down to the harbor to the *Fleetwind,* her third oldest son's ship. She sent one of the table-service girls upstairs to a storage room with a long list of items to bring down with her. Then she picked a number of bottles and jars and bags off the high shelves in the narrow room where cooking ingredients were kept, tossed them into a massive bowl big enough to wash a five-year-old boy, and came back to the cluster of couches and chairs where Elli and Merrigan waited in silence. She spread the ingredients out on a low round table and dragged it over to within easy reach of Elli's chair.

"I'd wager your spoilsport prince -- sorry, king -- has your description spread around the various ports, to keep you from getting on a ship and going after the knife." Ma picked up one bottle or jar or bag after another and took a pinch or scoop of each ingredient and dropped it into the big bowl. "I'll wager he's enough of a snot that he made sure you *knew* what he did with the knife, just to torment you. My guess is that he's counting on the longevity of mermaids, so that when he's a wrinkled old codger, you'll still be beautiful. When he's a widower, he can force you to marry him to get the knife."

"He could be banking on a few of the sillier legends of the sea people," Bib offered. "Such as, if a mermaid takes you down deep enough and you eat a certain kind of seaweed that only grows where no light can reach, you'll become mer and eternally young."

"Extremely silly, since that seaweed can only turn him into a mermaid, emphasis on *maid,*" Ma said with a nasty grin.

"What are you doing?" Merrigan asked, when Ma had dumped in a particularly strong-smelling vinegar. It made the mixture bubble and release even stronger aromas reminiscent of a nursery on a hot summer day.

"A disguise that will get our new friend across the ocean to steal that knife. I dare any magic spell to stand up against my great-granny Phoebe's hair tonic."

Merrigan dared any vermin within two miles to stand up against the smell. Fortunately, the stench died out quickly enough that only a few customers looked in from the dining room to ask if there was a problem.

Quincy, captain of the *Fleetwind*, showed up just as Ma was throwing a thick sheet around Elli's shoulders to protect her clothes and the surrounding chairs and books. He waited, rubbing his nose and pretending the stink didn't bother him. Ma used a pastry brush to glop the thick, slightly bubbling, brown concoction on the mermaid's hair and then work it through to her scalp. While Elli waited, her throat convulsing every time she took too deep of a breath, Ma explained her plan.

If she hadn't already had her breath taken away by the hair tonic, Merrigan might just have lost it altogether.

Mistress Mara, seamstress to royalty, would cross the ocean to Seafoam and kingdoms beyond, to seek her former home and cash in on several promises her former patrons had made to her. Naturally, a woman of her skill and age and delicate constitution couldn't travel such a great distance without a serving maid-apprentice. When they reached Windward, the capital and main port of Seafoam, the two would establish themselves in a reputable inn and then become part of the neighborhood, and trusted. Then they could find a way into the palace and retrieve that knife.

This was where Quincy came in. He crossed the ocean to Armorica regularly, and knew all the ports, large and small, fishing towns and major ports of commerce and quiet little villages so small they didn't have docks.

"Oh, yes, I know about Avylyn and Carlion and the other major kingdoms," he said, when his mother asked. His face lit up, as if he had been given an amazing gift. "Would you like to know about Jardien or Heiffelbein or --"

"No need. Just knowing there's someone on this side of the world who knows about my homeland, it's very encouraging." Merrigan blinked rapidly, fighting totally inexplicable tears.

"More important," Ma said, patting Merrigan's shoulder, "do you know a reputable inn in Windward where we can settle these two in safety?"

Merrigan hadn't thought it possible, but Quincy's face lit up even more. Yes, he knew of an inn where the food was outstanding and the rooms were clean and the innkeeper's family made sure their customers were safe and they kept out riffraff. He was friends with the innkeeper's sons and daughter, and would entrust Mistress Mara and Mistress Elli to their care, personally.

Ah ha. A daughter, she thought to Bib. *No wonder Quincy can't wait to go back. He's fallen in love. I wonder, does his mother know?*

Ma never misses anything, her companion responded.

Merrigan shuddered. She hoped there were at least a few things that had escaped Ma's sharp eye and even sharper instincts.

So it was that two days later, Mistress Mara bade farewell to the friends she had made at the Bookish Mermaid. She boarded the *Fleetwind* with her new apprentice, several crates of material, and all the essentials to set up a dressmaker's shop in the port town of Windward, in the tiny kingdom of Seafoam.

~~~~~

Elli didn't care much for sewing, and her attempts at singing hurt Merrigan's ears. She did find books fascinating, and confessed that she much preferred that method of storing information to the way it was done under the sea -- trusted to the memories of the great whales and to the spiny, blind creatures that lived at depths that would crush ordinary mortals. While their memories were perfect down to the inflection used when the information was relayed to them, whales were stodgy creatures devoted to protocol and manners, and the spiny creatures of the dark, cold depths had even spinier feelings. Sometimes retrieving the information stored in their minds was harder than reading books retrieved from sunken ships. Elli had wondered what was in the books, but the ink always faded away before she could teach herself to read.

Merrigan found some ironic amusement in discovering that she could be a fairly decent teacher if her pupil was clever and hungry to learn. She and Elli spent their time either holed up in their cabin or in the prow of the ship out of the way of the sailors. Merrigan designed fantastical gowns to catch the attention of the court ladies of Seafoam, while Elli learned her letters by reading aloud to her. Quincy had delightful taste in books, and four-fifths of the volumes lining one wall of his cabin were all fables and romantic tales of daring and adventures, rather than manuals devoted to the seafaring life. Four books were full of poetry. That made sense, since he seemed besotted to the point of turning mute, when it came to the subject of the innkeeper's daughter.

Merrigan blamed self-preservation and cleverness when she quizzed Quincy about his sweetheart until she had a good idea of the girl's height and build. She designed and sewed a dress for her
~~~~~

that was just a little grander than an innkeeper's daughter would wear, but not so grand she would feel uncomfortable. She doubted she acted out of gratitude for Ma and Tiny's help, so she helped Quincy's courtship. There was no real profit in being nice to the lower classes just for the sake of being nice to them.

Still, there was a vague disquiet deep inside, when she presented the dress to Rosa, the innkeeper's daughter, and she and her mother insisted that Merrigan and Elli had to have the grandest room in their inn. That was what she intended, wasn't it?

Rosa brought all her friends to see Merrigan and the material she had brought with her, and exclaim over the dresses she had designed. Of course, the other clothes were far too grand for them to ever dream of wearing, but many of them worked for rich merchants or were servants in some of the grand houses of Windward. They promised to speak with their mistresses about the fashionable seamstress who had come from far over the sea. Merrigan left hints that royal employers had sent her on her journey. By the end of the day, word spread through Windward that a royal seamstress had arrived, and she would be happy to share what she had learned before she returned to her employers.

"Now we'll see how fast the fish are biting and how hungry they are," she remarked to Elli that evening, as they headed downstairs to the dining room. The mermaid girl laughed at her figurative language. She had been trying to rid some of the sea-based metaphors out of her vocabulary during the voyage, while Merrigan had been picking them up from the sailors.

She returned to their room after dinner, leaving Elli sitting by the fire, listening with delight to a long, involved tale from Miles, Rosa's oldest brother. She stopped in the doorway, the question she had for Bib frozen on her lips.

A massive dog with eyes as big as rum bottles sat beside her bed, head bowed over Bib, who was spread out open on the quilt.

Merrigan blinked, rubbed her eyes, then looked again. She finally thought to close the door, and moved farther into the room. The dog was an enormous, muscular breed that looked like it could take a bite out of a building, or even drag it into the street. She could only walk to the foot of her bed because the dog took up most of the sitting area next to the fireplace. Merrigan was too stunned to feel afraid.

"Good evening, Princess," the dog said in a growly sort of slobbery voice that threatened to drip drool. He bowed his head to her, nearly knocking Bib onto the floor.

"Good evening, dog." She decided it might be prudent to curtsey. "Are you all right, Bib?"

Merrigan braced herself to find out that Bib's original master had regained his magic and had sent this huge dog to take him back home. She considered flinging herself onto the bed, under the massive jaws of the dog, risking a bite or even being inundated with that threat of drool, to grab hold of her friend and keep him from being taken away.

"Quite all right, Mi'Lady. Rolf and his two brothers are old friends. They are bound to a tinderbox that once belonged to my master. A witch stole it during the chaos. I'm delighted to meet up with him again. All three have had some exciting adventures."

"Then we sat in a cave for seventy years or so," the dog, Rolf, added in a tone that was part growl, part whine.

"True. The witch made a very serious miscalculation and she lost control over the tinderbox. She had to find someone willing to go down into the hole in the ground to get it, who wasn't interested in the tinderbox for his own sake. Most people took one look at her and either ran in fear or were stupidly greedy and thought they could cheat an old woman. Why does everyone think the elderly are witless or helpless?" Bib chuckled. "Appearances are deceiving, aren't they, Mi'Lady?"

Rolf laughed too, a panting sort of sound that necessitated his tongue hanging out. It was an enormous tongue that Merrigan thought she could use as a hand towel.

"So whoever helped the witch get the tinderbox out of the hole in the ground managed to take it away from her?" she guessed.

"A soldier, newly released from the army and still young enough to enjoy the rest of his life. He's staying here at the inn. Rolf here has an interesting story. He and his brothers take turns going into the palace every night to fetch Princess Dulcibella back here to the inn for their master."

"To do what?"

"My master is a romantic," Rolf said. "He is wooing the princess. They play checkers or walk, while he listens to her silly chatter and tells her she's smarter than everyone thinks she is."

"Is she?"

"Everyone in Seafoam expects her to be an absolute dunce, so of course, any brains she was born with are fading away." The big dog snorted. "Like seafoam."

"Why do they *expect* her to be stupid?" Merrigan climbed over the foot of the bed and sat on the mattress. She hoped Miles' story lasted a good deal longer and Elli stayed downstairs, so they wouldn't be interrupted.

"That's the curse of the kingdom. The king was a younger son, cast off by his stepfather and robbed by his older brothers and stepbrothers. He came to Seafoam, which was in ruins. Generations ago, some upstart who wanted to be king tried to dismantle the protective magic. It turned everything inside out. Someone in the royal family had created a spell to keep them from ever losing the throne. Essentially, Seafoam will vanish if there isn't someone of the royal bloodline in residence, at all times. The royal family thought they were clever, and when everything started falling apart, they whipped up magic to let them sleep until someone fixed things. They slept for maybe five years, until the current king got through a wall of briars, found the princesses, and kissed the oldest and smartest." The big dog snorted, his mouth dropping open in a wide, wet canine grin, so his tongue lolled out for several seconds before he licked his chops and resumed speaking.

"The former king and queen decided they would rather be sailor merchants, so they took off on a ship and haven't been heard from since. The two younger princesses grabbed a chest of gold and set off in search of a king to marry, and haven't been heard from since, either. They're probably prisoners of an enchanter who collects princesses."

"So what is the curse that makes this princess stupid?" Merrigan asked, to keep from remarking that she had met the two princesses, and she felt sorry for whoever had captured them.

"Well, it became tangled with the magic that requires a member of the royal family in residence. As the heir is, so will the rest of the kingdom be. Someone tried to trick the heir into marriage, and when she outsmarted him, he warped the spell, to turn all the royal women into dunces. Arabella married the first prince who came along and crossed the ocean to get as far from Windward as she could. Proved she had some brains. Everyone expects Dulcibella to be incredibly stupid. Every time she hears someone say how silly she is, she grows more silly. Honestly, the soldier I work for is good for her, and good for the kingdom."

"As soon as Rolf and his brothers sensed my presence," Bib explained, "they decided to come to me for advice."

"What sort of advice?" Merrigan asked.

"Our master is smart enough to know he doesn't want to be in charge of a kingdom, or be stuck with a silly princess. He likes her, but how much work will it take to convince her she's smarter than she thinks she is? It takes all the king's hard work and concentration to counteract the queen's silliness, otherwise Seafoam would be in a horrid mess. She does silly things and he wears himself out fixing her messes and keeping people from believing she is an idiot. What they believe becomes reality. Do you see what I'm getting at?"

"All too clearly. What do you expect me to do?"

"Our master is hesitating too much. Dulcibella likes him. She wants to marry him, but can you imagine the ruckus if she tells her parents she's in love with a soldier? Just wait until she tells them she goes to bed, and the next thing she knows she's waking up in a bedroom somewhere, with this man, and they sit and play checkers and talk. Then she curls up on his bed and when she wakes up she's in her own bed."

"Well, I imagine they will employ several tactics to try to figure out where the princess goes each night, or prove that she's just having a strange, recurring dream."

"And you know how that will go." Rolf shook his head, threatening to knock Bib off the bed. "They'll find our soldier and lock him up for kidnapping Dulcibella. He's 'nothing' but a soldier. They've conveniently forgotten that the king was a youngest son and started out with nothing but his wits and a magical handkerchief that granted three wishes."

"What do you think I can do?" Merrigan wondered if the king still had that handkerchief. Once magical objects with a wish limit went into a new set of hands, the magic started all over again. What she could do with three wishes ... She wondered what the king had wasted his three wishes on. Definitely, one wasn't making the queen and his daughters smarter, or trying to unravel the spell affecting them.

"Teach the soldier how to act like a prince, and dress him up like a prince," Bib said, when Merrigan looked at the dog and the dog looked back at her, leaning closer. She cringed away, expecting drool to fall on her at any moment.

"Talk to my master and convince him that it isn't so hard being king. Dulcibella only had to mention once that whoever she marries will be king, and my master panicked. She didn't say anything more about it. She's actually clever when it comes to wheedling and teasing and wearing people down to do what she wants. But in a nice way," Rolf hurried to add. "You might even like her, if she didn't think she was utterly stupid. It makes her cry a lot. My master is the only one who can make her laugh, lately."

"Sounds like she's in love," Bib offered in a cheerful tone.

"Why would you think I could convince a battle-hardened soldier that he wants to take on all the drudgery and finicky, headachy work of being king of Seafoam?" Merrigan asked.

"Your father is a powerful king and you were married to a king. Surely you picked up something along the way."

"My late husband made quite a few stupid mistakes," she retorted.

"Then tell my master all the mistakes he made, so he can avoid them," Rolf responded and grinned at her.

Merrigan wished dogs wouldn't grin. It always entailed their drippy tongues hanging out. She didn't want to know what the floor looked like underneath Rolf's mouth.

Still, so many possibilities had opened in front of her. Rolf had some freedom to move about. Could she borrow him to help her? Could she get him to look for the knife that would let Elli's hair grow back? Could he find the wishing handkerchief for her? Could he bring them out of the palace? Or since his master sent him for the princess, was she all he could retrieve from the palace?

"Oh, there he goes," Rolf said, sitting up and glancing toward the other side of the inn, as if he could see through the walls. "He's getting ready to strike the tinderbox and light the candle. Tonight is my turn, so I'll have to be going soon."

"Can you get me into the palace?" Merrigan asked. "Since you're going in to get the princess, could you take me with you, leave me there, and pick me up when you bring her back?"

"Don't see why not," he said, and a second later turned transparent and dashed through the wall.

"What are you going to do?" Bib asked.

"Look for Elli's knife." Merrigan slid off the bed and went to the pegs on the far wall where her and Elli's few changes of clothes had been hung up to air out and lose some of their wrinkles. The dark gray was perfect for pretending to be a servant in the palace. No one paid attention to servants, except other servants. This late into the evening, chances were good most of the servants would be settling in for the night, or they had gone home.

First, she would determine if there was a uniform for the servants. If so, she would take a set for herself, to help her blend in better. Then she could walk about more freely. Merrigan doubted the palace would be even one-fourth the size of her father's palace. She doubted it would take her very long to locate the throne room or the treasure chamber in the Windward palace. Likely this little country of fishermen might not even have enough treasure to require a treasure chamber. Probably the king kept it in a large chest. If she was lucky, the knife and the magic handkerchief would be stored together.

"Ready?" Rolf said, sliding to a stop in the room again, just as she finished buttoning the high collar of her gray dress.

"Umm ... how ..." Merrigan stepped up close to the big dog and gulped delicately. His back was higher than her head. She supposed she could step up on the bed to climb up on his back, but how was she to hold onto him? He did have a collar under all that tangled hair, didn't he? Falling off him before she got into the palace, or even while going through a solid stone wall, would be highly inconvenient.

"Just hop up and touch my collar. I tuck the princess's hand under my collar and she stays on with no problem at all."

"Very well." Merrigan raised her skirts and stepped up onto the bed. The mattress sagged slightly under her feet, but she had no fear of stepping through the gaps between the ropes that supported the mattress. With a hop, she got up onto Rolf's back, digging both hands into the thick, tangled fur around his neck. She found the collar and immediately stopped sliding.

"Ready?" he asked.

"Good luck!" Bib cried, before Merrigan could respond.

Then they were off, moving in a blur. Every time Merrigan thought she could see a wall coming toward them, they were through it before she could brace herself for impact. It was a somewhat exhilarating way to travel, but she wouldn't recommend it to anyone. In what felt like only a few galloping steps, they stood inside the small courtyard of what would be a manor house of a prosperous merchant in Avylyn. Merrigan slid off, revising her estimate of how long it would take to search this palace.

Rolf nodded to her, then reared back on his hind legs and leaped, up onto the roof of the wing directly to her right. Two more leaps took him up two more stories, to a balcony that Merrigan thought sure would snap under the dog's weight. He passed through the wall. She found it rather disturbing to watch in the moonlight, so she turned away. Now, where was she in relation to the throne room or wherever treasures would be kept?

She chose the nearest, most likely door. It led her into what she assumed was the receiving room, where petitioners awaited their chance to stand before the king. There were padded benches along both walls, several doors leading off the long room, and a decent runner down the middle to soften the sound of boots on the flagstone floor. Merrigan found the furnishings rather charming in their simplicity, though she could never understand the attraction of decorating with nets and seashells. The long murals of ocean vistas, however, she found soothing. They would be even lovelier in the daylight, rather than in the long streaks of moonlight from the windows high on both walls.

She took the first door to her right off the reception room, deciding to take her search counterclockwise. It would be easier to remember where she had been if she did things systematically. The first room looked like a secretary's chamber, shelves of stacked papers, inkwells, quill pens, blotters, and an entire wall of drawers with abbreviated words marked on little bits of paper attached to the front of each drawer. Not a likely place to hide magical items. There might be more to this room than appeared in the moonlight that spilled over her shoulder, but she couldn't take the time to find a candle or lantern, or risk someone seeing the light and coming to investigate.

Merrigan suspected it would take her several trips to do even a basic search.

The second room looked like a sort of miniature kitchen, or a pantry for serving visitors. She saw stacks of plates and shelves of cups and pitchers. The third door on the right wall turned out to be a long passageway from another wing of the palace. Merrigan saved that for another night of exploring, and hoped there wouldn't be any need. She might walk into the servants' wing. Granted, that would shorten her search, because no one hid treasures in the servants' domain, with all the dirty clothes and dirty dishes and mending and tools. Then again, that passageway might lead to the royal family's living quarters. She could imagine the king hiding treasures there. Perhaps a hole under the floor of his sitting room? Or perhaps it would have been safer to hide something under the nursery floor? The queen's sitting room? The schoolroom?

There was only one door in the wall directly opposite where she had entered the receiving room. The throne room. She was mildly impressed. The craftsmanship was simple and dignified. The woodwork gleamed, in the cornices and the beams decorating the vaulted ceiling, the high-backed throne wide enough for two to sit, the dais with one step -- high enough to signal the presence of royalty, but not too high. Quiet dignity. She wondered if the current king had designed this throne room, or it was a holdover from a previous king who had ruled with austere dignity. The decorations of a throne room could reveal quite a lot about the king.

She was wasting time, critiquing the fashion sense of the very people she needed to steal from. Merrigan walked the perimeter of the room, trying to decipher through gray shadows and black shadows and silvery streaks of moonlight where a good hiding place might be for a magic knife and an enchanted handkerchief. The knife was supposed to be encrusted with jewels. Where would a king of fishermen display something so gaudy, so out of character for his kingdom, or would he hide it?

"No, please," she whispered. If King Devon stayed in character, he would have had the jewels removed, sold, and the money used for the good of the kingdom.

Hadn't Quincy pointed out repairs to the cobblestoned streets and the new breakwater and docks, built since his last trip to Seafoam? Where would the money for such things have come from, other than adding to the taxes? The people wouldn't speak of their rulers with honest admiration and respect if the king had raised their taxes. The money had come from somewhere else. If the king sold the jewels, where was the knife?

"Please, please," she whispered as she sped up her walking tour of the perimeter of the room, "please don't have melted it down, or worse, given it to one of your guards? Or decided to use it for a filleting knife when you went fishing!"

She flinched and pressed both hands over her mouth, and it seemed that her voice, though a whisper, was still shrill enough to ring off the vaulted ceiling.

Discretion urged her to retreat, out of the throne room, out of the receiving room, and back to the courtyard where Rolf had left her. Merrigan spent the rest of the night curled up in the shadows on a bench, until the moon slid behind the high roofs of the palace. She thought long and hard until she started to doze, then jerked herself awake, and repeated the process.

She needed to get into the palace in daylight, when she could see details better. How was she going to gain not just admittance, but the freedom to wander around and poke into things, open doors and raise lids? She needed to be invited to sew for the queen and princess. Tomorrow, she would make some noise, get some attention, let the entire city know a master seamstress, worthy of royalty, had come to Windward.

However, Merrigan had learned the hard way that no plan was entirely flawless. Something always destroyed a plan, simply because other people operated by their own choices and reasons, and they could not be controlled. More the pity. She needed a backup plan.

Starting tomorrow, she would confront Rolf's master. It was useless to try to convince him he would enjoy being a king. She would have to play upon his sense of duty and honor as a soldier, so eventually, he would march up to the doors of the palace and demand Princess Dulcibella in marriage. With the support of the soldier -- what had Rolf said his name was, anyway? -- Merrigan would have open access to the palace. She might even be able to simply ask for the knife and have it handed to her.

First, she had to make sure the solder looked worthy of becoming heir to the throne.

Contemplating all that work, just to get hold of the knife, exhausted her. Merrigan had nearly fallen asleep, for the fourth time, when Rolf dropped down to land in the courtyard in front of her. She was so delighted to see him, because it was cold in the courtyard, she hugged him before she climbed up onto his back. At the inn, Elli was stunned at the sight of Rolf filling up their room, but had the good sense not to scream.

She burst into tears when she heard Merrigan's plan, hugged her, and swore she was the most wonderful, kind, clever, generous woman in the entire world. She promised once she had her tail back, she would swim to the deepest crushing depths of the sea to find the rare green pearl that was reputed to counteract any poison, heal any wound, and break any curse. No matter how long it took her, and it had taken the last successful hunter eighty years, she would find the pearl, to thank good, kind, generous, clever, brave Princess Merrigan.

Eighty years? Merrigan shuddered and told Elli to wash her face and go back to bed. By the time the grateful little mermaid found the pearl, it wouldn't do her any good because Clara's curse would nearly have run its course. In eighty years' time, what good would it do her to return to Carlion to reclaim her throne? No one who had sneered and found joy in her downfall would be there to grind their teeth in frustration, chagrin, and fear.

"Well, we have a long day and a lot of work ahead of us," Merrigan said, once Rolf had left and there was air to breathe in the room again. She picked up Bib and put him on the low table by the window, as he had requested, so the rays from the rising sun would touch him in the morning. "It's best we all get a good night's sleep, what's left of it. We need to find a way to convince the soldier --"

"His name is Warden," Bib said.

"Thank you. Convince Warden that we are here to help him, and we aren't madwomen trying to complicate his life."

"We could tell him the truth," Elli offered, as she slid back under her blankets.

"The truth?" Merrigan bit her tongue to hold back the bitter chuckle and the retort that the truth was a pitiful tool used by those who had no other resources. That was something Leffisand would say, and look where his cynical attitude and outlook had gotten him.

"Tell him we need a hero to help us find the knife so I can get my tail back and we can break the curse on you. This kingdom needs a strong king, and he's so kind and honorable. Princess Dulcibella is so much in love with him that if he doesn't marry her, she'll probably die of a broken heart."

"Oh. *That* truth." Merrigan turned away, unsure of her expression, and hid it by splashing water on her face and then rubbing hard with the towel.

"If her green tears don't convince Warden," Bib said, "then hearing me speak might do the trick. Or the fact that you know about Rolf and his brothers. Warden thinks he's the only one who can see them or talk to them, because he holds the tinderbox."

"If he would be king someday, then he needs some basic lessons in magic, so he doesn't trip over more curses and spells and enchanters in the future." She shuddered as she slipped out of her dress and hung it on the peg, and climbed into her bed in her undersmock. "The more magic used on a kingdom and on a royal family, the greater the chances even more magic will happen there, and to them, and attract enchanters and adventurers, which will guarantee more spells and curses and ..." She sighed and punched her pillow for emphasis. "There should be a school to teach heroes, so they don't make foolish mistakes."

"That would be fun," Elli said. "You could be headmaster, Bib. You know everything worth knowing."

"Ah, no, thank you for the lovely compliment," Bib said, his pages rustling with laughter, "but I am many thousands of books away from knowing everything. Someday, though ... I might learn enough, access enough books, hear enough stories ... What a nice dream."

Merrigan wished they would be quiet, so she could chase some dreams of her own. As if they heard her, both her companions were silent after that, and she soon fell asleep, to dream battle plans for the next several days.

Chapter Nine

Merrigan woke when the rising sun touched her face. For several seconds she lay there, eyes closed, stretching luxuriously. Then she realized how far into the morning it had to be, for the sun to cross the room. Why hadn't Bib awakened her when the sunrise touched him on the table? She sat up fast enough, with enough force, to nearly throw herself out of bed.

Bib was gone. So was Elli. That frightened her a little more than Bib not waking her. He should have known they needed to get an early start, to make sure Warden, the soldier didn't leave the inn before they had a chance to talk to him.

Merrigan shuddered as she scrambled out of bed and hurried to wash her face and braid her hair and get dressed. She contemplated all the things Elli and Bib could be doing right now. Had they conspired while she was away, planning how the mermaid would steal the magical book at the first chance and go off to seek their fortunes? Just what did that idiotic girl, who didn't know a lying, cheating prince when he sweet-talked her, think she could do with a book, of all things, in the sea? How could they have treated her like this, robbing her, foiling all her plans, all the hard work she had put in, after all the things she had done for both of them? What right did they have to go haring off on their own?

How could they leave her alone? Weren't they her friends?

Merrigan slid to the floor, shivering, feeling empty and sick to her stomach.

She was alone. Why did they leave her alone?

Was this part of Clara's curse, that once she finally found someone she actually liked to be with, they left her alone, to start all over again?

"Mistress Mara?" The knock on the door startled Merrigan. For a few heartbeats, she stared at the door, wondering why it was so blurry, and wondering who Mara was.

Then she remembered the false name she used, because she refused to let anyone other than Bib know that Queen Merrigan of

Carlion had been reduced to such awful circumstances. She blinked, and hot wet trickled down her cheeks.

What was she doing, sitting there on the floor and crying? Tears never solved anything.

"Yes?" She flinched at the creaky sound of her voice, and struggled up off the floor. Until this moment, she certainly hadn't felt like an old woman. Now, she ached all over. Another part of Clara's curse? Was the seer sitting by one of her visionary pools, laughing at the story being played out for her entertainment?

"Would you like your breakfast here in your room?" Rosa asked. "Elli said you were up very late last night, making plans for setting up your dressmaker's shop, so she said we shouldn't disturb you for a while. Should I leave you to sleep a little longer?"

"Oh, no, thank you." Merrigan staggered over to the washbasin to splash cold water into her eyes. Fortunately, they weren't as red and swollen as she feared. "Where is Elli?"

"Oh, she's in the front room, chattering away and showing off the clothes you designed. You're going to have to hire a dozen girls to help you, with all the orders you'll have by the end of the day, mark my word." Rosa chuckled. "You're lucky to have an apprentice like her."

"Yes, I am. Lucky," she said, tugging the door open. For a moment, Merrigan had the oddest urge to hug the apple-cheeked, smiling girl. "Well, I had better get down there and see to business."

Elli and Bib, she realized with one glance, had taken matters into their hands and some of the work out of hers. A tall, weathered man, with a few distinguished silver streaks in his ebony curls and a rather rakish scar across his left cheek, sat in the corner by the fireplace. He listened to Elli talk with all the girls who had come to look over Merrigan's designs. He held Bib on his lap, and from time to time, his lips moved slightly, as if having a conversation. Merrigan didn't doubt that Bib had started in on those king-making lessons that Rolf had suggested.

Dear Bib. How could she ever have doubted him, suspected him of treachery and abandonment, for one moment? He was devoted to her. Merrigan stumbled momentarily, crossing the threshold into the room, when she realized she hoped more than gratitude for repairing him made Bib devoted to her.

Rosa brought her a hearty breakfast and Miles appointed

himself errand boy, bringing paper and inkwells and quill pens, so Merrigan could write down the names of the girls and what sort of dresses they were looking for, and then to make sketches of possible designs. She wasn't so busy she didn't see the glances Miles and Elli exchanged. She hoped no one noticed the slightly greenish cast under the mermaid's pretty blushes.

That night, Rolf's brother, Dolf, woke her up after she had only two hours of sleep, to ride to the palace.

This time she had a clever, discrete little magical light conjured by a spell hidden in Bib's pages. It hung over her right shoulder and dimmed whenever anyone came near the door of the room Merrigan happened to be searching. She could conduct a much more thorough search, with the help of the light. She retraced her steps of the previous search, just to be certain.

~~~~~

The next day, two ladies of the court came to consult with Mistress Mara and her apprentice. They were pleased by the designs of the sample dresses Merrigan had made, and asked if they could take them back to the palace for the higher ranked ladies to examine. Of course, Merrigan agreed.

That night, Ualf, the oldest and biggest of the dog brothers, with spinning eyes bigger than serving platters, took Merrigan to the palace. She searched the throne room and the next room off the receiving room, going counterclockwise. Still no success.

In the days that followed, Warden took king-making lessons from Bib and Merrigan hired four of Rosa's friends to do the basic sewing on the ordered dresses. Her nighttime searches of the palace moved to where her father said the work of running the kingdom took place. Of course, in the palace in Avylyn the rooms for the secretaries and ministers did fill an entire wing, two stories tall. Here in Seafoam there were three rooms for the secretaries and clerks and records, and another room as large as all three together where the king met with his ministers every morning. Merrigan took an entire night just to search that room, although common sense told her the king would hide a jewel-encrusted knife or an enchanted handkerchief in some place a little less public.

On the tenth day since arriving in Seafoam, Merrigan and Elli and the hired girls were hard at work in the back room of the inn, which Rosa had convinced her father to let them use as a workshop
~~~~~

without charging them any rent. Merrigan had advised the girl that while she appreciated the generosity, such a gift couldn't be good for the inn's business. Rosa had laughed and told her that whenever a woman came to the inn for a fitting or to order a dress, her husband or son accompanied her. They couldn't sit in the main room of the inn without ordering at least a mug of cider or a pastry, could they?

That morning, Merrigan was ruminating over the arrangement, trying to wrap her mind around why Rosa would admit that the inn was not only benefiting from her dressmaking work, but they had enough profits to share. She didn't think the innkeeper girl foolish at all, but rather clever and forward-thinking. Quincy had as much as said that Rosa would inherit the inn when her father was ready to retire because she was so much better at running the business than her brothers. They would all be smarter to go to sea full-time, instead of dividing their time and strength between the inn and fishing. If Rosa was so talented at business, why share her profits? Merrigan concluded that such a decision was just who Rosa was, part of why she was so good at her business, and why the inn was so popular. It was an odd way of handling life and business, but if it worked ... Merrigan wished it could work for her.

She paused, her hand trembling for just a moment, at the oddness of the thought and the wistful feeling that made her eyes ache and feel warm and wet.

"Mistress Mara?" Rosa scurried into the room, weaving between the three long tables set up for the girls to do their sewing.

"Is something wrong?" Merrigan put down the needle she had been holding and staring at without really seeing it for the last ten minutes or so.

"Oh, no, nothing wrong at all. Queen Adele has sent a carriage. She wishes to know if you would be kind enough to come for luncheon and to discuss sewing for the royal family." Rosa smiled broadly. "When you have time. She specifically said you weren't to hurry, and if it was inconvenient, she can send the driver and coach another day."

Merrigan bit back a bubble of laughter and the remark that this just proved what a silly woman the queen was. Her second reaction was an astonishing wave of gratitude for such courtesy.

"Not inconvenient at all," she said instead, and stood slowly. "The queen is so kind and considerate, it would be rude to make her wait. Elli, I think you should change into --"

"Oh, no, I can't." The mermaid went so pale, the gill lines in her neck stood out like ink drawings. "Please, can't you deal with them by yourself?"

Merrigan squashed down an urge to slap the girl and tell her to grow a backbone. How was she going to survive in the world, whether it was under the sea or on dry land, if she let such a little thing as standing before royalty frighten her? After a few heartbeats, she found it much easier to smile at the girl and assure her that it would be all right to stay behind. After all, Merrigan reasoned, feeling her good humor return, Elli was smart to fear royalty. If more people had a healthy fear of royalty, the world would be in much better shape.

She left Elli in the sewing room to oversee the hired girls, took the time to change into her dark blue dress and comb her hair. Then she gathered up the pad of bound paper Miles had obtained for her, inkwell and quills, and her measuring tape. She tapped on the door of Warden's room, where he was having king-making lessons with Bib. After ten days of devotion to grooming, deportment, and the new, military-style coat and trousers Merrigan had made for him, he did look the part. Bib was an excellent teacher.

"Would you like -- do you need an escort, Highness?" Warden said, bowing to her after she told them where she was going.

For a moment, she was tempted. It would certainly raise her status in the eyes of the royals if she showed up with such a dashing escort. Then she shook her head, realizing what a disaster that could be. Right now, Dulcibella still believed her nighttime visits to the inn, to talk and play checkers and take nighttime walks along the shore with Warden, were all just dreams. Merrigan didn't doubt the girl was just flighty enough she would take one look at her suitor and faint. Not a good introduction to his future in-laws.

"No, thank you. The first time you go into the palace, it will be with an invitation addressed to you, to discuss the terms of marriage to the princess." She patted his arm. "Thank you, though. That was very gallant and well-spoken. You will make a fine king."

It took all Merrigan's self-restraint not to sit up tall and wave to the populace as she rode to the palace. Yes, people stopped and gestured at her. Several people who knew her face and name called out to her, and children ran after the carriage. Merrigan reminded herself she wasn't royalty on display. She was merely a seamstress being honored by a ride to the palace.

Someday, she promised herself, she would indeed ride through the streets of Windward on a grand, triumphal return to Seafoam. She would wave with dignity and a royal smile of blessing on these people. She would toss coins to the children, and the people who called out to her now as friends would grow pale with wonder and bow to her.

The king's chancellor, Morton, met Merrigan at the gates of the palace. He bowed to her, offered his arm to help her down from the carriage, and carried her bag for her. He asked her about her voyage and remarked on the great respect the throne had for Captain Quincy, as he guided her through the reception room and down the long passageway to the royal family's living quarters. He took her all the way into the dining room, where Queen Adele and Princess Dulcibella waited, announced her presence, handed the bag to a servant, and bowed to everyone as he left.

Merrigan had the oddest feeling that when he said he looked forward to speaking with her again, it had meaning beyond mere politeness.

Then she had no time to think about anything but designing dresses and discussing the fashions of larger kingdoms on both sides of the ocean. Queen Adele and her daughter were cut from the same cloth -- or more accurately, pressed into the same spun sugar candy mold. Enormous green-blue eyes, high cheekbones, cascades of honey-colored curls. Fortunately, their broad hips ruined the picture of too-good-to-be-true, and they had a genteel sort of horsey laughter rather than the insipid little twitters Merrigan loathed from other princesses.

They weren't quite as flighty as Merrigan expected, and they asked intelligent questions about clothes and fashions and the cost of the new wardrobes. They showed some restraint, wondering if there was enough in the personal budget to cover all the new clothes they wanted. Merrigan was hard put to keep from pointing out that the "enormous pile of clothes" they ordered was a mere pittance, compared to the vast wardrobe she had owned, and changed regularly with the seasons. Two new public outfits each for Adele and Dulcibella, three for wearing at home in private, and three new sets of clothes for King Devon and Chancellor Morton. Plus underclothes and nightshirts, and perhaps when spring came, sturdier clothes for a planned voyage along the coast to confer with the neighboring kingdoms.

Merrigan was there for most of the afternoon. She examined the current wardrobes of the royal family, giving advice on alterations to make them more fashionable and last another year or two. Then she sketched designs for new clothes and examined cloth that all three weavers in Windward brought for consideration. Adele and Dulcibella made sure she wasn't overtaxed, that they weren't taking up too much of her time, and insisted she should say what she really thought and not hold back for fear of royal anger.

She was convinced the two of them couldn't come up with a temper tantrum to save their lives. That odd, wistful, hungry sort of feeling flittered through her several times during what really was a pleasant afternoon. What was it like, she wondered, to grow up in a place where she knew people really did like her because they *liked* her, and not because it was their duty? A place where she didn't have to constantly weigh everyone's words and expressions and try to guess their thoughts, the games they played, and what cruel things people said about her behind her back.

She felt a little regret when the afternoon came to an end. Chancellor Morton appeared in the doorway of the sitting room, to escort her back through the palace to the carriage. He rested his hand on hers, tucked into the crook of his elbow, and Merrigan didn't think anything of it, busy answering his questions about the decisions the women had made.

She didn't think anything of the oddness of a chancellor bothering his head about clothes or escorting a seamstress to the carriage, until Chancellor Morton climbed into the carriage with her. Even stranger, he sat down next to her, instead of facing her. The driver flicked his whip and the carriage jolted forward, and turned left out of the palace gates instead of turning right.

"We need to have a discussion, Mistress Mara," Morton said. "The view from the cliffs is lovely at this time of the year. Some people don't like the wind, but I find it bracing. You will enjoy it with me, won't you?"

"The sound of the wind will ensure a private conversation,

won't it?" Merrigan fluttered her eyelashes, and he laughed. Not an evil sound, but strangely comforting.

Here was the man who truly ran the kingdom, she decided. He made it possible for King Devon to be so effective and well-liked.

"I would very much like to know where you found that lovely little light spell that you use," Morton said, once the carriage reached the long road that ran alongside the seaside cliffs.

Sitting next to her, he didn't have to raise his voice, despite the whining of the wind around them. Merrigan reminded herself she was an old woman and her gray hair wouldn't look any worse for being battered by the wind. She loosened the strings of her hood rather than fighting to keep it on her head the whole time.

"Ah ... so you're the one who has made the light flicker, I presume?"

"Only until I added a ring of silence and stealth to the invisibility cloak. What are you looking for, and what does it have to do with that soldier and his magical dogs who kidnap the princess every night?" His smile widened and he paused a moment to rake his tangled white hair off his forehead. "A man who can teach Dulcibella to play checkers as well as she does now, well ... I have high hopes he can counteract the stupidity spell. King Devon has done an amazing job of it, but the poor man is growing old and weary. It's time for him to retire."

"So you're not going to throw Warden into prison?" Merrigan nearly laughed with the relief that made her lightheaded. Just for a moment or two.

"Far from it. I've been trying for years to erase some of Dulci's silliness, ever since Arabella dashed my hopes and ran off with that scheming prince from over the water. When she started showing a growth in common sense, along with a tendency to sleep later than usual every morning, I took to spying on her. It wasn't that easy to follow the dogs until I contrived a bag of birdseed and hung it on the back of her nightgown. The silly girl never noticed it. The next day, I followed the trail of birdseed to the inn, then that evening I waited at the inn until the dog returned, and determined what room he went into. Your soldier is rather a romantic, almost too noble for his own good." He sighed. "And that might just be what will save Seafoam."

"By showing some restraint and not taking advantage of your

princess, he's counteracting the silliness curse?"

"In the distant past, a frustrated suitor cast a spell on the royal family, to punish them for not handing over whichever royal daughter he wanted. They've only had daughters for the last two hundred years or so, and every time the poor girl is seduced before the wedding, the silliness just grows and the king is sucked into the downward spiral."

"Serves him right," Merrigan muttered. "There's a proper way of doing things. If you want the princess and the kingdom, you have to earn them through daring, not seduction. I've made a study of fables of magic, and there's a sort of protective spell, not really mentioned, but hinted at, if the hero waits until the wedding night."

"I should like to meet your teacher."

"You will." She felt a little flutter at the thought of Morton and Bib together. The two would probably get along famously. She only hoped it wasn't so well that the chancellor would try to keep Bib in Seafoam, to advise him. "Can I presume you approve of Warden?"

"Oh, absolutely. The changes in him since taking up company with you are quite admirable. I should hire you out as a groomer for heroes and would-be kings. The only question is, what are you looking for when you sneak through the palace each night?"

"You know enough about me to know about my apprentice, Elli."

"Odd-looking, yet pretty. The innkeeper's boy is nearly lost for love of her. I'm guessing she has some sea folk blood?"

"Mermaid. The prince who married your Arabella gave a jewel-encrusted knife to King Devon. That knife was used to cut off Elli's hair when she refused to be seduced. Until we get the knife back, she's doomed to two legs and can't even swim."

"Is that so?" Morton nodded slowly, his eyes narrowing in thought. Then he laughed. "Serves him right, then. I was feeling a little sorry for Arabella's prince. The last reports from over the sea say the common sense in his kingdom is slowly fading. It seems the curse on the royal family isn't limited just to Seafoam."

"Most likely, he seduced Arabella."

"She was silly enough to let him." He sighed. "Well, I must admit to a great deal of relief. I've been living in fear the last few years that I would be forced to marry Dulci. That's part of why I've been trying to build up her common sense, to protect me and the kingdom. Do you know if she's in love with Warden, and he's in love with her?"

"Oh, he most definitely is. According to the dog brothers, he was ready to leave because he thought himself entirely unworthy of her, and the thought of running a kingdom properly terrified him worse than any battle he had ever been in."

"There's a man with the kind of common sense this kingdom needs."

"Indeed. Once I offered to help him become worthy, he jumped on it like a starving man on bread. The pains he has taken to learn deportment, to learn statecraft, it's quite admirable. If he weren't already so heroic -- you need to ask him about the wars he's been in, you'll be impressed -- if he weren't already so heroic, the work he has done ensures it." She sighed.

"What's wrong, Mistress Mara, king-maker?"

"He has one vanity that makes him rather endearing. Warden is rather nervous about seeing Dulcibella in the light of day. His gray hair, his weathered appearance, that scar. He looks older than he is, and he doesn't want to displease her. Candlelight does wonders for softening our flaws. You wouldn't happen to have a spell or a magic ring or something that would make him look a little younger, scrub away a few of the years?"

"As a matter of fact, I do." Morton held out his hand and they shook, though Merrigan did hesitate just for a moment. After all, they hadn't really agreed on any bargain. She had to trust that the chancellor was as honorable and sensible as he appeared.

That evening, a messenger came from the palace with a small package for Merrigan. She tried not to let her disappointment overwhelm her, when the box was too small and too light to hold the knife. It contained a ring, with the instructions that if Warden wore it for an entire moon straight without taking it off, it would become invisible and impossible to remove until his death. Even more important, his physical appearance would improve gradually, so there would be no shock at sudden changes, for those who knew him.

Warden went down on one knee when Merrigan gave him the ring and explained the properties and rules for making the magic work. He caught hold of her hand and promised undying loyalty and gratitude all his days. It was a very pretty speech, and proved that Bib was an excellent teacher. The book deserved the title of king-maker far more than she did.

Two nights later, when the most drastic of the wrinkles had faded from Warden's face, Princess Dulcibella came to him with a small bag of silver shavings hanging from the belt of her robe. Rolf was on duty that night, and he told Merrigan about it before he went back to disperse the bits of silver. She told him about her talk with the chancellor, and advised him to leave the trail of silver, and trust that his master would be welcomed at the palace the next day.

The next morning, Merrigan was expecting a small squad of guardsmen to march up to the inn and follow the trail to Warden's room. Instead, a pretty servant girl in palace livery, her face swollen and red with crying, stumbled into the dining room where Merrigan, Elli, and Warden were having breakfast. Bib sat on an empty chair between Warden and Merrigan, where he could join the conversation without anyone realizing there was a talking book in the room.

"Dulci, what are you doing here?" Warden shouted, standing up from the table so quickly he nearly knocked it over.

The girl was indeed Princess Dulcibella. It showed her good sense that she snuck out of the palace in disguise. That good sense dissolved in sobs and a tidal wave of tears as she flung herself into Warden's arms. Somehow, Merrigan and Elli got the two of them into the sewing room without too much fuss. Rosa came running after them, with Bib cradled in one arm and holding a pot of soothing chamomile tea in the other. Dulcibella sobbed and sniffed and babbled disjointed sentences through the first cup, and spilled at least a third of it on herself, her hands shook so. After that, though, she managed to calm down enough to stop crying, wipe her face, blow her nose, and snuggle closer into Warden's lap before she started talking coherently.

"Of course I know how to get here, and of course I know none of our visits were dreams, you silly darling," she said, tucking her head under Warden's chin. "I might be doomed to be an utter featherhead someday, but Morton's been trying to make me smarter and I've been trying to read at least one educational book each week. Then I met you, and somehow it all seemed to stick better. Does that make any sense?" She raised her head enough to look at Merrigan, Elli and Rosa, who had had the good sense to close and lock the door so the curious couldn't intrude.

"Perfect sense," Rosa said.

"Maybe I'm a featherhead, but I'm hopelessly in love with you, and I hope you feel a little bit of fondness for me."

"Lost," Warden blurted. "Hopelessly lost. I'd do anything for you, Dulci. I wish there was an enchanter to defeat or a dragon to kill, to prove it to you."

"Idiot," Merrigan muttered. That earned a chuckle from Rosa.

"You'll get your wish," Dulcibella said. "Morton announced at breakfast that his magic mirror revealed I am kidnapped every night with the aid of three enormous, fierce dogs. He put a magic bag on my robe last night and it created a trail, and any moment now, my father's guardsmen are going to come arrest you!"

"All for show," Merrigan interrupted, when it looked like the princess was about to burst into tears again. "All to save face. Chancellor Morton knows about Warden and the nightly visits and he approves of you two being together. The only problem is that you can't simply have a soldier walk up to the gates of the palace, a soldier no one has ever met before, and announce he's going to marry the king's daughter. It just isn't done."

"What am I supposed to do after I'm arrested?" Warden said. "Or shouldn't I let them arrest me?"

"Oh, definitely let them arrest you. I'd run upstairs and get your tinderbox and change into your new clothes, so you present a fine, handsome figure when you're taken to the palace. They'll probably march you on foot through town, instead of using a carriage. That will give everyone a chance to see you. The king will have to pretend to be furious -- after all, you've been kidnapping his daughter every night."

"It's not really kidnapping if I knew what was going on, is it?" Dulcibella cried.

"That's something you should only reveal to your parents." Merrigan's head hurt a little from thinking so fast. Honestly, why were people around her so helpless? "We will need some people to spread the story about how Warden has fallen in love with the princess and has been using magic to make himself worthy of her, and how terrified he is that the king will hang him for the insult to the throne. Oh, and they should talk about what a hero he has been all his life. Make him very admirable. By the time the court is convened, half the town should be banging on the gates, demanding that he be pardoned. And if we're lucky, demanding a wedding."

To Merrigan's relief, Princess Dulcibella showed some common sense by not crying out that she didn't have anything to wear.

<div align="center">~~~~~</div>

Merrigan knew she should be pleased, flattered even, when the dust settled and Queen Adele insisted she be the one to create Princess Dulcibella's gown for the wedding. She fumed more than she had in moons as she and Elli and the four hired girls worked long hours to create a memorable gown in short order. Granted, they cobbled together the gown from ten gowns previous Seafoam princesses had worn, so that saved enormous time. Alterations were much simpler than creating from whole cloth.

Taking apart the heirloom bridal gowns and fitting the pieces together into something modern and fashionable was rather like working a puzzle, and Merrigan remembered she had adored puzzles when she was a child. That was the sticking point: she had loved them as a child. The adult didn't find them quite so fascinating. Maybe if her eyes didn't ache with dry weariness and her fingers hadn't been poked full of holes from needles and pins until she decided to wear gloves to keep the blood off the cloth, she might have relished the challenge just a little bit more. Her back ached and her head ached and she *felt* old and shriveled.

That was frightening.

Even more frightening, at times something inside her reared back like an offended cobra, and silently shrieked at her to stop. She was a queen -- she shouldn't be reduced to slaving over a gown made of bits and pieces from ancient gowns that were unfashionable when they were new. And what was worse, creating a gown for a princess in a minor kingdom that wouldn't have been worthy of ten minutes of discussion in the council chambers of Carlion or Avylyn.

Hmm, I don't know about that, Bib commented. *I've been doing a lot of reading, now that I have access to the palace library. Your father is an amazing ruler, with his eye on everything, every kingdom, every war, every merchant route. He likely has several books chronicling the history of Seafoam, just in case he needs the information someday.*

"Eavesdropping is not nice," Merrigan snarled under her breath.

No one heard her, as they were busy exclaiming over Princess Dulcibella during that day's fitting. Merrigan focused on the princess. Smiling was easy. Yes, despite everything she had to work with, the gown was lovely. Dulcibella would be the loveliest bride this year. Not just among the small coastal kingdoms, but compared to any princess throughout the entire continent. Merrigan felt some pride in her design work. She did have talent, didn't she?

Isn't it nice to use that talent to make others happy?

For a moment there, she thought Bib had slipped that thought in when she wasn't alert and on guard. Then Merrigan sank back in the big, cushioned chair the queen insisted she use, to be comfortable during the long ordeal of sewing. Odd, that warm feeling soothed the achy, sharp, cold spots inside her, when she saw how happy Dulcibella looked. She had done that for her.

Well, didn't the girl deserve to be happy? She had been working harder than anyone guessed to overcome the curse of silliness some self-centered, nasty, frustrated suitor had cast over some ancestress of hers who had exercised good judgment in refusing to marry him. Dulcibella displayed uncommon good sense by falling in love with Warden. He could have used the tinderbox and the dog brothers to take advantage of her and manipulate circumstances to his advantage, but had chosen to woo the princess and be honorable. He was more than worthy to take over the kingdom after King Devon stepped down.

You do realize that helping people find happiness will go a long way toward reducing the severity of Clara's curse? Bib offered.

I thought you insisted we should call it a spell, not a curse, she shot back, with a bubble of laughter in her throat.

The magic book chuckled quietly, rippling his pages so his cover bobbed up and down but didn't quite flip open.

Chapter Ten

That evening as the seamstresses left the palace, Merrigan felt contented enough that the little niggling sensation of something wrong caught her attention. The feeling of something out of balance, rather plaintive, a touch of loneliness in the air, had been there every time she visited the palace, but until then she had so much on her mind, she ignored it. Now, with the knife promised to Elli and the dress nearly ready for the wedding, she could pay attention. Elli and the other girls were chattering away about their own dresses for the wedding, and didn't notice when Merrigan slowed her steps. No one saw her when she stopped. Odd, how she had never noticed that door in the wall of the long hallway leading from the royal family's wing to the main body of the palace. She looked up and down the length of the hall and calculated the placement of the wings and rooms. If she wasn't mistaken, there should be an area behind that door as large as an entire wing of the palace. It was in the exact middle of the palace, surrounded by wings on all sides. In fact, just the right place for …

"A queen's garden," Merrigan whispered.

Her knees tried to fold and she stumbled forward, to clutch at the doorknob, as a waterfall of memories spilled through her mind. Her mother's garden had been in the center of the palace of Avylyn, as all proper queens' gardens should be. The heart of the palace, the heart of the kingdom.

"Bib … was this door here before?" she whispered, and reached into the bag to pull him out and open him. His "sight" improved greatly when his pages were open. The book was silent so long, Merrigan feared something was wrong. Perhaps wrong with her.

"Forgive me, Mi'Lady," he said, so quietly he could have been speaking into her head. "I believe you are very right. This door was not visible until now. The changes in the palace, in the royal family, have caused other changes."

"It's been invisible, just like --" She choked, but forced the words out. "Just like the door to my mother's garden vanished. Not just locked up, when she died. It vanished when there was tampering."

"When your Nanny Tulip tried to use you to open the door contrary to proper timing, when conditions were wrong."

"She did no such --" Merrigan closed the book and slowly, carefully slid him back into his bag hanging at her hip. "Please, Bib, tell me it wasn't my fault that the door vanished, and the garden filled with thorns. Please?" She took a step backwards, then another, then another as the book stayed silent, until she pressed against the opposite wall.

Elli and the other girls were gone. By now they were likely waiting outside for the carriage to come and take them home. Merrigan couldn't hear them. Of course, part of that could be blamed on her thundering heartbeats.

"It is your fault, Mi'Lady, in the same way that a needle is to blame for ugly embroidery. You were a tool in the hands of someone who considered herself justified to tamper with the magic." The book shuddered inside the bag.

"How do you know all this?" she whispered.

"I know almost nothing, Mi'Lady. I'm sorry. There is so much written in the magic tangling you, so many layers, all of it smoke-filled and nearly impossible to read. You thought of the garden and the door that vanished, and the thorns that filled the garden, so you couldn't even stand in the nursery balcony and look down. I saw bits and pieces of your life."

"So I was used. Dratted majjians. It has to be majjians."

"I believe so. They used your royal blood, they used your magical position as the youngest. They attacked the magical heart of the kingdom through your mother's garden, and it shut itself up and shut itself in and shut the world out, to protect itself."

"But Nanny Tulip wasn't a majjian. Was she?"

"I cannot see clearly in your memories, Mi'Lady. You were a child. Lonely. Feeling unloved, even though your father and brothers and sisters loved you greatly."

Merrigan snorted at that, and didn't care who heard her. She had eavesdropped often enough through her late childhood and teen years, she knew exactly what her brothers and sisters thought of her, and what a trial she had become to her father. Only her mother and Nanny Starling and Nanny Tulip had ever fully loved her, with no reservations or conditions. Leffisand had adored her, but she doubted he loved her any more than she loved him.

Stop nattering and whining, Merrigan. You're thousands of miles away from Avylyn. There's nothing you can do about Mama's garden, and you certainly can't show your face at home looking as you are. Break the curse, then go home. Then maybe you can find some answers to fix the mess you helped make. Even if you were used horribly, abominably.

She couldn't do anything about her mother's garden, but what about this one? At the very least, it would be good practice for when she went home.

"And this garden, here? Was it attacked too?"

"I am sorry, Mi'Lady, I can't tell. I will need more study."

"Well, I know someone who likely has the answers, if there are any answers." She took a deep breath, crossed the hallway to the door, and pressed her hands against the wood. Merrigan only flinched a little when she thought she felt a heartbeat. That had to be a good sign. The garden was alive, likely deeply asleep, rather than dead and dry and hopeless.

Elli came back inside to look for her. The other four girls lived close enough to the palace they chose to walk home, rather than wait for the carriage. Merrigan sighed for the days when she had been strong enough, energetic enough to be able to walk anywhere. She remembered long walks across the countryside when Prince Bryan had visited. They had spent entire days adventuring, riding and hiking and climbing trees and wading across streams and telling each other stories they had discovered in their fathers' libraries. When had she changed so that she disdained adventures and hikes? While she knew her body was still the same as when she looked like a young and beautiful queen, and Clara's curse only made her *appear* old and fragile and dried up, it also affected her spirit. So she felt old and shriveled and wrinkled and tired easily.

Merrigan and Elli found Chancellor Morton in his office, sorting through a carved wooden box that looked rather old. The carvings were worn smooth in some places, the details hard to see through the patina of age. Merrigan thought she could make out frogs and swans and ravens and vines.

"How may I help you, ladies?" he said, standing to give them a polite bow, and flipped the hinged lid of the box closed.

"I would like to know about the queen's garden. Specifically, how long it has been locked up, and how long the door has been invisible," Merrigan said.

That's rather cruel, Mi'Lady, Bib said, when Morton goggled at her a moment, then seemed to lose a little color. Still, there was a touch of laughter in the book's voice.

Queen Adele's great-grandmother was to blame for the door vanishing. Morton told them the story as he escorted Merrigan and Elli back to the royal family's apartments. When she was young, pale skin and fragile voices and tiny waists were all the rage. She refused to learn how to tend the garden from her mother, because she claimed the sun would darken her skin and weeding and watering and transplanting would give her a farmer's appetite and muscles. When she became queen, she locked the door. When her daughters expressed interest in the garden, she told them the plants inside were dangerous, and a terrible curse had been placed on all the women of their family, so they got spots and their noses ran and they sneezed uncontrollably if they did any garden work. By the time her granddaughter had the good luck of falling for a semi-reasonable man who laughed at the story, the door was only visible at the full moon. It vanished entirely from all sight and memory, other than the kingdom records, soon after she died.

The queen and king looked blank when Morton bowed and announced to the royal family that the queen's garden had awakened. Adele knew nothing about the magical healing plants that needed to be tended, the pool of water that connected with other magical pools spread across the continent, or the sanctuary such a garden provided for rare magical creatures such as swans or white ravens. Even talking frogs.

Dulcibella, however, knew a few things, thanks to all the educational books she had been devouring for years, to combat the silliness curse. She insisted she had to see the door immediately. Was it possible to have the garden open, and perhaps have the wedding ceremony take place there? Wouldn't a royal wedding give the garden an infusion of magic that would benefit the entire kingdom?

Merrigan had no idea. She remembered so little of what her mother had taught her, during those idyllic days of her childhood. When Queen Daylily had died, her garden had shut itself off from the world. However, the garden here in Seafoam proved to be awake enough to hear Dulcibella's squeal of delight and her nonstop chatter, and reacted to the princess's emotions. The door shimmered, the light coming from it visible before Dulcibella, Merrigan and Elli turned the last corner. As they approached, the door swung open, sending pieces of old rotted boards flying, and chunks of rusty lock falling to the paving stones. Perhaps that was the garden's response to the old woman who had shirked her duties and then lied, to keep others from fulfilling theirs.

Merrigan crept into the garden, when Dulcibella and Elli nearly danced over the threshold with excitement. She staggered to the closest stone bench and sank down on it, half-expecting it to collapse under her. She looked around, at all the dry twigs poking up from the ground in circles, showing the hedge circles that once created sanctuaries for pixies and winkies and other tiny magical creatures. The plots of bare ground where magical healing herbs had once grown. The dry husks of trees lifting bare arms to the sky. The tangles of dry rose vines still clinging tenaciously to the inner walls of the garden.

The depression in the ground where the pond had once been, silver in the moonlight, blue under the sun, providing water for the whole garden and a hiding place for frogs. Merrigan remembered when a horde of desperate princesses invaded her father's palace, looking for a prince enchanted into a frog. She laughed, and wept a little as she told Elli and Dulcibella about the odd incident.

"It's not dry," Elli said. "I'm better with sea water, of course, but I can feel the water, waiting to come back." She gestured at the dry, dusty bowl of the pond.

"How?" Dulcibella said.

There's no harm in simply asking, Bib said. *All anyone can do is say no. Unless of course they're frightened or angered by the request. Then they might get angry, but I doubt that is the case here. However, it might be wise to start out by apologizing for the silliness of her great-great-grandmother, and then ask.*

Merrigan repeated the advice aloud, and Dulcibella showed her good sense by stopping to think before acting. She stepped into the depression and found the center point, knelt, pressed both hands into the spot, and very prettily apologized for the neglect and lies of her ancestors, and promised she would do the best she could to rectify matters.

"If you could help me fight the silliness curse, I would appreciate it very much," she added. "I want to do my duty as queen. You will help me, won't you? The people of our kingdom certainly don't deserve all the trouble they've had to suffer because of my family."

She waited in silence for a few moments. A rustling sound in the doorway of the garden got everyone's attention, and Merrigan turned to see the king and queen and Morton standing in the doorway, looking tearfully proud.

Queen Adele let out a little gasp when Dulcibella got up and walked back to the edge of the dry pond. She couldn't speak, and had to point. Everyone gasped, and then laughed, when they saw the streaks of mud on Dulcibella's dress, where she had been kneeling. Sure enough, water bubbled up in the center of all the dust and dry dirt.

Dulcibella sent for Warden, and they spent the evening searching the king's library for everything they could learn about the queen's garden in Seafoam, and queens' gardens in general. Merrigan spent the evening trying to recall everything she could of her mother's garden. When she returned to the palace in the morning, her duties changed from overseeing the final details of the wedding dress to revitalizing the garden. While the pond was halfway filled with water, and the trees had the first buds of leaves popping out in a soft green haze by morning, the other parts of the garden didn't seem to be awakening. Merrigan and Morton consulted together for only an hour, determining the plants that could be found in Seafoam to be transplanted into the garden. The more rare and necessary plants that weren't native would have to be sent for.

Twilight softly fell in gray and lavender shadows, by the time Merrigan was willing to give in to the aches in her legs and back, and limped to the door of the garden. Large patches of green had replaced the abundance of twigs and sticks and dust. The pond was full, reflecting the first curve of the moon as it peered over the gables of the palace. Merrigan thought she saw a few flickers of fireflies. They could have been other magical creatures, sparkling as they ventured into the garden. She was quite happy with ordinary fireflies.

In the doorway, Merrigan looked around one last time. Her

eyes blurred as she couldn't fight off the bittersweet memories of her own childhood. How different would her life be if her mother hadn't died, if the garden hadn't closed its doors, if she and Nanny Tulip hadn't been used by evil majjians to attack the garden?

Plop. The sound was unusually wet and small. Several more plops followed. Merrigan shivered and turned to face the pond. Several small, dark forms hopped up the path toward her. She retreated over the threshold, a thick sensation aching in her throat. Was she about to scream, or perhaps vomit? For a moment, she could taste all the frogs' legs she had eaten, during that awful, shameful, regretful time in Carlion, when she and Leffisand had been battling that wretched, cursed, magical apple tree.

Five frogs. All a dark greeny-brown, none of them longer than her thumb. They stopped halfway up the path, where the dust of years of neglect had been swept away to uncover lovely painted green and blue and lavender tiles. They reared up on their hind legs, and Merrigan braced herself against the doorframe. She regretted advising Morton that, to avoid further problems in the future, the door to the garden should be completely removed and taken far away. She wished for the option to slam that door closed. Those frogs were going to jump on her, she just knew it, and she feared she couldn't take another step to flee.

Staying up on their hind legs for a good four heartbeats, the frogs extended their right front legs, crossed their chests ... and bowed low to her. More tears filled her eyes.

"Tell --" Her voice cracked. She coughed. "Please, tell Veridian -- tell him -- I'm sorry."

The frogs croaked in unison three times, then dropped into normal froggy crouches, turned somersaults over each other, and hopped back to the pond.

"Why did you never mention that you were friends with the prince of frogs when you were a child, Mi'Lady?" Bib asked.

"I suppose ..." She sighed, found her handkerchief tucked up her sleeve, and dabbed at her eyes. "I suppose I was ashamed and tried to forget. And then there was the whole ... oh, it's so shameful. I ate frogs' legs for so long, demanded them, just to make sure I never ran into a frog while I was living in Carlion."

"If it's any comfort, Mi'Lady, I think what we saw just now means you're forgiven."

"Yes, I think it is some comfort."

She had some doubts about that, however, when her dreams that night and several nights until the wedding, were of misty, twisted, indecipherable memories from childhood. Merrigan woke to the sounds of brassy honking overhead, and at first thought it came from her dreams. Her ugly little gray, awkward duck, whom she had named Honk, had made the same sound. He had followed her everywhere, waddling around the palace, sticking his long neck and oversized bill and feet into everything. She had adored him. Or rather, she had adored him until her world changed, her mother died, and she listened too well when Nanny Tulip told her how to be a proper princess.

Bib flipped open to offer her a lace-edge handkerchief that smelled of the spicy leaves of her favorite bush in her mother's garden. Merrigan couldn't remember the name of the bush, but she did love the sweetly delicate, slightly peppery aroma. She blotted her eyes and told Bib about Honk, how she had been so cruel until finally he flew away, never to return.

"Veridian, and Bryan, and the children I used to play with among the palace servants and the nobles and ..." She sighed one last time. "I'm afraid, Bib, I have a dreadful, cruel habit of driving people away. If I have no friends, it is my own wretched fault."

"Forgive me, Mi'Lady, but you are sadly mistaken."

"Hmm?" She blotted her eyes one last time and sat up, sniffing delicately.

"You will never drive me away."

Bib had to produce a second sweetly spicy handkerchief, and Merrigan had to resort to dousing her face in water until she came near drowning, to soothe her red, tear-swollen eyes.

She felt better when she learned that the honking hadn't been entirely in her dreams. A pair of swans had arrived on the dawn breezes from the sea, and settled in the queen's garden. A sure sign of blessing and the return of healing magic to Seafoam. She had helped to do that. She had done something good.

~~~~~

The day of the wedding, Chancellor Morton presented Merrigan with Elli's knife. All the jewels encrusting it had indeed been removed. The money had to come from somewhere, after all, to pay for the festivities that included the entire town. Merrigan
~~~~~

tried not to feel a few flickers of resentment, because didn't she deserve a few jewels for helping to resolve several sticky problems for the kingdom? Then Bib pointed out that she had no idea how to remove the jewels without damaging the knife. Besides, he suspected the jewels had been put there to help stunt the magical powers of the knife.

"Do you mean to tell me if it was still covered with jewels, it wouldn't help Elli?" Merrigan dropped the knife on the table next to Bib and scrubbed her hands on her skirts.

They had returned to their room at the inn. Elli, Miles, Rosa and Quincy were still out dancing and enjoying the wedding festivities. Merrigan felt rather tired, maybe a little sad, and had decided to go upstairs and rest.

"It is possible." Bib flipped his pages open. "I think if I'm touching it, I can study it better and be absolutely sure."

"That villain. That wretch. That … snot!" Merrigan picked up the knife by the end of the handle, with two fingers, and placed it in the center of Bib's open page. "I hope Arabella's portion of the curse is so large, his entire kingdom lacks the sense to come in out of the rain."

In short order, Bib confirmed the scheming prince had tried to limit the magic inherent in the knife used to cut the mermaid's hair. However, whoever he hired to do the job had bungled. The most he and the jeweler and the minor enchanter had managed was to cast an unsteady I'm-not-really-here spell on the knife. Merrigan elected not to tell Elli about that part of the prince's nasty schemes. After all, she had started to fall in love with him, and might still have a few tender feelings.

"The world would be a much better place if men weren't such useless, childish fools and women didn't fall in love with them," Merrigan mused.

Then Elli and Miles burst into the room with flowers and a skin of wine and an enormous meat pie to share. Merrigan's eyes got misty when they declared they didn't think it right she should be alone while all the kingdom was celebrating. After all, without her cleverness and hard work, this day never would have happened.

The marriage of Dulcibella and Warden seemed to have opened a door, because betrothals were happening all over the town of Windward. Quincy and Rosa were downstairs right that moment, obtaining her parents' blessing.

"But I thought Rosa was going to run the inn. How can she do that if her husband is traveling the high seas most of the year? She isn't going to abandon the inn to travel with him, is she?" Merrigan cried. The odd, dropping sensation, she decided later, was from fear that Rosa and Quincy's marriage was doomed from the start.

"No." Miles chuckled and caught Elli up in his arms, spinning her around before putting her back on her feet and planting a kiss on her tiny, upturned nose. "Quincy is giving up the sea to stay here and run the inn with Rosa. I'm going to become his partner and take over the *Fleetwind*." He dropped to one knee, startling a squeak out of Elli and a groan from Merrigan. "And I hope you'll be willing to sail with me all the rest of my days, my love, my seafoam maiden." He kissed her hand, front and back.

Honestly, Merrigan thought to Bib, *where do commoners learn such courtly gestures?*

Still, she rather admired Miles for his gallantry. Then she pitied him when Elli just stood there, staring at him, her eyes getting bigger in proportion to the dimming of Miles' smile.

"But -- I'm -- Miles, you should know -- Mara, what do I do?" Elli wailed, turning to Merrigan. She didn't free her hand of Miles' grip, and that had to be a good sign.

Bib flipped his pages open and revealed the knife lying there. It glistened. Merrigan did not want to know how the book had managed to shine the knife. It boggled her mind.

"Is that it?" Elli asked.

In unison with Miles.

She turned to stare at him.

"Yes, I know about the knife." He stood and kept her facing him. "I know you need it to regrow your hair and get your tail back. I know you're a mermaid."

"Well, you're one of the few observant, sensible people in this town," Merrigan muttered.

"Not really." He grinned and nodded to her. "Quincy told me, when he guessed I was -- that we were -- he told me if I broke your heart, he'd use my guts for bait. I could never make you stay on dry land. All my life, I've dreamed of going to sea, to hear the song of the waves. How can I take that away from you? But if I'm on the sea, if I'm a captain with my own ship ... well, we can be together whenever you come up into the air. Even if it's only one day in ten years, it'll be worth it."

"I take back what I said." Merrigan sighed but couldn't fight her grin. "You're a ninny just as much as she is. That is an entirely different curse and has nothing to do with mermaids."

"Elli, what I'm trying to say --"

"Yes," she squeaked, sounding more like a dolphin than ever. She grabbed hold of his collar, pulled herself up to his height, and kissed him until the gill slits opened in the sides of her neck.

Miles was red-faced and slightly dizzy-looking when Elli released him. Then he whooped and spun her around four times, until he ran into the side of Merrigan's bed and stumbled. He nearly dropped her and they both ended up giggling and clutching at each other, struggling to regain their balance.

Merrigan shuddered, feeling as if she might be ill. She wanted to laugh at them and scold them. She wanted to hug them and absorb some of their happiness. In the end, she settled for picking up the knife from Bib and holding it out to the two happy ninnies.

Elli burst into tears, snatched up the knife, and flung her arms around Merrigan. The air buzzed, then turned into a shimmering, chiming sound that dropped in the scale until it became the roar of a single enormous wave crashing down around them. When Elli released her and stepped back, Merrigan thoroughly expected to find both of them drenched. Instead, they were tangled in the squirming, growing curls of thick, glossy, sea-scented hair sprouting from Elli's head. In seconds, it fell around her like a cloak, and moved as if pulled by distant sea currents. She chuckled when Miles and Merrigan stared at her moving hair.

"You don't think we swim so fast just with our tails, do you?"

"I -- well, I never really thought about it." Merrigan took a step back. As much as she liked Elli, there was something uncanny about her hair moving like that. It reminded her of tales of the gorgons, and she could easily envision that hair reaching out and strangling her, quite by accident. "What are you going to do now?"

"I think we should go swimming," Miles said.

Elli laughed like dolphins chattering, caught hold of his hand, and they dashed out of the room. Merrigan sank down on the side of her bed, feeling rather like a slowly deflating balloon. The smell of the meat pie filled the room, once the fresh sea scent of Elli had faded away. Somehow, it just wasn't very tempting, even though she was hungry. Merrigan shook her head, knowing it wouldn't do her any good to sit and feel sorry for herself.

"That's what it is. I'm feeling sorry for myself. I need to keep moving west, heading home." She sighed and stepped over to the table where Bib waited, softly glowing. "Well, Bib, it's just the two of us again. What do you suggest we do next?"

"Set yourself up as a dressmaker."

"I thought we already did that. And didn't you hear me? I want to keep moving closer to home." Home, she knew now, clearly meant her father's court, not Carlion.

"Once you finish your commitments to all those girls who want new dresses, I suggest you establish Elli as your heir, so to speak. Leave her here to set up shop whenever she decides to stay on dry land with Miles, because he certainly can't be at sea all year, can he? Outfit yourself with a wagon and plenty of cloth and supplies. You can go from country to country, earning your keep, sewing and designing clothes as you go. When you think about it, everyone loves seamstresses and treats them well, because a well-made suit of clothes makes everyone feel so much better. Don't you agree?"

"Yes," she said with a sigh. "Yes, I do. Bib, you are brilliant." She stroked down his spine, eliciting a purring sound from him that made them both laugh. "I don't know what I would do without you, my dearest friend."

~~~~~

A fortnight later, Elli and Miles were married on Quincy's ship, a day's journey out to sea, so Elli's mer relatives could attend. The Sea King himself came up onto the ship. His wedding gift was to turn the cursed knife into two magical bracelets around Elli and Miles' wrists that would never come off. Now Miles could swim with Elli and breathe underwater. As their love grew stronger, so would the magic, until someday he would have a tail of his own and be able to stay with her, as long-lived as all the sea folk.

After the ceremony ended and the dancing began, the Sea King took Merrigan to the prow to speak privately.

"You're learning the oysters' lesson, Princess," he said, as his skin turned green. "The girl asked me if I could undo the spells wrapped around you like poisoned seaweed. They're so tightly bound to the essence of you, cutting them could kill you." He
~~~~~

frowned, as his long, silver-green hair turned to strands of seaweed. "That might be the key. You have to die."

"No, thank you." She tried to delicately tug her hand free of his, as it was feeling decidedly cold and fishy.

"There's a bug you drylanders know. It dies and it's beautiful after it dies. Think about that." He winked at her, then flung himself backward over the railing. His legs merged into an enormous tail and waved as he went headfirst into the water without a splash.

~~~~~

Warden and Dulcibella seemed deliriously happy together. King Devon and Queen Adele appeared delighted with their new son-in-law. Rosa and Quincy set off after Elli and Miles' wedding, to let the entire enormous clan at the Bookish Mermaid know of their marriage and his decision to follow his mother's footsteps as an innkeeper. That left Miles and Elli to begin the venture that had earned shouts and tears of delight from her many relatives when they proposed it. They would travel up and down the coast, finding sturdy, honorable young men who loved the sea more than their lives, and would be willing to pledge their hearts to the many lonely mermaids longing for a husband and children.

Merrigan wished them well. She had laughed when they pleaded with her to stay with them and guide them in the venture, because after all, hadn't she done amazingly well with three couples already? It was on the tip of her tongue to confess to them how badly her one attempt at love and happiness had turned out, but she couldn't destroy their good opinion of her. She suspected she would never unwrap her heart enough to let someone else touch it. A queen couldn't afford to love, after all. She couldn't afford to be so vulnerable.

She tried to buy a wagon that an old woman could handle by herself. Chancellor Morton wouldn't hear of it. He presented her with a cart just the right size, and a lovely little donkey, fitted out with a magical harness that hitched itself to the wagon every morning and unhitched itself every evening. He couldn't send any guards with her because the guardsmen of Windward were as much bound to the kingdom as the royal family. However, he gave her a magic cloak that was impervious to knives and arrows and swords, once she had closed the brooch that fastened it and turned it three times. It was a princely gift.
~~~~~

So much so, Merrigan wondered if Morton, with all his wisdom and insight, had seen through the curse enfolding her. She knew better than to reveal her true identity. Even if someone could be trusted with her secret, how could she guarantee the wrong people wouldn't overhear, and use that knowledge against her?

No, she decided, the day she drove out of Windward with her cart full of cloth and all the bits and pieces to be a successful seamstress. Better that she and Bib make their way through the world on their wits. The victory when she regained her life would be all the sweeter.

Three days later, she crossed the border of Seafoam. That evening, she was alone in the forest. For the first time, there was no inn, or a hospitable farmer and his family eager to help an old lady traveling alone. Morton had given her the old wooden box she saw him examining in his office, and told her it would serve her when she had need. Merrigan searched it and found a bundle of sticks that, according to the instructions on the paper wrapped around them, became a lovely little fire when she crossed them over each other. In the morning, all she had to do was kick them apart and they turned into sticks again, unscorched. She hung a pot over the flames to make tea, ate some bread and cheese and an apple for her dinner, and was quite content. With the impervious cloak Morton had given her, how could she not feel safe?

By the light of the flames, she dug through the box, and chuckled when she realized it was larger inside than it was outside. Morton had put a good dozen books in the box, and several maps. The books discussed the many small kingdoms displayed on the maps. She let Bib absorb all the information in the books and maps, and then they had a lively discussion about options.

"We don't want to go through Sylvanglade," he announced, and *tsk*ed several times.

"Whyever not?" Merrigan's heart gave a couple rapid thumps.

"Such a sad story. The heir brought home a princess under a sleeping curse before her crucial seventeenth birthday."

"And?" she prompted, when the book stopped there.

"Well, curses like that can't be outrun. It unfolded just like the angry witch decreed, and most of the kingdom is sleeping now."

"Not just the palace? Not just the capitol city, but the kingdom?" Merrigan shuddered, imagining the terror washing over people the moment they crossed the border into Sylvanglade and they found themselves falling asleep. What did it look like from the other side of the border? Piles of people lying along the road, even their horses asleep in the harness?

"I don't have all the details, but yes, it's expanded beyond … ah, here come the details." Bib sounded somewhat uncomfortable. "It seems the crown prince and the princess had an awful argument the day of her birthday. She wanted to get married before her birthday, for true love's kiss to ward off the evil spell. He resented how her parents bullied him into taking her to Sylvanglade. He had rather looked forward to riding through the barrier of thorns and perhaps fighting a dragon and being a hero. She declared she hated him and he responded that he was glad, because he wouldn't marry her to save her entire kingdom from an entire flight of dragons."

"Now that's a great, ignorant ninny. Didn't anyone ever tell him that you shouldn't make oaths like that when evil spells are about to awaken?" She shuddered and imagined all the green fields and lush forests of Sylvanglade, wrapped in the unnaturally quiet, constant twilight that accompanied a sleeping spell.

Bryan had told her all about his home. He had given her drawings of the places he loved, and books about his kingdom's history. Before everything turned sad and cool between them, they had made plans for her to visit Sylvanglade. Odd, that after all these years, she still remembered those conversations and books and pictures so clearly.

"Because of the vehemence of their argument," Bib continued, "the sleeping spell is growing. All that anger sort of gave it a boost. It only took over the palace when it unfolded, but as time passed, the tendency to fall asleep for no reason crept outward into the capital, then the countryside. It's been going on for three years now and has completely swallowed eight towns, and portions of six more. At the rate it's going, the entire kingdom should be swallowed up in sleep in eight more years."

"Was everyone caught in it?" Merrigan's hand shook slightly as she lifted the pot off the fire, and dipped up some tea. She needed something hot and bracing right now. "The entire royal family?"

"Hmm … it says most of the younger princes were out on adventures or on diplomatic missions. It doesn't say which ones. Not that it matters, when you really think about it. Being a prince without a kingdom is powerful magic. Whatever they do, as long as they remember to act like princes, they will succeed and become heroes. It's sad for their family and kingdom, but when you think about it, they are much better off now than they would be as the third and fourth and fifth sons."

"Bib ... sometimes you can be quite mercenary," she murmured, and stared unseeing into the fire as she sipped her tea.

Five nights later, Merrigan climbed down from the cart at the end of the day in another stretch of woods with no inns or friendly farmers. She unharnessed the donkey and tethered her in the middle of a thick patch of sweet grass, and paused a moment to stroke the donkey's nose. The sweet creature nuzzled her once and snorted. Merrigan was sure it was her way of saying thanks. She walked around to the back of the cart to unload the magic box and take out the sticks for her fire. The shadows clustered in the trees overhead turned into six men who leaped down at her.

One snatched up the harness from the seat of the cart. Another yanked the donkey away from her grazing. Two pulled the cart toward the road while Merrigan let out a shriek. The last two leaped on her, swinging cudgels at her knees and head.

The cudgels snapped against the magic cloak. The two leaped on her, punching and kicking, but howled in pain and came away with bloody knuckles. One tried to pull the magic box from her hands. The cloak's protection enclosed it, so the bandit couldn't keep a grip on it. His partner tripped Merrigan. She didn't let go of the box, however.

Meanwhile, the other four harnessed the donkey to the cart and shouted for their comrades to come. Two drove the cart and the other two ran alongside. The two attackers flung handfuls of pebbles and forest trash in her face, then ran after their comrades. In moments, the evening forest shadows closed in around Merrigan as she gasped and struggled to sit up without letting go of the box. Soon even the sounds of running feet and the angry, protesting brays of the donkey faded into the distance.

Chapter Eleven

Her cart, her donkey, her food, her inventory of cloth and sewing notions, all gone.

"Bib!" she shrieked.

The satchel with the magic book was still sitting on the cart seat.

Her only friend in the entire cruel, unfair world -- gone.

Merrigan let go of the magic box and fell over it with a wail. She cried her eyes swollen and sticky. Cried her voice hoarse. Cried until she could hardly breathe and the front of her dress was damp and she thought she might be sick. Cried until she thought she might just be losing her mind -- because it was the strangest thing, she actually felt better, despite her aching head and sore throat and churning stomach.

"Oh, Bib, I'm sorry," she moaned, when she had caught her breath. "They likely don't know how to read, so they'll probably rip out your pages and use them for kindling. I failed you. I let them kidnap you."

"Is it really kidnapping when they didn't even know they had me, and they certainly couldn't keep me?" Bib said.

Merrigan tried to shriek, but her throat hurt too much and she didn't quite have enough breath. She settled for scrambling away from the dark lump that had appeared before her.

"Bib?" Her voice cracked in a most unbecoming way, but she didn't care. Cautiously, she reached out and rested a hand on the dark lump -- it certainly felt like the leather of his satchel.

"Right here, Mi'Lady. How?" he said with a rippling chuckle. "It's all in the bond we've created. Do you really think my former master would leave me vulnerable so anyone who walked into his library could steal me?"

"Well, you have to consider they'd have to go through a dozen magical wards, at the very least," she mumbled, wiping her face.

"You bound me to you when you repaired me, and I have chosen to bind myself to you. We are friends."

"It just shows how low I have fallen in the world, that my only friend ..." Merrigan sniffled and wiped her nose on her sleeve and for once didn't care what it looked like. "I'm sorry, Bib. That was cruel. I truly am the selfish brat my brothers and sisters always called me. You are my dearest friend, in some ways the only real friend I have ever had, and I am glad you -- well, you do like me, don't you?"

"Enormously, Mi'Lady. I see great and good things hidden within you."

"Your eyesight is much better than most. Such good things must be hidden very deep indeed. I certainly don't see them."

"They need excavating, so to speak, Mi'Lady. Well, now that we're back together, I suggest we make you as comfortable as we can for the night, then in the morning find the nearest village. There should be an official of some kind who can help us."

"Most likely, some of the brutes who robbed me are his sons or nephews. That seems the way of it, out here so far from civilized towns. Those with any kind of power and authority abuse it."

"You never know. Luck might be on our side this time."

Merrigan was pleased to discover that she had stored quite a few necessary things inside the magic box, taking advantage of its expanded interior. Her teapot and the tin of tea. Scissors, pin cushion and measuring tape. A paper packet of sweets the wife at the last farm had given her, in thanks for mending her husband's coat, along with three boiled eggs, half a loaf of bread and a block of cheese as big as her fist. All tossed into the magic box because it had been open at the time. Merrigan wished she had thought to put her little bag of gold and silver coins in there, along with her extra clothes and blankets. Fortunately, the cloak was warm and thick, coming between her and the rocks and branches and uneven ground. Merrigan made a decent dinner for herself. She discovered a little waterskin tucked into one corner of the box, just large enough for two mouthfuls. Then laughed a little harder than was reasonable when it spilled out a stream of water that didn't stop until she squeezed the neck and stuck the plug back in the mouth.

"Did you know it could do that?" she asked Bib, as she set the pot of water over the flames of her magical fire.

"No, Mi'Lady. I think we have been remiss in exploring all the wonderful things Chancellor Morton gifted us with."

"Remind me to do something wonderful for him, when I have regained my throne. Even considering all the help I was to him in resolving Seafoam's problems ..." Merrigan sighed and closed her eyes and rubbed them with her fists. "Bib, do you think, with all the wonderful little magic tools at his disposal, Chancellor Morton knew who I really was, and that's why he helped me? Not to be kind, but because it was his duty to a queen?"

"To be blunt," Bib replied after a short silence, "I think he has far too much on his plate to care about the trials of, if you will excuse me, Mi'Lady, the former queen of a kingdom far from Seafoam. I think he is first of all a kind man, and wise. One who knows how to repay invaluable help. If he had magic strong enough to discern your true identity, then he would have done more for you than he did. He was being kind and grateful to Mistress Mara, not to Princess Merrigan of Avylyn."

"You must be right," she whispered. She managed a weak little smile at the realization that it didn't bother her when he referred to her as a princess, rather than a queen. She was just too tired to fight over such details -- or maybe it just didn't matter anymore.

~~~~~

A merchant's caravan caught up with Merrigan when she stopped at a spring just past noon, to rest and have something to eat. The merchant's daughter was a sweet creature wearing far too many ribbons on her traveling dress. She squealed with delight when she heard Merrigan tell her father she was a seamstress. Before Merrigan quite knew it, she was ensconced in the largest of the wagons, plied with a warm meat pie and sweets while Gilda interrogated her about fashion and the latest designs. She nearly swooned when Merrigan admitted she had made the wedding gown for Princess Dulcibella of Seafoam, and had sewed in the royal courts of Avylyn and Carlion.

At the next village, Merrigan climbed out of the wagon with the assistance of Gilda and her father, Master Gilbrick, who both treated her as if she were quite fragile. A very nice change in circumstances. She barely heard them as they made plans for her to stay in the inn with them. Her attention caught firmly on the sight of three of the six bandits, on display on the village green. One sat in the stocks, the second stood in the pillory, and the third wore her donkey's magic harness, which attached him firmly to the shattered
~~~~~

remains of her cart.

A fourth member of the band, she found out from the innkeeper, was in bad shape, having been kicked brutally in the face and ribs by her donkey. The big, friendly man brought them their dinner himself and delighted in telling the merchant and Gilda and Merrigan all the details of the ruckus just the night before. The six young men, known in the surrounding five villages as troublemakers, had arrived just after moonrise, arguing loudly. As far as anyone could tell, four of them were mocking the other two over how a little old woman had bested them, bloodying their knuckles and breaking their cudgels. The two were angry enough about the teasing that they turned on their partners. Then the donkey got into the fight. The noise of the brawl brought the constable running, along with a troop of guardsmen on their way to report to King Fredric. The sergeant of the troop recognized two of the bandits as deserters, and immediately took them into custody. When their friends tried to help them, they were easily subdued. The judge for the five villages was due to come to town in four more days, and the foursome were being held until then.

"What about the cloth and other items they stole?" Merrigan asked. "Were they lost?"

"How do you know the cart was full of cloth?" The innkeeper took a step back and looked her up and down. Before she could respond, his face lit up and he let out a bellow of laughter that gained the attention of nearly everyone in the main room of the inn. "Bless me if you aren't the little old woman who fought them off. Please tell me you are?"

"Excuse me, Mistress Mara," Merchant Gilbrick said, "but proving the contents of the cart are yours could be difficult. I don't want to cause trouble, but I've run afoul of local authorities while trying to take back my rightful property that was stolen."

"Hmm, true," the innkeeper said. "Constable Fitz is a decent enough man, but he's got a dozen women of reputable families clamoring for him to declare that cloth abandoned property, so they can claim it. They'll fight you all the way."

"Where is my donkey? She'll know me," Merrigan said.

The donkey had fled into the night as soon as she kicked the one man in the ribs for the third time. No one was sure where she had gone. Merrigan and Gilda went up to the room they were to share, while Gilbrick and the innkeeper went to speak with Constable Fitz. Merrigan wanted to confront the four remaining bandits. She hadn't exactly gotten a good look at four of them, but the faces of the two who had attacked her would stay strong in her memory for a good long time to come. She just hoped they weren't the two who had been hauled away as deserters, to face King Fredric's justice.

"What's more important is if they recognize you," Bib offered, when he and Merrigan were alone together for a few moments.

To her delight, the man in the stocks and the man in the harness did recognize her when she stalked up to them the next morning. The one in the harness shrieked and tried to flee while still on his hands and knees, while his friend in the stocks went stark white, then bright red, then let out a stream of curses. Constable Fitz, a rugged yet pious man, slapped the curser across the mouth with his meaty fist, knocking him backward off the log he was sitting on.

"Good enough identification for me, Mistress," he said, tipping his floppy cap to Merrigan.

The women of the village, who had hoped to get their hands on the cloth from her cart, were not happy. Merrigan listened to the advice of Merchant Gilbrick and Bib and offered to sell the cloth to them, with a sizeable discount if they commissioned her to design the clothes to be made from it. The local seamstress was happy, as she would have the sewing income. That seemed to please everyone. Merrigan let Gilbrick handle the sales, and he negotiated for one-third again as much as she would have charged. Gilda and her father insisted on taking Merrigan under their wing and making her part of their traveling party.

They made their home in Williburton, a decent-sized country north of Carlion, east of Avylyn. It was also west of Sylvanglade, though why Bib had to point it out to her, Merrigan didn't know. She was delighted to travel with them and get that much closer to home. Gilda treated every word that fell from her lips as if they were gold. At least, everything Merrigan had to say about fashion, which colors were best for Gilda's complexion, and what countries produced the best cloth.

After only a few days, Merrigan learned Gilbrick was even more a slave to fashion than his daughter. He nearly swooned over fine quality material and subtle designs in the weaving. Some merchants lived for the thrill of the bargain, while others hoarded gold with the ferocity of dragons. Gilbrick lived in the pursuit of the finest cloth and most exquisite dyes.

"Someone so single-minded," Bib remarked, "is setting himself up for trouble. He needs to find some other passions in life. He's giving off the magical equivalent of a beacon fire, just begging for someone to come cast a spell on him. Or worse, swindle him."

~~~~~

The journey to Alliburton, the capitol of Williburton, Gilbrick and Gilda's home, should have taken a little more than a moon. The journey took three moons, because Gilbrick stopped at every city and town and tiny village along the road. He left Gilda to oversee his apprentices, who did the actual work of setting up the portable stalls, setting out their merchandise to display, and haggling with the customers. Gilbrick wandered through other sections of the market district, or in the rural areas, walked beyond the village. After the fifth such stop, Merrigan asked Gilda why.

"It's obvious your father is looking for something," she said, as the two of them settled down for the night in the opulent main wagon. Gilbrick's ventures into the last village had taken so long that they didn't leave until the first hint of sunset. The merchant caravan had traveled until dark and set up camp.

Quite frankly, Merrigan couldn't understand why they didn't camp along the road every night and save the coins that an innkeeper would charge. The wagons were sturdy and snug, the long couches served quite well as beds, they had plenty of food, and Gilbrick's cook was a sight better than many of the cooks in the inns they had frequented so far.

"What is he looking for? He never comes back with anything, though sometimes he seems quite pleased. Perhaps whoever he was talking to gave him clues in his quest?"

"Papa is seeking magical cloth," Gilda said in a whisper, her eyes shining. "Cloth too beautiful to behold. Fine enough that an entire bolt will pass through the eye of a needle, yet strong enough it can withstand arrows and swords."

"I should think clothes made from such cloth would be very uncomfortable. If it acts like armor, I imagine it would ventilate like armor, too." Merrigan's nose wrinkled up just at the thought of the stink. "Besides, how would you cut that kind of cloth to make
~~~~~

clothes? All it would be good for is to use as a tent, and even then you couldn't stake it down against high winds because you couldn't pierce it to attach the stakes."

Gilda stared at her for several seconds. Then she burst into tears. Merrigan couldn't quite muffle her sigh as she put an arm around the girl and patted her back. Gilda was ordinarily a cheerful creature, yet when she did cry, she could go on for hours. It was best to comfort and distract her as soon as possible.

One of these days, she's either going to flood us out with her copious tears, Bib observed, *or her howls will attract wolves or orcs or something much nastier.*

Merrigan couldn't muffle her chuckle, but Gilda didn't hear over her sobs. Soon enough, though, she got the girl to wipe her eyes. There was something almost amusing about Gilda in tears. Her explanation for why she was crying usually turned out to be silly enough to make even Gilbrick laugh, and he took her far more seriously than anyone else.

"What did I say to hurt you?" Merrigan had learned early that taking some blame on herself made Gilda calm down more quickly, because the sweet, silly girl wouldn't let anyone say anything against Merrigan. Even herself.

"Oh, you didn't -- I mean, you did -- oh --"

She sniffled and rubbed at her eyes and dug through a low box tucked under the couch until she found an enormous handkerchief, which she used to blow her nose. Merrigan found some comfort that while Gilda's face didn't get swollen and red when she cried, she blew her nose loud enough to call dragons out of the sky.

"It's the cloth. If my father ever succeeds in finding the cloth of his dreams, well … I know he'll spend everything he has to obtain it, and then what good will it do him if he can't use it for anything? Oh, Mistress Mara, you're so incredibly wise. You must help me protect my father. I adore him so, but sometimes he just lacks for common sense. It frightens me."

Now that's saying something, Bib said.

You -- hush! Merrigan muffled her laughter into a cough, and set about comforting Gilda. She promised to try to think of something to help her keep Gilbrick out of trouble.

Unfortunately, she proved to be very little influence on Gilbrick on the long, wandering journey back to Williburton. She tried to convince him that if the cloth in the local market wasn't remarkable, then someone weaving in a tumbledown shack out in the forest likely couldn't produce anything worthwhile. The argument never seemed to work. Gilbrick insisted that obscure, remote locations were more likely to have the magical cloth of his quest. Sometimes he found cloth that changed color to reflect the mood of the wearer, but it wasn't durable or waterproof or didn't go through the eye of a needle. Once he found cloth fine enough to go through the needle, but when daylight touched it, it faded into mist, along with the hunchbacked man who wove it. Twice, Gilbrick learned of someone who was reported to spin thread to be woven into the hoped-for cloth. Each time he got there, a prince had arrived ahead of him, freed the spinner from an enchantment, and carried her away.

Merrigan wondered sometimes why she had agreed to help Gilda, other than to prevent more weeping. Perhaps she was falling ill, because no sensible person could actually be fond of such a silly girl, could they? Merrigan did find some satisfaction in convincing Gilda that less was more when it came to the ribbons, bows and flounces on her clothes. The simpler her gowns became, the more elegant and mature Gilda appeared and acted. By the time they came within sight of Williburton, Merrigan suspected a silliness spell had been put on the girl by some business rival of her father.

The caravan stopped for the noon meal in the high mountain pass looking down on Williburton. Merrigan, Gilbrick and Gilda were discussing arrangements to set up Merrigan in her own shop, when a messenger caught up with them. His horse was in a lather and he wore the emblem of Gilbrick's merchant network -- a golden wagon wheel with a coin for the hub. The young man looked pale, yet ecstatic, and he trembled. Gilbrick shot him one question after another, never letting him get a word in for at least five minutes. Gilda finally resorted to hopping onto her father's back and slapping both hands over his mouth to make him shut up.

Maybe she's right, Bib said. *She is the sensible one in the family.*

Merrigan had to agree.

"Master, there's nothing wrong," the messenger finally said, after Gilbrick mumbled and struggled for a few moments but couldn't shake Gilda free. "I was sent to tell you some weavers have come to town --"

Gilda let out a squeak and released her father, who was struck silent. They held onto each other as the messenger went on. For a moon now, the weavers had been setting up shop at the far end of the merchant's district where Gilbrick had his warehouse. They set up their looms, but didn't buy any thread. No one thought anything odd about it, because the well-dressed couple kept busy selling dozens of bolts of cloth. Fine cloth of amazing colors.

The day the outriders from Gilbrick's merchant caravan returned to the warehouse, to say their master was returning, the two weavers made an announcement. They had been preparing for years for their crowning achievement. They had spent five years alone obtaining the wool from sheep that grazed in the famed Meadows of the Sun, then three years befriending mermaids, who gave them the shells of ancient oysters to create a magical dye that would change color to suit the temperament of whoever it touched. They had spent half their fortune obtaining a spinning wheel from the castle of a princess who still slept under a curse.

Merrigan flinched at that bit of news, immediately thinking of the creeping, growing curse on Sylvanglade.

Bib, you don't think that's the same spinning wheel?

No. Impossible. How could they have gotten into the palace without being overtaken by the spell? Taking away the spinning wheel should have violated the rules of the spell, and as far as I know, the curse is still on Sylvanglade and still growing.

Merrigan thought it highly amusing that princes down through the ages hadn't figured out that all they needed to do was move or destroy the spinning wheel to free the princess. She imagined quite a few royal marriages weren't as happy as they wanted people to believe, simply because once the boy kissed the girl, they had to get married. How much simpler things would be if the king could offer a wagon full of gold or a magic sword to the hero if he didn't care to marry the princess. And what if the princess had an older brother? Was the heir to the throne summarily disinherited so a stranger who kissed his sister could take over?

Focus, Mi'Lady, Bib said. *This sounds like trouble.*

Merrigan flinched, and mentally slapped herself for getting distracted. Fortunately, Gilbrick and Gilda were full of questions that let her piece together what she hadn't heard.

The two weavers claimed they had come to Alliburton on the

advice of a seer. The magical currents in air and ground were favorable for creating thread produced on the spinning wheel, and then weaving the thread into the most beautiful, magical cloth the world had ever seen. Since they arrived, the weavers had been spinning the thread by moonlight. The day the messenger left, the two weavers had closed up their shop and shuttered the windows so no one could see them at work. They would weave for three days, then display the magical cloth for one day only before packing up and returning to their home far over the ocean.

Of course, the steward and the warehouse managers had sent Bigsley, the messenger, to find Gilbrick and bring him home immediately. They were in a panic at the thought that their master might not arrive home in time to see the magical cloth and persuade the weavers to sell it to him.

"All but for Aubrey." Bigsley's mouth pursed with distaste.

"Why not Aubrey?" Gilbrick blurted. He looked stunned.

"Who's Aubrey?" Merrigan wanted to know.

"One of Papa's apprentices. He's worked his way up from sweeper to messenger to clerk to inventory keeper in just five years," Gilda said, her lower lip trembling and her eyes glistening with impending tears. "He's brilliant -- he's so talented -- he's witty and -- he's absolutely wonderful!" she ended on a wail.

I believe she's in love with this Aubrey, but he's committed the unpardonable error of doubting Gilbrick's quest for his amazing cloth, Bib observed.

Merrigan had to wait until the caravan returned to the highway, heading for Alliburton at all speed, before she could find out. Bib had got it on the first guess. The only thing more copious than Gilda's tears were her gushes of admiration and adoration for Aubrey. After the first half hour of listening to all the amazing, clever, kind things Aubrey had done, Merrigan stopped listening. She pondered what she had learned about the magical cloth.

Such cloth is feasibly possible, Bib said, after they conferred over the details together. Gilda had finally fallen asleep and the merchant caravan continued down the highway. *What I can't understand is why someone would go to so much trouble to make cloth with so much inherent magic woven into it. The magic elements should conflict with each other. The dye alone would imbue ordinary thread with amazing abilities. I've never heard of anyone coming back from the*

Meadows of the Sun with a single blade of grass, much less enough fleece to spin thread. The sheep who graze there are meat-eaters and stand twenty feet tall. They don't sleep because it's never night in the Meadows of the Sun. Which explains why they're always in such foul moods.

That's understandable. Merrigan shuddered at the memory of several times she had been forced to go just two days without sleep, and how her vision and hearing seemed to warp. Living like that constantly most likely drove the sheep mad. *Still, if someone did manage to get the fleece from just one sheep, would the thread be magical?*

I expect it would be used to create light, or even start fires, rather than cloth. Something is very wrong with the weavers' story. I will have to see the cloth to analyze it before I can give you any answers.

~~~~~

Merrigan felt as if she hadn't slept in several days, by the time Gilbrick's merchant caravan arrived in Alliburton. She had managed to doze throughout the night, but the swaying of the wagon as it turned corners and the jolts as it bumped over holes in the road made for uneasy sleeping. Then there was Gilbrick's increasingly louder fretting every time they had to stop to clear fallen trees out of the back roads that he insisted were a faster route to the capitol.

The caravan approached the city gates, just after the moon had set. A watchman on the wall let out a shout, soon taken up by other shouts, then trumpets. There were far too many people awake at that time of the morning. Why did momentous events always occur in that dim, cold period of the morning before night gave up and dawn sent its first silver splinters over the horizon? Gilbrick nattered to himself as the caravan neared the gates, never slowing. Merrigan opened up the sliding panel between the wagon and the driver's seat, positive that Gilbrick was talking in his sleep and didn't see the gates ahead of them. What else could explain why he didn't slow?

"Oh, dear, not this again," Gilda said, staggering up behind Merrigan.

"Again?" She seriously considered grabbing Bib and leaping off the back of the wagon before there was a collision. Merrigan didn't think the magical cloak that protected against swords and arrows and cudgels could protect her if the wagon rammed into the gates and its entire contents fell on her.
~~~~~

"It's very bad for his pride when this happens." She reached around Merrigan and caught hold of the sides of the panel, bracing both of them.

Merrigan appreciated the girl's consideration, but did she really want to be caught here if Gilbrick was about to ram into the city gates?

"His pride? What about his body?"

Gilda just rolled her eyes and shook her head.

The uproar from the people on the wall and more voices coming from beyond the city gates grew louder. Gilbrick's wagon drew closer. The horses slowed slightly, only because they pulled up an incline. A creaking-groaning sound pierced the clamor of voices. A glow of torchlight appeared down the middle of the gates. They were opening. The shouts turned to cheers.

"He'll be impossible to live with for at least a week." Gilda retreated to her couch, where she set about putting on her stockings and shoes and then brushed her hair into place.

Merrigan stayed at the opening behind the driver's seat, watching. Gilbrick stood up in the box, holding the reins with one hand, and waved his hat to the cheering crowds. He swept up the last hundred yards, then through the city gates, and onward without stopping for the guards. As far as she could tell, the guards who should have stopped to inspect or at least question them were cheering and waving just as fiercely as the common people.

"What does the king think of all this?" she asked Gilda as the wagon finally slowed and bumped down the main streets, heading toward Gilbrick's warehouse. Merrigan sat down. "It can't be good for one man to be so popular, so influential, that the rules don't apply to him."

She shuddered to think of the disasters that could have overcome Avylyn if nobles and merchants and scholars became so popular that their voices swayed the people to stand against her father. That was part of why Leffisand had worked so hard to foster suspicions and dissent among different groups, and even tried to turn countries against each other. People who were constantly sniping and suspecting each other never joined forces in rebellion.

It was a sad, lonely life for a king. Sometimes she wondered why anyone would want the responsibilities that seemed to outweigh the glory and power.

"Oh, no one is really sure what King Auberg thinks." Gilda paused to tie her shoe. "He's been so busy since the crown prince vanished."

"Vanished? Why?"

"The usual. Some minor wizard or enchanter or whatever got offended because he or she wasn't invited to the christening, showed up and pronounced a bizarre curse on the prince. When he reached twenty-one, he vanished." Gilda straightened, frowning thoughtfully.

Merrigan sighed and tried not to be disgusted that even when she frowned, Gilda looked adorable.

"It's all very hazy, which everyone says is part of the curse. No one remembers his name. The places where it's written down in official records are so blurry no one can read them. No one is quite sure what the curse entails, what tasks the prince has to perform. Some people say the curse is the delusion that we have a crown prince, and we're just living under some enchantment that needs to be broken and free us from a perpetual dream." She shrugged and stood up to gaze at the road ahead through the open panel. "We'll be there soon, maybe another ten, fifteen minutes."

"What do you say?"

"About the curse? Oh, well ... I remember going to the palace when I was little, when Mama was chief seamstress to the royal family. There was a boy ..." Her thoughtful frown grew deeper. "It's sad, but his face is just a blur now. I know I liked him very much, and he was kind to me and would give me sweets. He would show me all around the palace, and we would go riding on his horse. It was a white horse, with blue eyes and silver bells on his blue bridle and ..." She sighed. "He gave me this locket." She tugged aside the neck of her dress to reveal a golden oval on a thin chain. "Someday, when the curse is broken, both our portraits will go in it. He said as long as I wore the locket, as long as I remembered that he existed, he had a chance of coming home again."

Merrigan shuddered to think that a lost prince had to depend on such a flighty girl. Yes, Gilda was good-hearted and loyal and sweet, and as frustrating as she sometimes could be, staying angry with her was impossible. Still, what made her qualified to be the lifeline to pull a prince out of a vicious enchantment?

"There ought to be a law that no one with magical powers of

any kind should be allowed near any christening taking place, on pain of death. More mischief happens at christenings than anywhere else, all the rest of the year," she muttered.

"All I can remember of the curse is that the prince can't come home until he helps to make the blind see at last." Gilda sighed and shrugged again. "For a few years after he vanished, King Auberg sent messengers to every healer hall throughout the world, on the chance that the prince was being forced to work with blind people. That doesn't make much sense, does it? I suppose that's what happens when you're desperate."

Merrigan could understand desperation.

The wagon slowed at last. Gilda brightened and gathered up her cloak and staggered toward the door at the back. Merrigan cautiously stood and stretched and finished straightening her clothes. Gilda's words got her thinking.

Maybe ... maybe the illusion that surrounded her, so everyone saw and heard a little, thin, bent, white-haired old woman ... was becoming real? Sinking into her bones, so to speak? She shuddered at the idea. Bib claimed that her hair seemed to be darkening in spots, and some of the sunken spots in her cheeks had plumped, but she couldn't see it no matter how hard she stared into mirrors and willed her own, true face to appear. That just proved what a good friend Bib was, to encourage her, even if he had to lie.

"And here we are," Gilbrick announced, jumping down from the front of the wagon as it finally creaked to a stop. He raced around to the back in time to help Gilda and Merrigan climb down. Like a triumphant warrior, he spread his arms wide, in welcome.

The warehouse facility belonging to Gilbrick was three massive buildings, three stories high. They faced a central area with plenty of room for wagons to come in and be loaded, several at a time from the massive doors at the front of the warehouses. Everything was clean and neat, and despite the evidence that horses constantly inhabited the cobblestoned yard, did not smell of horse droppings and other filth that came from heavy traffic.

Young men and women came running from all three buildings. They all wore dark gray trousers and skirts, with white blouses, and long, gray vests with Gilbrick's symbol of the wheel and coin blazoned on the right breast.

Merrigan was overwhelmed by the apparently genuine, joyous

welcome of the apprentices and workers, the overseers and older men and women who managed the accounting books and inventory and processed orders that came from distant cities. Whatever his faults, Gilbrick's people loved him. She compared his homecoming to times she and Leffisand had returned from trips to other kingdoms or distant cities in Carlion. There had been plenty of pomp and pageantry when they departed and returned, but none of the joy she saw here.

"I'm simply tired." She gave herself a mental shake, to focus on the present moment and not grieve what would never be again.

Gilbrick introduced her to his people and assigned two girls to settle her in the guest quarters in his house. Then he beckoned for his senior managers and they stepped aside, out of the way of the laborers unloading the wagons. Gilda sighed and tried to smile at Merrigan. Clearly, the girl was increasingly concerned about her father. The latest news was that the weavers wouldn't open their doors or take the curtains off their windows to let the city see their miraculous cloth until noon. Gilda seemed to grow a little more cheerful after that. She persuaded her father to go home, wash, eat and rest, and try to attend to business.

"I wish they wouldn't ... encourage him," she confided to Merrigan, as Gilbrick stepped back once more to confer with the older men who oversaw his business. "It isn't that they're obsessed with the cloth, but they'd do anything to make him happy."

"It's a fine thing to be so greatly loved," a young man observed from behind them, in a melodious baritone voice.

"Aubrey." Gilda's face lit up as if she had swallowed a mouthful of sun. She turned, and for a moment Merrigan thought she would hug the overly tall, gangly, pockmarked young man. Instead, she hurried to introduce him to Merrigan, and announced Aubrey was one of the most talented, intelligent young men who had risen through the ranks of Gilbrick's little kingdom

That earned a deep blush as Aubrey bowed to her with an elegance entirely at odds with his awkward, overgrown appearance. While everyone else looked neatly turned out, pressed and tucked and wrinkle-free in their livery, his cuffs were wrinkled and frayed, his vest was a size too large and his trousers rode so high Merrigan could see the thin spots in his stockings. Still, there was no disguising or mistaking Gilda's feelings for the young man.

Merrigan envied her. Just for a moment.

"Ah. Aubrey." Gilbrick stepped over to join them, finished with his senior managers. "I hear you voted against sending for me, so I could be here to see the cloth that might satisfy my years of searching. What do you have to say for yourself, lad?"

"Sir." Aubrey gave him a grave, head-and-shoulders bow. "I couldn't wish any greater happiness for you than to have your desires fulfilled, but I find it hard to believe all the wonderful claims these weavers have been making about their cloth. Not the process of creating it, and certainly not the properties granted to whoever possesses the cloth. I don't want you disappointed, that's all."

"You're a good lad." He patted Aubrey's cheek and had to reach up to do so. "You're too young to be such a pessimist. What's the use of living if you always expect the worst of people, if you constantly expect to be disappointed?"

"I would say, sir, that if you expect the worst to happen, then when your expectations are disappointed you are better off."

"Ha!" Gilbrick nodded and looked back over his shoulder at the other managers who had gathered around. "Common sense and a sense of humor, and a bit of a philosopher thrown in for good measure. Mark my words, the lad is going somewhere amazing someday." His smile faded slightly as he turned and hooked his arm through Gilda's. "Keep in mind, lad, there's a fine line between a realist and a cynic. Now, give us an hour, then come to breakfast. All of you! We'll have a grand conference and make plans to act on all the amazing things I've seen and heard about on this latest trip."

With that, he offered his other bent elbow to Merrigan, and the three headed down a slate pathway between two warehouses. A fourth building in the cluster owned by Gilbrick turned out to be his house, slightly smaller than the warehouses, which just meant it was enormous. Merrigan estimated it could hold forty guests, along with the staff needed to keep it running smoothly.

Chapter Twelve

Halfway through breakfast, two boys who had been dispatched to keep watch on the weavers dashed into the massive dining room. Gilbrick interrupted himself, stopping short and turning whiter than the blouses of his staff.

"They've finished early, sir," the taller boy announced. "They're going to open the doors any moment now."

"Why?" Gilbrick said with a gasp. "Come along, everyone! Business can wait." Tugging his napkin out of the collar of his shirt, he dashed away from the table with such speed and force, he knocked over his throne-like chair.

"Why?" Aubrey caught hold of the messenger boy's sleeve to keep him from running off to follow everyone else. "Why now, instead of at noon like they originally planned?"

"As soon as the town crier announced Master Gilbrick had returned, they opened their doors and shouted they were done, everybody should come see." He frowned. "Do you think something's wrong, sir?"

"I hope not." Aubrey watched the boy run off, so it was just Gilda and Merrigan with him in the dining room. "Maybe I'm naturally suspicious, but it seems to me they were waiting for Master Gilbrick to return."

"Oh, Aubrey, what can we do?" Gilda cried.

"See what this cloth looks like and what it's supposed to do," Merrigan said. "It may be a lot of stuff and nonsense."

"But what --" Gilda stopped with a gulp and rubbed her eyes just as they started to glisten. "Right. We have to see what the weavers claim before we know what to do."

"Shall we?" Aubrey offered them his bent arms, and the three set off together.

The walk to the weavers' shop was short, but long enough for Merrigan to solidify some suspicions. She was willing to believe that half the people on this side of the world knew about Gilbrick's quest for mysterious, magical, incredibly beautiful cloth. These weavers could have come to Alliburton specifically to fool and rob the clothing-obsessed merchant.

When the three reached the shop, a sizable crowd had gathered on the steps in front of the door and trailed down the street. This looked like a main thoroughfare through the artisans' district of the capitol city, and Merrigan decided the weavers couldn't have asked for better timing. What if this was what they had really wanted? What if it was their plan to send everyone into a panic by revealing the cloth earlier than planned?

Gilbrick never noticed when his daughter arrived. Aubrey guided them through the crowd so they could get to the top of the stairs and stand in front of the doors with Gilbrick. Merrigan wasn't quite sure how he did it, but he had a knack for getting people to move aside. People who seemed ready to come to blows over holding their position in line smiled and moved aside when Aubrey addressed them.

"Welcome!"

The man who stepped out through the narrow opening between the double doors of the shop looked as thin as a rake. His smile struck Merrigan as far too wide for such a thin man. She wished she had Bib with her, but she couldn't very well take a leather satchel full of book with her to breakfast. Besides, he had been indulging in his own sort of breakfast, harvesting information from Gilbrick's impressive library. Aubrey had hurried them off down the street so quickly she hadn't thought to go back to fetch the magic book.

"How very gratifying to see the support and interest of all the lovely people of Alliburton who have taken us to their hearts, especially when we were mere strangers just a few moons ago." He bowed, and Merrigan fully expected to see oil dripping from him. "Ah! And can this indeed be Master Gilbrick?" He held out his bony, long-fingered hands to clasp Gilbrick's between them. "Sir, it is indeed an honor to have you here at the unveiling of our masterpiece, the result of a lifetime of effort and dedication. Sir, you are known the world over as a man of discernment and infinite worthiness. A king among men. You honor our humble workshop with your presence and your interest."

Gilbrick reddened and made a short, jerky bow to the weaver. A moment later, a woman stepped out, as thin as the man. Just looking at her, Merrigan's fingers stung, as if she had cut them on the woman's sharp features. The weaver introduced her as his beloved wife, his inspiration and helpmate, a seamstress beyond compare, who had been honored to design clothes for the most powerful royalty on the other side of the ocean.

"Hah," Merrigan muttered. She would have been disappointed if they claimed to have designed clothes for royalty on *this* side of the ocean. The possibility of verifying their claims, even if it took moons for messengers to return, would give them a cachet of truth. Making claims about countries most of the people here had never heard of just proved they were liars. After all, no one should have believed her claims about sewing in Avylyn's and Carlion's courts. Look what had happened to the people who did.

The trick here was deciphering why the weaver and his wife were lying, and what they hoped to gain.

At long last, with great flourishes, the weavers flung open the shop doors. The curtains hiding the display windows fell. A long, loud sigh swept through the crowd waiting on the steps in front of the shop, and those in the first eight or ten rows, who could see into the windows. Gilda let out a little gasp and leaned into Aubrey. The young man stood utterly stone cold still.

The massive looms at the back of the shop were empty. The shelves that had once held large quantities of fine cloth -- empty. The display tables in the front of the shop -- empty. The counter where an ordinary cloth merchant or tailor would measure out and cut bolts of material -- also empty. There was nothing else in the shop other than dust that swirled through the rays of light streaming through the windows.

The weavers hurried to the largest display table and moved with exaggerated care. For a moment, Merrigan could almost believe they were handling something delicate and draping. She could almost see the cloth between their fingers. Was it possible they had woven invisible cloth? Yet if they did, what good would it be? The cloth didn't turn anything invisible, because the table was certainly visible.

"Aren't these the most amazing colors you have ever seen? Isn't the shimmer amazing, unlike anything you have ever witnessed? See how the colors move as the cloth moves." The weaver went into raptures, describing the subtle shading from deep purple into lavender and then into rose, with streaks of amber here, the softest green of newly furled ferns there.

Merrigan crossed her arms inside her impervious cloak and shivered, hoping with all her might that whatever inimical magic might be at work in this place, the cloak would protect her. All the people who stood just a few steps away from the supposedly glorious cloth, the work of a lifetime, were silent. The ones behind Merrigan, however, whispered, hissing like the waves on hot sand, as one person after another repeated what the weaver said, passing his words to the people standing far back on the street.

"The most valuable characteristic of the cloth is that it ensures everyone in your employ, everyone entrusted with vital positions of responsibility and power, are absolutely worthy of their positions," the weaver said, stepping forward and bowing to Gilbrick and other well-dressed people standing inside the shop. "Never again will you fear that you have promoted someone too far above his station, or that those you entrust with vital missions will fail you. Only he who is worthy of his place, his duties, his rank, and his wealth can see this most miraculous cloth."

Merrigan choked back a shout of "Ah ha!" She held perfectly still, frozen in place by the sudden, overpowering stink of utter terror that exploded from everyone around her. She looked at those on either side of her as far as she could without turning her head. Every face paled, just enough to be noticeable. Every set of eyes widened. Sweat beaded several foreheads. More than a few people licked their lips, and glanced slightly to the right and left. Merrigan watched them as they stared at the empty table, the beaming weaver and his wife, the people around them, then back at the table. The weavers stepped back to the table and held up -- seemingly -- folds of the glorious cloth with the magical power of discerning worthiness.

"Astounding." Gilbrick's voice sounded like his throat was full of dust, while sweat darkened his hair and collar. "The value ... of such a miraculous ... such a work of art ... the value is incalculable. Don't you agree, Worton?" he said, turning to his senior manager.

"Sir." Worton swallowed hard and glanced sideways at the weaver and his wife. "Yes, sir. Beautiful beyond belief."

Merrigan wanted to shout they were all idiots, there was no cloth there.

Yet what if she was wrong, and all of them could see it?

As others around her chimed in after Worton and praised the beauty, the array of colors, the shimmer of the cloth, she wondered what they would do to her if she said there was no cloth there. For a moment, she slipped back to those cruel hours after Clara had cursed her, and brutes laughed in her face and said she was insane.

Sweat drenched her face, despite a chill that filled her marrow. She couldn't breathe. Carefully, moving slowly, bowing her head so she didn't look anyone in the eyes, she turned and slipped down the steps, through the crowd, and crept back to Gilbrick's grand house.

She curled up on the rug in front of the fire burning merrily in her guest room, wrapped a blanket around herself, and told Bib what had happened.

"What kind of magic is at work?" she said, ending on a sigh. "Is there something wrong with me, that I couldn't see the cloth? Or is everyone else wrong?"

"Just think for a minute, Mi'Lady. You are in a lowly but honest position. How could you ever be considered unworthy?" the book responded.

"True ..." Merrigan wrapped the blanket a little closer. "So is everyone else a fool?"

"They want to avoid looking like fools. They want it so badly, they're willing to lie, and they're afraid to accuse everyone around them of lying."

"I should think that would be more comforting than thinking you're the only unworthy person in the entire city."

"Honesty is rarely comforting."

"I'll tell you what isn't comforting -- the thought of half the people of this city, clamoring to wear clothes made of invisible cloth." Merrigan shuddered. "Forget about the crimes against fashion. The thought of all those ugly, misshapen, fat bodies wearing nothing but their underpinnings. Or the folk who dislike underpinnings!" She thought she might be ill.

An hour later, she learned she should have focused her concern and fear in an entirely different direction.

Gilda came to her in tears. Gilbrick had insisted on buying three bolts of cloth from the weavers, to have clothes made for himself, for Gilda, and as a present for King Auberg. Including fresh underpinnings. When Aubrey protested, insisting that there was no cloth, Master Gilbrick dismissed him from his service. None of the managers and senior apprentices stood up for Aubrey.

I wash my hands of her, Merrigan commented silently to Bib. *The silly child is upset about the wrong thing entirely. Her father is going to make her, and himself, and the king run around naked!*

You would be upset if you were in love with Aubrey, the book responded, sounding slightly amused.

Love makes even bigger idiots out of people who are already idiots. Thank goodness I was only partially in love with Leffisand, and it stopped before I went too far to be saved.

Really? Bib responded. *Do you truly believe that?*

Merrigan couldn't respond. Gilda had stopped weeping and said something that she had to ask her to repeat.

"Papa wants you to design and sew the clothes," Gilda said, her face brightening. Obviously, her love for Aubrey wasn't very deep, if passing on such news eased her spirits.

"No." Merrigan was amazed at how good it felt to say that.

"What do you mean, no?"

"I won't soil my hands --" She let out a gasp of exasperation at the contradiction of what she was saying. After all, how could she soil her hands on cloth that didn't exist?

"Are you saying you won't make the clothes for my father and for me -- and for our king? After all I've told you about him, how he's suffered so much since losing his son? After all my father has done for you?"

"I won't make the clothes because I can't make the clothes because there is no magical cloth."

For three eternal seconds, something like relief softened the worried lines around Gilda's mouth and eyes. She opened her mouth to speak. Then she hiccupped, pressed her wet handkerchief to her mouth and muffled a wail. A moment later, she fled the room.

"This is a madhouse."

"Indeed, Mi'Lady. I believe it would be wise to leave before we are asked to leave. Either from inimical magic at work or people's unwillingness to be thought of as unworthy. Insisting the cloth does not exist could make people angry. Enough to attack," the book hurried to add.

Merrigan had very little to pack, so she was ready to go in less than a quarter of an hour. Possessing a magic box that could hold anything she put inside it made packing easy. She put everything she possessed in two bags on long straps -- one satchel for Bib, and the other for the box. There were no household servants visible as she made her way down the stairs and across the grand entrance hallway, to the front door. They were likely huddled together, fearing for their positions since they couldn't see the cloth.

"Mistress Mara." Aubrey appeared from the shadows between the warehouses as Merrigan pulled the door closed behind her. "Please tell me -- you saw no cloth also?"

"Of course not. There was nothing to see."

"Thank you." His face lit up, so for a few seconds he was quite the handsomest young man she had ever seen. Merrigan's heart skipped a few beats. "I beg you, help me save Gilda."

"Save her?" Merrigan shook her head. "Just how do you propose to do that? And save her from what, exactly?"

"We have to keep Master Gilbrick from humiliating himself, utterly destroying himself over this cloth. Once his reputation is destroyed, it won't matter that he's been a respected, successful merchant for thirty years -- just a few hours of foolishness will destroy him. If he falls, so will Gilda."

"Hmm." She had very few options to consider, and she wasn't ashamed to admit she liked Gilda enough to want to protect the girl from her silliness. "If you'll find me a place to stay, since I'm no longer a welcome guest here, I'll see what I can do."

What we *can do, you mean,* Bib commented.

Of course. We're partners in protecting the fools of the world from themselves.

~~~~~

Aubrey brought Merrigan to a warehouse on the far edge of the old merchants' district. As they walked, he filled in the information that Gilda had been too upset to tell her. Gilbrick had announced that he wanted Mistress Mara to design the clothes. The weavers had scrambled to convince him that only they were able to cut and sew the "cloth of discernment," as it was being called. Only they could keep the cloth from losing its magic during the process. That had convinced Aubrey he wasn't being foolish or blind, but that this was an elaborate scheme. Gilbrick had indeed been
~~~~~

persuaded by the weavers and agreed that they would be entrusted with the making of the magical clothes, but he still wanted Merrigan to design them and oversee the work.

"I should have agreed to do it," Merrigan said, as they turned down the street with the warehouse at the far end. "At least I would be in a position to keep an eye on those two cheats."

"Oh, no, Mistress. That would just put you in danger. Eventually, they would realize you were trying to gather evidence against them. All my studies, all the books of history, indicate such people do anything to protect themselves. They consider murder justified. I would not willingly put you in harm's reach. Not even to protect my beloved."

Who still talks that way nowadays? Merrigan wondered.

A merchant's apprentice who reads the histories and studies how people think? Bib responded after a moment of thought. *This is someone who isn't what he seems. Besides yourself, of course.*

Oh, really? I hadn't noticed.

The magic book laughed, his pages vibrating enough to buzz through the bag where he pressed against Merrigan's hip.

The warehouse had been divided into smaller compartments. The massive tiers of shelves had been turned into beds. Scores of beds, each enclosed with boards and blankets for privacy and warmth. The beds, Merrigan soon learned, were filled with children. The shelves were high enough apart from each other, in effect each child had a small room of his or her own.

Aubrey was helping a dozen other people run an orphanage.

"You ..." Merrigan swallowed down the ridiculous accusation she was about to make, that Aubrey was going to let her stay there as an orphan. Maybe before Clara's spell she could have passed for eighteen, but certainly not now. "You want me to make clothes for the children, in exchange for shelter?"

Actually, it was a very kind offer. The young man had just lost the position he had probably spent his life working toward. How many other merchants in the city would take him on, after Master Gilbrick had expelled him? Yet despite this massive loss, the shock it had to be for him, he offered to help her.

"I hope if the children take to you, maybe you will become a teacher. Train the girls to become seamstresses. Who knows? Maybe if enough children are skilled enough, we could set up a shop here --" He grinned and gestured back into the shadowy depths of the warehouse, beyond the long line of lanterns hanging from poles on the shelves. "We certainly have enough room. If we could find several ways for the children to support themselves, we wouldn't have to depend on charity." The pleased, eager expression that made his face almost handsome faded into weariness and a type of frustration Merrigan knew all too well from personal experience. "Sometimes, I feel like we're invisible."

"So you want me to take on apprentices, so to speak?" She nodded, turning the idea over in her head. "I could do that."

At least she wouldn't be required to wash little hands and faces, change diapers, cook, or clean up after the ranks of children she saw scurrying around, attending to chores. She met the adults who acted as foster parents, overseeing cooking and cleaning and washing and mending, tending the ill and providing schooling. Some of these people were well-educated and displayed good deportment, erasing a fear of Merrigan's that this would turn out to be one of those horrid places that pretended to help the helpless and destitute, then used them for nefarious purposes.

Within an hour of walking into the orphanage, Merrigan decided the children were being taken care of very well. They were all neatly dressed, clean, and even if the food wasn't plentiful, no one was starving. As she watched, thirty or so children settled down at the long rows of trestle tables, pulling out slates and chalk and books. If they weren't so shabby, she could have compared it to her schoolroom in her father's palace, where the children of nobles joined her and her siblings for the best education possible.

An older man, who had been working over the massive kettles of soup for their supper, stepped up in front of the long rows of tables with a book open in his hands. The children raised their heads and quieted. Merrigan was impressed to see many of them even looked interested in what the man was about to say.

"Is he a teacher as well as a cook?"

"Nasius was one of the premier lecturers at the university in Krackenfranq," Aubrey said, lowering his voice and gesturing for her to follow him. "They let him go because they have some ridiculous idea that old things aren't as worthwhile as new things."

"He doesn't look all that old to me."

"Hmm, no. And he was let go five years ago. The new leaders

of the university decided to rid out the library, and he protested them tossing out books that were more than one hundred years old." He grinned when Merrigan let out an involuntary cry of horror. "They were considered too old to be relevant."

"Krackenfranq has always been a nation of elitist idiots who want to be at the leading edge of any innovation. The only leading edge they have ever attained is stupidity, and the scorn of all their neighbors. My father only allowed their ambassador to speak to him for two hours at a time, once each moon." Merrigan froze, stunned at what she had let slip past her lips.

"I thought I recognized a touch of ..." Aubrey patted her shoulder. "We all have burdens and curses to bear. Some of us are cursed with invisibility and obscurity. Somehow, being invisible makes it easier for us to see everyone else, and to see more clearly. Mistress Mara, we would be honored if you would share your skills and help us give these children some hope for a better future."

"Thank you. Yes." She thought of the regimentation Gilbrick employed in his warehouse. There was something frightening in all the uniformity. Merrigan decided she much preferred the shabby, make-do conditions of this warehouse full of children who had been cast off. So many of them likely had minds and skills quite as good as the other children their age in the city, able to pursue an education to become scholars and diplomats, soldiers and artisans, merchants, wherever their skills led them. The only thing that stopped Aubrey's orphans was the lack of parents to arrange for apprenticeships, and funds to pay for their education or training.

Merrigan felt a little queasy when the words, "It's just not fair," kept echoing through her head at odd times throughout the day.

The front of the warehouse had been partitioned into a general living area for the children. They worked on the various activities they had found to add to the income for their massive "family," sorting through rags and salvaged odds and ends that the wealthy tossed from their homes. Many of the children were dressed in the discarded high fashion of two or three years before, cut down to fit, or else simply hemmed up and belted in. Some children, she learned later, wore the same dress or the same trousers for several years, letting down the roughly tacked hems or moving the holes in their belts as they grew. Some were self-taught tinkers, repairing broken pots and pans, fashioning tools to assist them. Some learned carpentry by fixing broken stools and small cabinets and even a chest of drawers that it had taken four boys to haul home. Some were even learning to make shoes by taking discards from the tanneries, cobbler shops, and saddlers, and following the patterns of the shoes they wore or dug out of the city's trash heap.

One back corner of the warehouse was the washhouse. The children took turns all day, hauling water in buckets from wells three streets away, to fill massive cauldrons that sat on fires all day, heating the water. With so many children, doing laundry to keep them in clean clothes and providing hot water for baths every third day was a full-time occupation. Every child was expected to pitch in, helping with the laundry in some way, either hauling water, scavenging wood and coal for the fires, scrubbing the clothes, tending the drying racks, and filling the bathing tubs. Merrigan was amused to discover that the punishments levied by the foster parents didn't include extra time in the laundry room. The children liked being clean, they liked the luxury of hot water, and the laundry was the warmest area of the warehouse, after the kitchen, when winter winds howled and rattled the walls.

Clothes for mending came straight out of the laundry room. Aubrey consulted with Pansy, the constantly humming, tiny old woman generally in charge of the girls. She found a bed for Merrigan near the laundry, among the girls who had shown an aptitude for sewing. Her bed was on the bottom shelf of a stack of five, and Merrigan was grateful. While some of the girls seemed to enjoy clambering around like the pet monkey her oldest brother had doted on, she shuddered at the thought of having to climb a ladder every night and every morning.

Aubrey introduced Merrigan to the sewing team of seven and explained that she had been a guest of Master Gilbrick but had found it necessary to leave the household. Two of the girls burst into tears. It turned out they had already heard that Aubrey had been cast out of his apprenticeship. They had been depending on him putting in a good word with Master Gilbrick, to eventually convince one of his seamstresses to apprentice them.

"Don't you worry about that," Merrigan said, when Aubrey gave her a helpless, almost terrified look. Was it the girls' tears that knocked him off balance, or did he have such a soft heart that he felt as if he had betrayed them by losing his job? Men, no matter how wonderful, could be dunderheads. "Between us, we will build a reputation so tailors and dressmakers will be begging to learn from you."

That cheered up the girls in general, and helped the weeping ones to stop dripping and sniffling. Of course, they wanted to hear all about the miraculous cloth that was the talk of the city and had been so eagerly anticipated for weeks. They didn't entirely or immediately accept Merrigan's word that there was no cloth, that it was all a nasty trick. She decided that was wise of them. After all, she had just met them. As the day went on and Merrigan got settled with her students and they set up their sewing room to their satisfaction, news came in from other children who had gone out into the city. Everyone was in raptures over the colors of the cloth, the way it shimmered in the light, the delicate texture, and the miraculous things it could do.

Merrigan decided there was a kind of rough but solid wisdom among those who were all but invisible in society. One by one, the older children crossed the city to the weavers' street, to glimpse the cloth on display in the shop window. One by one, they came back, scratching their heads, puzzled. After all, none of them could see it. One by one, they agreed with Merrigan -- they were the lowest of the low in all of Alliburton, and there was nothing that made them unworthy of their position. Therefore, if they were worthy, they should be able to see the cloth. But they couldn't. Therefore, there was no cloth.

What amused Merrigan was the clincher in the argument. Someone pointed out that Aubrey couldn't see the cloth. If their beloved Aubrey couldn't see it and insisted there was no cloth, well then, there was no cloth. Therefore, all who said they *could* see it were fools and liars.

With the children as spies, Merrigan didn't need to leave the safe confines of the warehouse. Her seven girls became her eyes and ears in the world. After only three days, she took to calling them "dwarves" in her mind, because there was something sadly un-childish about them, their common sense and cleverness and responsibility. They went out on chores for the other foster parents, ran errands, carried messages for merchants and shopkeepers and artisans to earn a penny or two, and gathered up all the gossip and news of the city. Then they came home and told the adults.

Merrigan decided the people tending the warehouse orphanage were the most well-informed people in the entire kingdom. Even King Auberg and his council didn't know as much as the orphans did. Between their small size and shabby clothes and yes, sometimes general filthiness, people ignored them. Someone ignored long enough became invisible. Then people talked more freely, and the children heard amazing, frightening, amusing, and sometimes profitable things.

Merrigan's "dwarves" learned to search for news of the weavers, the amazing cloth, and Gilbrick's order of clothes. Every evening the weavers announced the progress that had been made on the clothes. Empty dressmaker forms stood in the windows of the shop. According to the weavers, the most amazing, elegant clothes the world had ever seen covered them.

As the suits of clothes neared completion, Aubrey and Merrigan discussed how to deal with the impending embarrassment for Gilbrick and Gilda. Preventing King Auberg from putting on the non-existent clothes was another task entirely, and Aubrey assured Merrigan they wouldn't have to deal with that crisis unless they failed in stopping father and daughter from displaying their invisible clothes, and their utter gullibility.

"If I'm right, King Auberg will never receive those clothes. Rather, the charade of receiving them," he said, when she continued to press him for the strategy to protect the king.

She supposed he was right. After all, no one ever saw King Auberg. Between the constant search for the lost prince and running the country, the king was fully occupied. She supposed some of the king's ministers were honest enough, humble enough, wise enough, to look at the miraculous suit of clothes and admit nothing was there. The question was if they were brave enough to say so, and face the ridicule and censure of those without the courage to be as honest.

The day the weavers announced the clothes were ready to be delivered to Gilbrick's home, Merrigan went to visit Gilda. Her seven dwarves accompanied her, dressed in new clothes, which she had guided them in making. Merrigan was quite proud of them. Maybe her girls weren't dressed in matching outfits, but they were clean and neat, their hair braided, shoes and stockings in good condition, and walked with their heads high and shoulders back.

She had also given them lessons in deportment.

Gilda was just coming back from her father's warehouse when Merrigan and her entourage arrived. The young woman stared for several seconds as Merrigan approached, her face pale. For a second or two, Merrigan feared the silly girl would faint. Then Gilda let out a sob and hugged her hard. At least she had enough self-control not to soak her clothes. In short order, they were all invited into the parlor for tea. Gilda wanted to hear how she was, where she had gone, how she was doing. She claimed she felt awful when she learned Merrigan had left the house, and terrified that something awful had happened to her, because Gilbrick had sent all over the city to find Mistress Mara, but she had vanished.

"After all, Papa said you were very wise to refuse to make the clothes for us. The weavers are the only ones who know how to handle the magical cloth without damaging its miraculous properties." Gilda paused as one of the housemaids stepped into the parlor with a long tray holding the teapot and cups and a wide assortment of pastries.

Merrigan's two oldest girls hopped to their feet to take the tray and served for all of them. She was very proud of them. They would make splendid serving maids in grand houses, if they couldn't apprentice with a seamstress and set up shops of their own someday.

"Where have you been for the last moon?" Gilda said, her voice tending toward a wail.

"Did you know Aubrey helps to support an orphanage on the wages your father paid -- or rather, used to pay him?"

"Orphanage?" Gilda glanced over the girls. Her eyes widened. "But -- they don't look like orphans."

"What do orphans look like?" Merrigan smiled when Gilda slowly shook her head. "You expect all orphans to be dirty and ragged and thin, and live in ditches or in trees? Thanks to Aubrey and his friends, nearly one hundred of this city's orphans are fed and sheltered, clothed, kept clean, and educated. I'm delighted that he asked me to help teach the children a useful trade. I may not be designing for royalty, but this work is more than satisfying."

She wasn't ashamed to admit she felt a certain bit of satisfaction in twisting the knife, metaphorically. Gilbrick had spoken so many times about Merrigan being a seamstress to royalty, she knew that was the main reason he wanted to work with her. Gilda flushed and bowed her head a moment. Yes, the girl did have some common sense. Not much more than her father, but enough that Merrigan wanted to protect her.

"I hear you are to put on the clothes tomorrow, and display them for all the elite of the city," she said.

"Oh, yes. Papa insists."

"You don't sound very excited."

"I'm just … it feels wrong, somehow." Gilda shuddered delicately. "Is it … is it right to so very blatantly point out the flaws in our peers? To rub their noses in the proof that they are unworthy of their positions? Is that fair?"

Three of Merrigan's girls giggled into their cups of tea.

"I'm not so much concerned about fair as I am about … embarrassment," Merrigan said.

"Oh, yes, Absolutely. We wouldn't want to embarrass anyone." Gilda's pink cheeks darkened for several seconds.

"I'm talking about your embarrassment."

"Mine?" She went pale, so that the smears of sleeplessness under her eyes stood out against the alabaster of her cheeks, as if someone had punched her in both eyes.

"Gilda, please, for your father's sake if you don't care about yourself or about me. Because I have become quite fond of you. Truly." Merrigan stopped for dramatic effect and delicately licked her lips. "Consider how many people will come to the unveiling tomorrow, who may be unworthy of their positions. They have been lying all this time, claiming they could see the cloth, but never could. Are you envisioning the possibility?"

"Oh, yes. Terrible. How embarrassing for them." Gilda bit her lip. From their raw condition, Merrigan guessed she had been doing an awful lot of that lately.

"For *your* sake, do this one thing for me." Merrigan leaned forward, implying she was saying something that others perhaps should not hear. That had always had the effect of making people listen twice as intently. "Gilda, make sure you and your father wear underclothes tomorrow."

"Well of course we would. The weavers promised us they are making underclothes to go with our new clothes. It would be highly unsuitable … Oh." She flushed such a bright red, Merrigan felt the heat of her cheeks from the other side of the parlor.

All seven dwarves giggled, so their teacups rattled in their saucers.

"Think of all the unworthy people who will see you and your father in the ..." Merrigan pursed her lips, feigning delicacy. "Well, in the all-together. I assure you, the unworthy will not be as embarrassed as you, and they will be just as unwilling as before to admit what they can't see -- or admit what they *can*. Do you understand me? Is my meaning clear?"

"Oh -- Oh -- Mistress Mara --" Gilda burst into tears.

By the time she had calmed down, she soaked four of the handkerchiefs Merrigan made sure her girls carried with them.

More important, Gilda promised she would refuse to model the new clothes unless her father agreed to wear his oldest underclothes, the winter style that started high on his neck and even covered his feet. She promised not to let the weaver's wife, who was assigned to help her dress, convince her to put on the new underclothes made of the miraculous cloth.

"I'm disappointed," Aubrey admitted, when Merrigan reported on the meeting two hours later.

"How? They'll be decently clothed and their reputations will only be bruised, not entirely shredded, with a charge of public indecency thrown on top of everything else," Merrigan said.

"Oh, no, not that. I'm delighted it worked so well. You are an utter genius, Mistress Mara." The young man shook his head. His sorrow softened his bony features and gave him an aura of nobility that was quite appealing. "No, I was hoping to hear the weavers would not be involved in dressing Master Gilbrick and Gilda. If I were playing such a cruel trick on someone, I would not wait for the deception to fall apart, and flee at the last minute. I would be packing up my wagonload of gold and fleeing the city tonight."

"Maybe they will anyway," young Timo the Mouse offered.

Chapter Thirteen

The boy, who was a head shorter than his yearmates, had a habit of hiding in shadows and listening where he wasn't invited. This time, he was under the table where Merrigan and Aubrey and the other foster parents were conferring.

"He's right," Nasius said in his pleasantly rumbly voice. "They're liars. They've been lying all along. Why not make everyone think they'll be here in the morning? We should post guards over them tonight, to make sure they don't leave before everything falls apart and the crowds clamor for justice."

"But what can a gang of orphan boys do to stop them?" Merrigan said.

"We don't have to stop them." Aubrey's smile took on a nasty glee that changed her image of him. She liked it. "Our children just need to raise such a ruckus that they can't go anywhere in the city without everyone around them knowing who they are. And hopefully, wonder why they're leaving, when they're supposed to be there for the unveiling of their miraculous clothes."

~~~~~

An invitation came for Aubrey, Merrigan, and her seven girls to come to witness the unveiling. Aubrey was torn. He wanted to lead the teams of orphans watching for the weavers to flee. During the visit with Gilda, Merrigan had been dismayed to learn that Gilbrick had paid the weavers with almost half his hoard of exquisite, rare bolts of cloth from all over the world. It was all too easy to imagine the frauds starting up their scheme somewhere else, convincing people they were skilled by selling all that beautiful cloth they hadn't made. For all Merrigan knew, that was how they had been operating for years: take beautiful cloth from their last dupe and use it to trick the people in the next town or country; get rich on it; then convince another Gilbrick to hand over his stores of more beautiful, rare, expensive cloth.

"On the positive side, they have to handle two wagonloads," Aubrey said, as he watched the teams of children head out into the
~~~~~

city to their assigned watching posts. "The more wealth they have to handle, the harder it will be for them to vanish."

Merrigan kept busy and fought her inexplicable nervousness during the waiting, by cutting out the first of dozens of winter coats. Gilda wanted to help the orphanage, now that she knew about it. She sent ten bolts of sturdy, woolen cloth back with Merrigan and her girls, to make coats for the children. Plus the handcart that held the cloth. It was a princely gift, and Merrigan hesitated to mention that those ten bolts would only provide coats for half the children. Well, it was a start. Maybe by the time she had the first batch of coats made up, Gilda would feel guilty about something else and provide more cloth for the rest of the children.

"That's ... odd," Bib said.

Merrigan worked alone while her girls were at their lessons. She had him sitting out on the table, talking with her. Bib had been sitting on a thick stack of maps of the city all morning, absorbing all the information, the routes, the traffic patterns, to try to predict which way the weavers would go when they fled the city.

"What is?" She paused in snipping the selvage edge of the cloth.

"There's magic. Quite a nasty spell. Badly applied. It's getting closer."

"What kind of spell?" She put down the scissors. They wouldn't be much good against magic, would they?

"A cheater's spell."

"Hello?" A heart-shaped face surrounded by a cloud of amazing, brilliant red curls, peered around the canvas wall that surrounded the sewing area. "Are you Mistress Mara?"

"I am."

"Millicent said I could help you. I'm new here. I'm good with a needle." She stepped into the sewing area, hands clasped at her waist, bouncing nervously on the toes of her slippers. She looked like she was between twelve and fourteen. "I'm Belinda."

"She's the source," Bib said. "She has several spells to disguise her, but they aren't dispelling the nasty magic someone cast on her."

"Is that ... a talking ... book?" Belinda's voice dropped the squeaky little girl exuberance.

Her outline flickered, and for several seconds she wavered back and forth between a twelve-year-old and a dainty grown woman. Her face elongated and shortened, her cheekbones sharpened and then vanished under baby fat, back and forth. The most disturbing part of the momentary flickering was how her breasts pushed out her bodice just enough to be noticeable, and then flattened again. It looked like a small animal bounced around inside her clothes.

"Either take off the talismans maintaining your disguise," Merrigan said, closing her eyes to fight the nausea, "or steady your control over them. I don't need to lose my soup on my sewing."

"Please tell me that isn't pea soup I smell." Belinda turned her head in the direction of the kitchen. "I'm allergic to peas of any kind. If I touch them, I break out in spots. If I smell cooking peas for too long, my nose runs and I sneeze for hours. If I eat it ..." She shuddered, then sank down at the table and hid her face in her hands. "I am deathly sick, and it's nearly impossible to run when they find me."

"That's the spell, isn't it?" Bib said.

"What spell?" Merrigan could barely restrain herself from shouting. "When who finds you? And why do you need to run?"

"You're a princess, aren't you?" The book flipped open and pages riffled until they displayed a page with writing on it.

"Spare me. The old 'princess and the pea' gambit?" Merrigan nudged Belinda's arms so she could fold up the cloth and get it out of the way. It didn't look like she was going to finish cutting out the coats today. "Isn't that usually used to prove a princess in rags is a real princess? Who are you hiding from?"

"Princes." The girl took a deep breath and lowered her hands. Her appearance steadied back into the almost-too-cute twelve-year-old. "Third and fourth and fifth-born sons who have no chance whatsoever of inheriting a throne. I'm my father's oldest daughter. Oldest of six daughters."

"Whoever marries you becomes king after your father. No chance whatsoever that you'll be crowned queen and you can keep your husband a prince, make sure he can't take over?"

"My father is so utterly old-fashioned. I barely escaped being stranded on the top of a glass hill, waiting for a prince who passes a dozen tests and can ride a magical black steed to the top of the hill and sweep me up into the saddle. None of my sisters wants to take my place as the prize. They all were allowed to learn useful occupations like spell-casting and managing libraries and two of them were allowed to become sword maidens. I had to concentrate on maidenly pursuits and politics and persuading hide-bound old counts and dukes to play nice with each other. I love sewing, but I wasn't allowed to do anything but embroidery for four years before I finally had to flee for my sanity. I swear, I'm very good with a needle for useful things." Belinda gestured at the dark, thick, sturdy coat material. "Please, let me be useful."

"What do you look like without the disguising spells?" Merrigan shook her head and waved a hand, as if brushing away that question. "Forget that. I caught a glimpse. I don't think I want to see you … melting back into what you really look like. It really is a clever disguise, making you look like a child."

"Someone had enough sense to track you by your talismans," Bib said. "I think that's part of the problem. They wrapped their tracking spell around your disguise spells. Everything is twisted. Tangled."

"Extremely twisted. I haven't been able to eat or even smell or cook anything with peas in it since I went on the run," Belinda said. "Whenever I eat pea soup, it's like lighting a beacon fire and they all find me."

"Unfortunately, peas are very cheap and nutritious and filling, so guess what most people donate to feed the orphans?" Merrigan murmured.

She honestly wanted to feel sorry for Belinda, but the whole situation struck her as quite humorous, in a nasty, see-how-we-can-twist-magical-traditions sort of way. The best she could do was refrain from giggling from time to time.

By the time the girls finished their lessons for the day and returned to the sewing area to get to work on the coats, Merrigan, Belinda and Bib had come up with a good cover story. They weren't able to untangle the tracking spell the princes had put on the fugitive princess. It was too tightly twisted around the disguise talismans. To untangle them, Belinda would have to remove all the talismans and stop using the disguise through two cycles of full moon and new moon, according to all the information on disguise spells Bib could find. Until they could come up with a new disguising talisman, they would have to find excuses why she couldn't eat pea soup or peas porridge or put in duty shifts in the kitchen. Only the nobility, who had access to the best-educated and most modern of healers and physicians, understood the concept of allergies. However, Merrigan thought she could convince the warehouse's foster parents to accept Belinda's eating restrictions. After all, Nasius was a well-educated man, and even if he specialized in philosophy and poetry, he had read something about medicine and medical developments.

The seven girls accepted Belinda with cheerful good grace and set about helping her gather up blankets and pillow, washcloth and towel and other necessities from the storage shelves, to make her bed shelf-room comfortable.

Just before dinner, the boys on watch duty all around the weavers' shop were relieved by the next shift, and returned to report that the couple had stayed in their shop all day. Merrigan and Aubrey's relief was short-lived when the oldest of the group, Lars, added, "But there's some mean group of men what looks like they're made out o' stone -- know what I mean? They been going in and out o' the back all day, hauling away sacks and crates and such. Just put somethin' on their shoulders and walk away, and they don't come back for hours. Don't know where they gone. Must 'av been a long walk."

"The city gates." Aubrey muttered several guttural words under his breath, and for a moment his angular face took on a stern, chiseled look that made Merrigan feel slightly queasy.

The same queasy feeling she got when Belinda's features had shifted back and forth.

There were times before her widowhood, when she had raged against what she considered the injustice of magic and declared herself allergic to magic. What if the repetition had made that true, and she was allergic to the spells cast on Belinda? Yet if that were true, was there a spell on Aubrey, too? Yet who would cast a spell on a mere apprentice?

That thought caught on something at the back of her mind. The problem was she had too much to worry over to pursue the hazy *ah-hah* feeling trying to strike a light in that dark, brooding tangle.

Before Merrigan could recover her breath, Aubrey gestured for the boys to follow him, and dashed out of the warehouse. Most of the other children and adults who might have noticed were busy setting the table or herding younger children to wash up for dinner. Nobody asked any questions, and that was another nice thing about living here in the orphanage warehouse: people helped and cared, but they didn't intrude.

Truth be told, despite their insistence on being too optimistic for common sense and taking up responsibilities no one had put on them, Merrigan somewhat admired the odd assortment of folk who ran the orphanage. Even more odd, despite their noise and smells and uncanny ability to get dirty ten seconds after putting on clean clothes, she even liked the children. Most of them, anyway. She was actually rather fond of her seven girls. They even giggled when she referred to them as her dwarves, because they were much too clever and mature to be merely little girls.

Aubrey came back just as Nasius and Robard were preparing to send someone to look for him and the boys. The boys were all excited and chattering and filthy-sweaty from running. Aubrey, on the other hand, looked exhausted and as stricken-pale as a man who had seen his own specter standing on a freshly dug grave. All but for two angry red spots in his bony cheeks and a growing fire in his eyes.

"What happened?" Merrigan asked him, when he returned from washing up and changing his shirt. The noise from all the children gathering around the tables gave them some privacy.

"The shop is empty. The weavers are at dinner in the Scepter Rose, where the entire city seems to be stopping by to congratulate them on a job well done." He snorted. Quite eloquent expression of his feelings. "I have boys posted at every door and window so they can't sneak out without us knowing."

"All those men carrying bags and crates --"

"Carrying away all the cloth and gold. Nobody noticed a man walk away from the shop, they'd only notice wagons. These people are entirely too clever. It's too well-planned."

"They've done this before." She shuddered, thinking about the gold and all that rare cloth, a lifetime of collecting, that Gilbrick had traded for nothing but embarrassment. His coffers would be greatly reduced, and he would have a brutal struggle to rebuild his reserves, with his reputation so thoroughly destroyed. The thought of Gilda suffering because of her father's stupidity infuriated her. Why did women have to suffer for the blindness and obsessions of their menfolk?

Ah, Leffisand. If I ever loved you, I have quite gotten over it. If only I had told Nanny Tulip to shut up, and had been wise enough to love Bryan.

"They'll do it again." Aubrey's voice cracked. "It isn't enough to try to stop Gilda and Master Gilbrick from shaming themselves tomorrow. We have to stop the weavers before they flee beyond the tales of what happened here. They might even cross the ocean, to a country that won't hear about what happened here for years, if ever." He sagged back against the wall. "What do we do?"

"I ... have some friends in Seafoam," Merrigan said. "I made the princess's wedding dress, and I know the captain of a ship. Maybe ..." She shrugged, unsure what she was about to propose. Maybe this was more of Clara's interfering magic, nudging her to get involved in things that were none of her business and certainly none of her responsibility?

A surge of heat that resolved into anger yanked the words from her tongue. Was this what had been happening all along? What had guided her steps? Some magic *making* her help people? Had it been fooling her into thinking she was looking out for her own interests when she took the side of people she had come to like? Had she been *forced* to become a champion for others?

If she could have, Merrigan thought she might pack up and flee this town tonight, just like the weavers. In fact, maybe she should look for them. How hard would it be to track them down at the most expensive and popular inn? She could tell them she knew their tricks, and she wanted in. She could offer to use her skills and connections as a seamstress to royalty to add more believability to their story. Then when they were comfortable in their next scheme to steal from some trusting, good-hearted yet gullible innocent, she could reveal all and --

"Do you have any friends left at Gilbrick's warehouses?" she hurried to say, to cut off the full-blown plan screaming through her mind. It made her head hurt, and her stomach twist.

"Several friends," Aubrey said, frowning. "Why?"

"Any of the messengers? Anyone willing to leave immediately and ride all the way to Seafoam?"

"What if they don't go to Seafoam? There are a dozen other countries with three times as many ports they can sail from."

"Yes, but if the princess of Seafoam and the family that runs the premier inn in Windward and the captain of one of the largest ships in the port all join together and ask port masters and captains of ocean-crossing vessels up and down the coast to look for the weavers and not take them on board ..." She smiled as she let Aubrey finish the thought for her.

"Mistress Mara." He choked and tears brightened his eyes, strangely at odds with the fiercely exultant expression that made his face once again, just for a few seconds, look chiseled and determined and handsome. "You are a treasure. You are a heroine. You are better than ten faerie godmothers all rolled into one." He picked her up by her shoulders and kissed both her cheeks.

Merrigan quite lost her breath, her toes dangling several inches off the ground and a strange tingling, buzzing sensation fizzing through her blood and bones. Aubrey put her down and she sagged back against the wall while he dashed away, shouting for someone to bring him pen and ink and paper.

What just happened? Bib demanded, his voice loud in Merrigan's head. *Never mind -- it just showed up in my pages.*

How? Merrigan nearly asked the question aloud. She staggered to her sewing room, blessedly quiet now.

"Magic," he said, his voice muffled, coming from behind the curtain of her bed shelf. "Two magic spells colliding. Meaning Aubrey --"

"Is under a spell too." She settled down on her bed and rested a hand on Bib's open pages. "So ... did it do anything to my spell, or was that just the feeling of two hitting each other, nothing changed?"

"If I miss my guess..." His pages riffled, nearly trapping her hand for a moment. "Sorry about that. It helps if I do a little actual physical searching. I know that makes no real sense, but it seems to help me sift things through, sort them out and ... ah...hmm..."

"That didn't sound very definite or certain."

"If I miss my guess, there's an undercurrent to both your spells that matches."

"Meaning?" She might have shouted the question, might have picked up Bib and tossed him across the room, but Merrigan couldn't get through the unsteady sensation bubbling through her. All that from a couple of kisses? They weren't even on her lips, so they really didn't count, did they? They were brotherly, for all that Aubrey was definitely exuberant and grateful and celebrating.

"There's healing magic in royal hands, and even stronger magic in royal kisses, in the right circumstances. If I miss my guess, the breaking of your curse -- excuse me, the breaking of the spell to reform your character and destiny, has a codicil for a standard spell-breaking clause."

"Meaning?" A tiny flicker of heat shoved away some of the unbalanced feeling.

"You, Princess Merrigan, were just kissed by a prince. If Aubrey's heart wasn't totally fixated on Gilda, and he had kissed you on the lips, he might have broken your spell."

"Well ..." She wondered why the news left her feeling flat, a little sad, but not infuriated, cheated, insulted, as it would have a year ago. "I like Gilda too much to take her prince away from her ... Wait." Her head cleared a little more. "Aubrey is a prince?"

"All the indications confirm it. The ripples in the magic, the sense there is more to him than he appears, his general goodness and honesty and leadership skills. The best kind of prince. A prince under a curse. It's always the good ones who are targets of curses."

"You don't think ... What was it Gilda said about the curse on King Auberg's missing son?"

"It had something to do with seeing ... I think." Bib chuckled. "I seem to be affected by the spell as much as everyone. It seems to be a misdirection spell, an adaptation of you-don't-see-me and you-don't-remember-me."

So she wasn't ill or suffering some sort of aberration the few times Aubrey's features changed, just for a second or two. The question was, what should she do about it? Could she do anything?

Why do I keep thinking the problems around me are my concern?

She spent the dinner hour writing several letters to Warden and Dulcibella, to Quincy and Rosa, Miles and Elli, explaining the situation and asking for their help. As soon as Aubrey had her settled with writing materials and assigned two of her girls to make sure she was fed and no one bothered her, he had run off to Gilbrick's warehouse, to track down his friends among the messengers. When he didn't come back right away, Merrigan feared he had run into trouble even getting in, much less finding his friends. Or worse, everyone he approached laughed at him, mocked him, refused to listen. She nearly cried out in relief when the familiar face of Bigsley peered around the doorway. That evening when she had met him on the hill looking down on

Alliburton felt like a lifetime ago. He informed Merrigan there had been a scuffle among the messengers for the privilege of taking the messages to Seafoam, once Aubrey explained what had happened. Not all the senior apprentices believed him, but they had at least given him the benefit of the doubt and went off to check the weavers' shop and verify his story. Aubrey was still trying to convince Gilda to refuse to put on the magical clothes, when word came back that the shop was indeed utterly empty.

All three warehouse managers were at that moment, according to Bigsley, confronting the weaver and his wife at the Scepter Rose. Bigsley was of the opinion that they would be nowhere to be found, and he had been entrusted by Aubrey with getting the letters from Merrigan and heading out on the road immediately. The word needed to get up and down the coast to keep the tricksters from even approaching a ship ready to cross the ocean.

"He loves her incredibly, doesn't he?" Belinda remarked, once Bigsley had raced away on his horse. She and Merrigan stood in the doorway of the orphanage warehouse, looking out into the darkening streets, where shadows grew long and were swallowed up in encroaching twilight.

"Who?" Merrigan pulled her thoughts back from Seafoam. She wished she could ride with Bigsley, to see her friends again. She knew the spell would keep her from retracing her steps, and not for the first time she regretted leaving Seafoam at all.

"Aubrey. He loves the merchant's daughter. That's an awful lot of worry and work and fury for just admiration." She sighed and followed Merrigan back into the massive building, where the sounds of bedtime activities trickled out toward them.

Merrigan liked the giggles of children as they played their games to delay the moment when they had to climb under their blankets and close their eyes and mouths. When she moved on, she would miss the tedium. The comfortable routines. Even, oddly enough, the smells of sweaty little boys with twenty different stains on their faces and clothes. The little girls who insisted on climbing into her lap during the bedtime story, making her legs fall asleep with the weight of their hot little bodies.

"I wish ... I wish I weren't quite so picky," Belinda confided in her as they settled down in the sewing room, just the two of them, with a pot of sweet tea, so heavy with spices the spoon almost stood up in it. For the next half hour, while the sewing girls helped bathe the younger girls, they had a few moments to themselves. Since she was new to the orphanage, she hadn't been assigned duties yet, other than sewing.

"Picky?" Merrigan had to struggle to focus on what she was saying. "Picky about what?"

"His name was Bayl. He was five years older than me, and at the time, I thought that was incredibly old. I had just decided that I wasn't going to settle for the first younger son prince who came calling. I liked him. I think I liked him far more than anyone else I had ever met. Father didn't think much of him, since he was the fourth prince. At that time, he still had some hopes that I could make a marriage alliance, joining two kingdoms together." She sighed, offering Merrigan a lopsided little smile. "I liked Bayl enough that it actually hurt a little when I turned him down. Father was pleased -- can you believe it? Actually pleased when I turned down a marriage offer. He wanted me to hold out for a second-born prince from the kingdoms surrounding ours."

"They found other princesses?" Merrigan guessed.

"They found enchanted goose girls and swan maidens and millers' daughters who spun straw into gold. When Father started encouraging third-born sons, I held out for Bayl. For a while."

"He found someone else?"

"His family's kingdom fell under some awful enchantment. Everyone who has tried to get into the palace, then the capitol city, and finally anyone trying to go within a day's journey of the capitol …" Belinda shrugged. "They never come back. They're trapped."

"Sylvanglade?" Merrigan whispered.

"How did you know? Yes, Prince Bayl of Sylvanglade." She sighed. "Father got to the point where he insisted I had to take a prince, any prince, no matter how poor his kingdom. All that mattered was royal blood, and not the brain or the personality or even the cleanliness of whoever showed up claiming to be a prince. Then he threatened me with enchantments, to make the princes prove they were worthy. At one point, he decided to put me and all my sisters into the enchantment, thinking that we'd have better luck with a traveling band of younger sons, working together. He would let them choose which of us the princes wanted to marry, without letting them know who was the heir to the throne. Oh, were my sisters furious! Bythia was furious enough -- she has some magic of her own -- she threatened to put a curse on me, as if it was all *my* fault the rest of them would be forced to marry someone they didn't like. Well, now they all knew how it felt to be just a prize hanging from the highest branch, waiting for anyone who could jump high enough to snatch us." Belinda burst into tears.

Merrigan patted the girl's shoulder, unsure what to say to soothe her. After a while, she rubbed her back, then moved on to wrapping an arm around her. Fortunately, Belinda's tears stopped soon after she turned and snuggled her wet face into Merrigan's shoulder. Even more fortunately, she stopped crying before the other girls came back from helping with evening baths, so there were no uncomfortable questions.

"How old are you?" Merrigan asked, under cover of the chatter and giggles as the seven girls scrambled into their nightgowns and robes and slippers, before heading to the main room for story time.

"Twenty-five. Yes, I know, I'm ancient for an unmarried princess." She sighed. Then for a moment she grew thoughtful. The disguising spell rippled just enough that her own face showed through the mask of childishness. "How old are you? And what's your real name?"

"My -- my real name?"

"Oh, there's so much magic soaked into me, after all this time, I can tell when someone else is tangled up in a few spells. I figure you're royalty of some kind. The nastiest, most complicated spells get wrapped around us. Something about inherent magic in royal blood, I think. One of the tutors for Bythia and Barbarina, when they were first learning magic, had a funny theory. He believed there were some elitist majjians out there, or at least they wanted to be majjians, who were trying to dictate who got magic and who could use magic. So anyone who is born with magic potential, even if it's just to have magical things happen to us, we become targets. To somehow control all that power." She shrugged. "It makes sense to me, I suppose, but what do I know about magic? I wasn't allowed to learn useful things. I was just a prince trap."

"Aren't we all?" Merrigan muttered, thinking of Bryan. She found it wryly amusing, in a sad sort of way, that she and Belinda had the same sort of experience with the royal brothers. Those who knew better didn't think the boys who loved them were worthy.

"Besides," the other princess continued, "you have a magical book -- that has to mean you're a princess, at the very least."

"Yes." Merrigan felt that queasy-yet-light sensation wash through her. How long since she had told anyone her real name, besides Bib? "I used to be Princess Merrigan of Avylyn. I was married to the king of Carlion, but when he … well, honestly, my late husband was an idiot, one of the most selfish … well, I thought I loved him. He hung himself in his own lies. Only a fool believes his own lies, don't you think? When Leffisand died, he left me in such a mess and this is what happened when I tried to fix it." She gestured at herself, from head to foot.

"Oh, and here I've been dripping all over you. I'm sorry, Merrigan." Belinda flung her arms around her and rocked them both back and forth for several moments. "I'm so sorry. I swear, no matter what happens, I shall be here for you, and we will find a cure for your curse as well as mine. Let us be friends, shall we?"

She sat back, gripping Merrigan's shoulders, holding her out at arm's length with such a charming, pleading smile on her glistening wet face. How could Merrigan deny her?

Shouting erupted at the far end of the warehouse, where the children were gathering for story time. Merrigan and Belinda held hands as they ran to see what had happened. She wasn't surprised to see Aubrey come running, shouting for everyone to come with him.

"It's happening tonight. Any minute now. We have to be there. I need the children," he shouted, as he turned back to the doorway. "Mistress Mara, please, you have to come with me."

"What's happening tonight?" Merrigan demanded.

"The managers caught the weavers leaving the inn and accused them of leaving the city, and now they're pretending to be hurt, insulted, falsely accused --" Aubrey's handsome, stern, princely face showed through the bony illusion for a moment.

"They're going to unveil the clothes tonight?" she guessed.

In the end, they gathered up all the children over the age of five and under the age of twelve, and left them in their nightshirts and robes. The orphanage had two wagons. They crammed as many children as they could into the wagons, and for good measure tethered them in long lines, anchored to the foster parents, to ensure they didn't lose anyone. Merrigan concentrated on Gilda and the mortal embarrassment that would shatter her young friend, every time she considered this was too much work, useless, a waste of effort.

Their wagons pulled into the courtyard in front of the warehouses and drove into the loading area inside the one on the far right. Moments later, massive freight wagons pulled out from the far left warehouse. In the time it took to unload the children, three freight wagons became a platform, with planks thrown across them and then carpets. Merrigan and Belinda clung to each other as they stared at the streams of people flowing into the open area in front of Gilbrick's warehouses. Guardsmen wearing the livery of several noble houses forced their way through the rapidly growing crowd, making them give way for the nobles to come in and stand on the back side of the platform on the wagons.

"This is awful." Merrigan turned to look for Aubrey. He had to be in a panic over the massive audience gathered for the mortal embarrassment of both Gilda and Gilbrick.

The young man was nowhere to be seen. Then she was busy keeping the children together, stopping the milling crowd from stepping between the children and breaking the tethers. Merrigan held back a rising urge to shriek her frustration, simply because she knew no one would hear her in the rising clamor. Finally, they had to retreat back to the orphanage wagons inside the warehouse. There was no room to stand without being pressed from every side. The children were constantly under threat of being trampled.

Merrigan realized with a bubble of relieved laughter that climbing up into the wagons gave them all a vantage point. The only better place where they could see what was about to happen was to stand on the platform.

The crowd's noise grew louder, then suddenly dropped to a murmur. Belinda let out a cry and pointed, and Merrigan turned, nearly falling off the wagon, to see. Aubrey stood a head taller than many of the people around him, and he led a cloaked figure with his arm wrapped around her. Merrigan knew that had to be Gilda. They edged their way around the perimeter of the crowd, their progress made easier as the surging current of onlookers turned toward movement coming from the first warehouse. Four apprentices came forward, dragging a loading ramp covered in several carpet runners, and leaned it against the far end of the wagon platform. Four more apprentices came from the shadows of the warehouse, supporting a curtained framework. There was a gap between the curtains and the ground of about a foot. In that gap Merrigan saw an old man's legs, bare but for a pair of grand, crimson and sapphire and gold embroidered shoes, like a courtier would wear for the most formal occasions in court.

"Oh, no," she whispered. "Please, please, please tell me they didn't talk the king into trying on the clothes first?"

"No." Aubrey helped Gilda up into the wagon. "The king's clothes are still waiting to be delivered to him. At least, what the weavers say are the king's clothes. We know better, don't we, Mistress Mara?" He grunted as he climbed up into the wagon.

Gilda sobbed, leaning into Aubrey. The cloak's hood fell back enough to show her glistening, tear-swollen face. Merrigan gasped when she saw the red mark of a hand on her friend's cheek.

"Who hit you?" she snapped, and turned to Aubrey.

"The weaver woman." Gilda sniffled and flung herself from Aubrey to Merrigan. "Oh, Mistress Mara, you were so right. How can I ever thank you?"

"Right about what?"

"Well, that odious woman was so furious when she came in to dress me and I wouldn't take off my underclothes and exchange them for the ones she claimed she had brought for me. I kept feeling for them on the rod where she said they were hanging, but they just weren't there. She tried to rip my underclothes off me. She was so angry, and she laughed at me for being a prude and a coward. She said I was being a silly little girl, because we were both women and then -- well, I tried to explain that I was afraid there were people who wouldn't see the clothes and I didn't want to be embarrassed, and then she got really nasty!"

"As if she wasn't before," Aubrey said, a growl adding masculine music to his voice. He wrapped his arm around her shoulders again. "I arrived just as she knocked Gilda to the floor and was trying to tear her clothes off. She said some vile things about it being too late to start using her brain. I honestly thought she would shift into some vile beast. She already seemed to be foaming at the mouth." He sighed and turned to the platform, where the four apprentices carrying the curtained enclosure had come to a stop in the middle, and a hush rippled through the waiting throng. "We can only hope that Master Gilbrick at least had the sense to wear underclothes too, despite what the villainous weaver told him."

"Oh, Aubrey, what if ..." Gilda looked like she might burst into sobs again.

Aubrey met Merrigan's eyes, then he leaped off the wagon and fought his way through the crowd to the platform. He yanked off his outer coat as he went.

The curtain fell when Aubrey was a good twenty feet from the platform. Gilbrick spread his arms wide, turning slowly to display every inch to the waiting crowd, a wide, beaming smile contorting his face into something almost childish and pure in his delight.

Gilda let out a scream and hid her face against Merrigan's shoulder.

The crowd fell so utterly silent, the snorting and stamping of the horses in the stables beyond the warehouse came loudly through the night air.

Merrigan looked, from curiosity, the aching need to know and prove to herself what kind of fool Gilbrick had become. She was both relieved and disappointed.

The weaver had indeed talked the merchant into discarding the long linen shirt that even the upper ranks used for underclothes and sleeping. Gilbrick's legs and arms and chest were bare, bony in some spots, sagging in others, and an odd fish belly white. Merrigan supposed all older men came to look like that.

Chapter Fourteen

However, Gilbrick had retained a combination of loincloth and swaddling that encompassed his hips and went halfway between hips and knees. Merrigan couldn't see much more than that in the few seconds it took for Aubrey to leap at the platform, catch hold of the edge, vault up, and fling his coat around his former employer's middle. He snatched up the fallen curtains and pulled them up around Gilbrick as the impact of their two bodies colliding sent the merchant to his knees.

"You're not wearing anything!" Aubrey shouted, before Gilbrick could recover enough to shout the rebuke visible on his face. "There are no clothes, no magical cloth! You're not wearing anything at all."

"He's not worthy of his place," one of the apprentices holding the now-empty framework cried. A second young man joined in, but no one else. They pointed at Aubrey and laughed, but their laughter choked off under the glares of the other two apprentices.

"They always disliked Aubrey," Gilda whispered.

"They're bigger fools than the others standing there," Merrigan whispered back.

"Mistress Mara, please, tell me the truth. Is my father --"

"He's wearing nothing but that diaper and the curtains Aubrey threw at him."

Gilda whimpered, but managed not to burst into tears again.

Other voices cried out from the crowd, insisting the clothes were glorious, and Aubrey was a fool for claiming nothing was there. They died out just as quickly as they had risen up.

"Do you see anything?" Aubrey shouted, turning to the children in the wagon.

"He's got nuttin' on but a diaper!" a boy cried out with glee. Several of his friends joined in, then others, until all the children had spoken.

Gilbrick's face went so pasty white, he seemed to glow in the encroaching darkness. Even the torches set up to illuminate the grand display faded under the onslaught of embarrassed, then cruel laughter that trickled across the wide courtyard, then grew stronger, until it was a crashing wave. Aubrey wrapped the curtains further around Gilbrick and gestured for the other apprentices. They surrounded their master and escorted him into the shelter of his warehouse.

Merrigan went with Gilda simply because the girl begged her. They were delayed for a while that seemed like forever, until the crowd left and the wagons full of orphans could leave. The two crept through the gathering gloom and darkness as the torches died and people fled the scene of mortal embarrassment with a speed that spoke of their own uneasy feelings. There was no one in the warehouse where Gilbrick had retreated, and another door hung open. They went to Gilbrick's house. Gilda's steps grew steadier and swifter as the two entered her house, went through the reception hall and headed for the stairs to Gilbrick's suite of rooms.

Only Edgar, the most senior of the warehouse managers remained, sitting in a corner with his head in his hands. Aubrey stood by a dressing screen, handing clothes over it to Gilbrick, who raged incoherently. Every once in a while, there would be a thud and his voice would break into heaving sobs, then quiet, then he would rage again.

"He's dismissed everyone," Edgar said. "Every single person who claimed they saw the cloth and then saw the clothes when they were being made. Only reason he didn't dismiss me is because I'm half-blind and he would have known I was lying if I said I saw them." He raised his head from his hands and managed a trembling, old-man smile. "You didn't see the clothes, did you, gal?"

Gilda shook her head. She hugged him, then turned to Aubrey, who watched her somberly. By this time, Gilbrick had taken all the clothes and his raging had slowed to mumbles. Merrigan suspected he was simply too furiously embarrassed to step out and face the few remaining in the room.

"Aubrey ..." Gilda finally dropped the cloak that had enfolded her. She wore the simplest, plainest gown Merrigan had ever seen on her. When she held out her hands, Aubrey caught hold of both of them and went to one knee in front of her. "You are a hero, my Aubrey. How can I ever express my gratitude -- no, not gratitude. I adore you. I wish -- well, we are ruined, our reputation is in tatters, but I wish I had an empire to give you, in thanks."

"If you are ruined, then you have nothing to be thankful for," Aubrey said, and pressed one of her hands against his cheek.

Merrigan thought she might be sick from the overwhelming sweetness filling the room.

Although, to be honest, she admitted a small part of her nausea might come from jealousy. When had anyone looked at her as Aubrey and Gilda looked at each other? When had anyone gone down on one knee to her like that, and risked everything he had, everything he was, to protect her?

"You alone were loyal enough to risk everything," Gilbrick said, coming out from behind the dressing screen with tottering steps. He looked gray, like old, cold porridge. "You spoke the truth, when everyone else was afraid to be honest. Including me. Aubrey, if I had an empire, I would offer it to you. By morning, news of my foolishness, my mortal shame, will have spread through the kingdom, and then through all the other kingdoms where I have done business, where I was admired, where I was considered wise … and I will be ruined. All I can offer you is material wealth, and it is not enough to express my thanks."

Some people, Merrigan decided, came to nobility and a semblance of wisdom too late. Then they overdid it, to the point of foolishness again.

"Sir …" Aubrey blushed slightly. He got up off his knee, but retained his hold on Gilda's hands. "Sir, I have little to offer your daughter other than a warehouse full of orphans I am trying to help raise, but we are rich in love."

"You are rich in the wisdom and honesty of children." Gilbrick tried to smile, but his mouth was so stiff it threatened to shatter. "I beg you, Aubrey, marry my daughter, and I pray your love will take care of her better than I have."

"Shouldn't someone ask Gilda if she wants to marry him?" Merrigan said, though she knew the answer. She had always hated the fables where the princess had no choice in accepting the prince.

"I have always loved Aubrey," Gilda declared. "Ever since we were children, and he gave me …" Her face went white, and her eyes widened more than the eyes of the dogs serving Warden. She dug into the high neckline of her dress and pulled out the locket. "Aubrey?"

"Come with me, my love? If you remember -- my father --" Aubrey barely waited for Gilda to nod. Retaining his grip on her hand, he fled the room, nearly pulling her off her feet.

"Where are they going?" Gilbrick murmured, tottering to the doorway. The clatter of their feet on the winding staircase revealed their progress, leaving the house.

"Sounds like out the front door," Edgar said.

"I imagine to see Aubrey's father, now that the curse has been broken," Merrigan said.

"The curse?" Gilbrick gasped and sagged against the doorframe. "The curse! But how?"

"Gilda told me there was something about making people see. I imagine that little ... debacle a while ago fit that requirement."

~~~~~

The weaver and his wife managed to escape during the uproar as the news of the clothes that weren't really there spread across the city. Hundreds of people who had loudly proclaimed the beauty of the cloth and the perfection of the design of the clothes were mocked, brutalized in public opinion for days afterward. Tales of fist fights and friendships irreparably destroyed, apprentices dismissed, businesses shattered, advocates fired, and even officials deposed from their positions ran rampant. Merrigan was heartily sick of the whole subject. For a while, she feared that anyone who made their living weaving cloth or making clothes would be gathered up like the worst criminals and ejected from the kingdom.

Still, it was easy to ignore the uproar in the rest of the city because the warehouse had turned into a wonderland, thanks to the generosity of Prince Aubrey.

The morning after the debacle of the invisible clothes, the warehouse occupants were awakened shortly after dawn when the massive doors opened with a loud bang. Even the most adventuresome of the children were slow to roll out of their bed shelves at the disturbance, because no one had gone to bed before midnight, after all the excitement. Nasius and the other adults called orders to the children to stay in their beds and asked the older ones to watch over the littlest ones, while they ran in their robes and slippers to see who had intruded.

Three dozen servants in royal livery spilled through the doors, carrying crates and bales of clothes and bedding, pillows,
~~~~~

mattresses, books, toys, dishes, and swaddled cauldrons of hot food, fresh from the royal kitchens. Hot food such as the children had never seen in their lives. While the foster parents stood and stared, their mouths dropping open a little more with each new gift that appeared, a tall, handsome young man directed the distribution. He was evidently a prince, even without the thin gold band that sat at a rakish angle across his forehead. His square jaw and high cheekbones, green-blue eyes that glistened like jewels, the pure gold of his hair, the flawless complexion, the sternness of his mouth that seemed to be joyous at the same time, and the trumpet clarity of his voice. Anyone could tell he was pure royal blood, even without the rich clothes and the king's crest of a dragon coiled around a stack of books that adorned his surcoat. The foster parents bowed and curtseyed to him when the bounty had been put away and the royal servants left the warehouse again, and only the prince stayed behind. Merrigan stayed back, arms crossed over her chest, caught between laughter and delight and scorn, and she waited.

Some blindness obviously hasn't been cured, Bib remarked.

Honestly, didn't anyone remember what she had told them last night? They had discussed the entire revelation for what seemed like hours, before they could get the children to go to bed.

"Aubrey!" one of the littlest girls shrieked, when she had finally pushed her way through the crowd of children. Of course, they had disobeyed orders to stay out of sight and stood all around the kitchen area, silent with awe at the wonders given to them. The child giggled, her voice like bells chiming, and leaped at him. "My Aubrey!" She laughed as Aubrey lifted her up high, twirling her around, and then hugged her close.

After that, it was chaos as the children gathered around, wanting to touch him, hug him, tug on his royal clothes and make sure they were real. The hot food had started to cool by the time someone got enough sense to pull out the new dishes, enough for everyone, and serve up the food. Merrigan suspected no one even noticed, in the wonder of having sausages enough for everyone to have two each, and bowls full of a rich, fruity, hot cereal turned golden with honey, and bowls slopping over with cream, not milk that had to be mixed with water to make sure everyone could have a cup. There were muffins and a dozen different egg dishes and kippers and kidneys and sour, thick fruit soup and other dishes that

Merrigan could barely remember from the days of more-than-enough in the palace of Avylyn. The children ate until some of them looked a little green from the surfeit of riches. Aubrey's rich new clothes were rather wrinkled and smeared with breakfast by the time everyone had had a chance to hug him and get close enough to look in his eyes and make sure that yes, even though he looked so different, he was still their beloved Aubrey.

Gilda and Aubrey married two moons later. Merrigan and Belinda and their girls had the honor of making the royal wedding garments, for them and most of the court. They barely had time to finish all the clothes, but no other seamstresses or tailors in the entire city would do. The orphan warehouse had the protection of the Crown Prince, and everyone wanted to patronize the place.

No word had come yet of the fate of the weaver and his wife, but Merrigan had the satisfaction of receiving several letters from Warden and Miles and Quincy. Every sea captain and every port master and the coastal patrol ships had been put on alert, to ensure they didn't cross over the ocean to continue their deceptive practices. She was also pleased to hear how her friends were faring as they settled down into marriage and their chosen lives. And she wept a little, when all of them asked, with every letter, when she would return and visit them. For some odd reason, they all credited her with them finding their happiness and their true loves.

~~~~~

The day after the royal wedding, Belinda woke up everyone with a mad dash to the garderobe, where she clung to the wooden seat and heaved and gagged for a good ten minutes before the convulsions of nausea stopped. Merrigan had Lily go to the kitchen, to verify her suspicions. Sure enough, the cooking crew had been at work for half an hour and the ingredients that had been soaking overnight were just starting to bubble in the enormous cauldrons. Breakfast that morning was peas porridge, although certainly a much higher quality peas porridge than the orphans had eaten in the past.

"I don't understand," she sighed, once Belinda had curled up in her shelf bed again, after changing into a fresh nightgown. The one she had worn to bed was soaked with sweat. "How could you smell it from the other side of the building? And how could you have such a bad reaction? We had peas porridge for breakfast four
~~~~~

days ago. Gretchen spilled some on you when you helped feed her, and you didn't get sick."

"Princes," Belinda said, her voice reduced to a rasp like sand. "There are princes close enough to wake up the other half of the spell. When they get close enough to me, and I'm close to anything with peas, it sort of starts an avalanche of magic that just gets stronger as they follow it and get closer to me."

"What can stop it?" Merrigan had the awful feeling she knew.

"The ingredients of the triggered spell have to be separated," Bib said, his voice muffled under the covers of Merrigan's bed, which was end-to-end with Belinda's shelf bed. Their pillows were separated only by a slanting board that supported the shelving around them.

The three of them had been up late the night before, talking quietly, remembering other royal weddings they had attended or stories of royal weddings Bib had gleaned from history books. In the two moons since Belinda had come to the orphanage, they had become quite good friends. It was amazing all the things they had in common, their opinions on certain royal traditions, their frustration with magic spells and interfering enchanters and Fae, and the dictates of fashion.

"Separated as in …?"

"I have to leave." Belinda's voice crackled, but she admirably held off the tears. "Actually, it would be more accurate to say I have to run. The problem is, at this time of the morning, anywhere I run, chances are good someone is cooking peas porridge. But the longer I stay here, the closer they could get, drawn by my reaction to the peas porridge, which reacts to them getting closer, which makes me sicker, which just makes the beacon drawing them closer even brighter, which -- "

The panic blanching her face warned Merrigan in time, so she scuttled backwards and only got a heel in her chest when Belinda leaped from the bed and dashed for the garderobe again.

"Unfortunately, she's right," Bib said.

"How hard can it be for even a prince who celebrated too much last night to figure out that she's here?" Merrigan growled. "We should have thought of that -- a royal wedding draws useless second and third and fourth sons like …"

She scrambled for a fitting simile. Flies to honey did not suit.

Flies to a corpse, however, did. Yet, hearing Belinda give one last loud, dry heave, she didn't want to say it. She liked Belinda more than any other princess she had ever met. The girl had gumption and a lot of common sense and a dry, sharp wit. The stories she had to tell about playing tricks on her younger sisters were hilarious. Especially the rather messy, embarrassing tricks.

This time, Belinda didn't have to change her nightgown when she stopped heaving. The girls were awake by this time and they surrounded her with sympathy and helped to bundle her back into bed. One offered to let Belinda sleep with her doll, another offered to run to the nearest bake shop -- a long trip, even though she was one of the swiftest runners among all the orphans -- to find her something for breakfast. By now, everyone knew peas made Belinda ill.

Everyone knew ...

"Oh!" Merrigan could barely keep back a stream of curses that wanted to fall from her lips. She didn't know whether to be grateful for the time on the ocean with Quincy's sailors, or not.

"I don't know," Belinda said, when the girls had gone off to breakfast and the three of them were alone again. Merrigan had just explained what had occurred to her. "How could we have kept something like this secret? Children are curious, and they talk, and everyone thinks I'm a child too, so they have to wonder why I don't have to eat the same things they do. But I don't think we're in that much trouble. To find out that someone who is allergic to peas porridge is here, those dolts chasing me would have to ask lots of questions. Those princes have to win a kingdom through marriage because they don't have the ambition or cleverness to earn a kingdom the old-fashioned way. Killing ogres and dragons. Performing twenty hard labors for a Fae queen. Digging a kingdom out of the bottom of the sea or something else that requires some guts and brains and sweat." She sighed.

"How long have they been chasing you, Princess?" Bib asked.

"Oh, let's see, I ran away when I was ... Oh." She lost a little of the color she had regained. "You're right. If they're still holding on in the chase after five years, they might have learned to do some hard work. Or at the very least, they're desperate enough to listen to gossip, or even talk to people. Anyone they meet on the street."

"How likely do they think you are to hide among orphans?"

Merrigan asked.

"How many fables are there of groups of children under enchantments?" She shrugged. "I've hidden anywhere I could, disguised as any number of things. I was a goose girl, a miller's apprentice, a milkmaid, a gardener. I even took shelter among some friendly trolls for almost an entire year. You would think the smell would make me invulnerable to the scent of peas cooking. Those wretched princes found me when someone planted an entire field of peas over the trolls' underground lair. At harvest time, someone cooked freshly harvested peas and there was enough magic to make me ill. So ill, even the trolls didn't want me around." She let out a sigh that seemed to make her deflate among her blankets. "They won't stop until they find me. How many princesses can there be in this city?"

"The day after a royal wedding?" Bib chuckled. "You were in the palace, finishing up Gilda's dress. Didn't you glimpse the guest book?"

"I did." Merrigan shook her head. "It's pitiful, all the women who hold tight to the title of princess even though they're so many generations removed from the throne, a plague would have to wipe out half a city for them to have a chance to wear a crown."

"Look on the bright side, then. Those princes could be drawn off on a dozen wild goose chases, following all those paper-thin princesses as they head home."

"Many of them will be horribly disappointed because yet another royal wedding passed, and some prince didn't snatch them up. Although that's a thought. Some of them might have come here to find a royal bride, any royal bride, no matter how far from the throne. Five years is a long wait. They aren't getting any younger."

"Neither am I," Belinda said with a sigh. "You'd think Father would have the sense to give up on me and make one of my younger sisters the heir, more likely to attract a prince with the strength to take care of the kingdom. Bythia and Barbarina ..." She shuddered. "Even with all the magic those two learned, Father would never be persuaded to make one of them his heir. It's sad, really. A wicked enchantress in charge might just make our tiny little backwater kingdom a popular place to visit."

"Excuse me?"

"Oh, it makes perfect sense," Bib said. "The presence of evil magic tends to draw the darker sorts of magical beasts. Even if they don't immediately start to feast on farm animals and kidnap children to enslave, their presence would in turn draw adventurers and heroes. Along with them would come all the hangers-on, the support teams, the armorers and healers and minstrels looking for another heroic ballad to write to launch them into fame and a comfortable retirement. After them would come the admirers and hopeful dreamers and the boys who want to apprentice with heroes. It's somewhat of a trade guild all in itself, and profitable."

"Nonsense," Merrigan said with a sniff.

Still, she couldn't shake the thought, and the speculations that followed. Leffisand, she had to admit, had done some despicable things in his quest to consolidate his power and secure his throne. If he had continued in his course of evil deeds and schemes, would Carlion have eventually attracted magical monsters that attracted heroes to fight them? And in the wake of the heroes, bring in people who had to pay for inns to stay in and food to eat and new clothes and all that went with travelers and armor and battles?

The three talked for another hour, weighing options. The possibilities of the princes following a departing wedding guest. The chances they would realize their runaway princess stayed in Alliburton. And just how long until peas were again served in the orphanage. The effects on Belinda faded as soon as the children ate their breakfast. The question was if enough damage had been done to bring the hunter princes into this quarter of the city.

"We can't rely on your disguise to stay stable," Merrigan said, when Belinda had recovered enough to get washed up and dressed. "I don't think you should leave the orphanage for the next few days. Just in case."

"That's it," Bib said. His pages riffled back and forth, loudly enough to make Merrigan and Belinda flinch. "A disguise -- no, not a disguise, but a decoy! We'll need to borrow one of Gilda's tiaras."

"What?" both princesses said in perfect, shocked unison.

"It's utterly brilliant," the book continued, ignoring the stunned looks the two exchanged over his pages.

For all his wisdom and the access to written knowledge, the book couldn't possibly understand. Tiaras and crowns were enchanted. They were stolen and recovered. They were inherited. They were not borrowed. It simply wasn't done.

"The spell is set to find *a* princess, am I correct?" Bib continued, oblivious to their reaction. "It's not tuned specifically to you, correct?"

"I don't think so. It's been so long since it latched onto me, but ..." Belinda's eyes got wide and a slow smile wiped away the disgusted twist that had held her mouth.

"What am I missing?" Merrigan demanded.

"We let those idiots find a princess. A real princess. Just not the one they're looking for. If I'm right, and the spell specifies *a* princess tangled in a spell, and not specifically Belinda," Bib continued, "then won't they simply ignore the spell when it keeps insisting that *a* princess is here, and they find one, right here at this sewing table, and she isn't Belinda?"

"Me?" Her voice squeaked alarmingly. A totally ridiculous wave of fear swept over her. "But I don't look like -- I'm not -- this isn't my face anymore. I'm -- well, let's be honest, I'm a wrinkled, shriveled, white-haired, crooked old hag! With warts. What?" she snapped, when Belinda frowned thoughtfully.

"But Merrigan, you're not white-haired or crooked," Belinda protested. "You stand quite straight. And you have no warts. Isn't that odd? Bib, have you noticed ... well, maybe I was just distraught when I first arrived, but I could swear Merrigan isn't so ... so wrinkled anymore. And her hair is a lovely dark silver, streaked with sable. It's really hard to see under that cap she keeps it tucked up in all the time, but --"

"Stop talking about me as if I'm a dressmaker's mannequin."

"We need a mirror."

"We need a crown," Bib said. "That cap will come in handy. The moment that tracking spell brings one of those dunderheads stumbling in here, you stand up and give them some royal scorn. Whip your cap off, and show them your tiara. That spell will verify you speak the truth when you announce you're a princess. But since you're not *their* princess, well, they'll have to go away. The princess they want will be right there in the room with them, and they'll never notice."

"Announce I'm a princess." Merrigan's voice cracked. She shuddered. Maybe now she was getting sick. Was it possible for the tracking spell to have transferred from Belinda, or just widened its influence to affect her? "Do I have to tell them ... who I am?"

"Oh, Merrigan." Belinda wrapped her arms around her. The warmth and sympathy felt incredibly good. "Of course not. They don't deserve to know your name, and I understand completely. It's rather embarrassing, being under a curse. I can't understand why someone as wonderful as you would ever be put under a curse."

The laughter bubbling in Merrigan's throat had an acid taint. Just when she thought Belinda wasn't a featherhead, she had to say something idiotic. Her, Merrigan of Avylyn, the royal brat, the terror of the court? The princess who drove away increasingly desperate or masochistic suitors before she duped herself into believing Leffisand rescued her? Wonderful?

"No, of course not." Bib's glee faded, his tone turned thoughtful. "No, don't embarrass yourself, Mi'Lady. It should be enough for the deception to announce you're a princess. Slap them down with all the royal elegance you've been denied for so long. But first, we need a tiara. The simpler the better. What princess in exile, living in impecunious circumstances, would have more than just a circlet indicating her royal blood?"

"Hard to keep clean," Merrigan offered. Funny how hard it had been to breathe for a few moments. "Very difficult to keep on your head when you're fleeing ogres and bandits."

"That's the spirit." Belinda chuckled and squeezed Merrigan close.

Gilda and Aubrey had left on their wedding trip, but King Auberg was in the palace and more than delighted to help Merrigan. He had become something of a grandfather to the orphanage. He took such mischievous delight in coming to the warehouse in disguise, loaded down with treats for the children. Books for the studious ones. Tools for those headed for a trade. Wooden practice swords, bows and arrows for the boys who wanted to join the city guard or the army. Ribbons and trinkets for the girls who were old enough to sigh over such things.

"Merrigan of ... of Avylyn?" Auberg repeated, when she finished detailing her request. She had brought Bib with her to the palace for their private meeting. A talking magical book was always a guarantee that her story would be taken as truth. "Oh, my dear princess, I have indeed heard what has been happening with Carlion and Jardien and your father's kingdom, but ... the tales are that you ... well, there are several mad women wandering the mountains, claiming to be you. Rather vicious, foul-tempered women."

"Far too easy for people to believe those women are me, you mean." Her face felt warm enough, she imagined she glowed redder than the coals in the fireplace on the other side of the room. Merrigan was grateful for this private audience. She didn't want word to get back to anyone who knew her, even if it took years for the gossip to trickle across the continent.

"Mi'Lady," Bib said, his tones subdued, "if I may be so bold, you are no longer you. It takes a heavy grindstone to turn wheat into fine flour, but the results are admired by everyone. I imagine if flour could think, it would be delighted at ... well, perhaps that metaphor isn't quite working, but --"

"I know what you mean. Thank you, Bib. You have always been my truest friend." Merrigan shared a smile with King Auberg. "I'm not here for my benefit, Majesty, but for Princess Belinda. If we could verify the princes hunting her were indeed here for the wedding, and determine how many remain on the hunt, that would help us ever so much."

"Determine who is still here in Alliburton, to know how much threat remains." He nodded, a decisive movement that belied his thinning white hair and sagging jowls.

In the two moons since the curse broke, a general sense of haziness and distraction had lifted from the entire city. Merrigan had learned that the king hadn't really been distracted by the hunt to find and free his missing son. Rather, King Auberg had discerned early that the spell was thickest around the palace, and had prudently removed the heart of the government to another city. Whoever set the curse had wanted to cripple the kingdom, not just make the royal family suffer. The curse was flexible, set to discern where the most government activity was, and then settle around that physical location. King Auberg's ministers and officers and secretaries had to pick up everything and move to another city every ten moons or so. The rumors that the king was useless and letting others run the kingdom for him were partly to satisfy the enemy, and keep him from checking the progress of the curse. Now, the seat of the government was back in the palace. King Auberg was a man reborn, alert and decisive and fixing all that had unfortunately been allowed to lie neglected for years.

"Come with me, Princess." He stood and offered her his bent elbow, then shook his head. "Forgive me. How rude. If you don't mind, Sir Bib?" He scooped up the book from the stool next to Merrigan, and cradled it against his chest with one arm.

"You honor me, Majesty," Bib responded, as Auberg offered his elbow again to Merrigan.

Her face warmed with pleasure as she tucked her hand into the crook of his elbow. He escorted her through the wide archway into the next room of the royal apartments. They stopped in front of a massive wardrobe, with three sets of doors. King Auberg bowed Merrigan into a chair, set Bib down next to her, then tugged a long chain from inside his shirt and unlocked the middle set of doors. This section of the wardrobe was all shelves full of carved wooden boxes. He brought down one long box, about eight inches tall, and set it on a footstool in front of Merrigan, then took a key from a hidden panel in the left door and unlocked the box. Inside were five tiaras, varying in grandeur and beauty.

"These belonged to my beloved wife," he explained, after bowing his head over the box and its contents for several moments. "I intend to give them to Gilda for her birthdays, and when she and Aubrey have their first child, but I believe my Rosamund would be pleased to donate one to the cause of defending a princess in distress." He beckoned for Merrigan to join him.

The crown they chose was a deceptively simple one, of pink gold woven into a wreath. Emerald dust spotted the leaves, and tiny flowers made of chips of sapphires and rubies peeked out from among the leaves, creating a rainbow shimmer when the light hit it just right. Auberg smiled with a hint of tears as he raised the circlet and nodded to Merrigan. She tugged off the cap that covered her braided hair, bowed her head, and her heart seemed to stutter in those few seconds before the delicate weight of the wreath rested on her head.

"Ah, yes," Auberg whispered. He rested a gentle hand on her shoulder and guided her a few steps to the right. Another key opened the right set of wardrobe doors, and Merrigan flinched as she was confronted with a full-length mirror. She tried to focus just on the circlet in her hair, but she couldn't help noticing …

"Bib, you were right," she whispered. In awe, she touched her hair. Dark silver and sable had replaced the thin mass of snowy white. When she washed her hair, she tried not to look at it, doing everything by feel. Granted, there weren't any mirrors in the orphanage, and she hadn't missed them. Her braids had thickened from bodice laces to plump sausages. She wondered that she hadn't noticed the change when she brushed and braided her hair every morning and evening.

Merrigan knew she was wasting time, so she turned her gaze away, but not before she saw other changes in her appearance. Belinda was indeed right -- she stood taller, straighter, and had fewer wrinkles. Her nose didn't look quite so much like a hawk's beak. Her jaws weren't nutcrackers. And no warts.

"They might just believe me," she said, her voice crackling a little, as she turned to face King Auberg. "When the princes track down Belinda. When I take my cap off and they see the crown, they just might believe me when I tell them I'm a princess."

"Of course they will. Because you are indeed a princess. A real princess." His smile went crooked and he patted her shoulder. "I daresay, more of a princess now than you ever were."

Merrigan didn't want to think too long or hard on just what he meant. Like so many other things she had thought about and learned since Clara cursed her, she knew she wouldn't like these new revelations about herself.

By this time, everyone in the city seemed to know Mistress Mara on sight, friend of Prince Aubrey and Princess Gilda. Merrigan's face and neck actually hurt from smiling and nodding greetings to everyone who called her by name on the long walk back to the orphanage. She wished she had accepted the carriage King Auberg had offered her, but she had decided to walk to attract as little attention as possible. That had been wasted effort.

"Look on the bright side," Belinda offered, when she and Merrigan and Bib were alone just before dinner. "You proved that it won't easily fall out of your hair." She lightly reached up to touch the circlet, still sitting securely among Merrigan's braids.

Merrigan wrinkled up her nose at her, and a moment later the two shared some giggles. Ordinarily, she wouldn't be quite so lighthearted about being responsible for the lovely old circlet, especially when it was very obvious it had deep sentimental value for King Auberg. However, Bib was the perfect guardian for the treasure when Merrigan wouldn't be wearing it. Just like other things he had hidden in his pages for safekeeping, the circlet would be safe, with no damage to it or his pages.

Their mirth buoyed them up against the depressing news that came the next afternoon, when a guardsman in palace livery delivered a thick packet of papers from the king. Of the fourteen princes who had been hunting Belinda, nine had come to the royal wedding. Two had targeted princesses who were the only siblings of unmarried kings, meaning they could inherit the throne. Both princesses were rather long in the tooth and hadn't been considered beauties even in their heyday. Belinda declared that served her unwanted suitors right. Seven lingered in Alliburton. King Auberg had assigned trustworthy men to keep track of the princes, and he promised to send daily reports on their activities.

Merrigan thought they were very well off, considering the circumstances. Forewarned was forearmed. Then Belinda picked up another piece of paper from the packet. This was a list of royalty currently without a throne. King Auberg's secretary who had compiled the information noted that while the princes, princesses, dukes and other assorted nobility were of no threat to the runaway princess, he thought it worthwhile to watch their activities until they left Alliburton.

"Oh, no, no, no," Belinda murmured, staring at several lines at the top of the list.

"What?" Merrigan thought she might have to tear the paper to get it out of the other princess's hand.

Belinda's eyes filled with tears. She handed Merrigan the paper, slumped back in her seat, covered her face with her hands, and trembled as the tears dripped through her fingers.

Merrigan read through the list. Thanks to interfering Fae and enchanters, evil wizards and other majjians, the list of royalty deprived of their thrones stayed relatively short. They won someone else's throne, regained their own kingdom, vanished, or they renounced their thrones altogether, to pursue a simple life. She read the list three times, her gaze skipping over a specific line.

Stop being such a ninny. For good measure, she clenched the fist not holding the paper, digging her nails into her palm.

Chapter Fifteen

The pain helped, surprisingly. Merrigan read *Sylvanglade*, with a squeezing sensation around her heart. Then she saw Prince Bayl's name and understood entirely. Poor Belinda. How it had to pain her, to know the prince she loved was in Alliburton. She never saw him during the wedding festivities. Even if he had looked right at her, the disguise spells interfered. She tried to think of something she could do or say to distract Belinda, to --

Wait. Had she read correctly? She checked the list.

Prince Bryan of Sylvanglade was also on the list.

The brothers were traveling together.

Merrigan put the paper down and smoothed it out flat on the table for good measure. The slight trembling in her hands, the hollow sensation in her chest, made absolutely no sense whatsoever. What was wrong with her?

"I wonder how soon dinner will be ready," she murmured, and reached over to pat Belinda's shoulder. "We both need something in our stomachs, or at least some hot, strong tea, with plenty of honey. It's been a trying day for both of us."

"Oh, Merrigan," Belinda whispered, and knuckled her eyes dry as she tried to smile. "I am so thankful you're my friend. What would I ever do without you?"

Merrigan bit back a tart response that Belinda was in a sorry state indeed, to consider her a friend and be grateful.

You're too hard on yourself, Mi'Lady, Bib retorted, his voice stern and bracing in her mind. *You've put yourself in the arrow's sight, so to speak, for her sake. Only a true friend would do that. I daresay you've become worthy of that pretty bauble you're wearing.*

Dear Bib, always thinking better of me than I deserve.

The shivering sensation in her chest stopped. Merrigan managed to laugh at herself for nearly forgetting to put her cap back on, to hide the circlet, before she and Belinda went to the kitchen for that tea they both needed.

~~~~~
~~~~~

The problem with the decoy plan was that it did them no good if the princes hunting Belinda didn't come close enough to actually see Merrigan. After three days, King Auberg's men reported that the princes were still in the city despite most of the other wedding guests having departed. The "most" qualifier bothered Merrigan. Belinda had whispered Bayl's name several times in her sleep. The trio decided they had to do something. Bad enough that rainy, sloppy fall weather kept the children indoors, but waiting for the enemy to wander in was nerve-wracking.

"You need bait," Nasius said, when they listened to Bib and brought the old philosopher into the plan and the team. "Send up a beacon, so to speak."

Belinda shivered a little, and her throat convulsed in anticipation.

The words didn't have to be said. Merrigan was thankful that Nasius had joined them in the plotting. It was left to him to have the largest cooking cauldron filled with dried peas and put on to soak, to make the richest pot of pea soup the warehouse orphanage had ever cooked. Belinda blanched when the pot of soaked peas and seasonings and chunks of salt pork went on the fire. When she broke out in a sweat, Merrigan checked, and found the water had started bubbling. The ripples of convulsions in Belinda's throat made Merrigan queasy, just watching her.

They tried to sketch new clothes designs, just to calm their nerves. Sewing required steady hands they didn't have. The squeals of the children at their games made them jump, even though it was pleasant to hear them laughing and shouting and jumping and running into the shelf frames. The drumming of the downpour outside made pleasant, almost soothing counterpoint to the sound. From the corner of her eye, Merrigan saw several little bodies lift up the curtains over her and Belinda's bed shelves to climb in and hide.

"No. Not happening today. Not a chance," she muttered, getting up from the long sewing table with enough force to knock her chair backwards, and earned a shriek from Belinda. "Sorry," she threw back over her shoulder, and stomped over to the shelves. She yanked up the curtain and saw two little girls just sitting there, eyes wide, and getting wider as they waited for punishment to descend on them. The little white-blond girl clutched at the hands of her dusky-skinned partner-in-mischief.

The angry words died in Merrigan's mouth, and left a bitter taste behind. She could only imagine the fury twisting her face. What made the neatness of her bed more important than the children having fun? They were stuck indoors. It was cold outside, sloppy wet, and the noise of the rain drumming on the high roof had made lesson time difficult.

"You don't want to be on the bottom shelf," she said. "They won't expect you to hide higher than your beds."

Their giggles washed away a knot forming in her belly. Totally inexplicable tears blurred her eyes when they held up their arms, asking for help climbing up two shelves higher.

Belinda shook off her growing nausea to come over and help the little ones hide. She slipped coming down from the shelf above Merrigan's bed, and her left foot swung out and then in, trying to find purchase. It banged against the magic box, which had been disturbed by the little girls scrambling across Merrigan's bedding.

"I'm an idiot," Merrigan said, staring at the box while Belinda finally got her foot back into the notch in the shelf support bar and climbed down.

She snatched up the box and carried it over to the sewing table. Bib lay surrounded by a new batch of books sent over from King Auberg's library. The magic book was so busy absorbing more knowledge, he didn't notice Merrigan right away.

"We never thoroughly explored Morton's gifts, did we?" Merrigan said, tipping up the lid. She reached in and carefully removed the things she had used before, especially the sticks for the magically renewing fire.

"If you mean we never found the bottom of the box, no." Bib explained the box and the story behind it to Belinda, while Merrigan dug, removing one thing after another. Most items on top were her own, non-magical, simply put in the box because it could hold anything and everything.

Every time Merrigan found something she didn't recognize, she put it on Bib's open pages for him to analyze. A ring that, according to the ancient writing on both sides of the band, allowed the wearer to understand the language of the birds. Limited to northern climate birds, Bib added after further reading. Another ring for southern birds. A third ring for breathing underwater. A headscarf that improved hearing. Socks that allowed the wearer to leap as high as the third story of a building.

"Very useful for thieves," Belinda remarked, with a trembling smile.

"I have the feeling Morton used us to get potentially troublesome magic items out of Seafoam, along with helping us," Bib added.

Merrigan searched the box faster. Any moment now, the soup's influence would take Belinda from sweating to heaving. The whole purpose of searching through all the minor magical trinkets was to find something to prevent the nausea. Merrigan finally explained what she was doing, after finding a magic waxed paper bag that kept pouring out sweets until they had a pile taller than the box. As far as Bib could tell, the sweets in assorted flavors and colors had no magical properties other than soothing sore throats.

"But what if stopping me from being sick somehow ... I don't know, interferes with the tracking spell?" Belinda said.

"You don't know unless you ask." Merrigan wished with all her might that they would find something they could use, right this moment, as she reached into the box.

Belinda fled for the garderobe just as Merrigan's fingers touched a soft fold of cloth. She pulled the small bundle out and unrolled it to find a simple, conical sleeping cap. A note was pinned to it in Morton's distinctive, neat blocky handwriting: *Do not use when you are alone.* Merrigan put it inside Bib's pages for him to analyze.

"It is just what it appears to be -- a cap for sleeping. Very dangerous," the book announced, as Belinda came back to the table, looking a little white around the mouth, and the hair at her temples dark with sweat.

"Dangerous how? Could we use it as a weapon?" Merrigan said.

"Only if we could convince our enemies to put it on, then for the next man in line to take it off the sleeping man and put it on his head, and so on."

"But the first man would just wake up, so what good would it do?" Belinda said, stroking the long tassel of silky black threads.

"Taking off the cap doesn't wake you." Bib ruffled his pages so the cap slid off.

Merrigan shuddered, grateful Morton had put that note on the cap. What if she had put the cap on just to keep her head warm, say if she was caught in the rain?

"Surely there has to be some way of reversing the sleeping spell. Who would make such a thing?" Belinda wiped her shaking hand on her skirts.

"Reverse." Merrigan could almost laugh with the relief that shot through her. "Bib, if we turned the cap inside out and put it back on someone's head, would that wake them?"

"It should," the book said after a moment. "Turn it inside out and put it back on me." He sighed loudly, riffling his pages from top to bottom down one side. "I do hate these limitations to my powers of analysis. Someday, there's going to be something very sticky and wet and staining that I will have to study, and I dread thinking of the damage to my papers when that happens."

Belinda and Merrigan smiled, but neither could laugh. Merrigan's fingers itched as she turned the cap inside out and laid it on Bib's open pages. After a few moments, he announced that yes, she was right -- reversing the cap reversed the sleeping spell.

"You don't sneeze and you don't heave when you're asleep," Merrigan said, handing the cap to Belinda.

"But I've awakened myself ... Oh. Yes. When I'm deeply asleep, during the middle of the night, I'm not sick. The spell only starts working when I'm waking."

"You'll be more comfortable while we wait, and hopefully the bait will still work. Besides," Merrigan added, as Belinda walked over to her bed shelf and lifted the curtain, "we can't have you sneezing like mad when those idiots walk into our trap."

"You are brilliant," Belinda said as she lay down. "What did I ever do to deserve a friend like you?" She settled herself, tugged her skirts straight, and pulled up the blanket. She pulled the cap down over her thick curls and sighed. "Oh, I feel bet ..." A soft snore escaped her before her eyes finished closing.

"You're under a curse," Merrigan murmured as she stepped over to pull the curtain down to hide her from sight. "That's what you did to have a friend like me."

Later, when the peas had been boiled soft and chunks of ham and carrots and onions were added, Nasius suggested they put several bowls of soup around Belinda's bed, to increase the spell's reaction. A few snorts issued from the sleeper when the clouds of steam from the bowls first seeped through the curtain, then she quieted again. A far as Merrigan could tell, the other princess was comfortable, no suffering from the proximity of peas.

"What if the sleeping spell totally cancels the spell to bring the princes to her?" she said to Bib, when lunchtime passed and still no foreign princes had invaded the warehouse.

"They're dilettantes," he responded. "The rain only stopped an hour ago. My guess is that they've stayed indoors this whole time." He chuckled, a delightfully malicious sound. "You'd think that all the privations of hunting for so long would weed out the weak and unworthy, so that in the end, only one prince would be left, who has become worthy through effort, and Belinda would be happy to let him carry her back home to her father's kingdom. With all the warping done to her disguise spells and the quite frankly nasty, childish nature of the detection spell, I'm of the opinion that these young men are holding on out of vanity. They can't believe a princess wouldn't want them. Still, their basic nature is showing, when they won't hunt in the rain and cold."

"Meanwhile, Belinda suffers. Why do little girls want to be princesses? It certainly isn't fun or comfortable to be the target of magic spells. Not even for the lovely clothes."

"Especially when you have the skill to make them for yourself."

"True."

They were still laughing together when a ruckus erupted at the other end of the warehouse. Children cried out in alarm. Merrigan lost her breath at the jolt of fury that shot through her. There were plenty of older boys and foster fathers to defend them, and guardsmen nearby to come at the first call, and alarm horns to sound, thanks to Aubrey. Only a fool would break into an orphanage, and risk being buried under a wave of shrieking, kicking, punching little bodies.

Despite hearing the blat of a horn to summon the guardsmen, Merrigan headed for the front of the warehouse. Her travels had taught her that the most vicious brutes and bullies shared a weakness: terror of little old ladies who reminded them of their grandmothers.

"I know she's here," a nasally tenor voice shouted, as stomping, booted feet approached the dividing wall between the dining and study tables and the kitchen. "Just see all the magic swirling around that huge pot of pea soup. It's a sure sign."

"Sure sign of what?" Merrigan demanded, calling up the chill, sharp-edged mannerisms she had once used to get her way. She stopped on the far side of the kitchen and tipped her head back, straightened her shoulders and held her hands down straight at her side. These obnoxious third-class princes were about to learn what it meant to be in a battle royal.

She barely restrained herself from reacting. The prince in the lead of the hunting party had been all too right. Swirls of pea-green sparkles spun in the air over the cauldron of leftover pea soup, like a particularly thick cloud of insane horseflies.

"The enchantress said if there was interference, then she found a majjian to help her." Another prince pushed to the front of the group. He looked enough like the first prince to be a brother or cousin, with long ferret noses and stringy hair that had probably been fashionably curled before they went out into the damp and wind. They both wore shades of muddy crimson. "Does she look like a witch to you?"

"Has to be a witch," the first prince said. The others in the group muttered agreement. None of them moved any closer. "Where is the princess? Hand her over, and you won't get hurt."

"Hand her over?" Merrigan nearly laughed. Her voice flung icicles in the air. "Who are you to give orders to me? Do you fancy yourselves to be princes?"

A few of the idiots actually nodded, some with wobbly grins, like puppies praised for doing the right trick entirely by accident.

"Do you fancy yourselves worthy of a princess?"

Merrigan heard the stomping of feet and the familiar bass tones of the captain of the guardsmen on the day shift. She forced a scowl when she actually felt a little wobbly in the knees from relief. For this deception to succeed, they needed to get rid of the princes as soon as she had convinced them they were hugely mistaken. They had to leave before they had time to think, to try to look around the warehouse. Belinda's enchanted sleep helped enormously, but the guardsmen would clinch the deal. She hoped.

"But we've -- we've been hunting a long time," the second prince said, his head turning back and forth between his leader and Merrigan. "We've earned her."

"All of you? Marry *one* princess? Is that what the enchanter who gave you that spell --" She flicked her fingers in disdain at the magic sparkles, spinning frantically over the cooling soup. "Is that what he told you?"

"She, actually," another prince said. The others glared at him and he retreated out of sight behind their slightly broader shoulders.

"Oh, I see now. An enchantress decided to *help* you bumblers find a princess?" Merrigan jammed her fists into her hips and stomped forward. She nearly lost her scowl in laughter when the knot of them backed up.

All hail the undeniable power of little old ladies, Bib said with a vicious chuckle that bounced around in her mind and nearly shattered her façade.

"I have some sad news for you, little boys." Merrigan glanced past them, to dozens of children with eyes wide and mouths falling open in astonishment. Five guardsmen stood among them, grinning with malicious delight. She knew then, these princes had made a nuisance of themselves while they hunted for "their princess."

She took one step forward. They took one step back, tripping over each other. Giggles arose from the children, seen and unseen.

"The enchantress was playing games with your teeny tiny minds. She wasn't helping you, if this princess was ever yours to begin with. Any enchantress worth her salt wouldn't help you buffoons trap a princess. She's helping the princess escape, by distracting you."

No, more likely the enchantress has a grudge against Belinda, Bib countered. *That might be helpful in figuring out who was helping them.*

"But -- she promised -- the spell was woven just for our princess," the first prince said, his voice as wobbly as his chin.

"She lied." Merrigan's icy chuckle echoed off the high ceiling. "How do I know she lied?" She reached up and lifted off her cap. A satisfactory cloud of sighs and a long ripple of *ooohs* and *aahhs* erupted from the children. Multi-colored shimmers reflected off the pots and pans and brass surfaces of the kitchen, coming from the crown. "Because I *am* a princess, you buffoons. The spell brought you to the nearest princess, and that is all it did."

"But -- but -- " The lead prince looked like he might burst into tears. His brother, or cousin or whoever he was, did burst into tears.

"Are these intruders bothering you, Highness?" the captain of the guardsmen said, shouldering his way through the knot of stunned, pouting princes.

"Yes, they are. Thank you, Captain Watkins. I know I have no authority, and no right to ask, but if his Majesty would be so kind …" She shrugged prettily.

"Highness, King Auberg has made it abundantly clear to us that even with no throne to call your own, you are royal and your wish is our command." Captain Watkins bowed low, and his expression grew stern as he straightened up, so when he turned it on the princes, they blanched to a man. All he had to do was point, and they scurried out of the kitchen.

"Captain? A small favor?"

"Anything, Highness." He swept her another, smaller bow. The captain really did have a wonderful future as a courtier. He had the manners down perfectly.

"Those … ruffians are obviously being guided by magic. If you could find the source of that magic and remove it, they wouldn't be able to harass and frighten any more innocent women." She crumpled her cap in her hands. The tallest prince looked back at her, and the glint in his eyes made her think he wasn't nearly as repentant as he appeared or should be. "It's hard enough being deprived of my ancestral kingdom, but for those bullies to intrude in here and frighten the children and remind me of all I have lost … I couldn't bear it if another displaced princess were to suffer the same humiliation and pain."

"Anything for you, Highness." He bowed again and grabbed hold of the shoulder of the prince closest to him, to guide him out of the kitchen. The foster parents guided the children away moments later.

Merrigan sat down on the nearest stool at the long preparation table. Her legs felt rather weak. Echoes of her icy words hummed in her head and her chest. She didn't like the sound of her voice, and liked even less the feeling of familiarity the whole situation gave her.

"Mara?" Nasius paused in the doorway of the kitchen. Merrigan wasn't sure how long she had been sitting there, holding her hands clasped tightly together so she wouldn't feel them tremble. The sounds of the orphanage on a rainy day had returned to normal, if a little softer than usual. "Are you all right?"

"Are they gone?"

"Gone, and if we're lucky, on their way out through the gates as fast as the good captain can move them."

"Good. I think it went rather well, don't you?"

"Well?" Nasius tipped his head back and let out one of his rare, bull-bellow laughs. "Mara, you were brilliant! If I weren't still heartbroken over my Felicia -- if I were ten years younger -- I'd ask you to marry me right this moment."

"Don't be ridiculous." She surprised herself with a chuckle. The sound broke a logjam inside her. Warmth spread to her extremities and calmed the impending shudders. "If I were twenty years younger, you mean."

"Well, maybe it's the magic of that crown, the colors ..." He crossed the kitchen to her and held out his hand. "There are many kinds of beauty, and youth is the least of them."

"Oh, my." Merrigan accepted his help sliding off the stool, and gladly leaned into his arm to walk back to the sewing area. "Nasius, where were you when I was ... well, when my prospects were much kinder?"

Just to be safe, Merrigan and Bib agreed to leave the magic sleeping cap on Belinda for the rest of the day. Nasius kept watch on the cauldron of pea soup, monitoring the nearness of the intruding princes and their tracking spell by the speed of the sparkles in the air. The old philosopher let out another bellow of triumph two hours later, and came running to report that the sparkles of magic had vanished with an audible snapping sound. Later, Captain Watkins confirmed their theory -- King Auberg had had the princes searched and every bit of magic removed from their belongings.

"Female magic," a thin, dusty-voiced man announced when Merrigan, Belinda, Bib and Nasius came to the palace two days later to discuss the resolution of the problem with King Auberg.

The king introduced the man as Bergomass, the seer and enchanter. He had assigned himself to the kingdom of Williburton, mostly because he didn't like to move and he had a comfortable, roomy suite in the north tower of the palace. He also happened to be King Auberg's great-great-great-uncle. He preferred most people not even know he existed, and had a clever spell in force that didn't take much maintaining, so people looked at the north tower and never wondered about it. Some didn't even realize it was there. He liked a good game of chess, appreciated magic puzzles, and got on very well with King Auberg. He had been incredibly busy for years, focused solely on unraveling the curse that tried to erase even the memory of Prince Aubrey. Now that the prince had been found and restored, he had far less work to do and was in a good mood. The task and challenge of deciphering the spell used on Belinda was just what he was looking for.

"I agree that the enchantress who wove the spells has a grudge against you, Princess. Most likely she is someone who knows you very well. See here." Bergomass gestured at a long table with numerous items scattered across a surface made of intersecting strips of iron and silver. Iron to counteract inimical magic and silver to reinforce the restraint spells, to keep any active residue of magic from affecting anyone in the room.

He explained that each prince in the party had carried a little leather bag, sewn with silver thread, carrying locks of red hair and dried peas, arrowheads and several pages torn from a book. Closer inspection showed the leather bags had bits of embroidery on them. Bergomass decided the leather had come from one larger leather item, perhaps a lady's hunting outfit. The passages on the pages were familiar, and likely all came from the same book.

"Mine," Belinda said, her voice thick, after she examined the items. She wrapped her arms tight around herself. "My hunting outfit -- my arrows -- my hair -- my favorite book!"

"Who would be able to get all those things, to weave together such an insidious, accurate tracking spell?" King Auberg asked.

"Someone who lived in the palace, obviously," Merrigan said, when Belinda could only shake her head. She was pale, but the two bright red spots in her cheeks hinted she wasn't going to burst into tears this time. Fury was the dominant emotion vibrating out of her now. "Do you think your father might actually be behind this, so desperate to get you back and force you to take a husband ..."

"Female magic," Bib reminded them. "You said your sisters were studying magic."

"Bythia and Barbarina," Belinda murmured. "How could they? They love books even more than I do. How could they sacrifice a book, of all things?"

Merrigan muffled a snort of laughter. She knew Belinda wasn't being a featherhead. The weight of the revelation was so bitter, she had to focus on something inconsequential to survive.

They agreed Belinda would continue to wear the illusion spell. Word that a "real princess" was living in the orphanage might draw the attention of the curious and adventurers. With all the pieces and knowing the source of the inimical magic, Bergomass had no trouble unwinding the tracking spell and separating it entirely from the illusions. When they returned to the orphanage that night, Belinda asked for a bowl of pea soup to celebrate. She said it was delicious, but only ate half of it.

Merrigan brought the crown back to King Auberg, but he told her to keep it, that it needed to be worn. Gilda was a lovely girl and he was delighted to have her for a daughter-in-law, but the crown of woven vines and tiny flowers was simply not her style. Merrigan agreed to keep it for Belinda, when she would need to prove she really was a princess. King Auberg smiled and said the crown would go to whoever married first.

Sometimes, Merrigan just could not understand men.

Then she had bigger problems to worry about.

The next morning, Prince Bayl and Prince Bryan of Sylvanglade walked into the orphanage, and announced Prince Aubrey had asked them to come help. After the previous invasion of princes, the foster parents were naturally hesitant to accept them. However, the brothers had a letter from Aubrey. He had met them several times during his travels working for Gilbrick. They had always been kind, and because they had been touched by a curse themselves, they recognized him as a fellow prince. Their friendship and support had helped make the years of obscurity bearable. Since Aubrey would now be busy with his royal duties and unable to spend as much time at the orphanage as he wished, he asked his two good friends to take his place. Besides, they were without a kingdom or home.

"None of us are getting any younger," Bayl said with a half-smile and a shrug. Nasius had read Aubrey's letter aloud to all the adults gathered around the table in the kitchen, where they could have a little bit of privacy.

"Why did you wait so long after the wedding to make contact?"

Garber, who taught the boys carpentry and leatherworking and arranged for apprenticeships, rarely spoke. Merrigan was glad he did this time, because the same question had been circling through her thoughts.

"Quite frankly," Bryan said, speaking for the first time, "those good-for-nothings who gave you trouble the other day. We would have come right after the wedding. We were going to introduce ourselves to you at the wedding, and follow you home, but they saw us before we saw them." He glanced at his older brother, visibly hesitant.

"It's all right, Bri," Bayl said. "I was … I loved a princess once, but I was unworthy of her. She was disgusted by all the younger sons of kings who saw her throne but never saw her. Those seven were hunting her. Our paths have crossed too many times over the years, and they've been so frustrated in their quest to force her to marry one of them, they take it out on me. Us." He nodded to Bryan. "I don't know what I would have done all these years, without my brother's strength and encouragement. Those scoundrels know I would like nothing better than to find her and rescue her from them. We didn't want them following us here and assuming that my princess is here."

Merrigan wanted to believe him, that fate had brought Bayl of Sylvanglade to the orphanage just when Belinda had been freed from her tormenters. Still, she was relieved when the other foster parents took the responsibility to doubt and to question and to make sure there were no holes or thin spots in their story.

She had brought Bib to the meeting to check over the princes in his own way. She knew as soon as they introduced themselves that giving Belinda and Bayl their happily-ever-after just could not be this easy. There had to be more codicils and nasty tricks, especially considering the rivalry between those useless princes and these two worthwhile ones. While she would have liked nothing better than to slap the borrowed tiara onto Belinda's head, yank away the disguise talisman, and send her running into Bayl's arms, Merrigan knew better.

You were right to be cautious, Bib said, after sitting on the end of the table for nearly two hours. *There is a fine net of inimical magic that has been woven around those two for so long, it has soaked into them. Thanks to exposure to the pea soup tracking magic, I can verify that this interference spell comes from the same source. Belinda's two sisters want to make sure she and her prince either never find each other, or don't enjoy their triumph when they do.*

"What do we do? Is it safe to have Bayl here?" Merrigan whispered. She was so furious over being right, and the nasty spoiled brat attitude of Belinda's sisters, she couldn't focus enough to converse in her thoughts.

I believe as long as he does not identify Belinda, they should both be safe. I will need time to focus and research, and perhaps consult with Bergomass. First, though, I need to study the prince for a good long time. I am sorry.

"Don't be. A delay is far preferable to eternal separation."

In the end, the adults decided to accept the princes' help, on a trial basis. They agreed none of the children would be told the two men were princes, only that they were friends of their beloved Aubrey. Later, after the brothers were taken off to settle them, Merrigan had another thought.

Bryan of Sylvanglade had looked her in the eye. He had complimented her on handling those scoundrel princes so well.

He hadn't recognized her.

Well, how could he? Everyone but Bib and Belinda knew her as Mara, and despite the flattery of her friends, Merrigan knew she looked nothing like the young woman she had been. She had seen her face in the mirror. Bryan would never recognize her.

The years had been very kind to Bryan. Generous, in fact. She had admired the boy he had been, athletic, rugged, cheerful and kind, always smiling. No threat of overwhelming handsomeness. He showed the wear and weathering that was only natural for a prince whose kingdom had been swallowed up by a curse. Merrigan wished she had met the princess Bryan's oldest brother had brought home, in an attempt to sidestep the curse. She would like to take the selfish featherhead and slap her until she finally woke up and thought about others for a change, instead of herself.

Then she would like to find the twit's royal parents and give them a good scolding that would scorch not just their ears but their clothes. How dare they foist their curse off on some innocent king's family, putting his kingdom under the curse they should have been dealing with? Didn't they have any sense of responsibility? Magic was chancy, nasty, and a stickler for the rules. Anyone who tried to get around it got in even more trouble than if they had simply stood up straight and taken their lumps and faced the requirements of breaking the spell.

Oh, but Bryan did look good. He looked like a prince, no matter how plain his clothes, no matter the wrinkles around his eyes, the signs of a life lived on the road, fending for himself. Merrigan imagined he was a great comfort to Bayl, supporting him as he searched for Belinda.

Consider it a fresh start, Bib said in the quiet of the night, after Merrigan was finally able to climb into her bed and let her achy-weary limbs relax. Sleep threatened on dizzy waves that she welcomed with pleasure.

Fresh start in what? Merrigan closed her eyes and wished he wasn't quite such a talkative talking book.

Your friendship with your prince.

He was never mine.

He could be now.

Focus on making everything safe for Belinda and Bayl. They've both suffered enough to deserve some happiness, don't you think?

What about you? Haven't you suffered enough?

Ask Clara. Merrigan rolled over and pulled her pillow over her head. Not that it would really help. But he did take the hint.

~~~~~

The seamstresses settled down to get to work on holiday clothes for everyone in the orphanage. Although the first snows weren't due for several more weeks, they had to get to work now, because there were quite a lot of children to clothe. Merrigan looked forward to the enormous project, with such a wide variety of cloth and colors and all the supplies she would need. The children would be so excited, she knew. They were intelligent and aware enough to know the difference between the abundance of clothes that had been showered on them when Aubrey was restored to his position as prince, and the new clothes they would receive at the winter festivities. The difference between something adjusted and adapted for them, and something made for them. The donations showered on the orphanage warehouse continued, though slowed down to a more manageable flow. They had a nice stockpile of shoes and boots and coats. All the children had a change of nightshirts, so laundry day wasn't a mad scramble to get everything washed and
~~~~~

dried by nighttime. They each had an outfit for chores and everyday wear, and an outfit for special occasions, such as when the king and other high-ranking or wealthy friends came to visit.

"What are you smiling about?" Belinda said, her voice threatening to grow loud enough to be a wail.

"I'm sorry -- I was just gloating over all the goodies we have to work with," Merrigan said, patting the other princess's hand. "It's funny, but I've never been proud of anything but myself before. I like being proud of our home, of the children, all that we managed to do before we gained wealthy patrons."

"Hmm, I suppose so." She blotted her eyes with a visibly wet handkerchief. "He hates me," she whispered.

"Who hates you?"

"Bayl." Her voice dropped to a squeaky whisper.

"How can he hate you when he doesn't recognize you? You're wearing an illusion spell, remember?"

"But -- but -- he avoids looking at me. Every time I try to talk to him, he excuses himself and gets away as fast as he can. He won't look me in the eye, even when he's standing right there in front of me." Belinda looked around at the other girls. Her desperate whispers had been covered by the crunching of scissors going through cloth and the excited chatter as the sewing teams matched trimmings and buttons to cloth.

"Don't be a goose." Merrigan gestured with her chin at the girls on the other side of the table, since her hands were full pinning a skirt together for basting. "If you weren't so busy avoiding him half the time, and the other time pushing yourself into his face, desperate for him to recognize you despite that very good illusion spell, you'd notice that all the girls over the age of thirteen are nigh on drooling over him."

"Oh, I noticed." The whine slid into a growl.

Chapter Sixteen

"But you didn't notice that he's avoiding all of them, the same way he's avoiding you. As far as he knows, you're just another girl fawning over a handsome, heroic prince. Just another girl, and far too young for him. He's a man of great honor and high principles, your Bayl."

"Oh, I wish he were mine ..." She sighed, blotted her eyes one more time, and tucked the handkerchief into the collar of her dress, ready for more dripping and sniffling. Belinda picked up the dress pieces she was supposed to be pinning together for basting. "What am I going to do? It isn't safe for me to drop the illusion spell. Not until we're absolutely sure those scoundrels have put ten kingdoms between them and me."

"It's the enchantress out to get you we need to worry about."

"Enchantresses."

"What's that?" Merrigan stuck a pin in her finger and bit back a curse.

"I have been able to spare a few thoughts for something besides how rough-and-tumble gorgeous Bayl has become." Belinda sighed. "My sisters created the tracing spell. I have no doubt now."

"Why? I didn't get along all that well with my own brothers and sisters, but they would never do something so despicable. It's royal blood against the world and all that claptrap."

"Hmm, you would think so." She finished her pinning and got up to take the pieces down to the end of the table to the basting team. "I think the frustration of having their lives in perpetual waiting, until Father gets the succession to the throne settled, has rather turned them sour," she said when she returned to her chair. "You would think evil enchantresses would want the throne, all the wealth and manpower at their disposal. It's much harder to dislodge evil enchanters if they have some claim to the kingdom. You'd think those two would want me out of the way, rather than get me married and settled on the throne with a dimwit."

"Maybe they want a figurehead. They might have some spell

to make you as useless and easily manipulated as those idiots we chased away." For a moment, they shared a grin, still feeling that triumph. "Or maybe ..." She remembered Bryan smiling at her. Other suitors had tried to smile, but went away pale with fear or some other emotion that had always made her feel triumphant and strong, until now.

"Maybe what?" she asked, when Merrigan paused too long.

"Maybe your sisters simply want you settled because they have sweethearts of their own, and your father won't let anyone marry before you. More claptrap and tradition about not letting the oldest daughter look bad, unmarried at her sisters' weddings."

"Those two?" Belinda let out a most unladylike snort. "They had plenty of suitors, but they tended to think of marriage as a punishment, not the sweet joy I saw between our parents." She sighed, and Merrigan was disappointed to see the featherheaded, moping expression return. "The sweetness I could have with Bayl, if I had just had the wit to snatch him up when I had the chance. Had. Past tense."

"You *have* a chance." Merrigan glanced at the girls. All seven had made some adjustments to their dresses, adding ribbons and embroidery. "While I'm sure your Bayl is too honorable to give our girls the slightest encouragement, you might want to find a way to discourage them without breaking their hearts or hating you."

"Oh. Yes." She studied the chattering, happily busy girls. "We need to match them with boys closer to their own ages and stations. Falling in love is the only cure for a broken heart."

~~~~~

Merrigan had settled in the sewing area to think while the children were at their lessons. Bib was busy with his usual occupation, absorbing information from a new batch of books borrowed from King Auberg. Belinda was out running errands.

"Mistress Mara? Forgive me," Bryan hurried to say, when his sudden appearance at the sewing table startled a squeak out of Merrigan. "I was hoping to catch you in a quiet moment, but I didn't think ..."

Some men could blush without looking like overly sensitive twits auditioning for the tragic hero part in an epic poem. Bryan was one of them. Then again, he had good, healthy coloring and wide cheekbones, perfectly framed by that thin, dashing line of
~~~~~

beard on his jaw. Merrigan scolded herself to stop being a ninny. There was far more to a man than just good looks and a voice that was a mixture of velvet and waterfall. Leffisand had all those qualities and more, and look how he turned out.

"It's all right, Highness --"

"Please." He rested his hand on hers on the table. "I'm no more a prince than you are a princess."

"Nonsense. I've learned quite a bit since ... well, I've learned in my travels that there's more to being royal than a throne and a palace and a crown. Some good fortune will smile on you, as a reward for all the good you have done. I'm sure Princess Belinda is deeply grateful for the work you and your brother have done, trying to defend her, help her. What?"

The deepening frown on Bryan's face made her heart squeeze and constricted her throat.

"We never said what her name was."

"Oh. Really?" She swallowed hard. "Are you sure?"

"Dolt." A shimmering voice came from Bryan's coat. "If you had done what I told you, in the sequence I told you --"

"Yes, yes," Bryan said with a sigh and an adorably crooked grin. He opened his coat and brought out a small hand mirror, round, with a handle twice as long as the mirror itself, encased in silver and ivory. The kind of mirror a fashionable lady would take on journeys, to ensure she looked her best before descending from her carriage. Why Prince Bryan of Sylvanglade would carry such a thing, Merrigan had no idea.

Then two amethyst eyes and a pair of plump, rosy lips appeared in the mirror.

"So you're the princess who set those fumblewits running," the shimmering voice continued, and one amethyst eye winked. "Pleased to meet you, Princess."

"My name is Mistress Mara." Merrigan clenched her hands together in her lap, praying Bryan wouldn't see them shaking. Now was not the time for her true name to be revealed. Mirror slaves were notorious for nasty streaks, being sly and speaking cryptically. She hoped that nasty streak didn't include revealing people's true names at the most awkward time.

"Of course, dearie. Whatever you say. Now, where's Bib?"

"You know --" She swallowed hard and made herself meet

Bryan's eyes. "How did you find out about Bib?"

"I don't know who Bib is," Bryan said. "Crystal insisted when I woke up this morning that she had to find him. There's too much loose magic bouncing around this place to let them talk unless they're together."

"Bib." Merrigan nudged aside some of the books surrounding him, and poked his spine. "Bib, we have visitors."

"Crystal?" Bib's voice sounded like his spine would shred. "Can that really be you?"

"How are you, you old inkblotter?" The mirror shimmered. "Be a dear and let two old friends get acquainted for a little while, would you?"

"Yes, Highness." Bryan winked and grinned. "Your wish is my command."

"He's such a good boy -- when he isn't being a cheeky brat. The sooner we get your princess untangled and set free, the happier you'll both be." Crystal chuckled, ending in a satisfied little sigh when Bryan put her down next to Bib on the table.

"I'm assuming the mirror is another magical item stolen from Bib's former master, during the enchanters' war." Merrigan knew she was babbling but couldn't help it, as Bryan settled down in the chair next to her.

"Ah, that explains quite a bit. I assume the book has been guiding you, as Crystal has been guiding Bayl and me for the last few years?"

"That pretty much sums up the story."

"Oh, but I hate summed up stories, don't you? I like all the messy details." He slouched down in the chair, so his head rested on the back rail and his tailbone rested on the front edge of the chair. He stretched out his legs with his ankles crossed and clasped his hands across his belly. "Let's share some war stories while those two old conspirators are catching up."

Merrigan didn't consider her travels and adventures with Bib to be "war stories," but she was pleased to get chuckles from Bryan when she talked about the odd characters she had met, the justice levied on Judge Brimble and the cheating miller. He slapped his leg and snorted when she talked about the bandits who had thought they were robbing a helpless old woman and ended up facing justice and humiliation. He wanted all the details of how she and

Aubrey and the children had helped to protect Gilda, and approved of their efforts to catch the weavers.

Finally he consented to tell the tale of discovering Crystal. The mirror had been among the treasures of Sylvanglade for decades, but had been asleep until the two brothers, looking for mischief on a rainy day, snuck into the treasury. Bayl picked her up and declaimed some lines from an epic poem about a magician who fought dragons, while waving the mirror about like a sword. Crystal refused to tell them what exactly he had said and done to awaken her, but she had been their advisor, getting them in and out of trouble ever since. They had promised never to tell anyone she was with them, because she lived in genuine fear the enemies of her former master might find her. It had taken decades of maneuvering for her to get to the safety of Sylvanglade's treasure room.

"You trusted her and listened to her when she told you to lie to your parents?" Merrigan couldn't help interrupting.

"Well ... we were boys, at that age when we felt like everyone was prying into our business. We hated being left out of all the fun our older brothers were having." Bryan shrugged, a thoughtful frown creasing his forehead. "Besides, Crystal, like many magical objects of knowledge, can't lie. She can be awfully stubborn and a stickler for exact meanings, and if she doesn't like you, she won't offer any information beyond what you ask for."

"Ah, of course. Judge Brimble's uncle got into so much trouble because he didn't ask the right questions. So Crystal found all the adventures you were longing for."

"Harmless fun. A chance to grow up and learn some valuable lessons without getting into any real trouble." He sighed and sat up a little straighter in the chair, but still managing to look lazily relaxed. "She was training us to be heroes, and sensitive to magic. And most important, to follow the rules. Sometimes I do regret obeying her and keeping her presence secret so long."

"Why?"

"Sylvanglade is a rather small kingdom. We are -- or at least, we were -- more comfortable than wealthy. Enough to make us good neighbors. Neighboring kingdoms knew they could rely on us, but we didn't have anything to tempt invaders. We thought we were safe. More fools we." Bryan offered her a rueful smile. "Sorry. Shouldn't wander like that."

"I'm sorry. It must be heartbreaking, to know your family, your friends are trapped and there's nothing you can do about the curse."

"That's the worst part of it. Crystal warned us as soon as Branwell brought that twitterheaded Princess Talithia across the border. She can sense curses a league away, and she's especially sensitive to all the warping and complications when you don't obey the rules. We warned Branwell and we warned our father, but they wouldn't listen to us. They didn't think Crystal was trustworthy because she asked us to keep her a secret all these years. That put Branwell in a bad mood, and he took it out on Talithia. She was in a temper because the curse was trying to drag her back to her father's kingdom, where everything was supposed to play out in due order and ..." He sighed and shrugged. "Crystal felt the trap ready to snap closed and warned us. We barely got out in time."

"Nobody would listen when you told them to run?" Merrigan guessed.

"We've dedicated our lives since then to defending others. And defending a certain princess, whose name you know, even though it's a sacred vow between us never to reveal it to anyone." Bryan sat up and leaned toward her. "There's quite a lot that's mysterious about you, Princess Mara. Including that intriguing magical box. Crystal senses it is capable of holding this entire warehouse. If we could figure out how to get it through the opening," he added with a grin.

Merrigan felt a little queasy. Afraid yet elated. She wanted to be included in some new mischief he was about to make, all hinted at in the glitter in his eyes. For just a moment she slid back in her memory to their childhood adventures, when his eyes held that same spark.

"Tell me the rest of your story, and when those two are finished catching up, the four of us need to talk. There's a great deal of magic still in play, and danger we need to untangle."

"Uh huh." His eyes narrowed and his grin grew sly.

Belinda's suspicions were proven true, when Bryan related what he and his brother had discovered. Crystal had been able to deduce much from scrying the magic every time they got close to the band of good-for-nothing princes. Bythia and Barbarina had woven the spell to trap their older sister, and put her into the clutches of the least worthy prince of the bunch. The magic held a nasty core. The enchantresses wanted Belinda dead, to take her throne, but their father also had a searching spell at work. He would not only know when Belinda was found, but also who hurt her. Both sisters would be disinherited if they directly harmed their sister. A curse was tangled around the hunting princes themselves. It would cause a series of embarrassing miss-steps and accidents, so the princes and Belinda would end up dead. Only someone made from magic, like Crystal, could see through the weaving to the malicious intent. Anyone else examining the aftermath would conclude Belinda had been killed through stupidity colliding from multiple directions.

"So tell me the truth," Bryan said, after they went to the kitchen to make tea and bring it back to the sewing room, with leftover biscuits from breakfast. "She's here, isn't she? Hiding among the orphans?" He waggled his eyebrows at her. "I thought you might be her, in disguise, but Crystal says you're an entirely different kind of magic."

"She does, does she?"

"You two are a pair of ninnies," Crystal announced, when Bryan and Merrigan just sat and smiled at each other.

"Oh, definitely a pair," Bib said, his pages riffling in a whispery chuckle.

"What sort of consensus have you two come up with?" Merrigan asked. "Are we safe enough from the enemies to take off some masks?"

"Bib is a wonder when it comes to diagnosing magic, but he hasn't had the experience with the whole nasty tangle that I've had over the years," Crystal announced. "As much as I hate to admit it, things could get much grimmer before they get better."

"The sisters?" Bryan asked, pausing with his mug of tea nearly to his lips.

"They've had time to seethe and add to their spells. By now, it's a matter of honor to them to wipe out -- our friend," Bib said, after a slight pause. Merrigan guessed that Crystal had warned him that the brothers didn't dare to even speak Belinda's name. "She's frustrated their plans and efforts for too long. Despite all Crystal has done, there are a few threads of magic attached to Bayl she hasn't been able to loosen. Her sisters will know when he's found and unmasked her. They have several contingency spells watching from far off, ready to snap into action and separate the two sweethearts."

"Oh, now that's not fair at all," Merrigan said.

Bryan muttered some curses into his tea, then tipped the steaming mug back and emptied most of it down his throat.

"Do we make things more treacherous if we tell your brother our mutual friend is here?" Bib continued after several moments of unhappy silence. "While it might make things more pleasant for him, can we trust him not to confront her? Or try to identify her?"

"I'm surprised he hasn't picked her out already," Merrigan said. "She looks like a much younger version of herself, that's all."

"That's easy to explain," Bryan said. "One spell on us decrees that until she reveals herself, neither of us will recognize her. Even if, as you said, she looked like a younger version of herself."

"A variation of the you-don't-see-me spell," Crystal said, "but woven in such a way it only reacts when the brothers and your friend are close enough to see or hear each other. Rather vicious, if you think about it."

"She thinks he hates her," Merrigan said. "She looked into his face, she talked with him, and he smiled at her and patted her head, treating her like a little girl. No wonder she's on the verge of tears half the time since the two of you arrived."

"It's to force her to confront him. Torture her until she breaks down and makes herself vulnerable." Bryan scowled into his mug. "You can't imagine how it tears him apart to know he probably looks her in the face a dozen times a day and he can't say anything, can't even speak her name, because it would put her at risk."

"Oh, I can imagine all too clearly," she whispered. Then she thought of something. "But she's told him her name. Several times. She isn't using a false name, which is rather reckless. He doesn't call any of the girls by name, now that I think of it."

"That's the really nasty part," Crystal said. "The spell makes him hear every girl say her name is *hers*. So when he *does* hear her name, he has no way of knowing it's really her."

"Until she drops her illusion. Oh, I would love to slap that sleeping cap on both of those nasty twits and lock them in a dungeon for the next hundred years or so."

"Sleeping cap?" The magic mirror wobbled from side to side, as if she were trying to sit up. "What are you talking about?"

"We've been busy discussing other things," Bib said. "Forgive me. That box contains some useful bits of minor magic. We used the cap to make our friend sleep during the invasion of the princes. We baited them with an enormous pot of pea soup, to activate the spell. She couldn't sneeze or heave while she was asleep."

"Clever." Bryan's face relaxed into the good humor that Merrigan thought made him so much more handsome.

"Hmm, a stopgap measure," she said. "We can't tell her he's unable to recognize her. It'd just make her more weepy than she already is. Would she risk her life to help him recognize her? How much temptation can she stand?"

"What if you made it clear that he was doing it to protect her?" Crystal suggested. "Let her know he is just as much tangled in enemy magic as she is."

"I would like to give her some hope, ease some of her hurt," Bib said, "but not if it just puts her in more danger."

"Why don't we ask my brother what he wants to do?" Bryan said.

When the others agreed that the older prince should have some say in what was told to Belinda, he got up to go look for Bayl. Merrigan sipped at her tea, watching him walk away, and wished … she wasn't quite sure what she wished for.

"I was such an idiot when I was younger," she whispered.

"Indeed you were, Princess Merrigan," Crystal said.

"Bib!" Merrigan slammed her mug down on the table, fearful she would drop it.

"I didn't tell her, Mi'Lady," the book responded. "She's a magic mirror. She sees everything."

"Even into the past?" She clutched her hands in her lap to resist the urge to snatch up the mirror and slam her down onto the stone paving of the warehouse. Unfortunately, magic mirrors were impervious to such attempts at breaking them.

"I see you as you are now. I can see the magic strangling you, and how you truly are -- the face of your soul and spirit and heart," Crystal said. "Pick me up, Princess. If you please?"

"Why? I know what I look like."

"You know what you've seen. I can show you what you can't see."

She hesitated. After all, how long would it take for Bryan to find his brother and bring him back here to talk? If she didn't comply, Merrigan suspected Crystal would take matters into her own metaphorical hands. She might even reveal the truth about Clara's curse, Merrigan's identity, even the travesty of her marriage to that charming but foolhardy schemer.

"Very well," she muttered, and reached over to pick up the mirror from where she lay against Bib. The silver and ivory hummed under her hands. Sparkles of blue and green and purple magic spun around the surface of the mirror, down the handle, then traveled up Merrigan's arm and enfolded her. For several seconds, she could see nothing but the sparkles. When she blinked them away, she saw her own, her real face.

Yet not her face. Her features were all sharp-edged and glossy, like jewels. She was young and beautiful and regal, but with an overall impression of coldness.

The image of herself reminded her of the Fae she had encountered before going into Smilpotz.

"That is the woman you used to be," Crystal said. "Here is the woman you are now."

The image softened. There were still hard planes, but no sharp edges, and the glitter and gloss of polished jewels had faded into warmth. The colors and tones were flesh and blood. Merrigan shivered when she saw she did look older -- of course, how could she expect all the travel and working to support herself not to age her? Yet there was something regal and admirable about the woman who gazed somberly from the mirror. A sense of warmth and mischief, where the jeweled woman had been chill and her humor had a malicious edge to it.

"What will I be in the end?" Merrigan whispered.

"That depends on the choices you make. I thought you said your princess was clever."

"She is. But everyone is clever in different ways," Bib said. "They're coming. Wipe your eyes, Mi'Lady."

Merrigan nearly snapped that she hadn't been crying, but she blinked and realized that yes, there was dampness in her eyes. She put Crystal back where she had originally been.

"Does he -- he doesn't mention me at all, does he?" slipped out before she could tuck that errant, totally ridiculous thought back into hiding.

"When he's tired and lonely and jealous of his brother's happiness," the mirror said.

"Happiness?" Merrigan flinched, thinking she heard footsteps.

"Men are silly sometimes, when they're being heroic. Bayl finds much of his strength in knowing that even though he can't be with his princess, he's serving her, and proving his love. He has the hope of winning her freedom and her love someday. He's clever enough to realize her sisters targeted him because she did feel something for him. If you want to hurt your enemy, use someone who has already touched her heart."

"I never gave him a bit of hope, did I?" she whispered. Yes, now she did hear footsteps.

"When you were young. You changed and he was gone too long, and what chance does he have, really, as the youngest prince of a kingdom that nobody will ever rule again?"

"Don't tell him, Crystal. Please. Promise me."

"Don't tell him what, exactly?"

"That it's me." She tapped her breastbone. "Inside this -- this -- old hag."

"Mi'Lady," Bib said, a touch of laughter in his voice. "You were more a hag when you were beautiful. Now, you're simply lovely. And you're not half as old as you think you are."

Then the two princes stepped into the sewing room. Merrigan watched Crystal from the corner of her eye the entire time they talked, terrified the mirror would reveal that Mistress Mara was Princess Merrigan of Avylyn. After all, she hadn't promised.

In the end, speaking in euphemisms so they wouldn't awaken the inimical magic wrapped around Bayl, they agreed on what Merrigan would tell Belinda. Bayl couldn't recognize her, and he begged her not to reveal herself to him until they could be sure both their curses had been entirely undone. Crystal and Bib believed Belinda would be comforted by the news. Bayl only cared about not hurting her, while Merrigan thought about what a featherhead she had turned into since her prince arrived.

To her surprise, Belinda was quiet and thoughtful when she gave her the news and explained the dangerous situation. Merrigan took her for a walk to have that discussion, despite the rain that fell in a cold mist all day. The two walked close together, gray enclosing them so it felt as if they were the only ones out on the streets as afternoon turned to evening. Every sound was muted with the hissing of rain and the gurgling of water in the gutters.

"Would it be ..." Belinda stopped and tugged her hood back a little to look up and down the nearly deserted, foggy street. Most shops had already closed. The ones still open were dim blots of golden warmth through watery air. "Would it be dangerous if I wrote him a letter? Would it awaken the magic if he wrote to me?" Her mouth trembled, and for a moment Merrigan feared she would burst into tears again. Then Belinda squeaked a laugh and threw her arms around Merrigan for a brief, wet hug. "He's been looking for me -- he remembers me. Oh, I don't deserve him, not after all this time, all this work and suffering and ... but I'm a horribly selfish person. I want him!"

Merrigan made a point of repeating the conversation to Bayl when the five conspirators met again the next morning, while the clatter of the kitchen crew starting breakfast preparations covered their whispering conversation. The glow in the elder prince's face created a twisting, aching, almost weepy sensation in her middle.

The first exchange of letters was carried out with all the stealth of spying in enemy territory among goblins and trolls. Bib and Crystal examined Belinda's letter for anything that might trigger the inimical, watchful spells on either side. If she wrote anything chancy, they had her rewrite it. Then they did the same for Bayl's response. That became the standard practice. Merrigan counted that necessity as another strike against the two vicious enchantresses: Belinda and her sweetheart couldn't even pour their hearts out to each other in writing. To ensure that Bayl had no chance to guess which girl among the orphans was his Belinda, Merrigan and Bryan acted as intermediaries. Belinda gave her letter to Merrigan, who passed it to Bryan several hours later. When Bayl wrote his letter, Bryan passed it to Merrigan, then kept his brother busy so he wouldn't see Merrigan give it to Belinda.

The job of intermediaries threw Bryan and Merrigan together. If she wasn't constantly watching for him, waiting for the signal that he had a letter to give her, he was watching for her signal in return. Then when the recipient was busy reading the latest letter, the sender wanted to be alone for a while. Merrigan thought it somewhat silly and melodramatic, and Bryan agreed when she mentioned it to him after three weeks of exchanging letters.

"Still, he's in a much better humor than he's been for years now."

Bryan leaned back against the support post of the pavilion where they had taken shelter from the rain-becoming-snow, on the edge of the festival grounds in the center of the city. He had offered to accompany her when she delivered a set of gowns for the christening of the twin daughters of Lady Geramia. Talking about their mutual concerns and friends was easier away from the orphanage, even if they still had to talk in euphemisms.

"To have hope ... it's painful, but it's a welcome pain. Compared to no hope whatsoever."

"Certainly a handsome young man such as you has some hope? One day soon, this whole ugly tangle will resolve and your brother and his sweetheart will be together, safe, settled -- you aren't going to spend the rest of your life looking after them, are you?"

"Oh, yes, a favorite uncle, growing old by the fire." He shuddered with mock horror, and for a moment they paused, caught in each other's eyes.

Merrigan ached for something she couldn't put her finger on.

"I find it hard to believe there isn't a princess out there, pining for you," she said, and a moment later wished she had cut off her tongue before saying something so foolish.

"Once. Where she is now ... I hope she's happy and safe somewhere." He gestured out across the silvery sheen of sleet that threatened to cover the festival grounds in ice. "I am just selfish enough to hope she thinks of me, once in a while. Maybe even wonders where I am. And yes," he let out a single chuckle, "I'm selfish enough to hope that sometimes, no matter how happy she is, she wonders what would have happened if I had been brave enough to ask, and she had said yes."

"She would have been an idiot, a featherhead, to say no to you."

"It doesn't matter, does it? I didn't ask. I had nothing to offer her, even when Sylvanglade was free of enchantment. Now, who knows what her fate is? I feel as if I failed her. We were friends when we were children." He sighed. "Yes, I failed her."

"No, you didn't. She failed you." She wondered if the odd aching in her head and in her throat was what people meant when they talked about twisting a knife a little deeper.

"I wish I could fall in love with someone else, but I am doomed to be the loyal friend, sacrificing all for the sake of the hero." He tried to laugh. "Mara? Are you all right?"

"Of course. Why wouldn't I be?" She fought the urge to wipe at her face with her mittens, afraid to discover the hot ache in the back of her head had escaped in the form of tears.

"It must be the dying light. You look so pale." He offered her his bent arm. She accepted the silent suggestion that they continue their long walk back to the orphanage.

"You make me wish ..." She waited until they had come down the steps from the pavilion and started down the icy brick-paved pathway. "I think there must be some truth in the saying that it is better to have known true love and then lost it. The sweetness, however short-lived, makes up for the pain."

"If I ever thought she loved me, maybe I could agree with you."

"Oh, no matter how selfish and spoiled your princess might have been, somewhere deep inside, she did love you. As much as she was able. No one could be so utterly self-centered and stupid they wouldn't recognize your fine qualities and love you. Even if just a little bit," she vowed.

"Thank you." He caught up her hand where it was tucked into his elbow, and pressed a kiss in the gap between sleeve and mitten, before settling it firmly back in place. "Where were you when I was soothing my broken heart with plans to hunt dragons and gryphons and make a heroic name for myself?"

"Making mistakes of my own." Merrigan laughed with him as they trudged down the pathway to the main street.

"All of youth must seem foolish and selfish, looking backwards, I suppose." He sighed, and they walked along for several minutes in companionable quiet. "What was he like, the man you loved and lost?"

"I didn't know how to love. Truly love. Before ..." She gestured at her face. Let him assume she meant when she was young, rather than before the curse hit her. "I was married, for a short time. We ... understood each other, as much as two nasty children could. We thought it was the two of us against the whole misguided world. Suddenly he was gone. He was so viciously clever that he became inexcusably stupid."

"You started to love him. Enough to hurt for him."

"That was a lifetime ago, when I was a very different person."

"He was a fool for not loving you completely," he said, resting his hand over hers in the crook of his elbow and squeezing it.

"You, Prince Bryan, are gallant and flattering and I don't know whether to laugh or cry."

"If only ..."

"Yes." She turned enough to see past the sagging sides of her deep hood, and found him smiling a little sadly at her. "If only."

~~~~~

The days passed, becoming another week, and Merrigan scolded herself for being a sentimental, selfish twit. She fell into more and more situations where she and Bryan were together, walking somewhere in the increasingly wet, cold weather. Running errands for the orphanage. Escorting children to lessons or visits with possible adoptive parents, or simply needing to stretch their legs and get some fresh air.

As the weather grew increasingly unfriendly, the children spent more time indoors. The noise of children seeking new entertainment irritated Merrigan more than she liked to admit. She swore she could hear them chattering and shrieking and laughing, knocking over building blocks or singing their nonsense songs and chanting puzzle rhymes at each other even in her sleep. She longed for some place she could go for solitude, and some peace and quiet.

Nearly every time she escaped the orphanage, just for a short walk, hungry for some solitude, she usually found Bryan ahead of her on the street. Or she turned, with the sensation of being watched, and found him following her. He waited for her, or she waited for him, and they talked and walked, sometimes for an hour, or two. Many conversations drifted to their regrets, wondering where that "someone" in their pasts might be right that moment. She admitted to Bryan that she had come near to loving a boy, but had let herself be persuaded that he had nothing to offer her. She remembered aloud for him those few short, sweet times they had spent together as children, yet with as few details as possible, so he wouldn't guess. When he remarked on how similar her memories were to the ones he had of his princess, she fought not to laugh because she feared she might weep. Her only consolation was that he smiled when he talked about the girl she used to be. If he had cursed her for her cold heart, Merrigan didn't know what she would have done.
~~~~~

Once, she managed to follow him into the city without him noticing her. They ended up in a small chapel, warm and softly bright with hundreds of candles. Bryan bought five candles, the expensive, bright green ones. He found a spot where previous candles had burned down and out in the long rows of shelves. Merrigan was touched that he took the time to clear out the expended candles and put the pieces in the barrel for that purpose, instead of just brushing them onto the floor as so many people seemed to do. Bryan set up the candles, then took his time to get a spill and light it from the central flame of the chapel. He lit each of the candles in turn, and let out a deep sigh as he waved the spill to extinguish it.

"Merrigan ..." He took a step back, gazing at the flames. "Be happy."

She fled before the sobs escaped her aching throat. If she made a sound, Merrigan was sure she would collapse in the slush and sleet and still be there when he left the chapel.

The only person more miserable than herself, she realized one day, was Bayl. She followed Bryan when she delivered the latest letter from Belinda, who was busy helping to bathe the babies that afternoon. The squeals and giggles and splashing sounds could barely penetrate the chatter and clatter and laughter of the children at play, and the shouts and sharper clatter of the ones who were arguing. The weather was having a negative effect on some of them, so that the foster parents prayed for clearer weather, just so the children could go outside to play. Merrigan intended to keep going once she saw the letter safely delivered to Bayl, and had her cloak in her hands. She didn't think to stop when she saw Bayl tuck the letter into his shirt with one hand, snatch up his coat with the other, and nearly run to the main door out of the warehouse.

Chapter Seventeen

Merrigan made no effort to follow him, but his deep footprints in the thickening slush and icy mud outside were clear and went the same direction she had planned to go. She didn't slow her steps, but listened for the sound of him ahead of her as she walked down the long side of the warehouse, heading away from the main street. The splashing of booted feet faded, so she didn't expect to see him when she turned the corner, into an open field. Many of the carting businesses and merchants in that part of the city pastured their horses there. Bayl stood in the open, arms spread, head tilted back to the sky. She shuddered, sensing the pressure building in him.

"No, don't," she whispered, unsure what she feared about to happen.

"Belinda!" he cried, the last vowel turning into a howl that fractured into a sob. Bayl dropped to his knees, head bowed, bracing himself on his arms as he crouched there in the mud and thickening slushy snow. "Belinda." His voice shuddered, dropping to a whisper so Merrigan more felt than heard the name. "So close. Can you hear me, love? Belinda…"

A sensation washed over her, as if all the world held its breath. Then for two seconds, utter darkness splashed across the field. It rippled out from Bayl as if he was the point where a massive rock was flung into a mud puddle, sending it splashing out in all directions.

Mi'Lady? Bib's voice sounded thin, scratchy, torn -- the sound she imagined all his pages would make as they were ripped, a dozen at a time, from his binding. *Mi'Lady, are you all right?*

Merrigan couldn't seem to gather her thoughts enough to concentrate and respond. She took one more glance at the prince. She remembered how her father wept when her mother died, and did not want to hear Bayl sobbing now.

No, wait. He wasn't sobbing.

He wasn't there.

A massive, churning black shadow swirled around the spot

where he had knelt, and then spun up into the sky, to vanish.

Stupid, stupid, stupid ...

Now they knew at least one of the contingency spells that Belinda's sisters had cast, in case Bayl did find her. Was it possible that Belinda heard, if only with her heart, when Bayl said her name? Did that trigger this malicious bit of magic?

Merrigan turned and ran, back into the warehouse. She nearly knocked several children over as she kept running, down the narrow aisle between different living areas. Back to the sewing room and her shelf bed, where she had left Bib and Crystal having another long talk.

"What did that fool do?" Crystal cried, before Merrigan could do more than tug aside the curtain across her bed.

"You felt that too?" Merrigan flung off her cloak and dropped down next to the two magical beings. Now she shook, hard enough she thought she would be sick.

"The more important question," Bib said, "is if the enchantresses felt it."

"What did he do?" Bryan demanded, sliding to a stop in front of Merrigan's shelf. He went to one knee and caught hold of her shaking, cold hands. "Mara, are you all right? What did my idiot brother do?" He shook his head. "No, I can imagine. We need to brace ourselves for attack."

"What attack? He's gone." She stumbled, her tongue tangling, as she told them what Bayl had said, what she had seen, ending with, "They've won."

"That kind never considers themselves winners until all hope is utterly shredded," Crystal said. "They've taken Bayl away, but if they felt the reaction, those two hags have to know Belinda is nearby. They'll come looking and deal with her, to make sure she can't find and rescue her prince."

"All right then. We need advice. Some magical help. Defense." Merrigan could almost have laughed at the fractured way she talked. "It's time you met Bergomass." However, when she tried to get up, to take Bryan across the city to meet the enchanter, her legs didn't want to support her weight.

She hated being so weak. Her sewing girls came to report that a massive snowstorm had swept in, surrounding the warehouse with howling winds and dropping gobs of snow that threatened to bury them by nightfall. They couldn't have gotten across the city in that mess outside, but Merrigan wouldn't forgive herself.

Bryan admitted he knew it was hopeless, but he had to try to get some clue to what had happened to Bayl. He took Crystal with him. Belinda showed up a short time later, the baby bathing finally done for the day. She exclaimed over the signs of shock on Merrigan, and immediately fussed over her. When Bib asked how she felt, they discovered Belinda hadn't sensed the reverberation of magic.

More than a dozen people were caught in that part of the city, blinded so they couldn't find their way. The storm swept them into the warehouse. Most buildings around the orphanage were uninhabited, with no one to respond to shouts for help, no heat, no blankets, and no smoke from fires burning. Nearly everyone who stumbled up against the orphanage doors reported they had smelled the bread baking for dinner and followed their noses.

The next few hours were a tangle of scrambling to get frozen, drenched strangers into dry clothes and settle them near the heating stoves and braziers. Merrigan hated the tight, coiled sensation in her chest that kept curling tighter with every task to help make the refugees more comfortable. She wanted to snap every time one of the other adults asked her to oversee something. Find another blanket or to send a child to haul wet clothes to the laundry to dry. Or send a boy to bring in more charcoal for a brazier, more wood for a stove. Knowing she was being ridiculous just made the sensation worse. Knowing something was wrong with her, blaming these poor people for the predicament they were in, just made her more irritable. She tried not to look at the strangers, and somehow that was the worst part of it. She wanted to dive into her bed, tug the curtain closed across the shelf, and hide under her blankets.

The pressure eased once everyone was dried and warmed up and dinner had been served. Once Bryan and Crystal returned, safe even if covered with slushy ice. They hadn't found anything, not even an echo of the magic that had snatched away Bayl. Still, Bryan was safe indoors, and she felt much better. She could breathe again.

Her uneasiness, however, seemed to transfer to the children. They wouldn't sit still for more than a few mouthfuls of food at a time. She couldn't understand it. Usually the presence of strangers in the warehouse put them on their best behavior, wanting to impress possible adoptive parents. The usual dinner chatter, the clatter of spoons in bowls, munching and slurping, and requests by adults to "chew with your mouth closed, please," became raised voices. Chairs scraping on the stone flooring. Arguments and thuds of milk mugs on the tabletop. Barked orders to sit down and finish their meals before they were sent to bed without anything to eat.

"I just don't understand," Belinda said, near tears, as the seamstresses took refuge in the sewing room, trying to find some peace and quiet once the washing crew got to work.

"It's the storm. Or whatever brought the storm." Merrigan shivered from a cold that had nothing to do with the weather. The clatter of wooden bowls hitting the floor resounded through the warehouse, followed by the howls of someone who got his ears boxed and someone else shrieking it wasn't his fault. She tried to find some humor in the situation, and could only be grateful their bowls and mugs tonight were wood, not the good crockery.

She wondered for the first time why Belinda hadn't noticed that Bayl hadn't come to dinner. Was some nasty magic working, blinding her? Or had she just been distracted by the extra noise and fussing from the children?

"If it weren't storming like that," Verbena offered, her long-fingered, agile hands pressed over her ears, "I'd be running for my life. It has never been so noisy awful before."

"It's all our fault." The speaker's creaky, powdery sort of voice startled all of them.

Several girls let out squeaks or yelps. Merrigan clutched her pincushion and nearly flung it at the source of the voice before she really looked.

Four little, wrinkled, crooked old women stood in the doorway of the sewing area. Their hair was still damp and their borrowed clothes were far too big for them. They looked like kittens someone had tried to drown. Their noses were too big and their mouths sank in from missing teeth, so Merrigan wondered how any of them could speak clearly. She stayed where she was, grateful that she looked like a little old woman too, while her girls showed their good manners and got up to make the women welcome.

Merrigan kept busy pinning a pair of trousers for basting and let Belinda and the girls answer the questions from the women. She didn't like their too-bright eyes, so big in their shriveled faces. They kept looking around the table, studying the girls as if they were boiled sweets to be devoured, asking their names, where they were from, how they became such clever seamstresses so young.

"You've all been so good to us," one of the women said. Merrigan couldn't tell them apart. They all sounded the same. She only knew she disliked the voice.

Belinda looked uncomfortable, too. That was a relief. Merrigan feared something was wrong with her. Why was it so hard to think clearly?

"We don't know what we would have done if we hadn't found your home," another woman said. She smiled, displaying an incongruously bright, full set of teeth.

Merrigan shuddered. She was positive that all the women had been toothless when they appeared as if out of nowhere just a few minutes ago.

"We wanted to thank you for being so kind to us, just poor old beggar women."

What were beggars doing in this part of town? There was no one to beg from, in the warehouses. Merrigan flinched, feeling as if her ears had popped.

Can you hear me? Bib's voice sounded oddly raspy, like his pages had been rubbing against each other long enough to start shredding.

Yes. She barely stopped herself from speaking aloud.

Then she understood and she shuddered as she looked at the old women. Why hadn't she noticed before that they were two sets of identical twins? Surely someone would have remarked on them coming in from the storm -- unless they *hadn't* come in with the other people lost in the sudden snow?

Stop them! Crystal cried.

"Shut up!" one of the women shouted, rising from her chair and standing suddenly two feet taller.

None of the girls reacted. Merrigan held still and held her breath, as the woman looked around, turning and glaring as if she could see through the walls. The woman's gaze passed over her. She nearly laughed aloud. Being just an old woman made her invisible. No threat at all.

Merrigan waited, watching them. A shimmering sound seeped

through the air, growing stronger with every heartbeat.

"We wanted to thank you. We've only got a few treats to share, and you girls were especially nice to us, so we want you to have them." The woman shrank back into herself, once again short and crooked.

Moving in perfect unison, both sets of twins reached into the pockets of their oversized skirts and brought out enormous, brilliant red, perfect apples. In unison, the eight girls let out sighs of delight.

Merrigan frowned and concentrated on the apples, looking from one to the other. Something seemed odd about them, and not just the fact that old beggar women wouldn't have such large, perfect, beautiful apples this far past harvest. Certainly not eight apples, all exactly alike.

That's it, Bib said. *Only one is real.*

The fog filling her brain vanished as if before a chill, refreshing breeze. Seven apples turned transparent. Only one remained solid and glossy. She could actually smell the sweet-sour, rich perfume of the apple. It made her mouth water.

Nothing in the world was going to convince her to bite into an apple that was clearly enchanted. Did they really think she was so stupid?

"Just like with the peas," a richly malicious voice whispered, clashing with the shimmering that grew stronger in the air. "It's a test. Only a real princess can see the real apple. Only a real princess can pick it up. Only a real princess can bite into it. Don't you want to prove you're a real princess?"

"No," Belinda whispered. "Not … safe."

"But one bite will fix everything," the woman whispered, and now Merrigan could see another image, behind the mask of the wrinkled little, smiling, harmless, beggar granny face. Dark eyes glittered with triumph over those full, cruel lips. "No more hiding. You and your prince, together forever. Don't you want that?"

"Yes."

"Then prove you're a real princess," one woman from the second set of twins whispered, her granny mask fading. She chuckled as Belinda reached out for the second apple in the row of perfect images.

What happens if she bites it? Merrigan thought, and then

repeated it in case Bib wasn't listening. She found it hard to do anything except watch the movements in front of her, slowed like they were mired in frozen honey.

Standard sleeping spell, Crystal responded.

Meaning? Merrigan caught her breath. It was a basic curse, old enough to be an irritating cliché. To break a sleeping spell required true love's kiss. *But her true love is gone.*

Yes, another voice whispered, chuckling, the sound cold and sharp-edged. Like the image of her former self revealed in Crystal's surface. *Gone. She'll sleep forever.*

"Take it," one of the old women urged, black eyes glittering, focused on Belinda like a cruel cat focused on a fear-paralyzed mouse. "Prove you're a real princess and take a bite."

"I'm a real princess," Merrigan announced, fury unfreezing her mind and her muscles. She lunged across the table to snatch the apple just before Belinda's fingers touched it.

"How?" the first woman shrieked, her disguise shredding. Two beggar women vanished entirely as she reared up like an offended cobra and her eyes widened in shock. "Only a real princess --"

"You didn't hear me, you dunderhead!" Merrigan slid back and stumbled away, clutching the apple against her chest. "I'm a real princess. More real than you two ever were. At least I never tried to kill my sisters!"

"You can't stop the spell," the second one snarled, her disguise and illusion shredding. Two tall women stood there, dressed all in black, silver, and crimson, with hoods hiding their hair. Their faces were so twisted with fury that their resemblance to Belinda sickened Merrigan. "Once magic starts, it can't be stopped. The spell wasn't perfect when we stole it. Too many holes in it. Too many escape clauses. We fixed it, though. And Father will never know. She'll follow that apple to the ends of the earth, until she takes a bite." A cackle escaped her. "The princess has to sleep."

"*The* princess?" Merrigan sidestepped Belinda as her friend came staggering after her, eyes wide and unseeing, reaching for the apple. "Just a princess? Not a specific one? You couldn't weave it too tight, or the blood tie would make you vulnerable. So only a real princess could pick up the apple, find the real apple -- but you didn't dare specify *which* princess did you?"

An unholy shriek erupted from the two women as they darted

around the table, reaching for her. Merrigan stuck her tongue out at them, raised the apple to her mouth, and bit down hard. So what if it was an unladylike large bite? She had to make sure the magic worked.

Numbness filled her mouth. She almost laughed at her disappointment that the apple didn't taste nearly as good as it smelled. Merrigan forced down the mealy, bland mouthful and the numbness spread through her in one huge, overwhelming ripple. Belinda caught her as she fell, and sweet weariness swept over her and closed her eyes. Her last thought was that at least she was going to get a decent night's sleep. For however long that lasted.

Sleep.

Nightcap. Turn it inside out. Why hadn't she thought of that before?

Merrigan struggled against the sensation of falling into velvet blackness. She had to tell Bryan. If he took the nightcap from her magic box, and wore it turned inside out, he could go into Sylvanglade and reverse the sleeping curse.

Sleeping curse.

"Bryan," she whispered, shivering in a bitter, draining chill that she only felt as it evaporated.

"I'm here," he said.

Then he kissed her, slow and sweet, his lips warm and firm against hers, long enough for a delightful shiver to sweep through her body.

No, Merrigan realized, as her eyes fluttered open and Bryan sat back, smiling down at her. This was the *second* kiss.

He had kissed her awake.

"Hello, Merrigan," he said. "Fancy meeting you here."

"You know --" She sighed as he bent down and kissed her again. This time she managed to raise her hand, so heavy, everything about her moving slower than her thoughts, and she touched the side of his face. She could almost have wept when he stopped kissing her and sat back again, even further this time. "How do you know ... who I am?"

"Show her," Crystal said from somewhere nearby. "But not with me -- an ordinary mirror. Otherwise she'll think it's a trick." Her sigh bubbled with laughter. "Some people will never learn how to trust."

Bryan slid his arm under her back and helped her sit up. Merrigan took a deep breath and it cleared cobwebs from her brain. She was in her bed. She looked past Bryan and saw ... it seemed like nearly everyone in the orphanage had managed to crowd into the open area by her shelf bed. Belinda stepped up, her face pale and eyes red with weeping, but she smiled. Merrigan blinked and shook her head, then rubbed her eyes. Belinda had gone from a twelve-year-old to a grown woman. She handed Merrigan one of the mirrors from the bathing room.

"Oh." Merrigan sighed, seeing her own features for the first time in what felt like a lifetime. Her hair was just as black as before, her skin just as smooth and just the right combination of alabaster and peaches and roses, her eyes just as smoky dark brilliant.

"You've changed, Merrigan," Bryan said, taking the mirror from her limp hands. "The princess I knew would have erupted by now, demanding explanations, or at least demanding that everyone stop staring."

"That's because she's not the princess you knew," Bib said.

Before Merrigan could ask where he was, Bryan stood up and reached into the shelf bed over her head, and brought down the book and the mirror.

"I don't ... I don't really understand," Merrigan said. Yes, she wanted everyone to go away. She couldn't make herself meet those bright, inquisitive eyes, or face the expected expressions of accusation, the demands for an explanation. All those people she had worked with, lived with for so many moons, deceiving them. Surely they were furious with her.

"If you don't understand, how could you know that you could make the spell apply to you?" Nasius asked.

"Well, it worked against those idiot princes," she said. "And they said *a* princess could pick up the apple, not one specific princess, so I just ... guessed."

"You have a brilliant future as a magic-wielder ahead of you," Crystal said. "If you want to pursue magical studies."

"No, thank you. I've had quite enough magic in my life already."

"You're going to need to pursue some magical studies if you're going to help Belinda and Bryan find wherever Bayl went." The magic mirror sighed loudly. "Breaking the spell had enough backlash to give those two hags a comeuppance, but it didn't bring back the prince."

"Belinda ... I'm sorry." Merrigan put down the mirror on her bed and held out her hands. The other princess came to her and they held each other. "How much of a comeuppance?"

"Not nearly what they deserve," Bryan said, his voice a little hard, "but we've only just started." His sharp smile softened. "What you did for them, for us ..."

Merrigan fought down the sensation that a totally featherheaded kind of giggle was going to erupt from her at any moment. She couldn't do that. Not in front of her friends and the children. Certainly not in front of Bryan. She couldn't tear her gaze free of his. "You kissed me."

"Three times." His lips twitched and he shrugged. "I figured I should get as many as I could before you were awake enough to give me a black eye."

"No, but you woke me. How?" She fought the urge to lick her lips, knowing she would lose the taste of his kiss still lingering there. "I know enough about magic ..." She shrugged. "Shouldn't it be true love's kiss? There's no way you could ... you could ..." She hid her face in her hands, unable to say the words.

"Love you?" Bryan gently caught her hands in his, and they were wondrously warm and strong and gentle. He pulled her hands down, so she had to look at him. "Consider it a promise. A strong possibility. And maybe ... I like to think it wouldn't have worked if there wasn't something inside you, some hope, maybe you could try to ..." He reddened in that charming way of his that squeezed at her heart.

"All right, everyone," Nasius announced, waving his arms in a shooing motion. "I think that's enough staring. We're all sure that Mara -- sorry, Princess Merrigan, is just fine now. Let's give her some room to breathe."

"It's just Merrigan," she called, as the people who had become her family turned around, some of them visibly reluctant to leave. "I'm no princess."

"That's what you think," Crystal said with a rolling, triumphant chuckle.

~~~~~

Bryan had realized what was happening when the two
~~~~~

enchantresses struck, because of the lingering threads of magic still clinging to him. He felt the reverberations and followed them to their source. Bryan immediately ran to look for Belinda, since his brother wasn't there to protect her. He arrived in time to see Merrigan collapse, and then Bythia and Barbarina a moment later, in reaction to the shattering of their spell. He had the presence of mind to shout for the girls to sit on the nasty women while he used scraps of cloth and measuring tapes to bind and gag them. Then they searched Belinda's sisters and removed everything that might be used to hide a spell or some sort of inimical magic.

He had the presence of mind to turn Merrigan's magic box upside down and shake it until everything stored inside it had been shaken out. Everyone laughed later, when they examined the pile that covered the whole sewing table, ten feet long and five feet wide. Then he shoved the two enchantresses into the box, which obligingly widened enough to take them without hesitation. They were currently locked up in the box, sealed with several unbreakable leather straps that had come from it. They would stay there until he and Belinda and Merrigan could turn the enchantresses over to their father to face his judgment and their punishment. With Bib and Crystal researching and investigating, and trying to question the prisoners, perhaps by then they would have some clue as to what had happened to Bayl and where the nasty magic had taken him.

Making those plans had been easy. Just one little hitch: waking Merrigan so she could join them on the quest. Two full days had passed in discussing how to break the spell before Bryan got up the courage to admit how he felt about her, and try to kiss her awake.

Merrigan finally got up on her feet and went out to have supper with the orphanage family. She was more pleased than she could understand, when the children welcomed her just as boisterously as they had when she was Mistress Mara. She feared that regaining her own face would frighten them, would make her a stranger to them.

"Silly girl," Auntie Gretel said with a sigh and an exasperated shake of her head. "You've been growing younger for the past four moons, but it was so gradual that none of us really noticed. Not with the whirlwind of everyday living, when you're tending nearly a hundred children. It's not really that much of a change. We could see you under the gray hair and wrinkles. I have to admire you, managing as well as you did. It's hard enough growing old at the normal pace, but to be turned into an old woman all at once ..." She patted Merrigan's cheek. "Stronger women have crumpled."

Her words tumbled through Merrigan's thoughts for a full day, until she finally confronted Bryan.

"So ... you recognized me?" she said, finding him alone for the first time in what seemed like weeks.

Only two days had passed since she had awakened. Days full of planning, with King Auberg and Aubrey's eager help, and loads of advice from Bergomass. The enchanter was only too eager to help make sure the enchantresses faced their deserved punishment. Their vindictive magic had been interfering with the majjian springs throughout almost the entire continent. When the underground veins of magic water were blocked or soured, it unbalanced everything, the magical as well as the ordinary, everyday things and activities and people.

"Yes ... and no." His eyes twinkled and his lips twitched, threatening to change his somber expression into laughter.

The problem was that every time Bryan's lips twitched, she found herself wishing he would kiss her again.

"Just what is that supposed to mean?"

"We haven't seen each other since you were what, twelve? I only had a glimpse of the woman you would become. There was an echo of that woman underneath the old woman, so I always felt I knew you, but ..." Bryan shrugged. "My heart nearly stopped when I saw you fall, the enchantment shattered, and you were yourself again. I knew who you were. I was frantic. I nearly -- I actually thought of --" His gaze shifted to her lips.

"You wanted to kiss me right there? Right away?"

"I knew how I felt about you, but no idea if you even remembered who I was. True love's kiss doesn't work for strangers. Then I remembered all the things you said, talking about the boy you knew and ... I hoped."

"I'm glad you hoped," she whispered. "But just in case ... in case it was only a temporary cure ..." Merrigan's face heated and she could almost laugh at how timid she felt, afraid to speak the image that filled her mind and heart.

"Regular doses?" Bryan bent down slowly, his warm, strong

hand cupping her cheek just as slowly, and kissed her, even more slowly, until she could feel the ripple of magic washing through her from head to toe.

END

Coming titles:

Book 2:
Majjian Springs

Book 3:
Thorns and Magic

About the Author

On the road to publication, Michelle fell into fandom in college and has 40+ stories in various SF and fantasy universes. She has a bunch of useless degrees in theater, English, film/communication, and writing. Even worse, she has over 100 books and novellas with multiple small presses, in science fiction and fantasy, YA, suspense, women's fiction, and sub-genres of romance.

Her official launch into publishing came with winning first place in the Writers of the Future contest in 1990. She was a finalist in the EPIC Awards competition multiple times, winning with *Lorien* in 2006 and *The Meruk Episodes, I-V,* in 2010, and was a finalist in the Realm Award competition, in conjunction with the Realm Makers convention.

Her training includes the Institute for Children's Literature; proofreading at an advertising agency; and working at a community newspaper. She is a tea snob and freelance edits for a living (MichelleLevigne@gmail.com for info/rates), but only enough to give her time to write. Her newest crime against the literary world is to be co-managing editor at Mt. Zion Ridge Press and launching the publishing co-op, Ye Olde Dragon Books. Be afraid … be very afraid.

www.Mlevigne.com
www.MichelleLevigne.blogspot.com
www.YeOldeDragonBooks.com
www.MtZionRidgePress.com
@MichelleLevigne

Look for Michelle's Goodreads groups:
Guardians of Neighborlee
Voyages of the AFV Defender

NEWSLETTER:
Want to learn about upcoming books, book launch parties, inside information, and cover reveals?

Go to Michelle's website or blog to sign up.

Also by Michelle L. Levigne

Guardians of the Time Stream: 4-book Steampunk series
The Match Girls: Humorous inspirational romance series starting with **A Match (Not) Made in Heaven**
Sarai's Journey: A 2-book biblical fiction series
Tabor Heights: 20-book inspirational small town romance series.
Quarry Hall: 11-book women's fiction/suspense series
For Sale: Wedding Dress. Never Used: inspirational romance
Crooked Creek: Fun Fables About Critters and Kids: Children's short stories.
Do Yourself a Favor: Tips and Quips on the Writing Life. A book of writing advice.
Killing His Alter-Ego: contemporary romance/suspense, taking place in fandom.
The Commonwealth Universe: SF series, 25 books and growing
The Hunt: 5-book YA fantasy series
Faxinor: Fantasy series, 4 books and growing
Wildvine: Fantasy series, 14 books when all released
Neighborlee: Humorous fantasy series
Zygradon: 5-book Arthurian fantasy series
AFV Defender: SF adventure series
Young Defenders: Middle Grade SF series, spin-off of *AFV Defender*
Magic to Spare: Fantasy series